The new witches of Windale
stand warned . . .

Wendy Ward, a Windale coed castigated as "the little witch girl" who played with Wiccan ritual and summoned a dreadful past. The extent of Wendy's powers are unknown even to her—until she's forced to confront a rebirth of evil that threatens total destruction.

Karen Glazer, a former Danfield College professor who thinks that the horror is behind her. But her darling new baby Hannah harbors strange powers that are drawing them both back into Windale's past and the grip of fear.

Abby MacNeil, nine years old, yet old enough to remember the blood sisters who invaded her innocence . . . and the monsters who lived outside her dreams.

Gina Thorne, a teenager whose life is just beginning— and so are the nightmares. The sound of a baby crying serves only as a grim reminder of a terrible choice she made. But things will change. She can feel it night after night, overtaking her warm, sleeping body.

When it rains, it pours.

WITHER'S RAIN

WITHER'S RAIN

A WENDY WARD NOVEL

JOHN PASSARELLA

POCKET STAR BOOKS
New York London Toronto Sydney Singapore

This book is a work of fiction. Names, characters, places and incidents are products of the author's imagination or are used fictitiously. Any resemblance to actual events or locales or persons living or dead is entirely coincidental.

An *Original* Publication of POCKET BOOKS

A Pocket Star Book published by
POCKET BOOKS, a division of Simon & Schuster, Inc.
1230 Avenue of the Americas, New York, NY 10020

Copyright © 2003 by Joe Gangemi and John Passarella

ISBN: 0-671-02482-5

First Pocket Books printing February 2003

10 9 8 7 6 5 4 3 2 1

POCKET STAR BOOKS and colophon are registered trademarks of Simon & Schuster, Inc.

For information regarding special discounts for bulk purchases, please contact Simon & Schuster Special Sales at 1-800-456-6798 or business@simonandschuster.com

Front cover illustration by John Vairo, Jr.;
photo credits: William Rivelli/Photonica, Mitsuru Yamaguchi/Photonica

Printed in the U.S.A.

For

Emma Faith Passarella,

who came into our lives just when we needed her

ACKNOWLEDGMENTS

My thanks to: Joe Gangemi for convincing me Wendy's story wasn't over; the Garden State Horror Writers for surprising me with uncommon fellowship; the generous Lehigh Press employees who held a former coworker in their thoughts and prayers; Gordon Kato for his unfailing support and sage advice; Mitchell Ivers, my editor, for believing in this book; Danielle Naibert for the Wiccan perspective; Gail Hochman for the publishing perspective; Yvonne Navarro, Doug Clegg, and Jeff Mariotte for the authorial perspective; Jeff Richards for scouring the Web; Dan Keohane for the Massachusetts connection; Greg Schauer for taking the train; and Andrea for her love and encouragement.

Special thanks to Drs. Anthony Avellino, Ana Janss, Donna Stephenson, Ken Cohen, and Ben Carson for giving my family hope during our darkest days.

I saw pale kings, and princes too,
Pale warriors, death-pale were they all;
They cried—"La Belle Dame sans Merci
Hath Thee in thrall!"
—John Keats

And what rough beast, its hour come round at last,
Slouches toward Bethlehem to be born?
—William Butler Yeats

For he who lives more lives than one
More deaths than one must die.
—Oscar Wilde

WITHER'S
RAIN

PROLOGUE

WINDALE, MASSACHUSETTS
OCTOBER 31, 1999

     . . . *blood, as black as crude oil, flows with a life and a will of its own, seeking a course through the rubble of the collapsed building, aided by, yet not prisoner to, the pull of gravity, occasionally rising over a rock when no lower outlet avails itself . . . an incomplete entity, still the blood has awareness and a driving instinct to find the warmth of human flesh . . . absent from this awareness are the memories of what it has been or even how it has been reduced to this tenuous race for survival . . . over rubble and glass, dirt and weeds, the blood courses with the cohesion of quicksilver . . . almost senseless, it seeks by touch alone any indication of humanity's presence wherever it flows . . . without a warm, living human host, its temperature starts to cool and its millennia-old awareness begins to fade into oblivion . . .*

• • •

"Pull over, I'm gonna be sick," Angelina Thorne said from within a bundle of blankets on the passenger side of the blue Ford F-150 pickup truck. Shivering, her voice was a weak quaver.

"Sure, Gina." Brett Marlin swung the truck onto the shoulder of Main Street, passing a partially demolished gas station and an overloaded Dumpster at the edge of the lot before stopping the truck and shifting into park. As he loosened his grip on the steering wheel, his hands were trembling. He sighed, reached for his door handle, but Gina's hand caught his other arm. "What?"

Gina Thorne's face appeared ghostly in the dashboard light. Her usual pale complexion had been reduced to sick pallor by the evening's events. She had dark rings under her light blue, almost gray eyes. And her long, strawberry-blond hair hung in sweat-soaked tangles. "She was already dead, right? Before you put her in the . . . ?"

Brett nodded, unable to give voice to the lie.

"She was so small . . ."

"Too small," Brett said, nodding again. "Wouldn't have mattered if . . ." He let the rest of this thought pass between them unsaid. Part of the lie was his alone to bear, but somehow he thought she knew all of it.

"It's for the best, right?" Gina asked him, searching his eyes.

"For the best," he said, his voice hushed.

"Because we're only seventeen. We have Danfield together next year. Our whole lives ahead of us," Gina said, then clapped a hand over her mouth.

Brett reached for his door handle again. Gina shook her head, keeping him planted in his seat as she pushed her door open. Dropping the blankets, she staggered to the edge of the road, where the shoulder met the grassy incline that rose to the sight of the abandoned Windale Textile Mill. Since Gina wanted privacy, even after what they'd been through together less than an hour ago, and he was unwilling to be completely alone with his grim thoughts, Brett turned on the truck radio. He hit the scan button several times, searching for an upbeat song, and happened across the local all-news station.

"... *golf ball-sized hailstorm, which disrupted the sixty-fifth annual King Frost parade, ended as mysteriously as it began. The brunt of the freak storm was localized in the downtown Windale area and the main parade route, and was responsible for several serious injuries among the twenty thousand spectators. Many outlying areas were also hit by the storm, where it caused numerous fires, damaged cars and windows. Property damage estimates will have to wait until morning, although Mayor Dell'Olio, himself injured during the storm, expects the totals will reach into the hundreds of thousands.*

Elsewhere, an unrelated fire erupted in Windale General's Childbirth Wellness Center—"

"Jesus!" Brett gasped. His hand jerked forward and switched off the radio before he could hear any more. As guests of the Harrison Motor Lodge, he and Gina had been as far from downtown Windale as possible and still they had heard the sirens. Easy enough to assume the crowd gathered at the King Frost parade had gotten out of hand. When Brett checked out of the motel, the balding desk clerk had been dozing in front of a small black-and-white television set tuned to a cooking channel with the sound turned off.

Brett sat up straighter in his seat so he could see Gina, bent over the grass, retching. They had wondered if anyone would miss them at the parade. Not that any of their friends, or even their families, had ever suspected anything. Gina had been good about disguising her condition. And amid all the destruction in the town tonight, their absence would never be noted.

Dry heaves. And still her body wracked with uncontrollable spasms. She was sore and tired and just wanted to go home and sleep for a week. To sleep and forget about . . . everything. But first she had to get through the next hour or two. Only when her retching subsided did she become aware that she was crying, silent tears washing away the remnants of her mascara and falling as quietly to the grass beneath her. *Get a grip*, she told herself. *Can't let Brett see me like this. We decided this together. We did this together. Can't fall apart on him now.*

Gina climbed to her feet on wobbly legs, then reached into the pocket of her baggy jeans for the damp wad of tissues. First she dabbed her eyes, then she wiped her mouth. The residue of bile still burned her throat. She craved a breath mint or a shot of vodka, maybe both. About to return to the truck, she stopped at the faint sound of crying.

She pulled the truck door open and looked in at

Brett, whose sandy hair was a mess from him running his hands through it too many times. His square-jawed face was tight, his brown eyes wide with concern. "You hear that?" she asked.

"What?"

"Crying . . . I thought I heard a baby crying. I still hear . . ."

"Gina, wait—!"

She turned away from the truck, even as Brett opened his door, and turned toward the sound, toward the Dumpster at the edge of the old gas station lot. With the loss of its main source of revenue, namely the daily mill worker traffic, the gas station had closed shop. Now it looked as if somebody had finally purchased the property and was clearing the lot for some new enterprise. Her gaze was drawn up the hill, to the abandoned factory, where she thought she saw a tendril of smoke spiraling into the night sky. *Impossible*, she thought, *the mill's been closed for years.*

Gina returned her attention to the thin, reedy crying sound, so soft it teased at her consciousness, almost a memory, yet not quite hope. All the guilt and regret still hadn't changed her mind. Given the same set of circumstances, she would make the same choice all over again. As much as she hated admitting that to herself.

"Gina, stop!" Brett called. "You're just imagining this."

"I'm sure I heard something," she muttered, stepping softly, almost creeping. She peered over the lip of the Dumpster, staring down into the construction debris. Split boards, rusty nails, chunks of mildew-rotted lath, jagged strips of metal . . . no way anything could be alive down there. Still, she leaned forward, gripping the edge of the Dumpster, feeling the chill bite of the metal against her palm. A strange sensation, as if all her warmth were leeching out into the metal, overcame her. She shuddered.

"Gina!"

Something cool and slimy coated her fingers, covering her hand in the blink of an eye. Startled, she jerked away from the Dumpster. Her hand was as black as if she'd dipped it in a bowl of India ink, and ached with pins and needles. Unable to resist the simple urge, she raised the blackened hand to her nose and inhaled. Her eyes burned and her nose began to drip, as with a sudden nosebleed. But when she looked down at her hand, she saw the strange liquid was dripping *up* and stretching amoebalike, splashing across her lips and rushing into her mouth and nostrils.

"Gina, what is it?"

She wanted to scream but could not. She was paralyzed with fear and with something else, something approaching a drug-induced ecstasy. Trembling, as wave after wave of the black substance poured into her mouth and nose and eyes and ears, she felt her knees buckling. She moaned. Then someone tugged the ground out from under her . . .

It happened in an instant. Brett slammed his truck door shut and followed Gina toward the Dumpster, reluctant to give credence to her hallucination. If she was hearing an infant cry, it was definitely in her mind. Still, he was only a few yards behind her when she jerked her hand back from the Dumpster, a few feet away when she raised a black-coated hand to her nose. Even as she shuddered and moaned, he leapt forward, just in time to catch her as her legs buckled. The second time that night he'd had to carry her to the truck, the first being when they left the motel room. Years of weightlifting had given him enough upper-body strength to carry her effortlessly. He lowered her into the passenger seat, reclined the backrest a bit more, then tucked the blankets around her. A quick examination of her left hand showed it was pale but otherwise normal. The sheen of black he'd seen must have been a trick of the light and shadows.

As he drove her home, he kept glancing over at her, willing her to awaken. Finally, she blinked herself awake. She flashed him a dreamy smile, the same drowsy, contented smile that usually followed their lovemaking. A long time since he'd last seen that smile.

"What happened?" she asked.

"You collapsed, back there at the Dumpster," Brett said. "I thought maybe you cut yourself or something." He shrugged. "Probably just exhaustion."

"Yeah," she said, "I'm sure that's all it was."

"How do you feel now?"

She lifted his right hand from where it rested on the gear shift and squeezed it, hard. "Better," she said. But now her smile seemed almost predatory. "So much better, Brett. You have no idea . . ."

Puzzled, he watched her as long as he dared before returning his attention to the road. "Good," he said, finally. Maybe they could put this night behind them, as if none of it had ever happened.

"We're starting over," Gina whispered. "A whole new beginning. Only this time, we won't make the same mistakes."

. . . from the brink of darkest oblivion, awareness returns and expands with a rush as the black blood courses through the human's veins and arteries, spreading to the limits of this new host body, learning all its secrets from the inside out, yet already beginning the slow process of corruption . . . time passes and the changes begin to give the black blood purpose, awareness recovers a lost memory, a single thought, an identity by which it has known itself for three hundred years . . . and the name is Wither . . .

Wendy Ward's Mirror Book Entry
November 6, 1999, Moon: waning crescent, day 27

I don't know if I can do this anymore. Being Wiccan meant something peaceful to me before. Now I can't get past the fear. I'm afraid to go back into the woods. Afraid of the consequences. Can't very well be a proper Wicca when you're afraid of the forest. Until I overcome that fear, what's the point in continuing?

It's been six days since I . . . since Wither died. And I feel normal again. Well, physically normal, anyway. Still not sure about my overall sanity, although most people in town would say I lost my marbles years ago. Little witch girl. Whatever.

I shudder whenever I think of her crawling around inside my mind, sifting through my thoughts and memories, trying to replace me. Still have nightmares, but now they're regular nightmares, not the lucid dreaming episodes in colonial Windale, living actual days past in Wither's life. Those dreams were part of Wither's connection to me . . . and the bitch is gone now, for good. They say time heals all wounds, so I'll wait and see where I go from here.

Saw Alex in the hospital again today. He looks so helpless with both legs and his left arm in casts. Helpless, but adorable. Doctor told us he put a half dozen metal pins in Alex's legs, and Alex joked about never being able to make it through an airport metal detector without causing a scene. Glad he hasn't lost his sense of humor. I know he doesn't blame me, but I can't help blaming myself. Wither hurt him, tried to kill him, just because we were close. Even after they remove the casts, Alex is in for months of grueling rehab.

Karen—I should say Professor Glazer—took baby Hannah home, finally. She's a precious little thing. I promised Professor Glazer I'd be available for sitting. At least Hannah won't remember any of this. She'll have a chance to grow up normal.

Abby's a different story. She didn't exactly have a model childhood before and she's old enough to remember how her father treated her and what happened to him, old enough to remember the monster, Sarah Hutchins. I worry about Abby. Just hope the sheriff and his family can give her a good home.

Wendy Ward's Mirror Book
December 21, 1999, Moon: waxing gibbous, day 21
Yule

I tried tonight. I really tried. No, not in the woods. An indoor ritual. Sure, I *could* blame my stay-at-home ritual on the Gremlin, which is a mangled block of scrap metal, thanks again to Wither. Dad would have had a coronary if I asked to borrow his Beamer, so maybe I could have borrowed Mom's car. Don't know. Never asked. Not ready to go back into the woods. Not yet.

Nothing wrong with an indoor ritual. (Especially when it's freezing outside!) I waited until everyone was asleep. Took a late purifying bath. Purified the space and made a circle near my window, so I could see the night sky. I even put up a little altar with a sprig of pine and juniper. I cleared my mind, centered myself, felt at peace. Called the elements. I meditated for a while. I wanted to cast a healing spell, to speed Alex's recovery. He's still in a lot of pain. Then I realized I was stalling. Afraid to do any magic. And that made it all wrong. I thanked the elements and broke the circle.

Before, I believed in myself, believed that the magic worked, in small ways, sometimes noticeable ways. Until Wither came along. Until the night it rained, the night I believed I had made it rain. Thought I'd tapped into something special, some previously hidden amazing potential. But that was Wither's rain. I know that now. She was playing with me all along, amused by my little, useless games while she controlled all this dark power.

Can you lose something if you never really had it?

Wendy Ward's Mirror Book
February 2, 2000, Moon: waning crescent, day 27
Imbolc

Too close to the new moon to think about doing any magic. Another excuse not to do a ritual? Maybe. Lit all the lights in the house at sunset in celebration of Imbolc, then dozed off before turning them off again. Dad was not a happy camper. Said the whole campus could see the president's mansion up on the hill, lit up like a Spielbergian—yes, he used the word Spielbergian— UFO about to rendezvous with the mothership.

Speaking of dozing off, my nightmares aren't as frequent, but when they come, they're doozies! In the last one, Wither was a giant and I was bound head to toe on a large serving plate. She was slicing off pieces of my flesh and tossing them back into her gaping maw. I woke up screaming from that one and couldn't sleep the rest of the night. No wonder I doze off at odd hours!

Alex is getting around these days with a cane, which makes him self-conscious, even though he tries to joke about it. He tires easily. By the end of the day, his legs are exhausted and his left arm is stiff and sore. He'll always have a limp, but the cane is temporary. Of course, he'll never run on the track team again. But he's busy enough just trying to catch up on reading assignments.

Professor Glazer tells me Hannah's growth is off the charts. Even higher than when she was born. But she seems like a perfectly healthy baby girl. Art's been staying closer to mother and daughter, helping out. I think he's got a thing for my comp lit prof.

Oh, Mom and Dad bought me half a car. (Yes, this was before the house lighting incident.) I agreed to pay them back for the other half and pay for the insurance. Guess they were tired of me moping around the house. Ha! I never told them about the battle with Wither since I didn't think they would believe me. Not surprising since I have a hard time believing it myself, and I was there! If they did believe me, they'd probably never let me out of their sight again. Still, I had to explain the Gremlin getting totaled. So, I told them the Gremlin, famous for stalling at inopportune times, stalled when I was making a turn, that I lost control of the steering and the car rolled down the hill. Frankie and I escaped with some cuts and bruising. Trouper that she is, Frankie backed me up on this. So Mom insisted my next car be more trustworthy and practical. She decided on a Civic, so I insisted on the color. Black, naturally. It's a 1993 four-door, automatic with just under 100,000 miles on it. Hasn't stalled once. Almost makes me want to keep the interior clutter to a six empty-soda-can minimum. Despite the expected reliability of the car, Dad bought me two presents he stashed in the glove box: a cell phone "for emergencies only" and an automobile club membership. Since the Civic has front-wheel drive, it should be up to the challenge of these snow-clogged New England streets. Not a four-by-four, by any means, but those SUV beasts really guzzle the fossil fuels and are not kind to Mother Earth.

Wendy Ward's Mirror Book
March 21, 2000, Moon: waning gibbous, day 16
Ostara, Vernal Equinox

Spring is in the air! Drove the Civic down Gable Road today. Two times before I mustered enough courage to stop and visit my special clearing again. First I've gone back since the time I included Alex in my ritual, since the trouble with Wither.

Figuring I might freak out at night, I went during the day. And, believe it or not, I felt a sense of peace, as if I really did belong there. Shouldn't surprise me. Wither is gone. I'm free of her. Just need to get her out of my head. I collected some wildflowers from the area and brought them back to my bedroom.

Spring semester is winding down with some good news and some bad. Good: Alex might come back from Minneapolis for a summer session—Yay!—to make up for time lost during rehab. (Okay, so that part's not so good.) He had to cut his course load, dropping classes that gave him the most difficulty, rather than let his GPA slide into probationary territory. Hopes to make it up over the summer so he'll be back in the groove for sophomore year. Bad: Professor Glazer accepted a job offer from Stanford. (Well, bad for me since I'm gonna miss her.) She'll finish this semester, then move to California. And, turns out I was right about Mr. Leeson! Art will be going with them.

Oh—Big Surprise! When I visited Professor Glazer at home, I saw Hannah pull herself up and walk around the room, from one piece of furniture-support to the next. And she was baby babbling, though I could make out "mama" in there. While I was rolling a ball (baba) back and forth with her, she called me "Aunt Wendy." Okay, if you want to get technical, it sounded more like "Ah-weh." But she's not even five months old! Way ahead of schedule. Gonna miss the little cutie-pie!

Wendy Ward's Mirror Book
April 30, 2000, Moon: waning crescent, day 26
Beltane

Okay, so maybe tomorrow, May 1, is really Beltane. April 30 is the old-time date and this year it falls on a Sunday, so that's convenient. And who says I can't be old-fashioned some of the time? Busy, busy, busy with exam week and term paper deadlines looming ahead. Everyone is panicked. And study groups only seem to intensify the panic.

I returned to my clearing today for a meditation ritual, wearing my robe and a garland of flowers, just hoping to find some tranquility in the midst of all the chaos around me. It was a pleasant hour, but I fear it's the eye of the storm.

Professor Glazer sold her house and Art's already had an offer on his. Like me, he's a townie, and he's having a hard time leaving his home behind. I heard him talking about closing the house up, maybe having a caretaker look after the place. But I think they'll need the money for the new place in California. Professor Glazer had little equity in her place. (Equity! Jeez, I'm starting to sound like one of Alex's finance textbooks!) She and Hannah moved into Art's place. They'll be leaving the end of May.

Alissa told me she wants to spend the summer in Europe, but only if I agree to manage The Crystal Path while she's away. At least she trusts me not to run the business into the ground! Alex said he'd help me with the bookkeeping when he comes back for his summer session, so it's not looking as scary as I thought. On the plus side, I'll be able to pay off my half of the Civic, maybe even save enough to afford an apartment next term. (Frankie mentioned she'd go in half on the rental if she lands a decent job.) I get along with Mom and Dad. Still, it would be nice to live without constant parental supervision. I'll be nineteen on August 1 (just 3 months!), but sometimes I think Mom and Dad look at me and still see a little girl in pigtails with Band-Aids on her knees. If they only knew the things I've seen!

PART ONE

REBORN

CHAPTER ONE

"Are you sure you want to do this?" Wendy Ward asked Alex as she parked her black Civic in one of the faded herringboned slots on the fractured asphalt parking lot beside Marshall Field.

Wearing a predominantly green Hawaiian shirt over baggy, faded jeans, Alex Dunkirk held his dragon-head metal cane between his legs. He spun it within the circle of his left hand and grinned, his hazel eyes glinting with amusement as they peered at her over the Ray-Ban Wayfarer low on the bridge of his nose. "Gotta get back up on the horse, right?"

"True, when you fall off the horse," Wendy said. "When the horse falls on top of you, then I'm not so sure." Wendy wore a baggy silver blouse, black jeans, and silver Skechers with neon green piping.

She examined his face for a moment, noticing the fine line of scars around his forehead. He had bigger scars, she knew, on his left arm and both legs. Alex often joked that he'd received the Frankenstein monster special but the HMO wouldn't spring for the twin neck bolts. He'd been weaning himself off the painkillers, but always had at least a dull ache in his legs and left arm, especially before it rained. Working out with light weights was helping to build up his endurance, but he still tired easily. Sometimes he seemed so strong. Other times he seemed fragile. But she would never tell him that.

"If you want to catch Professor Glazer at the airport—"

"Okay, okay," Wendy said. "No more stalling." Alex pushed up his Ray-Bans as they climbed out of the car and walked side by side with her up the grassy knoll to Marshall Field. Grimacing all the way up the incline, Alex used his steel cane for traction more than support. Once they crossed the four track lanes, he flipped the cane back over his shoulder. But it was more than a cane. Alex had it specially made by a shop in Cambridge. If he pressed a recessed button on the side, the dragon-head handle snapped up, becoming a hilt for the eighteen-inch blade that slid out of the cylindrical housing. "Since flight is no longer a viable option," Alex had told her when he first demonstrated the convertible cane-sword, "I'll be prepared to fight."

Alex stopped and looked to the expanse of bare dirt

stretching the length of one side of the field. "So they're really gone."

Wendy nodded. "They tore down the bleachers and hauled away the pieces less than two weeks after you were attacked by Wither." She regarded Alex's thousand-yard stare. "What are you thinking?"

"Those bleachers saved my life."

"You were nearly crushed to death under them!"

"Nearly," Alex said. "But if I hadn't been pinned under there, she would have finished me off."

Wendy shuddered, slipped her arm around his waist and turned into his embrace. "I don't want to think about it."

"Do you?"

"What?"

"Think about her? Wither?"

Wendy sighed. "Spent the better part of the last six and a half months trying to forget about her. That answer your question?"

He chuckled. "Suppose so." Taking in the abandoned athletic field with one last sweeping gaze, "I thought it would creep me out. But I feel okay."

"Hmm," Wendy said, grinding her pelvis against his. "I'd say you feel better than okay, Mr. Dunkirk."

"Careful, Ms. Ward," Alex said with a quick kiss on her lips. "People could be watching."

"Let them." Wendy took his head in her hands and gave him a properly thorough kiss.

"As interesting as your proposition sounds, Ms. Godiva, this is probably the last place I'd pick to test the flexibility of my patchwork limbs."

Wendy frowned, released him and stepped back. "Good point. 'Ick' factor is way too high here. And we have that airport run."

The public address system at Logan International Airport announced that passengers for Flight 313 to San Francisco International should begin boarding . . . and still no sign of Wendy. Karen looked around, hoping to catch a glimpse of her favorite student.

Art Leeson slung the straps of two hefty carry-on bags over his shoulders, picking up Hannah's small bag last in his left hand. With his free hand he pushed his glasses up the bridge of his nose. "Ready?" he asked her, a disappointed look on his face. He knew how much she'd been looking forward to seeing Wendy one last time. She suspected Art himself wanted one last chance to say good-bye to the young lady who had been so instrumental in ending their Halloween nightmare.

"Suppose so," Karen said, picking up the child's car seat.

Hard to believe how much their lives had changed in less than seven months. Paul was gone, killed by one of the three-hundred-year-old Windale witches, rather, one of the nine-foot-tall demonic creatures who had been perceived as witches by their seventeenth-century neighbors because in those days the creatures had still appeared human. Since Paul's death, brought together by their shared grief, Karen and Paul's brother, Art, had begun to spend more and more time together. Friendship had grown into something more, something intimate. She still wasn't sure she was ready for marriage, but Art loved her and Hannah. And while she cared for Art a great deal, her emotions were too unsettled about what had happened in Windale, about what was continuing to happen to Hannah, for Karen to know her own mind. She hoped the change in scenery would bring her emotions into focus. Art deserved no less.

She glanced down the crowded concourse for any sign of Wendy, then sighed.

In a white, frilly dress and white stockings over black patent leather shoes, Hannah walked along a row a plastic chairs, touching her finger to each chair and counting softly, "One, two, free, four . . ." To look at her walking confidently and learning to count, one would think the little girl was three years old. Karen knew better. Hannah Nicole Glazer was less than seven months old. Other than her accelerated development, the doctors could find nothing wrong with her, pronounced her perfectly healthy. But Karen was learning there was a world of difference between healthy and normal. Sometimes she would wake up in the middle of the night in a cold sweat, thinking about Hannah and wondering if the whole ordeal with the ancient witch, Rebecca Cole, was really over. Were they really free of her? Or did Hannah carry a sinister legacy that would someday shatter their lives?

Hannah realized she was under her mother's scrutiny and looked up with a smile. "Go bye-bye, Mama?"

"Yes, Hannah," Karen said. "We're going on the airplane now."

"High inna sky?"

Karen smiled. "Very high, Hannah."

"Ann Wenny come," Hannah said, but it wasn't a question.

"Aunt Wendy couldn't make it, honey."

Hannah shook her head, defiantly. "Ann Wenny come!" She pointed behind Karen. "Look, Mama!"

Karen turned and for a moment, saw only the hurrying throng of strangers. Suddenly, an auburn-haired young woman dashed between an Asian couple and a luggage cart. She wore silver and black and was waving frantically. Karen smiled. *If only I had had as much faith in Wendy as Hannah does.*

Wendy was a little out of breath. Combined with the exertion of the jog through the airport was the fear she'd arrive too late to see off Professor Glazer, Hannah, and Art. She heaved a sigh of relief as she saw them preparing to board. The other passengers were moving in hushed conversations toward the boarding ramp. *Well, boarding tunnel when you came right down to it,* she thought.

"Hi, Wendy," Karen said. "We're boarding."

Wendy stopped, grabbed Karen in a fierce hug. "I know. Sorry we're late. Traffic was a mess and we had to park somewhere over in Rhode Island."

Karen smiled as Wendy released her and asked, "Where's Alex?"

"Coming," Wendy said. "Told me to run ahead so I wouldn't miss you guys." Wendy crouched down and held her arms open for Hannah, who ran to her and wrapped her hands around Wendy's neck. "I'm gonna miss you, you little cutie!"

"Ann Wenny go high inna sky?"

"Aunt Wendy has to stay here for a while, Hannah. So I want you to take real good care of your mother, okay?"

Hannah nodded, serious. "I hep Mama. See Ann Wenny again."

Wendy fought back a tear as her throat grew tight. "We'll see each other again, Hannah. Love you, sweetie!" Wendy hoisted the little girl into the air and handed her to her mother. "She's a great kid, Professor Glazer."

"I know."

"Best of luck at Stanford," Wendy said. "But Danfield will sure miss you."

The public address system announced a last call for Flight 313. "Karen," Art called. All the other passengers had boarded already.

"Thanks, Wendy. Have a good summer but don't neglect your studies come fall semester. No excuses about any sophomore slump. Besides, we all need to put the past behind us and move forward with our lives."

"One day at a time."

Karen glanced down at Hannah, who was playing with the lace collar of her mother's blouse as if she were trying to determine how it was made, and nodded. When Karen looked up again, her eyes were moist. "Take care of Alex, too."

Wendy nodded. "Don't forget to send your E-mail address."

Art stepped beside Karen and offered his free hand to Wendy. She took it and yanked him forward into a hug. "Bye, Art. It's been a pleasure."

"Sure has. Aside from all the evil witch monster stuff."

"Yeah, that I could have done without," Wendy said. "You've got a special lady there."

"Two special ladies," Art said, glancing at Karen and Hannah. He turned back to Wendy and brushed a strand of auburn hair away from her face. "Letting your hair grow?"

Wendy shrugged, embarrassed. "Something different. Until it becomes a hassle."

"It suits you."

Wendy laughed. "You sound like my mom. Hey, you guys better get moving. Those tickets are nonrefundable."

As they walked down the ramp to board the Boeing 757, Hannah watched Wendy over Karen's shoulder. Wendy gave her a little wave and Hannah curled her fingers open and closed, a slow-motion farewell. "See Ann Wenny again."

After they were gone and the plane had taxied away from the boarding ramp toward the runway, Wendy sat down in one of the molded plastic chairs, all of which were momentarily empty. She planted her elbows on her knees and rested her face against her palms. When Alex stepped up beside her, she was crying silently. He laid a gentle hand on her shoulder. "That does it," he said. "I'm buying one of those portable motorized scooters."

Wendy laughed. "You'll break your legs—again." She stood and walked into his embrace, tucking her head in the hollow under his chin. "Everybody's leaving."

"Not everyone," Alex said. "Not for good. Frankie will be back for fall semester. I'll be back even sooner."

"Promise?"

"Scout's honor."

She looked up at him. "You were a Boy Scout?"

"Well, if you're gonna get all technical . . ."

She punched his shoulder, the right one. Once, a couple months ago, she'd slugged his left shoulder and his face had gone ashen. He'd almost fainted from the pain. "Wait here for me?" she asked.

"Not going anywhere."

Wendy walked against the flow of traffic to the nearest rest room, which was currently empty. By some weird trick of acoustics, all the ambient sounds of a thriving airport were muffled. The whisper of her shoes and the sound of her own breathing seemed amplified, as was the steady drip from a faucet at the opposite end of the long row of sinks. The cold fluorescent lighting seemed to sap all color out of the long room.

She examined her face in the mirror. Her eyes were a little puffy and red-rimmed from crying, and her hair was disheveled from running along the concourse, but otherwise she looked okay. Since she never wore mascara, she avoided the crying hazard of sad-clown face.

She worried about Professor Glazer and Hannah. While they never really discussed Hannah's accelerated growth and intellect, the circumstances of the little girl's birth weighed on both their minds. Wendy half believed that Professor Glazer took the teaching position in California to distance herself from what had happened on

Halloween in Windale, as if moving thousands of miles away would be enough to make her life and Hannah's life normal again. Wendy already felt as if a piece of herself had gone missing. Of the three of them, Wendy knew she would miss Hannah the most. She had a bond with the little girl. Maybe she was just exhibiting an early maternal instinct. *Better keep that particular thought from Alex or I'll scare him half to death.* Wendy chuckled and told herself she was being silly.

After running cold water into her cupped palms, she leaned over and splashed it on her face. She looked up and saw, standing beside her and reflected in the rest room mirror, an old woman with loose gray hair, wearing a long white robe and sandals. Wendy gasped.

In a paper thin voice, the old woman said, "It's not over."

Wendy spun around to face the woman, but nobody was there. Except for Wendy, the rest room was deserted. Wendy clutched the edge of the sink for support, forced herself to take several deep breaths. She must have imagined the old woman. *But she was so real.* Wendy walked over to the row of stalls and pushed the doors open one by one, and found each of them empty, just as she knew she would.

Voices approached. Two women. A mother and daughter, maybe, chatting about the merits of the Grand Tetons versus Yellowstone National Park as they made their way to the sink to check their hair and makeup. They glanced at Wendy briefly, the older woman smiling for a moment before resuming her conversation. Wendy forced a smile, then hurried out of the rest room.

The first thing Alex said was, "You look like you saw a ghost."

"That's one possibility."

"What happened?"

Wendy shook her head. "Wanna drive the Civic home? I'm thinking a nap might be on my agenda."

"Half-hour drive," Alex said, tapping his leg with the end of his cane. "No problem. Sure you trust me with your new car?"

"More than I trust myself at the moment."

"But you're okay?"

"I'll be fine," Wendy assured him. "Just have to remember Professor Glazer's last lesson and put the past behind me."

Gina Thorne stepped out of the shower, wrapped a towel around her body and ran a brush through her long, strawberry-blond hair to remove any tangles. The bathroom was moist with steam and the mirror was a foggy blur, revealing barely a ghostly image of her face. Scattered on the floor were a half dozen empty plastic bottles of various bath and shower gels, their mingled scents wafting off of her exposed skin.

She walked down the hall to her bedroom, her bare feet leaving wet prints on the deep pile white carpeting. After closing the door she hit the remote control to turn on the nineteen-inch television, switched to an MTV beach party event and muted the sound. Next she turned on her stereo and scanned the stations till she found one playing a rap metal song by a band with a lead singer whose voice had probably been enhanced by a shot of drain cleaner. It was almost like aural, if not melodic, violence. She cranked up the sound until she could feel the bass in the floorboards.

In one corner was a trash can overflowing with her entire collection of Beanie Babies, each one stashed with a letter opener, their spongy-pellet guts littering the pale blue carpeting like lumpy confetti. The stuffed creatures were beyond disgusting. She wondered how she had ever tolerated them . . . or how she had ever accumulated such a pathetic, syrupy collection of music CDs. And she'd taken great delight in slashing the hell out of the Thomas Kinkade lighthouse print that had looked down on her bed.

After toweling herself dry she tossed the towel on the floor and examined her body in the full length mirror. It had taken several months, but she'd finally shed all the weight she'd gained during her concealed pregnancy along with an extra ten pounds. Although she had never been as fit as she was now, all her curves were more pronounced. Turning in profile to the mirror, she appraised the smooth curve of her rear end, placed a splayed palm against her flat stomach, before sliding her hands up to cup the swell of her breasts. It was as if she were seeing her body for the first time, with a stranger's eyes.

She slipped into a black bra, fastened the front clasp, then stepped into a pair of black bikini panties. Dropping to her unmade bed, she lit a cigarette and began to paint her fingernails cherry red.

Out of the corner of her eye, she noticed her bedroom door open. Standing in the doorway, holding onto the knob as he stared at her, was her thirteen-year-old stepbrother, Todd.

"What are you staring at, you little perv?"

Todd gulped. "Nothing much—loser," he said, finally. "Dad says turn the music down, you're giving him a headache. Mom says dinner's almost ready."

Gina stood and walked toward the stereo, aware of Todd continuing to stare at her in bra and panties. She lowered the volume and said in a threatening tone. "Next time, knock!"

"I knocked, bitch," he said. "Not my fault you couldn't hear!"

"Knock louder, or I'll slice your little root off while you're asleep."

"I'm telling Mom."

"Go ahead and tell her, Toad."

Gina slammed the door behind him, cursed under her breath, and turned up the volume close to where it had been before. She dressed in a sleeveless silk leopard-print blouse and a black leather skirt that fell to mid thigh, finally strapping on a pair of black stiletto heels.

Inevitably her mother rapped her knuckles on the door and opened it without waiting for Gina's invitation to enter. First thing she did was turn off the stereo. "You upset your brother."

"Stepbrother," Gina corrected. "And he deserved it. Little pervert was staring at me in my underwear."

At thirty-nine, Caitlin Thorne-Gallo was a raven-haired beauty who, during her marriage to the late Alden

Thorne, improved upon her natural good looks with a vigorous round of nip, tuck, and augmentation. Almost five years ago, Alden Thorne, founder and CEO of Thorne Biotech, spotted the recently divorced Caitlin Hayes in his own marketing department. After a whirlwind, three-month affair and despite a thirty-one-year age difference, Alden and Caitlin were married. A short but prosperous marriage for Caitlin, since Gina doubted her mother had ever loved the old coot. When Alden Thorne died two years ago of a heart attack, he left his considerable estate and majority holding in Thorne Biotech to his young widow.

Although Caitlin had waited over a year to marry Dominick Gallo, the regional manager in Thorne Biotech's tax department, Gina had heard the nasty rumors that the two had been having a clandestine affair while Alden Thorne was still alive. If the rumors were true, Caitlin had managed to keep the affair secret from her own daughter. Even so, Gina suspected that Gallo was simply playing gold digger to the gold digger. Karma and all that.

To Angelina, his sweet sixteen-year-old, adopted stepdaughter, Alden Thorne had left only a trust fund that wouldn't kick in until she was twenty-five years old. So Caitlin never missed an opportunity to keep her daughter in line by threatening to yank the financial rug out from under her at the slightest provocation. Gina had to endure seven more years of maternal badgering before she would have any sort of financial freedom.

"We're a family now," Caitlin said. She had been saying this since the day she remarried almost a year ago and, frankly, Gina was sick of it. "We need to get along with each other. Make this work. Will you at least try?"

"Whatever."

"Were you planning on going out tonight?"

"Brett's taking me out."

"I thought you were eating with us."

"Guess I forgot to mention it," Gina said; the thought of eating with her newest family was enough to nauseate her. "We have reservations at Roy's Steakhouse."

"Not the sort of place I'd expect to find a vegetarian."

"I gave that up, Mother. We're top of the food chain. Why pretend otherwise?" She shuddered at a sense-memory of biting into a slab of rare steak, the feel of warm blood trickling down her chin. At least she thought it was rare steak . . . and that the memory was hers. Lately her memories had been jumbled. Ever since that night at the Harrison Motor Lodge.

Caitlin glanced at the smoldering cigarette in the ashtray on the floor and heaved an indignant sigh. "You know I don't allow smoking in the house."

"Nerves," Gina said. She'd started smoking a couple months ago and couldn't get enough of it. Actually, there were a lot of things besides cigarettes she couldn't seem to get enough of, alcohol being one of them. "Finals coming up. Besides, next year I'll be in a dorm at Danfield and you won't have to worry about me messing up your perfect little life anymore."

"That's not what I meant," her mother said, and sighed again. "Listen, Gina, I think it would be a good idea if you had a talk with Father Murray. You haven't been yourself lately." She looked around the cluttered bedroom, silently cataloguing all the oddities she found there before giving up. "The smoking, the late hours, poor grades, leaving your room a mess."

Her mother, the hypocrite, had a maid come in five days a week, but Sylvia was restricted from cleaning either Gina's or Todd's room, supposedly to teach them some responsibility. Meanwhile, Caitlin never had to lift a finger.

Caitlin droned on, "Not to mention your recent rude behavior. Tell me, when was the last time you joined us at church?"

Last year, Gina thought. "I've been real busy."

"It's always some excuse," her mother said. "But Gina, while you live in this house, you obey our rules. If you expect me to foot the bill for your tuition to Danfield, I demand that you treat your stepbrother, your stepfather, and me with respect. And it wouldn't kill you to show a little gratitude."

Since her mother had ample means, Gina wouldn't qualify for any financial aid, so she had to play ball by her mother's rules. "I *am* grateful, Mother."

"Then show it. Talk to Father Murray."

Gina nodded. *Long enough to tell him to fuck off.*

"Thanks, dear, I appreciate it." Her mother kissed her on the cheek. "Don't stay out too late. You know I worry."

Gina closed the door behind her mother and banged her head against the door. "I gotta get out of here," she whispered. She sat before her vanity mirror and applied red lipstick to her full lips. The same shade she'd applied to her fingernails. She stared at her face in the mirror, once again with that odd, distant appraisal. Her pale blue eyes, almost translucent, stared back at her. Trembling, her hand reached out and pressed against the glass of the mirror. Anger flashed within her like a sudden spark and the glass shattered under her palm. Pulling her hand quickly away, she marveled at the broad starburst pattern that now fractured her reflection. She'd applied only the slightest pressure to the glass and it had burst. *Must be defective*, she reasoned.

By the time she finished blow-drying her hair, Dominick, her latest stepfather, called up that Brett had arrived. Gina grabbed a clutch purse and hurried down the stairs, anxious to be out of the house, under the twilight sky, free of criticism, constraints, and false familial bonding.

Almost standing guard, Dominick waited at the bottom of the steps. Although he'd doffed his suit jacket, he still wore his white-on-white dress shirt, scarlet necktie in a perfect little Windsor knot, charcoal-gray suspenders and matching pants over black, tasseled loafers. At thirty-six, Dominick Gallo was three years younger than Gina's mother. Just under six feet tall, with wavy brown hair and a well-trimmed mustache, he stayed reasonably fit through regular tennis and golf dates with some of his fellow managers. If not for a too long nose and the smug attitude he wore like a tailored overcoat, Gina might have considered him handsome. Regardless, he was a self-righteous pain in the ass covering up, she suspected, for an inferiority complex or a small trouser hose. When Caitlin decided to take his surname, Dom Gallo had puffed up his chest, but he probably could've done without the Thorne hyphenate. *Having everyone assume you're the boss lady's boy toy must do wonders for the self-image.*

He looked her over with his patronizing little smirk, as if she must pass his inspection before he'd let her out. Either that or he just wanted to be sure to get an eyeful. "School tomorrow. I assume you finished all your assignments."

"I'm caught up through Friday."

"Good to hear it. Be home by ten-thirty," he said finally. "And, Gina,"—he caught her bare arm and gave a little squeeze—"don't do anything to embarrass your mother or me."

She smiled pleasantly as she pulled her arm away. "Wouldn't think of it, Dom."

"Can't say I like your attitude lately, young lady."

Who asked you? Gina thought and squeezed by him before he could cop another feel. She bit her tongue and slipped out the door. Anything she said would only start a fight, ending in her being sent to her room or risking the loss of her collegiate funding. Getting to Danfield was secondary to just getting out.

Brett was leaning against one of the wraparound veranda posts. He turned as the right double-door swung open. While Gina had become more vibrant in the months since that night at the Harrison Motor Lodge, Brett had become more haggard. He smiled. "You look terrific."

"I know," she said. "Let's get the hell out of here."

In the pickup truck he leaned over to kiss her and she turned her mouth away, offering only her cheek. "Time to mess up the lipstick later," she said. "I'm ravenous."

He started the engine and drove out onto Main Street without saying a word. Finally, she sighed and asked, "What?"

"Nothing."

"Stop brooding and speak."

"It's just that you're so . . . different now. I mean, I'm glad, though. You've put it behind you."

She knew what *it* was. "Get over it, Brett. Or this won't work between us. I have no intention of wallowing in depression with you for the rest of my life."

"I know," he said. "You're right. It just . . . helps to talk about it, and you're the only one I can talk to, so . . ."

"I'm sick to death of talking about it," Gina said, exasperated. "We have a bright future ahead of us, but not if you keep looking over your shoulder." She reached into the lap of his Dockers and squeezed. "Be a good boy tonight and I'll give you a little surprise."

"What—I thought we weren't going to—?"

"Changed my mind about a lot of things," she said, crooking a smile. "Decided to seize the day." She squeezed him again, harder this time. "Among other things." She glanced out on Main and saw a row of fast-food restaurants. "Pull over!"

Brett swung the pickup onto the shoulder. "What's wrong?"

Gina massaged her temples, trying to ease the flare of pain she'd felt a moment earlier. Something about the restaurants had made her incredibly tense. She looked at their plastic signs and garish lights. McDonald's, Burger King, Wendy's . . .

She shook her head, brushed her long hair back from her face. "I don't know. Something . . . I can't remember now."

"Put the past behind us and move forward with our lives."
Karen's parting words had become a challenge for Wendy. Either by fate or coincidence, there was a full moon this night and Wendy had all but abandoned any kind of ritual or mirror book observations on the Esbats. After dropping Alex off at his dorm so he could finish packing for his flight the next day, she had stopped home for a purifying bath among scattered lavender petals. Then she'd driven the Civic out to Gable Road, parked on the shoulder, leaving a white T-shirt dangling from the driver's side window to convey a breakdown, before making her way along the game trail to her clearing. She was determined to finish before dark as a way of easing herself back into her clearing, back into her outdoor rituals.

From an ash staff, birch twigs, and willow binding she'd purchased at The Crystal Path, she'd constructed a small witch's broom. She used that broom now and with symbolic, sweeping strokes purified her space, which seemed all the more important since she'd been away so long. With peg, string, and funnel, she poured a thin line of flour to form her circle before unfolding her meditation mat. Since she planned an abbreviated ritual and wanted to maintain her nerve throughout, she chose not to go sky-clad for this particular Esbat, though she had no problem removing socks and shoes.

She welcomed the four elements, starting with Air to the east and proceeding clockwise through Fire to the south, Water to the west, and finishing with Earth to the north. As she proceeded, she gained confidence in herself, in her ritual. She'd only brought a few ingredients with her, enough to make a healing sachet for Alex, something he could take with him over the summer to Minneapolis.

First, the parsley and sage she'd purchased at The Crystal Path had to be consecrated. She offered the seeds and leaves to each of the four elements, before using her bolline, the white-handled ceremonial knife, to cut the leaves into tiny pieces. If she were making an infusion with spring water, she would grind them into powder with mortar and pestle. Instead, she slipped the snipped pieces into a white linen pouch, along with a polished rose quartz stone she'd washed in a fresh-water stream. She tied the pouch with a length of blue ribbon, blue being a healing color, and offered it to the north. She visualized Alex walking through a meadow, unencumbered by a cane, without discomfort or even a limp, holding the image until it seemed more memory than desire. "Mother Earth, bestow on this bundle the blessing of health and the power of healing." If only in her imagination, within the confines of her visualization, she felt a warm tingling in her fingers and along her arm.

Her one bit of magic complete, she needed to reabsorb the magical energies she had raised from within herself. She broke a gingerbread cookie in half and scattered crumbs on the ground beside her as an offering, followed by a few drops of milk. She nibbled on the other half of the cookie and drank the rest of the milk. Finally, she thanked the elements for their attendance and broke the circle.

Twilight was past and the shadows were lengthening, darkening, but she felt invigorated and safe in her special place. The taint of Wither was gone at last. She felt whole again.

Gina climbed out of the pickup truck, calling to Brett who was filling up the gas tank, "I want chocolate." She walked into the gas station's mini-mart, glancing at the bored teenager working the cash register. Gina thought she might have seen him in the halls at Harrison High but couldn't recall his name. She walked down the candy aisle and selected a Hershey bar. Pure chocolate, no nuts, nougat, wafers, raisins, or crispies. She ripped off the wrapper, snapped off a section down to the "S," and pushed it into her mouth with a low moan of delight. She finished that bar and ate another, taking a third for the road.

She walked up to the register, a pronounced slink in her walk, as she now had the clerk's full attention and wondered if he'd accuse her of stealing. He wore a grease-stained gray polyester shirt with "Kenny" embroidered on a patch above the pocket. Placing the Hershey bar on the narrow counter, she looked through her clutch purse for money and found only one crumpled up dollar bill. *This won't do*, she thought and had a bizarre idea. Staring into the clerk's brown eyes, she said in what could best be described as a pouty voice, "Can you make change for a hundred, Kenny?"

With a gulp, he took the bill from her hand, but not before she placed her other hand on top of his and squeezed. A flash of warmth passed between them and Kenny seemed a little confused. Glancing down at the dollar bill, he stammered, "We're not supposed to accept anything bigger'n a fifty."

"But you'll make an exception for me, won't you, Kenny?"

"Yeah," he said, nodding. "No problem."

He popped open the cash register, lifted the tray, and slipped the dollar bill underneath with checks and large bills. Tomorrow his boss would probably wonder why the hell he'd hidden a dollar under the tray and why his drawer was short. Kenny counted out five twenties and handed them to her. Again, she held his hand between hers and thanked him. "Oh, you forgot to charge me for the chocolate."

He shrugged, smiled, and said, "It's on me, miss."

"You're very sweet, Kenny."

As she walked out to the pickup truck, she was sure Kenny was checking out her ass. Small tradeoff for a ninety-nine dollar profit. *Girl's gotta have some spending money.*

Brett climbed into the truck, glanced at his watch, and said, "Better hurry. Don't want to miss our reservation. And I want to make sure we have time for, you know"—he took in the long line of her thighs—"other things."

"Don't worry, Brett," she said. "We'll have plenty of time to satisfy our appetites later. First, one more stop before dinner."

"Where?"

"Holy Redeemer," Gina said, a mischievous glint in her eyes. "I promised Mother I'd have a talk with Father Murray."

Flushed with a renewed sense of inner peace, Wendy drove her Civic into the nearly empty parking lot behind Schongauer Hall. Carrying a small backpack by the straps, she hurried up the steps of the eerily quiet stairwell to the second floor. The hallway was deserted. A jazz instrumental played in a dorm room at the other end of the hall. Finals were over and almost everyone had fled the campus for summer break. On the dry-erase board mounted beside Alex's dorm room door, was a note scribbled in block letters: ON PIZZA RUN. LET YOURSELF IN!

Alex's roommate, Jesse Osborne, had also left for home—Buffalo, New York—in his decrepit station wagon, leaving behind his dorm key, which Alex had lent to Wendy for just such an occasion. She let herself in and turned on the light. The room was small, utilitarian, each side almost a mirror image of the other, with a small bed and student desk against each long wall. Underneath each bed were four drawers that substituted for stand-alone dressers. The bookshelves over the beds and desks were empty of everything save a few scattered college newspapers. Wendy looked at a couple of them and saw they were open to the sports sections, found a couple pictures of track events and a few wrestling matches. Wendy recalled that Jesse had been on the wrestling team.

At the far end of the room was a window bench that overlooked the quad. *At least Alex's room doesn't have a view of the parking lot,* she thought. On one side of the bench was a shared closet. On the other was the door into the bathroom with a small sink, stool, and shower stall. A private bathroom was a luxury. Most of the dorms had communal toilets and showers.

Alex had already packed most of his belongings away in two cloth suitcases and an Old Navy duffel bag lined up on the padded window bench. He'd left out a toiletry kit and a change of clothes. On his desk he'd laid out paper plates, napkins, and plastic cups, along with a single red rose in a narrow glass vase. She smiled at the touch of romance amid all the disposable practicality. Possibly he remembered the time she'd told him roses were used in love magic. Or, it was just a rose. Either way, she appreciated the special touch.

She sat on his bed and unzipped the backpack. Inside were two dozen white candles, a box of wooden matches, another small box, the magical healing sachet, her linen robe, and a bottle of white wine she'd liberated from her parents' liquor cabinet. She wanted to have everything ready by the time he returned.

In less than five minutes, she'd scattered the candles across the desks, bookshelves, and windowsill, saying a quick prayer as she lit them that they wouldn't trigger the sprinkler system. She poured the wine into two plastic cups and slipped into her robe, hiding her street clothes in the backpack. She put away the rest of the matches and tossed the small box on top of Alex's toiletry kit. Finally, she turned off the cold fluorescent light, dropping the small room into a warm, amber darkness. She could imagine herself floating through the night sky, each tiny candle flame a distant star.

She was in the bathroom, finger-combing her hair when she heard Alex's key in the lock. *Well, it's not a complete mess,* she said, passing judgment on her errant mane.

"One large extra cheese—Wendy? Are you here?"

"Pizza man," Wendy said, stepping out of the bathroom. "I thought you'd never get here."

Alex placed the pizza box on an open corner of one desk, looked around at the assortment of candles and said, "I have the feeling I walked in on the middle of one of your rituals."

"Not the middle," Wendy said. "The beginning. It's the time-honored I'll-miss-you-so-hurry-back ritual."

"I'm not familiar with that one," Alex said, grinning. "You'll have to walk me through the protocol."

Wendy padded over to him in her bare feet and stood close enough to feel his breath on her face. "Oh, most of the ritual should come naturally. First you get a present."

"A present? I just love a ritual present. At least I think I do."

She took his hands and placed them on the ends of the cloth belt of her robe. "Unwrap it and find out." He tugged the belt loop and it came undone. She guided his hands up to the collar of her robe and helped him pull it open. It slipped off her shoulders and dropped to the floor. She stood before him completely naked, bathed in the golden light of two dozen candles.

With a peck on his cheek, she said, "Grab your toiletry kit and join me under the covers."

"You want me to shave now?"

"No, silly!" she said, slapping him on the rump.

He had a twinkle in his eye and not just from the scattered candlelight. "You want me to shave you?"

She paused for a moment. "Ask me some other time," she said, before slipping under the covers of his bed. "Now hurry up and get under here with me."

Alex walked over to his toiletry kit and clucked his tongue. "A twelve pack?"

"I enjoy the never-ending struggle for perfection," Wendy quipped.

He brought the box back with him, but even as he pulled his shirt over his head, he hesitated. "We haven't—I mean, I'm not sure I'm ready for—"

"It's been almost seven months, Alex," Wendy said. "I'm ready to give those patchwork limbs of yours a test drive."

Alex chuckled. "Promise you'll be gentle with me?"

"If you insist," she said, helping him with his button-fly jeans.

"You know, the pizza's gonna get cold," Alex said. "We could do this after."

Wendy had an added gleam in her eye. "We will."

Wendy was hungry for the taste of him, the feel of

him, the warmth of him. They had been intimate for the first and only time just hours before he'd been attacked at Marshall Field. She'd almost lost him forever that night and she couldn't bear the thought of him flying so far away, not seeing him again for months without being close to him one more time. Despite the urgency of her need to be with him, she had to maintain a slow, careful pace, watching his face for any signs of pain as she rolled on top of him or as he twisted underneath her. She found the best position was with Alex on his back while she straddled his hips, her knees supporting most of her weight. She helped him slip on the condom, then guided him inside her. As she found a slow, determined rhythm she leaned down and trailed her hair across his chest, then planted hot, breathy kisses along his throat. He ran his hands up her sides and cupped her breasts.

Afterward, she lay beside him, studying his face in the candlelight, memorizing his features, tracing the scar above his right eyelid with her index finger. "Oh, I forgot, I have another present."

"Maybe we should eat a slice of pizza first."

She leaned way out of the bed and reached for her robe on the floor, pulling it toward her by the cloth belt. Alex took the opportunity to give her bare ass a playful swat. "Hey! Save that stuff for later."

She curled into his arms and handed him the sachet. "Something to remember me by."

"I think you've already given me that."

She kissed his cheek. "You're sweet. But this will make you better, patchwork limbs and all."

He took the small pouch and noticed her broad smile. Arching an eyebrow, he said, "You were out in the woods tonight, weren't you."

"Small ritual," Wendy confessed. "One spell. Healing magic. Kind of a health talisman. Keep this close to you. In a pocket, under your pillow at night."

"I thought you were nervous about going out in the woods again."

"I was," Wendy said. "But it's time to forget the past."

"And move forward with our lives," Alex finished.

"Exactly." Wendy sighed in contentment and rested her cheek against his bare chest. "I realized tonight I finally feel at peace again. I finally feel safe."

For nine-year-old Abby MacNeil, the monsters had always been real. Sometimes they were even human. But not always. Almost seven months ago, one of the not-so-human monsters had killed her father, who was himself a creature that lived on in one of her occasional nightmares, if not during her waking hours. She remembered his name, Randy, but his face was fading away, a lost memory. He had never loved her as a father should love and cherish his daughter, had never been kind to her, and, when he had too much to drink, had touched her in ways that made her hate herself and hate him. She'd been a nuisance in his life, but he was all the family she could ever remember. And all she wanted was to forget he ever existed.

Art Leeson and Sheriff Nottingham had rescued her from the other monster, the ancient, dark monster called

Sarah, who could fly and smelled like the worst garbage she could ever imagine. The sheriff, who asked her to call him Mr. Nottingham, and his family had taken her in, but while she had become comfortable in their home, she still felt like an outsider, a visitor on a really long sleepover.

All six of them lived in a one-story frame house with three bedrooms. Abby had her own bed but shared a room with seven-year-old Erica, who insisted that Abby was her older sister. Five-year-old Max and four-year-old Benjamin had bunk beds in the smallest bedroom. Of course, the sheriff and his wife, Christina, had the largest bedroom, with their own bathroom. Rowdy, the Nottinghams' chocolate Lab, seemed to prefer the boys' bedroom most nights. The sheriff had built an addition behind the two-car garage and used that room as his office. Behind the house was a large deck with eight sides, shaped like a stop sign, and a bigger, fenceless yard that ended with a dark tree line.

Looking dark and enchanted under the full moon, the forest seemed to call to Abby just as it had before, behind her own house. Then she had found the gravestones of the three Windale witches, the witches who had become the not-so-human monsters.

Abby leaned against the deck railing and stared across the yard into the deeper darkness of the trees. She remembered dreaming of the forest, running between the mighty columns of trees with long, loping strides. When Mrs. Nottingham asked who wanted a piece of chocolate cake, Abby waited until Erica, Max, and Ben had run inside screaming, "I do! I do!" before calling after them, "I'm stuffed." Rowdy had gone with the majority, no doubt anticipating more table scraps.

"Well, let me know if you change your mind, Abby," Mrs. Nottingham called. "Time for baths soon."

Abby was already crossing the yard, mesmerized by the scent of the trees and the rich earth before her. As she stepped over some tangled underbrush past the tree line, the darkness seemed to open up for her, revealing treacherous, exposed tree roots and outlining low hanging branches that might have scratched her face or jabbed her eyes. Even as her vision adjusted to the darkness, her hearing became more acute, picking up the distant sound of a hooting owl as well as the rustling of a nearby raccoon. The air was alive with the buzz of insects and the rich fragrance of moist earth and fresh leaves. Soon she heard the trickling of a small stream and she let herself follow the peaceful sound, closing the distance to the source of fresh water. The full moon peeked between the crisscrossing tree boughs more frequently as she neared the stream and she knew the forest was thinning at last. In a few minutes, she stepped out of the trees and stood alone on the grassy bank of the meandering stream.

Abby sat on the grass and felt a shuddering in her body.

Less than seven months ago, before the not-so-human monster had kidnapped her from the hospital chapel, Abby had been in a terrible car accident with Art. She had been paralyzed, unable to move her arms or legs, and by the looks on the faces of her doctors at the time, they thought she would never walk again. In overheard, whispered conversations, she had listened to them talk about cancer or something else, strange growths that had covered her bones, unlike anything they had ever seen before. They never could explain what had happened to her bones or why they had healed completely soon afterward. She was a medical miracle, some of the nurses said, or at least a medical mystery. Maybe that's why she felt like an outsider. She had experienced something no other little girl ever had.

Abby shuddered again and felt an ache deep in her bones. One of her nightmares was that she would wake up and find out that she hadn't been cured, that she was still stuck in that hospital bed, a helpless prisoner to her own paralysis. *If nightmare monsters are real, maybe what you think is your real life is nothing but a dream,* Abby thought. *Maybe I'm dreaming now.*

Then she screamed.

In the moonlight, her eyes reflected yellow.

Her right hand burned so bad she thought it was on fire. She grabbed it in her left hand and held it up to her eyes. Beneath her flesh, the bones were moving, contracting, her fingers shortening, becoming blunt. The fine blond hairs on her forearm multiplied and became coarse, turning into white fur, a shade lighter than her hair. The crunching pain of shifting bones spread to her other hand, then her legs, hips, and even her jaw. She screamed again, but this time the sound came out more like a desperate howl, for she knew the awful truth of it.

Abby MacNeil herself had become a monster.

• • •

Gina Thorne entered the Holy Redeemer Church through the back entrance, turned at the corridor that branched off from the choir rehearsal room and walked to Father Murray's office. If she recalled correctly, he stayed in his office till eight o'clock on Wednesdays. She was careful not to make too much noise in her stiletto heels. Best not to ruin the surprise.

The frosted glass door was open only a few inches, obstructing most of the view into the office. All she could see was a mahogany bookcase. Instead of knocking, she gripped and opened the door. Father Murray shoved his desk drawer closed, almost dropping the cigarette he held in his other hand. He'd been sitting alone in the weak spill of light from a green-shaded banker's lamp, not expecting anyone. "I'm sorry, you startled me, young lady," he stammered. He wore a black shirt with a clerical collar. His hair was more gray than black and hadn't been washed in days, while his pale face was a study in fine lines and wrinkles, his bulbous nose etched in a splay of tiny red blood vessels. And he needed a shave. "May I help you?"

"I was told you wanted to see me, Father," Gina said, spreading her arms. "So here I am."

"I'm sorry, I don't recall your name."

"Gina," she said. "Angelina Thorne."

"My heavens," he said. "You have changed."

"Could you light me?" Gina asked. She took a Kool cigarette out of her clutch purse, put it to her lips, then leaned over his desk, far enough for him to get a complete view of her cleavage, far enough for him to catch a good whiff of at least three of her shower gels.

He opened the top drawer and took out a Zippo lighter, giving her a glimpse of what else he kept hidden in his desk. With a trembling hand, he lit her cigarette, then pointed to an uncomfortable looking wooden chair and said, "Please. Sit down."

She dropped back into the hard wooden chair, as unforgiving as a church pew, and crossed her legs, so the leather skirt would ride up, exposing even more of her creamy bare thigh. Father Murray looked away, making a show of straightening several stacks of paper, folders, and ledgers on his desk.

Gina inhaled and blew a stream of smoke up toward the sign on the wall, the sign that read NO SMOKING.

He followed her gaze and cleared his throat. "Oh, that. Well, it's after hours, don't you know. Nobody to complain."

"Lucky for us."

"Quite," he said. "Now, if I recall the situation correctly, your mother is concerned about your behavior these past several months."

"She'll get over it."

"I think it's her desire that *you*, as you say, 'get over it,' Miss Thorne. She tells me you haven't been to church at all this year. That you are rude, inconsiderate, stay out too late, and have let your grades suffer."

"My grades will be fine," Gina said. "I've made special . . . tutoring arrangements with some of my teachers and they are quite . . . pleased to give me the grades I deserve."

"Be that as it may, I want you to know it is not uncommon for teenagers to go through a rebellious period. Still and all, you wouldn't want to participate in behavior that would jeopardize your future. And you must be mindful of your mother's prominent position in this community."

And appearances are everything to Mother, Gina thought sourly.

"Don't worry, Father, I don't think she'll forget your offering plate."

"Insolence is an ugly trait, Gina."

"My insolence isn't why your hands are shaking, Father," Gina said. "Don't mind me. Go ahead. Take that little flask out of your drawer and finish what you started before I so *rudely* interrupted you."

"We are here to discuss your behavior," Father Murray said, his face becoming red in indignation.

Gina blew a stream of smoke into his face. "Careful. High blood pressure is the silent killer."

"Young lady!"

"Listen, old man," Gina said. "I don't have time to sit here and be lectured by a hypocrite. As long as we're discussing vices, just how many do you have, Father? Smoking, drinking, young choir boys?"

"Miss Thorne!"

"No, I suppose not," she said. "I saw the way you pretended not to check out my legs."

"This meeting is over!"

"Fine, then let me help you out, Father. I know you're anxious to resume your Bible study." Gina leaned forward, her brow creasing in concentration. Anger helped. The spark warmed her, made her whole body hot and tight with the need for violence. She watched in satisfaction as the desk drawer jerked open, as if by an invisible hand.

Father Murray gaped, then gasped as the silver flask rose from inside the drawer and wobbled in midair on its way to his face. He swatted it aside, as if it were a stinging insect, and jumped out of his chair. The screw cap, already loose, fell off as the flask struck the desk blotter. The metal container tipped over, spreading a puddle of whiskey. Gina took an exaggerated whiff. "Strong stuff, Father. I approve."

Father Murray's face was livid, his pale skin now a blotchy red. Gina imagined she could hear his heart thundering in his chest, rushing blood through clogged arteries, and it was beating too fast, working too hard. The priest was already breathless. With the power of another thought, spurred by her own rage, she tweaked his heart, made it beat faster and faster still.

Father Murray gasped again, but this time clutched his chest with his free hand. Blood spilled from his right nostril and over his lips to stain the stubble on his chin. Trembling, he fell back into his chair. His cigarette fell to the desktop and began to char the dark wood grain. "You—you are evil!"

"Now, now, Father," Gina said. "That's not a very politically correct thing to say. Remember, I'm the misunderstood, rebellious teenager."

But his voice failed him, followed a moment later by

his heart. Father Murray fell forward, his face splashing into the puddle of whiskey. Gina leaned forward in her chair, elbows on her knees, then looked at her own smoldering cigarette. "These things really are hazardous to your health." She pursed her lips and blew the puddle of whiskey toward the priest's smoldering cigarette where it lay at the edge of the desk. When the first drop made contact with the glowing ember, a blue flame caught and *whoosh*ed across the entire pool of whiskey. Father Murray's face happened to be right in the middle of that puddle. His clerical collar began to burn and his face darkened.

The scent of burning flesh intrigued her, but not enough to risk ruining her leather skirt, should the office's antiquated sprinkler system decide to kick in. She took a drag of her cigarette, shook her head and left the burning priest in his office.

Gina followed the corridor around the sanctuary area and entered the church by the door near the altar rail. Beside every other row of pews was a tapered stained glass window fifteen feet high, depicting the Stations of the Cross and other biblical scenes. Half of them had probably been donated by Alden Thorne. *And the old man had given her nothing!* Gina crossed to the nave and walked halfway down the length of the church before turning to face the crucifix she knew was there, the ten-foot long plaster Jesus with his crown of thorns, lit from above as if by heavenly light. She hadn't been to this place in months and would never come again. She knew that now. And as she stood there, the anger, the rage, and the hate boiled within her. The energy from all that fury had to go somewhere. The church pews began to vibrate against their floor bolts. Still it wasn't enough. Plaster statues of various saints in various states of martyrdom wobbled on their pedestals, then toppled over and split into pieces, losing limbs. But still it wasn't enough.

She squeezed her fists at her sides until the bones creaked and her fingernails scored her palms and drew blood. She gritted her teeth until her jaw ached and tendons along her neck throbbed. Finally, she threw her head back, arms raised at shoulder level, bloody fingers straining outward, and screamed with the intemperate wail of a banshee.

With an ear-rending explosion, every stained glass window burst simultaneously, blowing out of arched frames in thousands of jagged pieces, bits of multicolored shrapnel carrying messages of salvation and redemption too small to be understood.

At the same moment, the emergency lights and all the electronic votive candles popped, casting the church into unaccustomed darkness. And the long shadows were a comfort to Angelina Thorne. A comfort to her and the dark entity blossoming inside her with a growing memory of ancient evil.

CHAPTER TWO

As he left the town council building complex to visit Abby at the hospital, Sheriff Bill Nottingham swung his white Jetta to the side of the road and shifted into park to watch the construction workers walking along the roof of the Witch Museum. After several months, the reconstruction was only about half complete. Fire had gutted the place last year, but the mayor was determined to have it back in business by the end of summer, well in advance of the heavy autumn tourist season. In a few short months it should be better than new, the fire and tragedy of Halloween 1999 irrelevant, if not completely forgotten.

Too bad we can't rebuild people the same way. Try as he

might, the sheriff had been unable to put the memories behind him. If he closed his eyes, he could still see Abby bound in the crumbling barn like a spider's webbed morsel, prey to a witch that was not really a witch at all, but some sort of demonic creature, three hundred years old. Art Leeson had destroyed that monster, with a little help from the sheriff, if he was willing to give himself any credit. But what cost remained to be paid for that night? Abby's miraculous cure now seemed to be only a remission.

The sheriff pulled into the flow of traffic and made his way to Windale General. After parking the Jetta in the visitor lot, he swung by the gift shop to pick up a small bouquet of flowers featuring a stuffed polar bear cub with its arms and legs wrapped around the plastic vase.

Though Christina was scheduled to bring Abby home today, the doctors still had no idea what was wrong with her. After some blood work, a series of X rays and a CAT scan, Dr. Khayatian had pronounced Abby MacNeil a perfectly healthy nine-year-old girl. But the doctor hadn't been there the night of the full moon, hadn't heard Abby screaming. The sheriff had found her lying unconscious in the grass by a small stream. She'd been sweat-soaked, her clothing torn at elbows and knees as if she'd been attacked by some wild animal. But aside from some minor bruising, her skin was uncut and she'd suffered no serious, visible injuries. Nevertheless, she'd remained unconscious for almost three days and the doctors had no answer for that, other than some talk of exhaustion and dehydration.

Before turning down the corridor to Abby's room, the sheriff stopped to greet the three nurses standing behind the central nurses' island. One of them, Jill Schuller, had graduated from Harrison High the same year as the sheriff and Art Leeson. "Good morning, Bill," she said.

"How's she been?"

"Quiet, mostly," Jill said. "Staring out the window."

"What about her sleep?"

Jill nodded. "She asked for the girl again, by name."

Art had told him about Wendy Ward and her role in the events of last Halloween. The sheriff had even seen the local girl visiting Karen Glazer, one of her college professors. Still, he didn't believe Abby had had much if any contact with Wendy herself. *So why would Abby be calling for Wendy in her sleep?* Even though Dr. Khayatian had no idea what was afflicting Abby, the sheriff had a dark and certain suspicion it had something to do with the events of last Halloween. Despite wild rumors of Wendy dabbling in the occult, he didn't suspect her of any harmful intent. She might, however, provide some help in unraveling this new mystery surrounding Abby.

With a soft knock on the open door, the sheriff took off what Abby called his "Smokey the Bear" hat and entered her room. She was lying in bed, her head turned away from him. While she'd been unconscious, they'd hooked her up to an IV to keep her hydrated, but now she had a pitcher of water and a juice box on her bedside table and appeared to be taking liquids orally. For a moment he thought she was asleep, but as he rounded the foot of her bed, he saw she was staring out the window at a line of trees beyond the hospital's west parking lot.

"Hey, kiddo," he said. "Look what I brought." After a long moment, she turned her gaze away from the window and looked at the flowers and polar bear vase, netting him one small smile. "You can take him home with you today." That seemed to get her attention—the thought of leaving more than the polar bear perk. She pushed herself up into a proper sitting position. "Mrs. Nottingham is coming by in a bit with Erica to take you home."

"What about Max and Ben?"

"They're staying with Mrs. Schaeffer this afternoon." Mindy Schaeffer, the wife of his deputy, Jeff.

"Crash." Abby smiled. "They'll love that."

Bill chuckled. Whenever they visited the Schaeffers, both boys could inevitably be found mesmerized in front of Jeff's PlayStation, putting Crash Bandicoot through his paces. Bill placed the flowers on the table and sat on the edge of the bed, watching the young girl. Brushing her pale blond hair back from her forehead, he asked, "You ready to go home, kiddo?"

"Definitely."

"Any idea what happened out there? In the woods?"

Abby shrugged. "Don't know," she said. "I went for a walk . . ."

"You weren't scared out there? Alone? In the dark?"

"It wasn't too dark, at first," she explained. "And I'm not a little kid anymore."

"No," he said, "you're not."

"And I like the woods."

"It can be dangerous out there, kiddo." She was silent. "Do you remember what happened by the water? Why you—" He'd been about to say "screamed" but that seemed too scary a word, somehow. "—yelled?"

Abby shook her head, and he had the feeling—call it "cop instinct"—that she was holding something back. "Don't remember."

"See anyone else out there?" The thought that somebody might have tried to hurt her made his hands tremble. She'd already been through more than anyone her age should ever have to endure. "Maybe that's why you screamed?"

Abby shook her head. "I was alone," she said. "It was peaceful, until . . . I don't remember."

"I understand," the sheriff said, brushing her hair back again.

He looked up at a knock on the door.

"Hi, Sheriff," Wendy Ward said, holding a helium-filled Tigger balloon in one hand. She wore an emerald green pullover and a wraparound black skirt, or maybe it was one of those skorts, with ankle-high white socks and black running shoes. The sheriff remembered her in black and grays, with shorter hair. "Hope you like Tigger, Abby. They were all out of Pooh."

"Tigger's cool," Abby said, smiling.

The sheriff stood, having given equal attention to Abby's reaction at seeing Wendy and vice versa. If either of them were hiding anything, he couldn't tell. "Thanks for stopping by, Wendy," he said. "I thought Abby might like to see you. As I mentioned on the phone, she was out for quite a while. In her sleep, she seemed to be calling for you."

"Me?"

"Well, she asked for *a* Wendy," he said. "I just assumed she meant you."

"I'm not sure why," Wendy said, walking closer to the bed, her eyes locked on Abby's face, searching for something. Whatever it was, she didn't seem to find it. "Abby? Were you dreaming about me?"

Abby bit her lip in concentration. "I remember I was scared."

"What scared you?" the sheriff asked.

"Not me," Abby said. "I was scared for Wendy."

Wendy took Abby's hand in both of hers and Abby sucked in her breath as if the contact startled her. "Why were you scared for me?"

"Because she was after you," Abby said, a little agitated, reliving the fear of her dreams. "She was gonna hurt you, Wendy."

"Who?"

"The other one," Abby said. "The other witch. The one called Wither."

Wendy seemed to relax a bit. "She's dead, Abby. I watched her die. She can't hurt me or you or anybody anymore."

Abby sighed and fell back against her pillow, looking out the window once more, toward the trees beyond the west lot. "I know," she said, almost too low for them to hear. "It was just a bad dream."

The sheriff looked at Wendy. "Can I speak with you? Outside?" Wendy nodded, and he looked down at Abby. "Be right back, kiddo."

Abby didn't reply, but as he walked Wendy toward the door, Abby called out, "I have to help you, Wendy."

Wendy stopped and returned to the bed. "Why, Abby? Why do you have to help me?"

Abby looked at Wendy, her face solemn. "Because, Wendy," she said, "when I don't help you, you die."

Outside Abby's hospital room, Wendy leaned against the cold wall and tilted her head back to stare at the ceiling tiles and banks of fluorescent lights, anything to avoid the sheriff's penetrating gaze. *He thinks I'm keeping secrets from him. And sometimes I feel like I am, but I have absolutely no idea what they are. They're even secret from me.*

She chuckled bitterly.

Sheriff Nottingham put his hat back on and somehow it seemed as if that meant he was back on official police business, questioning a suspect. "Something funny?"

"No," Wendy said. "It's just the irony of it all. Every time I tell myself to put it all behind me, something happens to bring it back."

Alex had only been gone a few days and she already felt more alone than she had in years. She needed somebody to talk to, somebody who had been there, who understood everything that had happened. Despite everything the sheriff had seen, Wendy was too nervous to confide in him.

"What did you make of all that?" the sheriff asked, nodding toward Abby's room.

"Bad dreams," Wendy said. "Nightmares. It has to be nightmares. I saw Wither crushed under tons of stone. Abby was traumatized by everything that happened to her." The sheriff nodded, conceding this point. "It's gonna take some time for her to heal. And she's not the only one."

"I suppose so," the sheriff agreed. "But nightmares don't explain how I found her, out there in the woods, soaked with sweat, clothes all torn but not a scratch on her. They don't explain why she screamed so loud we could hear her all the way back at the house or why she was unconscious for nearly three days. Do they?"

Wendy could only shake her head. Nightmares couldn't explain Hannah's rapid aging. Or the mysterious old woman Wendy saw in the airport rest room. What had she said? *It's not over.* Wendy shuddered at the memory. She looked past the sheriff, at a folded newspaper on a visitor's chair in the hallway.

"You all right?"

Wendy nodded as she walked over to look at the *Windale Record* article that had caught her eye. The tragic death of Father Joseph Murray in his office at Holy Redeemer Church. Wendy skimmed the article. "You know about this?"

The sheriff glanced at the article and nodded. "Burned in his office, but the medical examiner determined the cause of death to be a heart attack. Apparently his arteries were in real bad shape. Without a quadruple bypass, it was just a matter of time."

"How was he burned?"

"Spilled whiskey on his desk," the sheriff said. "Smoking at the time. When he collapsed the whiskey caught fire, burned up his torso real bad, not to mention the desk before the sprinklers put out the fire."

Wendy looked up at him. "This says the fire was confined to the office area?" The sheriff nodded that she'd read it correctly. "But it also says all the stained glass windows were blown out, statues inside the church knocked over and destroyed."

"Vandals," the sheriff said. "Had to be vandals."

"Just like the steeple?"

"Steeple?"

"The church steeple," Wendy said, pointing to the mention at the tail end of the article. "Last September, the steeple was destroyed, knocked off the roof. It says Father Murray had heard sounds on the roof and when he ran outside to investigate, the steeple came crashing down onto the lawn."

"A string of bad luck," the sheriff commented. "Sometimes these teenaged vandals get stuck on something, like a dog with a bone. They keep coming back."

Wendy doubted teenaged vandals had been responsible for the church steeple last year, not after what she had come to witness. And that made her wonder about the stained glass windows and statues from several days ago. Could it be coincidence? Or something more?

Still, for all her speculation, Father Murray had died of a heart attack. Nothing more sinister than the end result of a poor diet, smoking, and a sedentary lifestyle. No reason to jump to supernatural conclusions. As she'd learned in her spring semester philosophy class, per Occam's razor, the simplest solution was usually the correct one.

So why am I still worried? she wondered.

Because, Wendy, when I don't help you, you die.

Alone in an aluminum rowboat, Wendy's hands rested, motionless on the oars. The rush of sun-dappled water surrounded her, carrying her boat along in a steady current. Silver fish darted beneath the surface on either side of her. The distant banks were lined with a green wall of oak, hickory, maple, and elm trees. She glanced over her shoulder beyond the bow of the boat, and saw a wall of mist rising into the cloudless sky. She had never been to this place before. Looking down at herself, she examined her clothes. A sleeveless, white cotton tank top, white denim shorts, and matching white tennis shoes. Atypical attire for her, to say the least.

"I'm dreaming, aren't I?" she asked no one in particular.

But she was no longer alone.

In the rear of the boat sat the old woman from the airport, still wearing her flowing linen robe and sandals. Around her neck she wore an emerald necklace, and on her right ring finger, an amethyst ring. She inhaled the fresh air, her white-gray hair fluttering in the gentle breeze. The bright sunshine revealed all the wrinkles and fine lines in her face, but somehow softened them, made her more vibrant than she'd appeared under harsh fluorescent lighting.

"A pleasant dream, though," the old woman answered.

"Yes."

"For now."

"What do you mean?" Wendy asked, looking about nervously, despite that she knew she was dreaming.

"Listen, Wendy," the old woman said. "What do you hear?"

"Water, rushing around us, splashing on the boat," Wendy said. "The current."

"And we go where the current takes us?"

Wendy glanced over her shoulder again, into the rising wall of mist. The rush of water had increased and in the distance, she could hear a rising roar of sound. She glanced back at the woman. "Waterfall?" With a gentle, approving smile, the woman nodded. Wendy gripped the oars, lifted the left and began to pull on the right one, slowly turning the boat until she was facing downstream and the waterfall. Dropping both oars into the water, she pulled in long hard strokes and, for a time, she bested the current, pulled the boat farther away from what she feared would be a precipitous drop.

Sweat appeared on her brow, ran in rivulets down her face, the salt stinging her eyes. Soon her cotton top was soaked with perspiration, across her back, under her arms and between her breasts. Her arms began to tremble with fatigue.

The old woman glanced over her shoulder now, to check the distance to the waterfall. "We're getting closer."

"Can you—help me?"

The old woman smiled. "That's why I came, Wendy."

"Who are you?"

"All you need know is that I am a friend." The woman sighed. "This is hard to explain."

"Try."

"It is difficult to reach you from so far away," the old woman said. "Easier in dreams, by far. Rest assured, we shall have time for all of it."

As the current became trickier, the rowboat started to drift to port. Wendy struggled to maintain control, but her arms refused to cooperate. She could only watch in dismay as the roar of sound seemed to wrap around them. "We're running out of time," Wendy reminded the woman.

"You have so much to learn," the old woman said. "For now, you need only know that, try as you might, you cannot change the current."

The water became rougher, causing the small boat to dip and rock, spraying them both with each plunge. Desperate, Wendy asked, "What's that supposed to mean? How does that help me?"

"The way ahead is treacherous and, I fear, unavoidable," the old woman said. "You must be prepared."

"How?"

"I will guide you," the old woman said. "But I grow weary . . ." With those words, the old woman simply faded away, leaving Wendy alone in the boat, which had taken on too much water to be maneuverable. Wendy shook with the chill, her arms leaden and all but useless. As the roar became deafening, the boat pitched forward one last time, over the edge, going to vertical and beyond, tossing her into the swirling white maelstrom below. She spun through the air, screaming . . .

. . . and slammed the back of her skull into the headboard.

Wendy rubbed her head as a knock sounded on her bedroom door.

"Wendy? You all right?" Her mother.

"Come in," Wendy called, raising herself into a sitting position. Damp with sweat, she threw her blankets down to cool off.

In a long white nightgown, Carol Ward seemed almost ethereal as she crossed to Wendy's bed and sat on the edge. "Nightmare, I take it?"

"Not sure," Wendy said, trying to recall the details of the dream.

"You woke up screaming. I think it's safe to say you had a nightmare."

"One of the falling variety," Wendy said.

"Off a building?"

"Over a waterfall."

"Well, at least it was scenic."

"Mother!"

"Sorry, dear," her mother said, fussing with Wendy's tangled hair. "Glad you're growing it out. Brush before you went to sleep?"

"Just my teeth," Wendy said, grinning. Her mother could become tyrannical about proper hair care.

"Maybe you should get a permanent," her mother said. "Would be low maintenance."

"Never," Wendy said, then arched her eyebrow. "Are you changing the subject?"

"From you plunging to your death?" Carol shrugged. "Isn't that what mothers are supposed to do?"

Wendy sighed. "Think it was a warning."

Frowning, "To always wear your seat belt?"

"Something like that," Wendy replied. "Be prepared."

"Well, if it's good enough for the Boy Scouts, I suppose it's good enough for my daughter."

Wendy quirked a smile. "Thanks, Mom."

Her mother kissed her on the forehead and said, "Good night, Wendy," before she left, closing the door behind her.

Unable to sleep, Wendy climbed out of bed and sat in the wicker chair by her window. Instead of a nightgown, she wore only a gray, oversized Danfield University T-shirt. The cooling sweat on her body was beginning to give her a chill, so she tucked her legs under her and crossed her arms to generate a little warmth.

The old woman in her dream had been wearing amethyst and emerald jewelry, the stones for dream magic and divination. Appropriate, considering her message and the method in which it was delivered.

With Abby's warning of a couple days ago still weighing on her mind, Wendy had a hard time dismissing her dream as meaningless. Especially since she had had episodes of lucid dreaming last year. *Then again, maybe Abby's words spooked me enough to cause the dream. Oh, I'm too tired to think straight.*

Wendy closed her eyes, trying to visualize the old woman's face, seeking some hint of familiarity in it. A *distant relative, maybe*, she thought. *I'll have to ask Mom to dig out the old photo albums.* She yawned. *Look for a match in the morning.*

She yawned once more and somehow, curled awkwardly in the white wicker chair, managed to fall back asleep. This time without dreams, without warnings.

WINDALE, MASSACHUSETTS
JUNE 1, 2000

Gina had instructed Brett to park the Ford F-150 pickup on one of the old, unpaved mill access roads. During the day, the winding roads provided some sport for off-road bikers, but nighttime usually found them deserted. As good a place as any to kill him, if it came to that. Brett knew too much. She had to be sure she could count on him to keep her secrets.

She had chosen the night and the location, utterly secluded, under a new moon and far from the benefit of any streetlights. When Brett switched off the headlights, darkness closed around them like a cloak. Brett left the interior cab light on to provide some illumination while he made his preparations. He rolled an old navy blanket across the sheet of plywood he kept in the bed of the pickup, no doubt trying to recall the last time they'd found a secluded spot to curl up together inside a roomy sleeping bag. It had been many months ago, over two months before the night at the Harrison Motor Lodge. *Mid-August last year*, she decided. It had been a humid night the last time they had sex. *So make that on top of the sleeping blanket.* Gina had kept Brett at arm's length since then. And after Halloween, Brett himself had been too unsettled by what they'd done that night to push the issue.

Gina stood beside the truck, waiting for him to finish, a bottle of peach schnapps in her hand. No particular reason. It was something alcoholic to drink, and sweet besides.

Brett hoisted her into the back of the pickup, then lay down on his back with a heavy sigh and twined his fingers together behind his head. Kneeling beside him in a sheer, cream colored blouse and pleated red miniskirt, Gina put her free hand on her hip. "Are you just gonna lie there flat on your back?"

"What?"

"We're having sex, aren't we?"

He sat up, eyes wide. "But, I thought . . . You haven't really mentioned it since the freak accident at the church."

She set the bottle down beside them, then pressed her fingers to his lips. "What did I tell you?"

"We don't talk about it," Brett said compliantly. "We were never there."

"Good boy," she said as she straddled his legs and unbuttoned his flannel shirt. "Like the papers said, Father Murray had a heart attack. Not our problem.

Wrong place at the wrong time. No need for us to get involved." She ran her hands across his broad, muscular chest. "Been lifting again?" He nodded. "Excellent. You need to stay in shape." *Just in case I need some muscle.* She tugged on his belt buckle, unfastened it, then pulled the zipper down on his jeans.

"Gina," Brett said, catching her hand. "I forgot—I mean I didn't think I'd need protection, since we haven't . . ."

"Don't sweat it, Romeo," she said. "I will *not* be getting pregnant again. Ever." She couldn't say how she knew, just a sense of something *different* inside her now.

"What? You're on the pill now?"

"Something like that." She could imagine she'd attained some sort of control over her own body, but it was more than that. She was changing inside, even as the images and memories bubbled to the surface like steam in a hot spring. She unscrewed the bottle cap and took a slug of the sweet liquor. "Want some?" Again he nodded and she tilted the bottle over his mouth, pouring it over his lips. He took several gulps, coughed, and turned his head aside. She laughed and set the bottle down again. "Don't go drowning on me, Brett."

He wiped his mouth with the back of his hand and shook his head. "I'm okay."

Gripping the legs of his jeans, she tugged down. He helped by lifting his hips while she pulled. When they were at mid-thigh, she pushed down on his abdomen. "That's far enough." He swallowed hard and nodded. "Now do me a favor, Brett."

A little breathy, "Anything."

"Grab my ass."

His callused hands slid up the smooth expanse of her thighs, slipped under her red pleated skirt and cupped her ass cheeks. She wasn't wearing any panties. "See," she said, taking another gulp of schnapps. "I came prepared. How about you?" She reached through the fly of his briefs and found him fully aroused.

"Gina, you're—you're sure about this, right?"

"Is there anything at all in my body language that begs the question?"

He looked up at her as she straddled his hips, skirt pushed up almost to her hips, a bottle of schnapps dangling from one hand. "I—I guess not."

She reached back and guided him inside her. "Glad that's settled."

"Me too," Brett said, a little distracted as she rocked back and forth astride him in a quickening rhythm. His hands guided her hips, but she controlled the pace, a tempo that kept him all but breathless.

Gina gulped more schnapps but the bottle was still about one third full. "You brought two bottles of this stuff, right?"

"What? Oh, yeah, another one's up front, under my seat. Why?"

"Waste not, want not," Gina commented as she shifted to an overhand grip on the neck of the bottle and smashed the base against the rust-speckled side of the pickup truck.

"What the hell—!"

The neck of the bottle now flared out into a ring of

jagged edges, dripping schnapps on the blanket. "You always want to talk about that night, Brett. So, let's talk." She shoved two particularly sharp points against his throat, hard enough to dimple his skin without slicing into the flesh. Instinctively, his hands rose from her hips and started toward her arm. "Put your hands back where I can feel them or I'll rip your throat out!" Slowly, he moved his hands back under her skirt to grip her buttocks. She resumed her energetic pace, her face becoming a little flushed as her excitement grew in direct proportion to his fear. "I need you to listen to me. Are you listening?" He nodded, then stopped as he felt the broken glass nip his skin. "Good. Because I need to know I can count on you, Brett."

"You—you can count on me, Gina," he said, his voice raspy from his fear and his own arousal. "You know that."

"Here's what I remember from that night," she said, squeezing down hard against his hips as a wave of pleasure coursed through her. His fear was more intoxicating than the alcohol or the sex act itself. "I gave birth to a baby girl in the Harrison Motor Lodge. You took her away, probably smothered her and left the body—"

"Gina—that's not—we agreed—"

"—in a Dumpster. I was too distraught to tell anyone."

"Gina!"

"Ooh, I like when you squirm around like that," she said, flashing a lusty smile. "But try not to lose your edge, Brett dear, I'm not quite there yet." To emphasize her point, she nudged the jagged edges of glass a little harder against his throat. A trickle of blood ran down behind his ear and he winced. With a soft chuckle, she smeared her left index finger with his blood, then sucked it off. "Yum. Salty."

"You are different," he said, his voice a shocked whisper.

"You're damned right I am, Brett," Gina said. She reached back, wrapped her hand around him and squeezed hard enough to cause him to grimace. "I'm taking control of my life."

"What do you want? For me to confess? Take all the blame."

"Not at all. We'll keep our secret, just as we planned."

He seemed relieved. "What then?"

"Pledge yourself utterly to me, and you'll have your rewards." She stroked him lightly, with only her fingertips. His body shuddered and he swelled inside her.

"You're—everything to me," Brett gasped, his hands sweaty and trembling on her ass. Gina increased her tempo, bringing him and herself along. "I've been in love with you for almost two years."

"Let's leave *love* talk to the poets," Gina said. "I don't need your love. I need your obedience."

"Fine," he said, maybe a little too fast. She grabbed his hair in her left fist and nudged the broken bottle a little deeper, causing a few more nicks, which trickled blood. "Please—please, I promise, Gina!"

Easing up on his throat a bit, she released his hair and resumed her feverish pace, a little breathless herself. For a moment he'd thought she was about to kill him and the rush of pleasure she felt was almost unbearable. She squeezed her thighs against his bare hips and bore down on him with the weight of her approaching orgasm. "Know this, Brett. If you are ever a question to me, if I ever doubt your complete loyalty, I will arrange another accident." She moaned in pleasure, completely enfolding him inside her. Despite the broken bottle against his throat, Brett's hips bucked beneath her with his own furious release. Ah, *the marvels of youth,* she thought.

As he began to shrivel inside her, Gina held the broken bottle beside his head, then leaned forward to lap up the thin lines of blood on his neck, like a cat at a milk dish. At last, she whispered in his other ear, "An accident just like the one that killed poor Father Murray."

Tossing the bottle aside, she placed both hands on his chest and lifted herself so she could stare deep into his eyes. Thinking of Kenny and his inflated dollar bill, she knew she had demonstrated the ability to control weak minds, but Brett was different. His mind was not necessarily weak, but, she hoped, pliable. And for her to control him, he had to be, at least in part, willing to be controlled. Sex was a primal key to energy and power and, given the right circumstances, control. The eyes looking back at her now were wide more with excitement than fear. She caressed his sweat-streaked face. "Good, wasn't it?" He nodded. "It only gets better, Brett. And the night is still young. I want to drink and fuck for hours. You have a problem with that?"

"Not—" He swallowed to clear his dry throat. "—not at all."

She had the sudden idea that she could groom him

to be her keeper, without understanding what the term *keeper* even meant. "Grab the bottle you stashed under the seat," she instructed, shaking off the stray thought. She reached back to stroke him and felt him twitch with the first hint of renewed arousal. "Then we'll see if I can kiss this and make it all better."

CHAPTER THREE

"Last chance," Alissa Raines said, dangling the keys above Wendy's outstretched palm. "Sure you can handle this?"

"As long as you promise to come back before fall semester," Wendy said. "I think I can handle the shop."

Alissa had long white hair bound in a loose ponytail and watery blue eyes set in a tranquil face. Nothing ever seemed to bother the woman, a state of mind she attributed to daily meditation and yoga. During the day, she usually wore a colorful scarf and wraparound skirt over an exercise leotard. Since she always kept an exercise mat in the back of the store, she never had to wander far to achieve renewed peace of mind. Now and then, Alissa would try to recruit Wendy into the yogic ranks, but Wendy deflected these overtures by promising to begin a *tai chi* regimen one of these days. After scrapping what she had come to consider her demonic exercise bike, Wendy had begun jogging and generally put in five miles a day, four or five days a week. Alissa considered jogging to be too undisciplined, but Wendy enjoyed an aerobic workout she could autopilot for the duration.

Displaying the smallest of frowns on her usually smooth face, Alissa dropped the keys into Wendy's hand. "Remember, you're the boss, so kiss flextime good-bye. The shop hours are now your hours. No coming in late or leaving early. Juggle Kayla and Tristan as needed. They're flexible, but part-time, so keep them under thirty hours per week. Try not to be in the shop alone for any extended period of time."

"Yes, Mother Raines," Wendy teased. "And what about my project? Do I have your blessing?"

Alissa frowned. *Twice in five minutes,* Wendy thought, *must notify the press.* "I don't know, Wendy. A Web site for The Crystal Path?" She shook her head. "Goes against my inherent Luddite tendencies. It feels wrong."

"Don't forget about the techno-pagans," Wendy said. "And more than one Wiccan out there has her Book of Shadows stored digitally on a personal computer."

"Do you?"

"Well, not right now," Wendy said. "But I've been considering it."

Alissa sighed. "Okay, we'll give it a try."

"Cool!"

"But I only want you working on it in the store, when business is slow. You're young. Don't obsess over this day and night. Enjoy your life away from work."

What life? No college, no Alex, and no Frankie for the next couple months. What she said was, "Thank you. Maybe I'll be able to wrangle some independent study credits out of the project."

"That would be nice," Alissa said. "Well, wish me luck across the pond. I've always wanted to tour Europe."

"Wish I could come with you," Wendy said, adding an exaggerated pout.

Alissa took her chin and gave a gentle shake. "Unfortunately, that new car of yours has left you penniless. Even so, I'd drag you along with me, but then I'd have to shut down the store."

"I could make a 'gone fishing' sign for the door and stowaway in your luggage."

"Wouldn't your parents miss you?"

Wendy shrugged impishly. "Hardly ever see them, anyway. One college function after another, banquets, dinners, garden parties, fund-raisers, I lose track." Wendy's father was the college president and one of the obligations that came with the president's mansion was endless entertaining and fund-raising, often one and the same thing. "Their social calendar gives me an inferiority complex."

"Poor dear," Alissa said, patting her cheek. "Maybe next year."

"Ooh, an annual tradition?"

"For what this is costing me, make that biannual,"

Alissa said. "Now, I have some luggage to gather and a plane to catch."

"I require a postcard from every city you visit, Ms. Raines."

"Postcards you shall have. Any last minute questions on store procedures?"

"I have everything memorized," Wendy said, then added, "somewhere on a clipboard. But, hey, if an emergency comes up, I'll ring your cell."

"I don't believe in cellular phones or pagers."

"They exist, Alissa. I've seen real people using them here in this very town."

"Ha, ha, funny girl," Alissa said. She stepped forward and gave Wendy a hug. "I'll miss you, Gwendolyn Alice Ward. Don't get into any trouble."

"Who? Me?"

Alissa leaned back and stared at Wendy from arm's length. "Is there something you're not telling me?"

Wendy shrugged. "A bad dream or two. Nothing like last year's doozies." *Besides, things are too weird right now to even begin to explain.* "And I don't want you worrying about me when you should be enjoying yourself. You've been dreaming of this trip your whole life."

Alissa smiled. "I have. Oh, I almost forgot. You and Frankie still thinking about renting a place for fall semester?"

"That's the plan, if we can swing it financially," Wendy said. One of the perks of being the president's daughter was that Danfield comped her tuition, with the exclusion of dorm room fees. They considered the president's mansion spacious enough for the largest possible presidential family. Just because Wendy wanted and needed her own space, they weren't about to give her a free pass. *Half the time, I can't even find a parking space!*

"Instead of an apartment, would you consider a two bedroom cottage?"

"Heck, yeah," Wendy said. "Would the landlord consider an apartment-sized rent deal?"

"He'll take it in trade."

Wendy grinned. "Hey, I'm an old-fashioned girl! What kind of trade?"

"A little elbow grease."

"Now, that is kinky."

Exasperated, "I'll be late for my plane, Wendy."

"Sorry," Wendy said. "Spill."

Alissa explained that one of her semiregulars, a term she preferred over Wendy's suggested *irregulars*, had a small cottage located within a couple miles of Danfield's campus. An older, eccentric gentleman who had made something of a name for himself writing books on past-life regression episodes, Clayton Quinn had made the mistake of lending the use of the cottage to a nephew who had attended Danfield several years ago. The nephew eventually formed a rock band called Bloody Pus, subsequently dropped out of college, toured with the band, appearing mostly in dives, never to find a record label willing to front them any studio money. Unfortunately, Brad Quinn—or Brad the Impaler, as he called himself on stage—and his band mates had refined the requisite art form of hotel room destruction by practicing on the little cottage.

"Ouch," Wendy said.

"Exactly," Alissa said. "Clayton travels all over, tracking down interview subjects for his books, but wouldn't mind pulling in some rental income from the place. As is, it's useless to him."

"So what does he have in mind."

"He pays for supplies, out of a budgeted account, you make the repairs, fix the place up, pay your own utilities and the place is yours rent free for three months."

"And after three months?"

"Three hundred a month through your spring semester," Alissa said. "After that, slight rent hike, probably an extra hundred, if you want to stay, but less than he'll charge somebody else."

"So I'd be grandfathered at a lower rate. Like rent control."

"Essentially. If you choose to stay."

"Hmm, a fixer-upper rental. Could be sweet. Can I check it out before I decide?"

"That's the idea. Pouch under the counter with his name on it. Keys, instructions, et cetera. Little bit of hard work, you could have the place in shape before classes start."

WINDALE, MASSACHUSETTS
JUNE 11, 2000

It's a complete disaster area,
Gina thought.

Dressed in a powder blue wool sweater with a V-neck, cutoff jeans, knee-high tube socks, and hiking boots, Gina scrambled over the rubble with an uncomfortable sense of foreboding. Using mangled twists of rebar for support, she pulled herself to the summit of collapsed concrete that had been the front end of the abandoned textile mill. The side and rear walls still stood over the shell of the old factory, but the front section, which had included the administrative offices, had all collapsed.

Her legs were trembling, but not from fatigue. Gina sat on a cold slab of concrete and wrapped her arms around her knees, trying to understand the jumble of fear, desperation, and rage that swirled inside her. Her only memory of the place was from a couple years ago, with a group of fellow high school sophomores. Sharing a few smuggled cans of beer, throwing rocks through a couple of the remaining windows out of sheer boredom. Nothing that would account for the strong emotions that threatened to overwhelm her.

Brett scaled the rocks, making the ascent with the nimble grace of a natural athlete, leaping over the crevices between collapsed slabs of concrete, unconcerned about potential injury and unencumbered by strong associative emotions. At that moment, she hated him for his confidence.

He crouched on the rock beside her, wearing a green and yellow rugby shirt, jeans, and black Nikes, and tried to figure out what held her interest. At last, he commented, "Not much here."

"Death," Gina said, meeting his eyes. "Death is here."

"Whose death?"

She looked away again. "Mine."

"Yours? Gina, you're very much alive."

"You know that feeling they talk about? Somebody walking over your grave?" Brett nodded. "That's how this place feels to me."

Brett chuckled, a little uncomfortable. "Like a premonition? Maybe we should leave before this pile of rubble collapses."

"It's too late," Gina said, rising to her feet. "I already died here." She started to make the awkward descent, but yelled back to Brett. "Now I need to know how it happened . . . and who was responsible for killing me."

Brett hurried to catch up to her. "Why?"

Standing on the factory floor at the base of the rubble, she turned to him and said in a tone that stopped him in his tracks. "Because, I'd like to return the favor."

"This place is a dump," Larry Ward said as Wendy led him through the small cottage. When she frowned at him, he amended the statement. "A dump with possibilities."

"Try to visualize how it will look after I fix it up," Wendy said.

"After *you* fix it up?"

Wendy wrapped an arm around her father's shoulder. "After *we* fix it up, *pater.*"

"That's what I thought you meant."

Only one story, the cottage was rectangular in design with white stone facing located at 333 Kettle Court, at the end of a cul-de-sac in a residential section of Windale, just off the main Danfield campus. A curved walkway led across a wide expanse of front lawn that boasted a maple tree and a recent mowing. But that was the only bit of maintenance the cottage had seen in years. Most of the front windows had been broken and subsequently boarded up with plywood painted white to be less noticeable from the street.

Inside the cottage, the carpeting had been so extensively stained that Wendy refused to even speculate on the nature of the contaminants involved in the patches of discoloration and clumping. In other places, the carpeting was torn or gouged or charred. The walls were the worst, with many gaping holes created by hammers, fists, feet, and other unidentifiable instruments of household destruction. Where the walls were undamaged, graffiti had been sprayed in a Day-Glo demonstration of the artist's extensive knowledge of profanity, both common and esoteric. Beer and soda cans, along with the occasional wine and whiskey bottles, were scattered throughout.

So much for first impressions, Wendy thought.

She led her father through the cottage. As they walked, he commented about the types of repairs required and what supplies they would need, scribbling related notations in a small spiral-bound notebook he'd had in his shirt pocket, occasionally taking measurements with a tape measure. "Paint . . . lots of paint . . . enamel and latex. You'll have to decide on colors. Drop cloths, rollers, brushes, turpentine. Drywall. Need to rip out all the carpeting . . . new windows . . . screens . . ."

Immediately to the left of the front door were a closet and a storage room. Then a short hallway led down to the utility room and a bedroom on the left, with the common bathroom and the other bedroom on the right. Both bedrooms had roomy closets. The bathroom featured an old-fashioned claw-foot tub but, in a nod to modern convenience, it had an adjustable showerhead nozzle and a bar for a shower curtain. Of the two bedrooms, she preferred the bedroom on the right side, since it faced the backyard garden, which had grown wild. The other bedroom was about the same size, but had a window looking out on the front lawn. The bedroom walls had sustained minimal damage, though the rugs would need to be replaced. But all the windows were cracked or missing and boarded over. The bathroom needed a fresh grout and a good scrubbing but otherwise no major reconstructive work.

The kitchen and dining area were centered at the back of the cottage, overlooking the terrace. Some of the kitchen appliances might even be functional. They would know when they had the utilities turned on. A half wall that had been half destroyed by unidentified members of Bloody Pus divided the right side of the cottage. The near side could function as a living room, with the far side, looking out on the remains of a screened-in porch, reserved for a family room.

Aside from the kitchen appliances and a washer-dryer combo unit in the utility room, all the furniture had been removed from the cottage. *Assuming Bloody Pus ever had any furniture here,* Wendy thought.

Wendy and her father stepped out on the stone terrace, overlooking the jungle that had once been a secluded backyard and garden. Here again, it looked as if someone had upended a few trash cans filled with aluminum cans, bottles, and fast-food wrappers. Beyond the yard was a line of coniferous trees, with a fragrant mix of pine, spruce, and balsam fir. Wendy's first thought was that once she whipped this outdoor area into shape, she could perform her rituals next to the garden, away from prying eyes. No need to drive all the way down Gable Road, leaving her car in faux abandonment on the side of the road.

She turned to her father. "So, what do you think? It's close to campus. There's a second bedroom for Frankie," Wendy said. "And best of all, the rent will be notoriously cheap, at least for the first year."

Larry ran a hand across his balding head and sighed. "I won't kid you, Wendy. It's a lot of work, even with me helping you."

"I know," she admitted. "Go beyond that. Visualize it all pretty."

"Do your mother and I bother you so much you have to leave home?"

Although he'd smiled to take the sting out of it,

Wendy could tell he was a little saddened at the prospect of her moving out. *Guess the empty nest moment comes a lot quicker when you only have one child,* Wendy thought. "You guys are great," she said. "I have no complaints. You know I love you both. This is just . . . a chance for me to be a little independent without taking a lot of risk. Only a three-month renewable lease, and you and Mom are only five minutes away in case of an emergency. Like, for instance, laundry day."

He chuckled, and she gave him a hug. "I won't be so far away," she said. "Feel free to visit anytime. In fact, days when you have some choice leftovers would be ideal times to drop in on me."

"Okay, Wendy," he said. "But don't even think you're moving in until the windows have been replaced, the locks have been changed, and you have a chain and dead-bolt on the door."

"Deal!"

WINDALE, MASSACHUSETTS
JUNE 12, 2000

At quarter to two in the morning, Brett swung his pickup alongside the curb outside Gina's house and shifted into park. "Feeling better?"

"Much," Gina said. She leaned into his kiss, teasing his lower lip between hers for a moment before biting down hard enough for him to yelp. Reflexively, his hand went to his lip and came away streaked with blood. "Don't tell me you're afraid of a little pain, Brett." She took his palm in her hand and, with one long stroke of her tongue, lapped up the blood. "Or a little blood?"

He ran his tongue across the wound and shook his head. "Guess not."

"Good boy." She rubbed her hand across the fly of his jeans and gave him a healthy squeeze. "Go home and rest. You want to be able to keep up with me, don't you, Brett?" He nodded, his tongue swiping his suddenly dry lips. "We're at the beginning of something here." She climbed out of the passenger side of the truck, then looked in through the window. "Something big."

"G'night, Gina," he said and drove away.

After the pickup's taillights turned the corner, she strolled up the walkway, fitted her key into the lock and opened the front door slowly. Everyone would be asleep by now and she saw no reason to announce her late arrival home.

As she slipped through the inner doors of the vestibule into the reception hall, a shadow detached itself from a chair in the dining room to her right and approached. By the size, she knew who it was. "Hello, Dominick," she said casually to her stepfather. "You really didn't need to wait up."

He'd been sitting at the dining room table in gray flannel pajamas, sipping scotch on the rocks. *If Dominick's drinking this late,* Gina thought, *he must be nursing his anger.* A bad day at work, so take it out on the stepdaughter?

"You're late," he said softly, his lips hardly moving. *He's trying to control his temper.* "I was worried."

"I'm touched."

He frowned, stepped closer to her, into her personal space. "Your mother and I asked you to be home by eleven. It's almost two o'clock."

She shrugged. "Lost track of the time."

"Tomorrow's a school day."

"Oh, please," Gina said dismissively. "The teachers don't even expect us to show up for these last three days."

Dominick put his hands on her shoulders and pushed her back against the corner formed by the wall separating the reception area from the dining room. "We expect you to listen to us, young lady! Our house, our rules. But you've been running wild. You're late—and you've been drinking!"

"So have you."

His hand blurred, stinging her cheek.

She touched her cheek, feeling the warmth there. *Just a little pain,* she thought. *Nothing wrong with that.* "You know, Dominick, if you really want to spank me," she said, taunting. "There are much better places."

His eyes were wide, almost wild, and, for a moment, she thought she saw a flicker of deliberation there.

Gina seized the moment and leaned against him, feeling the stubble of his cheek against the new warmth in hers, and whispered in his ear, "I won't tell Mom if you won't."

"What . . . ?" His voice was almost silent with disbelief.

As she slipped by him, she pressed her pelvis against him just enough to know he wasn't as completely in the dark as he would like her to believe. "Pleasant dreams, Dom," she said and blew him a kiss.

Turning her back to him, she walked up the steps with deliberate slowness, flashing long tan thighs in her cutoffs, waiting for any protest or invitation from below. The stairway had a midlevel landing where it reversed direction before continuing up. She paused there to look down and confirm that he'd been watching her slow ascent. *Speechless,* she thought. *Just the way I like old Dom.*

She needed a warm shower to wash away the residue of the day, dust, sweat, and other bodily fluids. Just to torment her stepfather, she'd left the bathroom door open while the shower ran. Afterward, she toweled off and walked naked down the short hallway to her bedroom, giving grudging credit to Dominick's ability to resist temptation. No doubt he thought she was setting him up and, to be fair, she probably was. She just hadn't figured out how yet. She closed her bedroom door, but left it unlocked, just in case he reconsidered her offer.

If he decided to pay her a late night—actually early morning—visit, he'd find her completely nude between her blue satin sheets. It had only been a few weeks ago that she discovered how luxurious satin felt against her bare skin. While she lay there, waiting for sleep or something more interesting, her mind drifted back to the condemned textile mill, the collapsed wall, the mound of debris that had filled her with not only a sense of doom, but also with a simmering anger, a desire to lash out at someone.

Gina felt as if the presence within her, an entity that embodied her newfound confidence and ambition, ached to remember . . . and the desire to remember was exhausting. She drifted into a troubled sleep and dreamed . . .

Elizabeth Wither, a widow who prefers the dark, stands in her own keeping room, before a gateleg table, dressed in head rail, widow's peak, doublet, and petticoat. Across from her sits a hard, middle-aged man, attempting to look comfortable in the wainscot chair and failing miserably.

The pale wash of moonlight reveals his faded gray eyes to her, filled with fear and respect in equal measure. She notes with satisfaction that his throat often becomes dry in her presence. Every few moments, he takes careful sips of beer from the leather blackjack she's placed before him. Enough to lubricate his throat, yet not enough to scatter his wits. Goodman Ezekiel Stone must never think himself my equal. He is merely a tool.

She pushes aside the flint and steel in her tinderbox, which is mostly for show anyway. Instead, her right hand reaches to the candle in its tall holder. She flicks the nail of her index finger across her thumbnail and a spark leaps to the wick. Ezekiel tries not to look startled, but she sees the nervous lump bob in his throat. She lights a stick of pitch pine from the burning wick and tosses it into the hearth. The flames catch, chasing back the shadows. On the hearthstones are small dolls, made from pilfered rags and stuffed with goat hair, some stabbed with pins. She turns away from the light. "Better?"

"Aye," *he says, squirming.* "A bit."

Even that little bit of fire witchery unnerves him.

In the firelight, she sees that he's dressed plainly enough in a city cap, looped doublet, leather breeches, and the dark cloak he fancies. In her service, he does well not to draw too much attention to himself. "What have you brought me?"

"Your paper. From that Rittenhouse mill in Germantown."

"Good," she says, taking the package from him. Paper is a rare commodity but she has the resources to acquire what she needs. Though wouldn't her neighbors be appalled to learn that most of the paper is bound for the fire? More so, should they discover she scrawls spells upon the pages beforehand. "Naught else?"

He clears his throat, uncomfortable. "If you speak of the . . . other, we have yet to set a price."

She leans forward, hands pressed to the table, her eyes burning with an intensity that makes him shudder. She hisses, "You would haggle over price when you know you will be handsomely rewarded for this above all else?"

"You—you wish only the young. There is great risk. If I am caught with a stolen child . . ."

"If you are caught you are twice damned, Ezekiel, for I shall not let you slip away so easily." Her hand closes on the haft of a knife, which has appeared on the table as if from nowhere. Ezekiel might suspect she has a sheath hidden in her clothing, but he can never be sure where she is concerned. The wooden haft is stained almost black from tides of blood. On each side, a serpent has been carved with forked tongue and extended fangs. The long blade gleams as she turns it in the candlelight. "There is power in the taking of innocent lives, in the devouring of innocent flesh. But Windale is too small as yet for such things to go unnoticed. I have not the anonymity of London's busy streets."

"I have scouted the larger towns, Salem Town and Boston. Fear not. I will find what you need. I merely thought you would wait until you formed the three, the coven before . . ."

"You would do well to think less, Ezekiel. Be sure, the three will form. Opportunities exist right here, women who will fall to me given the right . . . circumstances. But I will tell you no more or less than you need to know." She leaves the knife on the table, wondering if he will, given the chance, attempt to slit her throat with it. All fear and respect leave little room for betrayal. Someday the coven will require long sleep and she would have a keeper, a keeper properly trained and completely subservient.

She walks from the table to the hearth and kneels there, her back to him. If he attempts to come out of that unforgiving wainscot chair, he will make the devil's own noise, the last noise he will ever make. But he is still, as she knew he would be.

She passes a hand over a hearthstone, dispelling the illusion it is too heavy to budge, even to her, before lifting it free. The bag it conceals has its own considerable weight, the real weight of coins, not the false weight of enchantment. She brings the bag to the table and places it before him. Some men are bought with power, some with sundry and various pleasures, some merely with gold. Ezekiel is a simple man, for whom riches suffice. "Here is but half your price," she says, watching his broad smile bloom. "Bring what I desire, yet only on the new moon and well after dark, and you shall receive the other half." She picks up the knife and runs her finger beside its glittering edge, preternaturally sharp. "Come not at all and I shall find you, even if it be in the deepest recess of hell. Come empty-handed and I shall make other use of you. Make no mistake, Ezekiel, your skin is not yet too tough for the stewpot. Serve me well and you will have your rewards. Fail me just once and you will yearn for the fires of hell."

A slight creaking sound.

Disturbed from her dream, Gina rolled on to her back, flinging out her hand and murmuring a single name. "Wither . . ."

In a moment, she slipped into another dream, not so different from the first . . .

Elizabeth Wither strides across the town at an unseemly pace, her petticoat swirling around behind her. In front of the town hall, a drunkard is locked in the pillory, a "D" strung around his neck. She recognizes him as Goodman Osgood, the town cooper. He takes note of her passing as well and croaks, "I know what you are, Widow Wither! I see you—your apparition, flying, come to torment me at night."

She glares at him. "You see naught but what can be found in the bottom of a tankard of ale. And may you rot of it."

As she turns away from him, he yells, "Witch! She is a witch and she has cursed me!"

Wither glares at him again, but this time her face strains with effort, her fists ball, fingernails digging painfully into her palms. Goodman Osgood abruptly loses his voice, choking and spasming in the pillory. A trickle of blood leaks from his eye and he slumps in the wooden frame, a nuisance no more. She whispers, "I always knew liquor and a loose tongue would be the death of you."

A quick glance around reveals no one who might have witnessed the exchange, her flare of temper, and the deadly result.

Because she had sensed an opportunity to subvert Rebecca slipping away, she acted too precipitously with Osgood. At that very moment, if the scrying crystal and her own premonitions could be trusted, Rebecca was falling prey to one of her seizures right in the presence of their lecherous magistrate, Jonah Cooke.

With one last parting glance at the slumped corpse in the pillory, Wither thinks, Goodman Osgood's tongue is well silenced.

Her dreams already fragmenting, Gina awoke with the warmth of the sun bathing her skin, yet waited to open her eyes. Her alarm clock had yet to ring and her thoughts drifted in the quiet moments that remained, trying to piece together memories hidden just beneath the surface of conscious thought.

A mechanical clicking sound in the stillness disturbed her.

Instantly alert, she opened her eyes and sat up, noticing that the blue satin sheets were already pooled around her waist. She must have flung them aside while she slept. She'd also noticed a darting shadow just beyond her open door. Before she'd fallen asleep, the door had been open. But she hadn't locked it, expecting . . .

She jumped out of bed, slipped on a black silk robe that fell to mid-thigh and cinched it at her waist as she hurried down the hall to the bedroom on the far side of the bathroom: Todd's room.

She flung his door open, bouncing it off the doorstop. "What the hell are you up to, junior pervert?"

Still in pajamas, Todd was sitting at his desk, in front

of his blueberry colored computer. His digital camera was on the desk as well, with a cable spooling out from behind it to a connection on the computer. The moment the door slammed open, he'd hit a key combination to make the computer monitor go dark, but not before Gina glimpsed the sun-bathed image of a topless woman lying on blue satin sheets, eyes closed, one arm carelessly flung over her head. She had to admit it was a good picture of her, even if her hair had been a mess. "What are you up to, you little peeping toad?"

"Nothing," Todd said, face pale with guilt. "Just updating my Web page before school."

"Nude photos of me on your Web page?" She grabbed his chair and spun him around to face her. "For all your little pervert buddies to gawk at?"

"It's not—it wasn't you."

"The hell it wasn't!" She picked up his digital camera. The heat of anger flashed and her fist convulsed. Sparks sprayed out of the camera, its internal mechanisms fried. She tossed it aside and placed her hand on top of the blueberry colored monitor. "I saw it, Todd. My hair was a complete disaster. Definitely not ready for prime time. Don't you agree?"

"What . . . ?"

"Exactly," she said, allowing the welling anger to flow through her and erupt once more. After a prolonged sizzle, the computer popped with a spray of sparks. Wisps of smoke issued from the vents. She removed her hand, revealing a runny sludge of melted blueberry plastic beneath. "That should keep you out of trouble."

As she walked out of his bedroom, Todd found his voice. He screamed, "Fucking bitch!"

"Drop dead," Gina said without looking back. She chuckled, wondering if the words might actually pack more wallop than an idle threat. The confident presence within her surged, goading her to try, wanting her to will Todd's life away, just as she had willed Father Murray's heart to stop.

Denying the impulse, despite the sweet temptation, Gina returned to her bedroom and started to dress for school. Already Todd was screaming for his father and Caitlin, claiming Gina had ruined his computer.

Gina had just finished buttoning her pink cashmere sweater when her mother knocked on her door and said, "We need to talk."

Gina brushed the tangles from her hair, tilting her face side to side to check her makeup. "About Toad?"

"Gina!" Caitlin sighed. "Care to tell me what happened?"

"Not especially, Mother."

"Todd says you ruined his computer? He says you poured water in it or something, shorted it out."

"I don't have to defend myself."

Caitlin grabbed Gina's arm. "I disagree, Gina. I refuse to tolerate your blatant disrespect for everyone in this family and your casual disregard for their personal property."

Gina fought a sudden, visceral urge to claw out her mother's eyes. Her body trembled as she sought to control the rage boiling just below the surface. "Why would I break his computer?"

Releasing her arm, "That's what I'm here to find out."

"Fine," Gina said. "When Toad was blabbing about me, did he mention how he snuck into my bedroom with his digital camera while I was sleeping? How he took naked pictures of me to post on his Web site?"

"No," Caitlin said. "Do you have any proof?"

Sure. Before I fried his equipment, Gina thought. "Just my word. Don't suppose that's worth anything to you."

"Well, your credibility is on a downward spiral, young lady," Caitlin said. She threw up her hands. "So, fine. You're both grounded. After school, you're stuck here with us. One big happy family."

Gina shook her head. "Oh, please . . ."

"Gina, you really need to remember who's in charge here. That is, if you still care about your future."

Swallowing an outburst, Gina clenched her jaw shut until the wave of anger passed. Finally, she sighed. "Fine."

"Good," Caitlin said. "Maybe we can break out some board games tonight. Bond as a family." She smiled, turned away, then paused for a moment and looked back at Gina. "How late were you out last night? I fell asleep early."

So Dom never told you, Gina thought. *Guess he wants to keep his options open.* "Little past midnight, maybe."

"Too late for a school night and you know it," Caitlin said. "You only have a few days left, Gina. Let's go out on a high note, please."

"Right."

"And start thinking about how you can earn some extra money," Caitlin added.

"What?"

"To buy your brother a new computer. I'm not bailing you out, Gina. You need to take responsibility for your own actions."

Through a supreme effort of will, Gina forced herself to remain silent. Caitlin nodded, left Gina's bedroom, and closed the door behind her. Noticing a fine tremor in her hands, Gina made white-knuckled fists and pressed them against her temples. She stared at the stranger reflected in her mirror and whispered, "Maybe I should just kill them all."

Imagining a different gruesome demise for each member of her family helped her through the long, boring day at school.

Wendy Ward's Mirror Book Entry
June 12, 2000, Moon: waxing crescent, day 10

Sure it's a lot of work, but I'm excited about getting the cottage in shape. Already cleaned up all the Bloody Pus debris inside the house. (Where's a good biohazard suit when you need one?) Dad and I drove to Boston—to one of those home improvement superstores—and picked up several gallons of paint and painting supplies, along with a dozen sheets of drywall. (And we'll probably need more!) After I promised to fill up the gas tank, Mom lent us her Pathfinder for transport. Before we left, I called Bobby McGowan, paperboy and moonlighting lawnmower man, and hired him to clean, mow, and weed the backyard. Mom gave me the number of a carpet installer she's dealt with in her real estate adventures, but Dad suggested I wait until the painting is finished to replace the rugs. Makes sense. Even so, the old carpet is so oogie I want to gag!

Mr. Quinn's reclamation account money is for materials only. Told me to save all my receipts. However, as part of the free three months rent, I'm responsible for labor costs. Plan to do as much as I can myself. Dad says he'll help me put up the drywall. Figure I can handle painting the place alone, in my spare time, which means evenings and weekends, mostly, since I'll be managing The Crystal Path all summer.

Broke and tired. What a way to spend summer vacation!

That evening, Gina stayed in her bedroom as much as possible. After school, Brett had dropped her off at her house. Since she wouldn't be seeing him all night, she'd promised him a quickie on the kitchen table. Unfortunately, Sylvia had been cleaning the house when they arrived, and Gina had doubted the stout woman—with her severe, dyed-orange bun and sanctimonious frowns—would either approve the misuse of kitchen furniture or agree to participate in the frolics. So Gina had dismissed a disheartened Brett, waiting until Sylvia finished before smuggling a bottle of Bacardi rum up to her room. If her mother was determined to keep her in the house, Gina was as determined to stay in her bedroom, coming down only when she needed another chilled can of Coke to mix with her rum. *Family bonding be damned*, she thought.

On her third trip down to the kitchen, her mother called her from the family room. Gina heaved a sigh. "What, Mother?"

"In here, Gina. Now."

Bitch, Gina thought. She trudged into the family room with the unopened can of Coke. Since she was under house arrest for the night, she'd already changed into powder blue satin pajamas, which consisted of a sleeveless, V-neck top and short-shorts. She wasn't wearing anything underneath. Figured she could flash Dom without even trying too hard.

The three of them were sitting around a card table, playing Scrabble. She could tell by the many square wooden tiles on the game board that they were nearly finished. "What?"

Todd smirked. "Better start looking for a summer job to buy me a new computer."

Gina glared at him, imagined throwing the soda can at his pimply face hard enough to smash his nose, maybe bust a few teeth. The visual brought a cruel smile to her lips.

Todd looked away for a moment before his father said, "Enough, Todd. I told you Gina will empty her savings account to buy you a new computer. Then she'll have to find work to pay back that account."

Caitlin was smiling, trying to put a pleasant face on the disaster she called a family. "You've always enjoyed Scrabble, Gina. Why not join us for the next game?"

"You want me to pose in your little Norman Rockwell painting?" Gina asked with open contempt.

Staring down at the intersecting rows of tiles, she was struck by a sudden inability to make sense of the words they formed, as if she were suffering from aphasia. At the same moment, she was overcome with a violent urge. She took a step forward, slipped her fingers under the board and flipped it off the table, scattering the tiles in front of the fireplace. "I'd rather go to hell!"

In a heartbeat, they were all up and yelling at her, but Gina blocked them out, so much white noise. Or rather, their protests grew faint in light of her sudden revelation. She walked toward the fireplace, entranced. Dozens of the wooden tiles were scattered across the slate in front of the fireplace. Most of them, all but six of them, were letter-side down, displaying their blank backs. The other six were laid out in a staggered line, a weak sine curve, but with an eerie order. If she read them from left to right they spelled out a word, a word that resonated inside her, brought back memories of recent dark dreams that had been all but forgotten only moments ago. She whispered the word, "Wither."

Caitlin was standing in front of her, demanding, "—wrong with you, Gina?"

Gina shook her head. "I don't know," she whispered, which was true.

"Clean up these tiles, then go to your room."

Gina dropped to her knees and spread her trembling hands across the tiles, finding each one as cold as ice, leeching the warmth from her fingers until her hands were numb. She gathered them into a pile.

While Caitlin stood nearby, fists on her hips, Gina

carried as many tiles as she could hold in her cupped hands across the room, then held her breath as she dumped them on the table. Again, almost all of them landed facedown. All but seven, seven that spelled out another word, which she mouthed, "Awaken." She was the only one aware of the messages and she knew they were meant only for her. A third handful of tossed tiles produced a meaningless jumble of letters.

Nearby, Caitlin nodded. "Now apologize to everyone."

Gina stared at each of them for a moment. Beside her mother's undisguised anger, Dominick was a model of restraint. He always tried to appear temperate whenever Caitlin was around. Todd, with a hand in front of his face, was only partly successful in hiding the satisfied grin. "Mother, Dominick, Todd . . . I just want to say," Gina began, her voice soft and in control, settling her gaze on her mother. "Fuck off."

Caitlin slapped Gina across the face.

Gina enjoyed the sting and the flush of heat rising to her face almost as much as she savored her mother's trembling rage. Caitlin's lips were quivering. *She's losing it,* Gina thought. She had the urge to spit in her mother's face to put her over the edge. *Another time,* she decided. "Am I done now?"

"Get out!" Caitlin screamed. She grabbed a handful of Gina's hair to yank her out of the family room.

Gina's hand pried back her mother's little finger until Caitlin screamed in pain, then Gina shoved her backward. Caitlin stumbled, almost fell, her eyes wild.

Dominick said to Caitlin, "Stay here. I'll take care of

this." He grabbed Gina's arm and pulled her from the family room. She stumbled along with him into the reception area, but once they reached the stairs, she went limp, falling to her knees, forcing him to wrap her up in his arms and carry her up the staircase, an awkward, squirming bundle, her body pressed against his. Her skin burned, as if she had a fever. And the hotter her skin became, the colder his flesh felt and she imagined she was siphoning warmth right out of him.

He kicked her bedroom door open and tried to shove her into the room, but she had anticipated the move and clung to his arm. She staggered backward tugging him along and, with strength that surprised her, she pulled him down on top of her on her brass bed. Both her hands grabbed the hair at the back of his head and forced his face down to hers, crushing his lips against hers even as she ground her pelvis into his evident arousal. "You know you want it!" she whispered, a throaty dare or maybe an invitation. She wasn't quite sure.

As he tried to pull back, she bit his lip, drawing blood. With a yelp, he shoved himself off her. Breathless, "You're sick."

"What's that make you, Dominick?"

"You need a psychiatrist."

"That's not what I need right now, Dom." *True enough.* More than just to unnerve him, she slipped a hand inside the V-neck of her pajama top, cupped her breast and ran her thumb across the aroused nipple. She wanted to feel pain. She wanted to inflict pain. *Maybe that's what the message means,* she thought. *Awaken.*

Dominick's face was a tortured mixture of emotions, anger, lust, and fear foremost among them. If she had to guess, she'd say that fear was the most prominent at that moment. He backed away from her, her bed, and paused just outside the doorway. "Keep your hands off of your mother!"

"What about you, Dom?" she called. "Should I keep my hands off of you, too?"

He slammed her door shut and stormed down the hall.

Gina laughed. First it was an amused chuckle, then it became deeper and stronger, something empowered. Restricted to her bedroom, she had never felt more in control of her surroundings. *Killing them now would be such a waste,* she thought. *Waste not, want not.*

The image of the wooden tiles scattered on the hearth flashed in her mind, then was replaced by the hearth in her dreams, and the image of rag dolls, stuffed with goat hair. While her family talked about her downstairs, conversations with occasional words that drifted up to her like helium-filled balloons, words that included, "counseling, psychologist, drug treatment" she drifted into their bedrooms, rummaging through their clothes hampers, selecting one unwashed item each of them had worn but might not miss. Next she lifted their shed hair from brushes and combs. When she returned to her bedroom, she locked the door and removed from her top dresser drawer her travel sewing kit with its miniature scissors.

Sitting on the bed, she tore the cloth into flat strips,

then used the scissors to cut out the appropriate shapes for her family bonding ritual. "Awaken," she whispered, letting the ancient voice deep inside her mind guide her fingers.

WINDALE, MASSACHUSETTS
JUNE 16, 2000

Lying in bed in her flannel nightgown, Abby put the paperback book, *White Fang* by Jack London, down on her nightstand and rubbed her dry eyes. Across the room, Erica slept under her Franklin and Little Bear posters, curled among an assortment of stuffed animals. The whole house was quiet, everyone asleep, except for Abby, who had tossed and turned until close to midnight when she had stopped fighting her restlessness and had turned on her bedside lamp and picked up her book. Less than ten pages further into the story about the half-dog, half-wolf before she had had enough. Something was bothering her, something she couldn't name, a nervousness, butterflies in her stomach and an itch under her skin.

She stretched until her bones creaked a bit and made her whimper. An energy seemed to blossom inside her, urging her out of bed with a need to run as fast as she could. Crossing the room to the window, she looked for the full moon. As she craned her neck for a better view outside the window, she felt her arms begin to twitch and tremble and looked down at them, frightened. It's *happening again*, she thought. And I *can't stop it*.

Her heartbeat thudded in her chest and her face became flushed.

The trembling spread to her legs, muscle spasms, but more than that. Her bones were shifting, rearranging themselves under her skin. Her knees throbbed in pain and her fingers crumpled inward, her thumbs retracting. Her breathing had become a steady, animal pant and she whimpered again as her skull seemed flattened, her nose extending forward and darkening.

What's happening to me? Why is this happening to me? Make it stop, please make it stop!

She shivered as white fur sprouted across her arms, down her back, and across her thighs. Moment by moment she had a harder time standing erect and that, more than anything, made her desperate to escape, to get away from the confines of the small bedroom.

After fumbling with the lock, she managed to raise the window high enough to squirm through and fall to the grass outside. She could no longer stand erect. Instead she walked around on all fours, whimpering as her spine bowed outward. Clothing bound her, tripping her, until she twisted her powerful neck around and ripped the fabric away with long, pointed teeth.

From inside the house came the sound of Rowdy barking. She meant to tell him to be quiet before he woke everyone, but her admonishment came out as a deep-throated growl. She tried to speak but the words were meaningless yelps and barks. Her night-adapted eyes stared down at the ground and saw white paws where her hands should be. And walking on all fours was nowhere near as difficult as it should be. She moved across the yard, circling around to the back of the house with a fluid grace, the full moon casting her pale shadow on the grass. A canine shadow . . . no, not canine. Lupine. She had become a wolf.

Abby dreamed she was a wolf and ran into the woods behind the house.

But even in her dream, she heard the barking of the dog and the shouting of humans. With long, loping strides she left the sounds behind and chased the elusive scent of a raccoon. Later, the wolf emerged from the woods and slaked her thirst by lapping water from the cool stream. Tossing her head up, the wolf howled at the pale gray face of the moon, remembering a gauzy, confusing dream in which the wolf had been a human girl.

A girl whose name the wolf had forgotten.

WINDALE, MASSACHUSETTS
JUNE 21, 2000
MIDSUMMER

Wendy sat in front of the computer in the back room of The Crystal Path. Afternoon business had been slow after a brisk morning, and Kayla was minding the register up front while Wendy tried to make some progress with the Web site for the New Age store. She was still laying out the basic page design and had to look forward to—*or dread*, she thought—building the product database and linking it to the ordering system. But that was weeks away. *Panic for another day.* Instead, for the second time, she read the E-mail she'd received from Professor Glazer that morning.

TO: Wendy Ward
SENT: Tue 6/20/00 10:48 PM
SUBJECT: Relocation

Hi, Wendy,
A quick note to tell you that all three of us are settled in, more or less. What boxes we chose not to unpack we've hidden in the attic. Looking forward to the fall semester here. Art applied for a position at the university so we're keeping our fingers crossed.

Also, I wanted to let you know that Hannah is fine and says hello. (As does Art.) She always asks about you.

We took her to a few specialists here, you know, just to get a sixteenth and seventeenth opinion. For a time, I thought she might have progeria, the premature aging disorder that affects children. But the doctors assure me whatever is different about her is unrelated to that degenerative condition. They are polite, but so obviously clueless, offer assurances, but are no help at all.

I must admit Hannah seems perfectly healthy, just advanced physically and mentally. I'd say she probably sleeps more and eats a lot more than the average child her age, but it's hard to even know what her age really is. Everyone tells you your children grow up too fast . . . if they only knew! Because of the circumstances of Hannah's birth, I can't help worrying about her, about her future. I wish I understood what this all means. Art has been so supportive. We just try to take it one day at a time and hope my dear little girl stays as normal as possible.

Hope this finds you well, Wendy.
Take care,
Your old prof, Karen

Wendy sighed. Professor Glazer confided in her, Wendy believed, because she thought Wendy might somehow find the cure to Hannah's condition. Find a cure or prove that no harm would come to her daughter. Wendy hoped Hannah would be fine, but Hannah's abnormal growth was a result of fetal tampering by the witch, Rebecca Cole, who had employed dark magics to bring Karen to term in time for Halloween. Hannah had experienced accelerated growth inside the womb, and that accelerated growth was continuing almost eight months after her birth.

Since Rebecca had planned to use Hannah as her new human vessel, she may have wanted the accelerated aging to continue long enough to provide her with a mature human body far ahead of schedule. Hannah's growth might be just a lingering side-effect of the spell. Rebecca was dead. So maybe the rapid aging would stop soon. That's all Wendy could hope for, for Hannah's sake and her mother's. Best not to dwell on the emotional damage that rapid aging might cause Hannah.

From the front of the store, chimes sounded.

Wendy took enough time to type a quick reply, telling Professor Glazer that they were all in her prayers and that she was sure Hannah would be fine. "*Offer assurances but they are no help at all.*" Wendy sighed at her own impotence, but clicked the *send* button anyway.

As Wendy walked up the center aisle of the store, Kayla, who had yet to come across a body piercing she hadn't tried at least once, cast her a surreptitious gaze and rolled her eyes. Wendy noticed the customer, an attractive teenaged girl with strawberry blond hair, standing by the section of the store dealing with runes. Books on using runes for prognostication, along with kits that included rune stones, some of which were actually made of stone while others were wooden and still others were, and why even bother, made out of plastic.

Wendy stopped next to Kayla and whispered, "What's up?"

"Asked if I could help her with anything," Kayla said,

overenunciating to compensate for a tongue stud. "Gave me a look as if I were something she had to scrape off her shoe, and said, 'I doubt it. Go away'. That's an exact quote, in case you were wondering."

Kayla Zanella had a shock of spiky black hair, shaved at the side of her head. She favored undersized T-shirts or crop tops with distressed jeans. While her ears sported enough metal to appear cybernetic, silver posts pierced the outside of both her eyebrows, and silver loops adorned her right nostril, the middle of her lower lip, and her exposed navel. She'd told Wendy once that she'd purchased five of the loops. Against her better judgment, Wendy had inquired about the location of the other two. Kayla had replied, "One's on my left nipple and the other one is . . . downstairs."

Tristan had been sipping some of Kayla's double-kick coffee in the back room with them that day and, at that precise moment, sputtered all over the concert review he'd been reading. Like a shark smelling blood in the water, Kayla had sensed a golden opportunity to make Tristan even more embarrassed—or maybe she'd just been flirting with him, Wendy could never be sure. Kayla had whipped up her crop top to flash him her bare breasts and asked, "What do you think, Tristan? Should I have the other nipple pierced?" Tristan's eyes had gone wide a moment before his pale face blushed beet red. Looking away, he'd said. "I'm pretty sure this qualifies as sexual harassment." As she pulled her top down, Kayla had replied, "No, Tristan, that was sexual *enticement*. Sexual harassment would be if I told you to show me yours." When his face then achieved an even deeper shade of red, Kayla had laughed and clapped her hands, mission accomplished. The next day, apparently fresh from righteous Internet research, Tristan had informed Kayla that a woman who pierced her nipples ruined her ability to breast feed. Kayla had simply said, "I'll worry about that when they ban Similac."

Wendy glanced over at the young woman, who was reading the back of a rune stone kit, all but oblivious to them. Nevertheless, she kept her voice low. "Never seen her in here before," Wendy said. "But something about her seems familiar."

"She goes to Harrison," Kayla said. "A senior. Angelina Thorpe . . . no, Thorne. Everyone calls her Gina."

She would have been a sophomore when I was a senior at Harrison, Wendy thought. *Maybe that's how I recognize her.* Curious, Wendy walked over to the young woman. When Wendy was within six feet of her, Gina dropped the box and spun around as if she expected an attack, her eyes wide. Wendy held up her hands. "Sorry. Didn't mean to startle you."

Gina wore a snug, white knit sweater and a short, wraparound red skirt. She stared at Wendy for a moment, then dropped to a crouch without looking away from her, her hand fumbling around for the box. "Who are you?"

"I'm Wendy Ward, the manager," Wendy said. She'd meant to offer her hand to the young woman, but a sudden impulse caused her to clasp her hands together instead. For some reason, the thought of touching Gina's flesh was making Wendy physically ill. "Can I help you find anything."

"No," Gina said, shoving the box back on the shelf. She examined Wendy with an intent, unblinking gaze, as if trying to remember her every feature. "I wasn't expecting you . . . I mean, no, I have to be somewhere."

Gina backed away, as if she'd feel too vulnerable turning her back to Wendy. Her fists remained clenched until she reached the door and slipped out of the shop with a clatter of chimes.

Kayla walked over to Wendy and said, "What the hell was that all about?"

"She seemed surprised or frightened," Wendy said. "Not that she could shoplift anything in that outfit."

"One weird bitch," Kayla commented.

"That's not very enlightened, Kayla," Wendy said, smiling.

"She gives me the creeps."

"Yeah," Wendy said. "Me too."

A moment later, Tristan entered The Crystal Path, looking over his shoulder. "Not too shabby," Tristan said, "for a bat out of hell."

"The strawberry blonde?" Wendy asked.

Tristan nodded. Pale and tall, with a slender, almost frail build, he had ash blond hair and long, tapered fingers. Tristan Rogers always dressed in shades of gray, which seemed to rob him of what little color he had. "What spooked her?"

"Freaked out by our boss lady here," Kayla said. "But I think the feeling was mutual."

Wendy shuddered. If she never saw Gina Thorne again, she'd be one happy Wicca. "You guys want to mind the fort while I . . ."

"Do your midsummer thing?" Kayla asked.

Wendy nodded. "Where's the joy in performing a midsummer ritual after dark? Besides, right now I could use a good cleansing."

Heart pounding, Gina Thorne raced down Theurgy Avenue until the narrow heel of one of her pumps caught on an uneven section of sidewalk and twisted her ankle. Cursing, she leaned against a brick wall and massaged her foot. Inside The Crystal Path she'd been overcome with fear and hatred. The fear, and the unknown associated with that fear, had won out. Until she understood the strong feelings coursing through her, she had to put some distance between her and that Wendy person.

She's dangerous, the voice inside Gina warned. *She's the one.* But the voice also made a promise. *She must die.* Gina nodded to herself and whispered, "I have to kill her."

Even though Wendy wasn't living at the cottage yet, the backyard was in good shape. Bobby McGowan had cleaned the physical mess, removing all the trash before mowing the grass and pulling the weeds. Wendy had performed a cleansing ritual with her witch's broom to get rid of the psychic debris left over from the Bloody Pus days. All of which meant, she felt comfortable performing a midsummer ritual in the yard.

She'd taken a cleansing lavender petal bath at home

to prepare her before driving to the cottage. Since flour made for a poor magic circle in grass, even trimmed grass, she laid out a purple cord to form the circumference of her magic circle. Wearing a white robe with bands of red, orange, and yellow as she sat cross-legged on her meditation mat in the center of the circle, she took a few minutes to clear her mind of all distractions. When she felt calm and centered in the moment, she shrugged off the robe to be naked while she communed with nature.

Within the circle, to the east she placed a stick of sandalwood incense in her antique holder to represent Air; to the south, a burner, filled with kindling, to represent Fire; to the west, a silver cup filled with red wine to represent Water; and to the north, a cup of cooked rice, to represent Earth. She had invoked each of the elements, the four rulers, starting with Air to the east and proceeding clockwise through north, returning to east once again to close the circle. At each compass point, she had envisioned the nature of the element she addressed, communing with each element as she called on its presence for her ritual.

On midsummer's day, the sun was at its most powerful point, providing the longest day of the year. Midsummer was a time for purification and renewed energy, and was a powerful Sabbat for all kinds of magic. Wendy had in mind only two spells, a healing spell to aid Alex's own body in its repair of numerous injuries, and a protective spell, for Hannah. Technically, she was healthy and required no specific healing, but the taint of Rebecca

Cole hung over her with, perhaps, the potential to ruin her life.

During the protective spell for Hannah, a smooth turquoise stone clutched in her right, projective hand as she faced north, eyes closed to help her visualization, Wendy felt a wave of dizziness. She opened her eyes and saw the white-haired, old woman in the long white robe standing before her, within her circle, ghostlike, with the translucency of gauze. Yet Wendy was not frightened by her. Ever since her rowboat dream, she believed the woman meant to help her, not harm her.

"Who are you?"

"*In practicality, a teacher,*" the woman said. "*But you may think of me as the Crone.*"

The Crone was the third aspect of the Goddess, after the Maiden and the Mother, symbolized by the waxing, full, and waning moon. "Am I dreaming again?" Wendy asked.

"*No, but your ritual places your mind in a receptive state,*" the Crone explained. She shook her head with a strange sadness. "*So much for you to learn, yet our time grows short.*"

"Why?"

"*The evil has reawakened, Wendy,*" the old woman said. "*And it brings with it the power of corruption, the power of chaos. And chaos predates our natural world of order. You must be strong. You must be fierce.*"

The old woman kneeled, or at least appeared to kneel on the grass before Wendy, less than an arm's length away from her, hands resting on her thighs. Wendy could feel warmth radiating from the ghostly form.

"Why me?"

"*The evil knows who you are,*" the old woman said. "*I believe it even knows what you are.*"

"And what am I? Exactly?"

"*You are its natural enemy,*" the old woman said and gave a gentle smile, as if at a private joke. "*Its adversary. First it tried to corrupt you, which would have been the ultimate irony. But it failed to corrupt you. So it seeks revenge.*"

"Revenge? Not so good for me, I'm thinking."

The Crone nodded. "*Since it failed to corrupt you, its fear has taken over. The evil must kill you.*"

"It's afraid of me? Why?"

"*As it has awakened, so too will you.*"

"How? How do I awaken?"

"*I need your permission. To speak directly to your mind.*"

"If it'll help me understand," Wendy said. "Permission granted."

The Crone nodded and reached out for Wendy, holding her face in insubstantial hands. Wendy shivered at the feathery contact. "*Listen,*" the Crone whispered, leaning forward to touch her forehead against Wendy's. But the old woman's insubstantial head continued forward after contact, passing through Wendy's skin and bones and into her skull, until their heads completely overlapped. A voice roared inside Wendy's mind, a deafening, deranged rush of thought that threatened to drive her insane. "WENDY-YOU-WENDY-MUST-WENDY-LISTEN-WENDY-TO-WENDY-ME!!!"

Even though the sound came from inside her skull, Wendy clamped her hands over her ears. Still the blurring rush of thought assaulted her mind.

Wendy screamed.

Her body convulsed once, twice, then she fell over on her meditation mat, where her limbs continued to thrash. Her eyes stared into the distance, unseeing. She was unaware of the blades of grass pressed against her cheek, unaware of her fingernails clawing into the earth, unaware of the ghostly image of the Crone as it twisted and dissolved into the midsummer air.

When the tremors subsided, Wendy's eyes rolled back in her head, flashing the whites. Eventually, her eyelids drooped shut and the cool darkness tugged her down into the deep emptiness of complete oblivion.

PART TWO

ADVERSARY

CHAPTER FOUR

Nine-year-old Abby Mac-Neil lay in her bed in the Nottingham house with the covers pulled up to her chin. She was running a fever, so one minute she would be hot and sweaty, the next racked with chills. She stared at the posters across the room over Erica's bed and wondered what Franklin the turtle and Little Bear would think of a girl whose bones changed shape at will. Well, with a will of their own, since Abby felt she had little control over when or how they changed. That was the part that scared her.

Sometimes she thought she had imagined both episodes, the last one four weeks ago when she had frightened everyone in the house, including Rowdy, the

Nottinghams' chocolate Lab. Abby had been missing all night. In the morning, Mr. Nottingham had found her sleeping, practically naked, in the dirt, curled in the looping root of a maple tree. Nothing left of her pink nightgown but a few shreds of cloth. Her arms and legs mapped with fine scratches and sporting several faint bruises. No serious injuries, but that hadn't stopped the Nottinghams from taking her to the doctors and the hospital for more tests. They poked her with needles to take blood, made her pee in a cup and even had her lie down on a table that went into a shiny tunnel for a CAT scan, which was a test that had nothing to do with cats but let the doctors see inside her body. Ever since last year, when all the doctors thought she was going to die, Abby had hated hospitals. She wished everyone would just leave her alone. After all the tests, the doctors were still puzzled. Mrs. Nottingham told her the tests had come back normal, that Abby should be perfectly healthy. But the Nottinghams still worried about her.

Finally, they had Abby meet with a lady doctor who didn't use needles or big, fancy machines to take tests. She just talked. She asked Abby why she had left the house, where she had gone all night and what had happened while she was alone in the woods. Abby couldn't answer any of her questions, because she didn't know. Her only secret was her bones, her changing bones and she was too afraid to tell anyone about that. If she told the lady doctor, Abby worried that the woman would tell the Nottinghams she wasn't a normal little girl, would tell them that Abby MacNeil was some kind of freak.

Then they might send her away to an orphanage. Or worse. Maybe they'd give her to a traveling carnival, to be chained in the tent with the other freaks. Boys and girls would buy tickets to see the freak show, to make faces at her. She imagined the mean boys would jab sticks through her cage, poking her. Or maybe they would throw rocks at her, even spit on her. Nobody cared about freaks. The Nottinghams were the only family Abby had now and she was afraid they would send her away if they found out she was different. She *had* to fit in.

Abby became aware that she was scratching her right hand, the two middle fingers on that hand. She held up her hand to examine it by the bedside light. Those two fingers were the ones that had changed first last year, after the dream she had, the dream about the witch named Sarah Hutchins. They seemed normal now. Except they itched.

Abby remembered how it had started last year. First the fingers had become long, with hardened nails, and she had attacked Art Leeson in the car. *Would a normal little girl attack someone who was trying to help her?* The car had crashed and Abby had been paralyzed for a while, then the rest of her bones had changed. The doctors had suspected some sort of bone cancer. But they had never guessed the truth, that the witch Sarah was responsible. She had taught Abby how to move her arms again, how to walk again, and then the old witch had taken Abby from the hospital.

"Sarah's dead now," Abby whispered, an affirmation. "And I'm normal again."

Her two middle fingers twitched, the skin rippling, sprouting white fur. Abby squeaked in terror, covering her right hand with her left and pressing both hands to her chest. Tomorrow was the full moon. Her bones hadn't changed since the last full moon. After all the tests and all the time that had passed, she had almost been able to convince herself it had been nothing more than a bad dream.

Bones don't change shape, she thought, *and normal little girls don't turn into wolves!*

The door flung open as Erica ran into their bedroom. Rowdy, a brown mass of raw energy, bounded along behind her. Erica sat on the edge of Abby's bed, holding her Suzy Superstar doll close to her chest. "Hi, Abby. You weren't sleeping, were you?"

"No," Abby said.

"Are you still sick?"

"Just feel cold, is all."

Erica held out her doll. "Want to play with Suzy? She talks and sings."

"Not right now."

"Okay."

Rowdy hopped on the foot of the mattress, dropped to his belly and hunched himself forward in increments. He knew he wasn't supposed to lie on the beds, but he took his chances. Leading with his cold nose and wet muzzle, Rowdy nudged his head under Abby's arm, soliciting a mere scratch behind the ears which always ended up as a vigorous full belly rub. Without thinking Abby reached out for him with her right hand, then snatched it back to check her fingers. Finding them normal again, she let out a breath she'd been holding and petted the dog's head.

"Mom told me to ask if you want anything."

Abby glanced at the empty glass on her nightstand. "Maybe some more ginger ale."

Erica grabbed the glass. "Okey-dokey."

Abby's hand convulsed. She felt the bones shift beneath the skin, and the shiver of gooseflesh that happened when she was sprouting white fur. Rowdy's hackles went up and he emitted a low, rumbling growl, backing away from her. Abby pulled her hand back again and covered it with the left one.

"Stop it, Rowdy!" Erica said. "Can't you see it's just Abby?" Rowdy jumped off the bed, ran in a frustrated circle and let out a low whine of discontent. "Sheesh! Our dog's a scaredy cat," Erica said. "I'll get your soda, Abby." Erica tucked her doll under her arm to free a hand and grabbed Rowdy by the collar. "Come on, you dumb dog. Growling at a little girl. Sheesh!"

Abby almost smiled, thinking of Erica referring to her as a little girl, when Abby was a couple years older than Erica. Then the smile collapsed. She held her hand up to the light and saw her fingers crumbling downward to her palm, while her hand had become . . . a paw. Abby frowned in concentration, willing her fingers to become long again, to become normal again. The chill fled her body as her face became flushed. She began to perspire, gritting her teeth as she extended her fingers, stretching them out until the knuckles cracked with the effort. In small agonizing increments, the middle fingers seemed to become longer again, the bone segments beneath the flesh and her knuckles re-forming into normal fingers. At the same time, the small tufts of white fur thinned and retracted, leaving only the fine blond down of her human skin.

When her hand was back to normal, she let out a long breath and dropped her arm to the covers. Trembling with exhaustion, she drifted off to sleep before Erica returned with her drink.

As Kayla Zanella inserted an Enya CD into the player under the counter and adjusted the volume on the store speakers, Wendy grabbed a box cutter and sliced open a package containing three Galilean thermometers. The thermometers were long, hand-blown glass tubes filled with liquid, housing multicolored, liquid-filled glass floats that rose or fell depending on the ambient temperature. From the bottom of each float hung a gold-plated lead tag with a temperature stamped on it. The thermometer worked on the principle that temperature affected the density of liquids. Some floats would rise, while others settled to the bottom of the glass tube. The approximate temperature would be that listed on the tag of the lowest of the risen floats. Since they only measured temperatures from the mid-sixties to the mid-eighties, the thermometers were basically for indoor use. They managed to be elegant and modern, even though they recalled simpler times. Wendy spaced them out on the counter, setting the tallest one in the middle.

Another box had an assortment of power-bead

bracelets. Wendy slid them on the black velvet holder. As she read the little tags, she shook her head and chuckled.

"What's up, boss lady?"

Wendy held a couple of the bracelets out in her palm. "The same people who shudder at the mention of the word witchcraft don't give a second thought to slapping on a turquoise power bracelet for good health or a yellow jade bracelet for good fortune."

Kayla pressed her palms together, as if in devotion as she gave a slight bow of her head. "Grasshopper, you fail to understand the one power greater than witchcraft."

Wendy smiled, playing along. "Faith? Love?"

Kayla shook her head. "Marketing."

"Ah, yes," Wendy said, nodding. "Repackage the Wiccan heritage for the new millennium."

"Exactly," Kayla said. "Step into our changing room and try on your shiny new cynicism for the twenty-first century."

"*Wendy!*"

"What?" Wendy said.

"I said, step into—"

"No, I thought somebody called my name."

Kayla looked around the empty store. "I didn't hear anything."

"Probably just my imagination," Wendy said. She reached out to brush a lock of Kayla's spiky hair away from her ear. "Hey! You're wearing Celtic ear cuffs."

"Guilty," Kayla said.

"Cuffs? Isn't that some sort of sacrilege for an acolyte of the Church of the Divine Piercing?"

Kayla grinned. "A minor transgression, at worst."

"*Wendy!*" Louder this time.

"There it is again," Wendy said. "Somebody calling me." She had a disturbing thought. "Has that Thorne girl been back? Gina Thorne?"

"I haven't seen her," Kayla said. "And Tristan hasn't mentioned anything."

"*Wendy!*"

"You're sure you don't hear that?" Wendy asked.

Kayla shook her head. "Just you, me, and Enya, baby."

Wendy wandered toward the back of the store. "Turn the music down."

Kayla turned the volume down to an ethereal hush. "Should I come . . . ?"

"No," Wendy said. "Stay there."

Kayla shrugged. "You da boss lady."

The door to the back room was open. Wendy couldn't remember if she had closed it after taking a break from the Web site project. She'd been absentminded lately, ever since her midsummer ritual had ended in disaster.

Her memories of the ritual were a tattered patchwork involving the ghostly old woman who called herself the Crone, a thousand voices all screaming inside her head and a mind-splitting pain. Somehow the old woman had hurt her, a brief, overwhelming agony. Wendy had passed out in her backyard. If not for the gentle rain on her bare flesh, she wondered how long she would have remained unconscious. Long enough for a neighbor or Bobby McGowan to find her sprawled naked in the grass? A potential embarrassment avoided and best not contemplated.

Fortunately, the Crone had not reappeared since then. A bad case of the jitters had followed the Crone's appearance at the ritual. For a while, Wendy had jumped at every shadow, every sound. It had taken nearly two weeks for her to feel whole again. In the past month she'd recovered her peace of mind, so busy with the cottage renovations, that she'd spared little time worrying about the Crone or even about Gina Thorne. For whatever reason, they had both left her in peace, and she preferred it that way, settling into a hectic but normal life.

Now she was hearing voices. *Never a good sign*, Wendy admitted.

Her hand closed on the doorknob. She swung the door open and stared into the dark room, reassuring herself that the darker, blockier shadows in the back of the room were merely boxes and cartons of overstocked merchandise. The computer screen cast a pale glow across the center of the back room and the open space on the white tile floor where Alissa usually laid her exercise mat for her yoga exercises.

Wendy flicked on the light switch. A slight breeze scattered papers from the computer desk. At first, Wendy thought the wash of cool air had issued from the ventilation ducts, but she hadn't heard the thrum of the air conditioner's compressor. Only silence.

Beside the light switch, a gilt-edged oval mirror hung from a wall hook. Alissa always checked her hair and makeup there before coming to the front of the store. Now Wendy looked into the mirror. But the face reflected back to her was not her own. It was the Crone's.

"*Wendy!*"

With an abrupt scream, she lashed out with her fist, the hand holding the box cutter, its razor blade still extended. The blade snapped and the force of the blow cracked the mirror. "Get out!" Wendy shrieked.

The box cutter slipped from nerveless fingers and she wiped at tears brimming in her eyes before they could spill down her cheek. "Just leave me alone," she whispered. "Leave me alone, damn you!"

When she looked again, the distorted reflection in the cracked mirror was her own. Legs trembling, Wendy sank down into the computer chair. She leaned forward, forearms resting on her thighs as she took long, cleansing breaths.

"Say the word, boss lady, and I'll swing for the fences."

Wendy looked up to see Kayla standing in the doorway with an aluminum baseball bat over one shoulder as she took in the room with a sweeping gaze. "No, I'm okay."

"I heard something break."

Wendy pointed. "The mirror," she said. "Something startled me."

"Was it a spider?" Kayla shuddered. "The kind with the long, hairy legs?"

"Creepier," Wendy said.

"You kill it?" Kayla asked, glancing back and forth across the floor.

"No," Wendy said. "But maybe it will think twice before coming back."

"Hope so," Kayla said. "Hate to think you'd have seven years bad luck for nothing."

Wearing a red, crocheted tank sweater and cutoff jeans, Gina sat cross-legged on her bed, looking down into the shoebox balanced on her lap. Inside were the three small rag dolls she had sewn from strips of cloth worn by her mother, Dominick, and Todd. Over the past month, she had taken more hair from their brushes and combs to stuff inside the dolls, along with small snips of cloth to flesh them out. The dolls were featureless, with a simplistic human shape, bound together with crude stitching. Each doll had a black ribbon knotted around its head—tiny blindfolds. But the dolls lacked even an approximation of eyes. The blindfold was symbolic, a focus. And she had seen results, encouraging results.

Also in the box, in a faux leather pouch, was a set of Scrabble tiles that had failed to deliver on their earlier promise. For a while, Gina had debated buying a set of actual rune stones, prompting her visit to The Crystal Path and her encounter with that disturbing Wendy Ward person. But she'd decided against the confusing and ambiguous glyphs in favor of messages spelled out in plain English. So far, though, the new set of Scrabble tiles had spelled out only plain gibberish.

Gina heard Brett's F-150 pull up out front.

Sliding the shoebox back under her bed, she left her bedroom and padded down the hall in her bare feet, taking a moment to look in on Todd. "Hey, little toad, enjoying your new computer?"

Sitting at his desk with his back to her, Todd said, "It's great, Gina. You should try it out."

Gina chuckled. "I'll leave that to you, little toad. Have fun!" Never failed to amuse her, watching him sitting in front of his ruined computer, staring at the dark screen, hands flashing on the keyboard or sliding the mouse around on its pad as if something was actually happening inside the big plastic piece of junk. But Todd was happy and they all saw what Gina wanted them to see, so that kept Dominick and Caitlin out of her hair.

Yes, definite results, she thought and turned to walk away.

"Gary's coming over later," Todd said. "Can't wait to show him how fast this is."

"Gary?"

"Gary Gatti," he said. "My friend from school. He's coming over later with his skateboard." Todd looked over his shoulder to flash her a pimply grin. "He'll be blown away."

Oh, Todd, Gina thought. *Don't you know some things must remain in the family? Outsiders just wouldn't understand.*

The doorbell rang. Gina shook her head and ran down the steps to answer the door. "It's for me!" she called before her mother or Dominick poked their heads into the reception area. She pulled the door open, grabbed Brett by his belt buckle and tossed him inside. "What kept you?"

"Sorry," Brett said. "I had to fill up the tank."

"Who—who is it?" Dominick asked, his voice tentative.

Gina turned to him, anger flashing in her eyes. "It's Brett. Now go away, Dominick."

Standing at the opposite end of the reception area, Dominick's face was pale, with uneven patches of stubble along his jaw and dark circles under his eyes, as if he wasn't getting enough sleep. But Gina knew sleep alone wouldn't help his condition. She was tapping him.

Dominick nodded and even that simple motion seemed to take too much effort. "Okay, okay. Sorry to intrude, Gina, I was just curious."

"You and the cat, Dom," Gina said. "Better hope you fare better."

Dominick mumbled, "You kids go about your business then." He backed out of the reception area, eyes downcast.

"As if I needed his permission," Gina said, shaking her head. She swung the door closed and led Brett upstairs. In the hall, Brett craned his neck to look in on Todd, shook his head, baffled. "How do you do that?"

"He sees what I want him to see," Gina said. Then softer, "They all do. Life around the house is much simpler this way."

Brett nodded, following her into her bedroom with one backward glance at Todd. After she closed the door, Brett wandered over to her stereo. His hands strayed across the various controls without changing them. With his back to her, he cleared his throat and asked, "What about me? Are you controlling what I see?"

"Look at me, Brett," she said, a seductive lilt in her voice. He turned around. She was standing naked before him, her tank sweater and cutoffs in a careless pile at her feet. She spread her arms. "Do you have a problem with what you're seeing?"

He swallowed hard. "Not at all."

"Good," she said, sitting on the bed and patting the mattress beside her. "Now get over here and out of those jeans. Pleasure before business."

"Business?"

"It's time we started making plans."

Wendy wore a baggy gray Danfield College T-shirt with the arms cut off over a black sports bra, along with jade green shorts and black running shoes. After the unsettling vision in the mirror in the back room of The Crystal Path, she'd had a lot of nervous energy to burn. Right after closing the shop, she'd driven home and changed into her jogging attire. She'd finish her run long before twilight, take a quick shower, and have a light dinner. She always felt jazzed after a run. Well, once the initial exhaustion wore off. She'd read that exercise increased the body's metabolic rate for hours afterward, which improved digestion and caloric burn. Wendy always felt more alert, more focused after a good aerobic workout. Unlike weight training, which left her feeling achy and weak for days.

A week earlier, she'd taken the Civic out on the road, using its odometer to map out several courses two and three-quarter miles from the cottage. Giving herself more than one route to choose from helped to alleviate some of the monotony of jogging. After a stretching regimen, she walked the first quarter mile, before picking up the pace to long-legged strides, almost a run, if not a sprint. When she reached the traffic light at the intersection of Mage Avenue and Ash Street, with Spellcaster Video Rentals on the near corner and Mike's Sandwich Shop on the other, she would tap the metal pole for luck and head back. As a cooldown, she would take the last quarter mile at a brisk walk. That way she could stumble into the cottage, peel off her jogging togs and jump into the shower. Five minutes later she would be clean, clearheaded, and refreshed. No better tonic.

Except this time, the voice kept slipping into her head, into her consciousness, calling her name over and over again. "*Wendy ... Wendy ... Wendy!*" As if waiting for her to answer. Wendy gritted her teeth and pressed her hands to her ears, which not only made running more difficult but failed to block the voice. The Crone was speaking to her mind, not to her ears. *Either that,* Wendy thought, *or I'm just losing my marbles.*

"Wendy!"

"Leave me alone!" Wendy shouted, much to her dismay. Too late she saw several teenaged boys spilling out of Spellcaster Video Rentals, just in time to witness her bizarre outburst.

A pale, freckled redhead clutching no fewer than four plastic encased DVD rentals glared at her. "What's your dysfunction?"

"Theater major," Wendy called with a gregarious wave. "Just—uh, practicing my lines." *Oh, brother!*

She circled the traffic light, forgetting to tap the pole. Fortunately, her brisk pace put a lot of distance between her and the guys. But not before she heard another one comment, "Loopy bitch."

Wendy tried to put the incident behind her, picked up her pace, running so hard that her breathing became labored. But she couldn't outrun her own mind.

"Wendy!"

"Go away!" Wendy hissed, almost under her breath.

"Please," the voice said. "Forgive me."

Wendy faltered in her stride. "What?"

"My mistake hurt you. I'm sorry."

The voice—the thought—in her head sounded contrite. Wendy resumed her jogging. "Look, I can't talk now. People are staring." True enough. An old woman walking a schnauzer kept flashing Wendy surreptitious glances, as if wishing she knew the number of the nearest mental health facility. Maybe she's just trying to remember if she packed pepper spray in her ten-gallon purse before taking Fido out for his evening trot and squat.

The voice chuckled in Wendy's head.

"You heard that?" Wendy whispered.

"You need not speak aloud," the voice said. "I hear your directed thoughts."

"Like—" Wendy began, then stopped herself and thought the question at the voice. Like telepathy?

"Yes."

You can read my mind? Wendy thought, alarmed. I'm not sure I like that. Especially since I can't read yours.

"I can hear, or sense rather, your directed thoughts," the voice explained. "Your general thoughts are like static, or white noise to me, a chaos of words and images."

Now you sound like Professor Lordi, Wendy thought, adding a mental chuckle.

"You're getting better at this."

When will I be good enough to read your thoughts?

"That is problematical. I don't exist as you do."

So you are a figment of my imagination? Wendy thought. Then she said aloud, "I am going crazy." Wendy paused at an intersection, running in place to keep her heart rate up, as a pale blue Dodge van turned down the side street.

"I exist outside your imagination, Wendy, I assure you. But my thoughts originate from an altered state of consciousness."

Peyote? LSD? What are we talking about here?

"No hallucinogens, smoke, or mirrors are involved. Just trust that I've found a way to contact you. That's the important thing."

You said you made a mistake, Wendy thought. When you hurt me on Midsummer Day. What kind of mistake?

Less than a mile to go until the turn down her cul-de-sac. After the turn she would begin her cooldown walk. The voice remained silent while Wendy, thanks to her brisk pace, passed one block and another. Are you still there?

"Yes. Just deciding the best way to explain what happened during your ritual." Another pause. "I had hoped to save time by passing all the information to you at once."

How?

"With what I've come to refer to as an information overlay. Almost by creating the memories in your mind."

That sounds bizarre.

"It is an acquired skill, both in the sending and in the receiving. That was my mistake. I had forgotten that your mind was not prepared to receive information that way."

So you triggered my mental gag reflex.

A chuckle sounded in Wendy's mind. "Basically. Sometimes this altered state of consciousness of mine contains lapses or gaps. This was a dangerous gap. My attempt at an overlay triggered the equivalent of a mental circuit breaker in your mind."

Lights out, Wendy.

"Yes. My attempted shortcut backfired and I needed to give your mind time to recover."

That's why I haven't seen or heard from you lately?

"Exactly. If I had attempted contact too soon, the circuit breaker would have been tripped merely by my presence. You might have gone into shock . . . or worse."

Worse? You mean dead?

"A coma, possibly."

Wendy felt a flare of anger. *But you came back anyway? Knowing you could have put me in a coma?*

"I am sorry, Wendy. You must understand how important this is. You were ready to receive me again more than a week ago. Still, I waited . . . just to be sure. For me to wait any longer, to delay your training any longer, would put not only your life at risk but would open the door to an evil reborn."

Wendy arrived at the turn into her cul-de-sac just in time. Her legs felt heavy and lethargic. She rested her hands on her hips and walked along the edge of the asphalt road, staring into the distance.

"Wendy?"

I'm still listening, Wendy thought. I knew we'd get back to this eventually.

"As we must."

Because I'm the adversary?

"Good, you remember. I worried that the overlay had wiped some of your memories."

I remember most of the ritual, up to the moment you reached out for me, then a burst of pain, then it gets hazy.

"That's when I began the overlay. So let's continue from that point, shall we?"

How long before I can learn how to do the overlay thing?

"Just to learn how to receive an overlay would take the average person years. For you, maybe months."

Ah, because I'm special, Wendy said, trying for a mental snicker.

"Believe it or not, you are special. But we don't have the luxury of time for me to train you to receive. We'll have to do this the old-fashioned, linear way. One word at a time."

Just my luck, Wendy thought. Remedial telepathy.

"You have already made great progress."

I have?

"Yes. You are already an excellent sender."

An excellent linear sender, you mean.

"We all must crawl before we learn to walk."

Okay, so down to business. Where's my syllabus? How does my linear lesson begin?

"With you, Wendy. You are her adversary and she is yours. She grows more powerful with each passing day."

Whereas I remain puny and insignificant, Wendy quipped.

"You are helpless and unprepared," the Crone told her. "Never consider yourself insignificant."

Wait a minute, Wendy thought. You said her, not it. My adversary, this reborn evil is a she?

"Yes."

Let's not beat around the mental bush anymore. You're talking about Wither, aren't you?

"Yes. She is the ancient evil."

Wendy balked at the thought. But I destroyed her!

"You defeated her, in her oldest, most bestial form. But you failed to destroy her."

Wendy stopped walking, shaking her head as if the Crone were there to see the gesture. You can't know! You weren't there! I crushed that bitch under several tons of rock.

"Fire is the only sure way to destroy her evil."

Standing next to a candy-apple-red RAV4, Wendy dropped her head to her chest. She almost wanted to sob. We burned her. Frankie and I took gasoline from the Gremlin, poured it over the rubble. We watched it burn.

"You watched her remains burn. I sense that."

You're damn right we did!

"You must have been too late with the fire. Her essence escaped."

Essence? What the hell are you talking about?

"Blood. Her blood is her essence, it carries her corruption within it."

Wendy resumed her walk home. Her blood infected someone?

"Yes . . . you could think of . . . as . . . blood-borne infection. But corruption . . . closer to the mark. When . . . complete, the human host . . . gone and only Wither . . . remain . . ."

I'm losing you! What's happening?

Not only were words dropping out, but the strength of the words had begun to fade, almost to a mental whisper.

"I grow weary. Maintaining . . . state of consciousness . . . draining. After . . . rest . . . we will continue—Wendy? . . . wrong? . . . sense surprise . . . ?"

Wendy had begun to walk faster, just to be sure she wasn't hallucinating. *He's two days early!*

"Who . . . ?"

No, it's okay. Go rest. She whispered, "It's Alex. He's back."

Wendy began to run again, her pace increasing to a sprint as she neared her cottage. Alex had been sitting on the low stoop, his cane across his lap, a large suitcase and a navy-blue duffel bag behind him, against the wall. He stood and smiled as he saw her, taking a few steps across the lawn toward her. And maybe it was just her hopeful imagination, but his limp seemed a little less noticeable now. She lunged into his arms, wrapping her arms around his neck and planting frantic kisses on his cheeks. He dropped his cane, caught her around the waist, and, considering his medical condition, made an ill-advised attempt to spin her around in the air. Managing only about a quarter revolution before his legs gave out, Alex surrendered to gravity with a resigned laugh and fell back, carrying her down on top of him.

Wendy pushed herself up at arm's length and said. "You're a sight for sore eyes."

"And sweaty limbs, apparently," Alex said, noting the damp patches she had managed to transfer to his rumpled airline clothes.

"Sweaty limbs," she agreed, then rubbed a sweaty cheek against his face. "And sweaty cheeks." She poked him with her nose. "A sweaty nose . . . and sweaty lips," she added, kissing his lips and tasting the salty sweat between them. Before the kiss progressed to stage two on the passion meter, she broke contact. "That your cane between us or are you just happy to see me?"

"My cane is way over there," Alex admitted.

"Just as I suspected," Wendy said. "You are hopelessly lecherous."

"Guilty as charged."

Wendy pecked him on the cheek. "Wouldn't have you any other way." She climbed to her feet and offered him a hand. "Lest we scandalize the neighbors." He nodded, took her hand, and let her tug him up beside her. "Now, either I've experienced a serious lost-time incident or you're a couple days early, Mr. Dunkirk."

"I'm a couple days early."

Alex fell into step beside her as she fished her house key out of her shorts and unlocked the door. She gave him a playful glance. "So, they finally kicked you out of Minneapolis?"

"Released on good behavior."

She pursed her lips. "Oh, so you can't be naughty anymore?"

"You'll find I'm a recidivist by nature, Ms. Ward," Alex said, patting her rear end.

"I was counting on that," Wendy said with a wink. "Have a look around while I take a quick shower."

Alex paused. "You know, I could use a shower as well. Especially after our brief but sweaty interlude in the grass."

"And you were thinking . . . ?"

"Water conservation."

Wendy placed the tip of her index finger between her lips and gave him her best coquettish look. "Let the naughtiness commence."

Gina heard the unmistakable rumble of skateboard wheels on asphalt and cursed. She plucked at the tangle of sheets wrapped around her naked body and stumbled out of the bed.

Brett sat up and finger-brushed his hair. "What's wrong?"

"Gary." Gina pulled on her cutoffs, then slipped into her red tank sweater. "Gary is wrong."

"Gary?"

"Todd's gonna show him his new computer."

"That piece of junk he stares at all day?"

"Now you see the problem."

"What are you gonna do?"

"Hold that thought," Gina said. She unlocked her bedroom door, walked down the hall and knocked on Todd's door. "Hey, little toad, your buddy's here. Go outside and compare skateboard moves."

"But I wanna show him—"

"No, that can wait."

"But—"

"I said, *it can wait*. Now be a good boy." In a moment, Gina returned to her bedroom and closed the door again. She walked over to her window and opened the blinds.

In a black Metallica T-shirt, baggy green shorts, and scuffed sneakers, Gary Gatti hadn't approached the house yet. Instead he was attempting to flip his skateboard up from the ground into his outstretched hand, a feat he finally managed after three botched attempts.

After a rush of footfalls, the door slammed and Todd appeared below, his own battered skateboard tucked under his arm. As usual, he'd left his plywood stunt contraption out by the curb. Gina supposed it substituted for a skateboarder's half-pipe, but it was more quarter-pipe, since it only had one curve. On its own, it wasn't all that treacherous, especially when Todd remembered to wear his knee and elbow pads. Brett had parked his blue F-150 in front of it.

Gina glanced over her shoulder, sensing Brett approach her from behind, wearing only his black Jockeys and sporting a blood-smeared bite on his left shoulder. Gina's recipe for great sex required a pinch of fear and a dollop or two of pain. As a result, the bite on Brett's left shoulder was deep enough to lift a full dental cast.

Brett's weight-lifting regimen had provided the clay. Now her intimate contact with him allowed her to channel dark energies into him, all without his awareness, further sculpting his body, building his biceps and forearms, giving him a broad powerful chest over cobblestone abs, well-defined thighs, and strong calves. Beyond her own developing abilities, he was her primary tool and she was molding him, honing him into a lethal weapon. While she reveled in his tireless service as her lover, more important would be his role as her keeper.

The clatter of skateboards on plywood and asphalt interrupted her thoughts. She returned her attention to the thirteen-year-olds as they attempted various stunts off the curbside quarter-pipe. "Look at him," Gina said, shaking her head. "Thinks he's Tony Hawk."

Brett wrapped his muscular forearms around her bare waist and nuzzled at the side of her neck. "Life imitates video games."

Gina noticed a long truck rumbling down the street, Yankee Silver Springs Bottled Water painted in blue letters on a white background. Every few days the truck driver made a sweep through their development, Eden's Crossing, dropping off five-gallon water jugs and picking up the empties at each of his appointed stops. The neighbors often complained about the driver's reckless speed, demanding the township install speed bumps along the busiest streets in their suburban development. "Make yourself useful and grab the box under my bed."

Brett retrieved the shoebox, glancing at the rag dolls, the pouch and the loose string with an arched eyebrow. "This part of your plans?"

She nodded, keeping her gaze on the approaching bottled water truck, judging its distance to the boys on their skateboards. Brett's pickup would obstruct them from the view of the careless driver.

"What do you have in mind?"

Gina picked up the Todd rag doll and a loose ten-inch length of black thread. "I've decided that my family is too big by half."

The rumble of the truck became more noticeable. The driver had no stops through the end of the block, so he was picking up speed. Both boys were caught up in their own petty stunts, only peripherally aware of the approaching vehicle, secure in the false knowledge of an orderly universe and their own immortality.

Gina looped the length of thread around the legs of the Todd rag doll and waited for Todd to roll up his quarter-pipe. At the top of his arc, he gripped the bowed front of the skateboard and spun his feet around to roll back down facing the other direction, facing away from the truck. As he landed on the board, she tugged the loop tight and the rag doll's legs collapsed together. Gina felt a rush of heat along the inside of her forearms, a manifestation of her power. The tracery of blue veins under her pale skin had become dark, pulsing as black as India ink. Out in the street, Todd lost what little balance he had left. As the skateboard began the descent, Todd's center of gravity drifted too far forward and he staggered off the board, lurching into the street—

"Look out!" Gary yelled.

—as the truck barreled past the pickup truck and slammed into Todd.

Gina had been hoping her stepbrother would fall under the wheels—*all that water had to weigh an awful lot, surely enough to pulp a thirteen-year-old brat*—but he was propelled by the impact, flipping through the air before slamming into the asphalt.

The truck screeched to a halt, the door flung open and the driver jumped out, running over to crouch by the still form. White-faced, he looked over his shoulder and shouted at Gary to call 911.

Brett's arms fell away from her. "Is he—is he dead?"

"One can only hope," Gina said. She examined her forearms, noticed that the black veins had already constricted, begun to fade back to blue. "Time to make yourself scarce, Brett. We're sure to have a scene here, ambulance, paramedics, police even, with no end of questions."

"But they'll know I was here," Brett said.

"Don't worry about my family. I'll cloud their memory," Gina said. "Besides, it's not like you were involved. The truck driver may remember your truck parked outside, but so what."

"How can you do this?"

Gina smiled. "It's a gift, Brett. I've been given this power and it's still growing inside of me. It would be a . . . crime not to use it. Don't you agree?"

"I guess so," Brett said, as he tugged on his jeans and slipped his arms into the sleeves of his shirt. He cast a fearful glance or two her way and her smile broadened. Fear was just another way to maintain her control over him.

Gina returned the shoebox to its place under her bed, then straightened the sheets and blanket. "If it ever comes up," Gina said. "We were listening to music when we heard the screech of brakes and some shouting."

"Right," Brett said. He started to come forward, perhaps to kiss her good-bye, but thought better of it and gave a curt nod. "I'll call later, to find out . . ."

"Don't worry," Gina told him. "You'll know when I need you."

Gina followed him into the hallway, but waited at the top of the stairs, listening to the frantic shouts from below. She heard the door close as Brett slipped out, then called, "What's all the commotion?"

Gina's mother came halfway up the stairs, pausing at the landing, where the stairs doubled back. Her pale face was stricken. She looked as if she'd aged ten years in the last month. *Well,* Gina thought, *in a way, she has. All my extra energy has to come from somewhere.*

"My God, Gina!" Caitlin said. "Todd's been hit by a truck!"

"Oh, no," Gina said, pressing a hand to her mouth, afraid she might grin and ruin the moment. "Is he all right?"

"Told him not to play in the street," Caitlin muttered, turning away. "That stupid skateboard!"

Gina asked softly, "Is he dead?" *Please, oh, please!*

But Caitlin shook her head as she ran down the steps and out the front door. Gina followed at a slower pace. She waited on the wraparound veranda, leaning against one of the support poles as she watched the truck driver, Caitlin, Dominick, and Gary all gather around the still form in the street. She rubbed fingers along the inside of her forearm, feeling the residual heat of the power that had flared inside her.

The power was becoming stronger, but it was more

than power within her, it was a semiconscious entity, an *other* self existing inside her skin, a being who promised to share everything with her. Gina's only sane course was to go along for the ride, for while this other self needed Gina's body to survive, it was more powerful and dominant than anything she had ever imagined. Sometimes, during the early morning hours, when wrenched awake by terrifying dreams, Gina understood she had no choice in the matter, that she had run out of choices the moment the entity called Wither had invaded her. Otherwise, her moments of true self-realization only came in the wake of this *other's* expended power, as if its defenses sagged for a moment and Gina could see through the veil. But those moments were fleeting at best and, by morning light, became as tenuous as forgotten dreams.

She heard approaching sirens and that distraction was enough. Her moment of insight slipped from her grasp, pulled down into the darkness of disconnected thought. Now all she felt was disappointment that Todd had probably survived the impact. With a sigh, she walked across the lawn to join the others. *Have to keep up appearances, after all,* she reminded herself.

As Brett drove his pickup truck away from the Gallo house, he had to grip the steering wheel tight with both hands to stop them from trembling. Gina continued to surprise—and scare—him with her strange new abilities, and the predominantly sociopathic ways in which she used them. Prime example was the tragic accident scene receding behind him.

He'd left the house because Gina had commanded him to leave. Simple as that. Whenever he tried to remember exactly when he'd lost control of his life to her, his hazy memory failed him. And free will was a concept that had gradually lost meaning. Yet, the shock of watching the water truck slam into Todd had jarred Brett's complacency. For a few moments at least, a voice deep inside him, a voice filled with panic and dread, spoke loud enough to grab Brett's attention. All it said was, "Run! Get away!"

Running is not an option, he thought.

Receding. Diminishing.

All that mattered to him was pleasing Gina, obeying her every whim. Sure, the sex was great, better than ever, if a little rougher than it had been a year ago, but something else compelled him to be with her, to be there for her at all times. Something he could almost but never completely understand.

"A moth to the flame," the voice, already fading away, warned.

His hands steadied on the wheel when he realized his inner voice was selfish. It never stopped to consider Gina. He could never abandon her. She was so alive! And she needed him. He had to be there for her. Dazzling Gina . . .

CHAPTER FIVE

Wendy Ward's Mirror Book Entry
July 16, 2000, Moon: Full, day 14

I'm writing this in the wee hours of Sunday morning from my *new* home. Strange to think of this little cottage as home, even if it's only for a semester or two, but that's what it is. I've put in enough time, effort, and money to earn the right to call it home. Earlier in the week, I finished all the painting, just in time for the carpet installer Mom recommended. Two days ago, he finished the last of the wall-to-wall carpeting and it looks gorgeous. Forest green for the common areas, tan for what will be Frankie's bedroom (yes, I got her long distance color approval) and—hope this wasn't a big mistake—white for my bedroom. Painted all the walls antique white, except for my room, which is powder blue. I probably went over-board with the earth and sky theme but I'm a Wicca, so sue me. Anyway, the carpeting was my biggest out-of-pocket expense. True, the Clayton Quinn Home Renovation Fund paid for the carpeting, but I had to pay for labor. Dad and I accounted for the rest of the labor, and Dad accepts hugs as legal tender. For those really back-breaking jobs, I give him a bear hug.

Alex is still sleeping.

Yes, I let him stay over. Since he can't pick up dorm keys till tomorrow, he planned on staying at the Harrison Motor Lodge, but I haven't seen him in so long I couldn't bear to let him go. This was only my second night in the cottage, so I hope Dad doesn't pay me an early morning visit. True, I'm a big girl now, but I think parents, no matter how old you are, always remember the child in you.

Why am I up? I have this feeling she called to me in my sleep. The Crone, I mean. It's so quiet now, though, I can hardly remember the sensation I had upon waking . . . one moment I was sound asleep, the next wide awake and alert. Either she's still weak from our last conversation or I'm too distracted to *hear* her. I'd better put this aside and just *listen* . . .

"*Wendy . . .*"

Faint this time. *Careful not to startle me? Or calling me away?*

With one last glance down at Alex, sleeping in the bed beside her, Wendy ran her fingers through his tousled hair, gentle enough not to disturb him. Then she laid her mirror book on the nightstand, and padded out of the room in her bare feet, luxuriating in the feel of the deep pile carpeting against her toes. Unwilling to venture down the hallway in complete darkness, she left the bedside lamp on and the bedroom door wide open.

Wearing her yellow, rose-print pajamas with lace trim, she walked past the open bathroom with ginger steps, senses heightened, listening, then by the kitchen to her left and into the living room. Her pajama top was sleeveless and had a peasant neckline with ties and buttoned down the front. Thanks to Alex, the ties were untied and only a few buttons remained buttoned, so when a slight breeze swirled around the room, it was cool enough to raise gooseflesh on her exposed skin. She crossed her arms and rubbed them for warmth. "Are you here?" Wendy whispered, then repeated the question as a thought, *Are you here?*

Where the breeze had swirled, Wendy saw a haziness in the air, like lingering smoke in a crowded bar. The smoke began to shape itself into the ghostly image of the Crone. "I'm back."

It's early.

"You're not alone."

Wendy felt a tinge of red on her cheeks. *You're not my mother.*

"No, I'm not, but I thought it best if we talked while we had some privacy."

Sorry. Color me a little defensive.

"I'm not here to judge you, Wendy. Only to help."

Wendy sighed. "Okay, this is a little too bizarre," she said aloud. "It feels weird *thinking* at you when you, well, your image at least, is right in front of me. Mind if I just talk? I'll be quiet. Promise."

"*Fine.*"

"And since the only furniture I have out here is a card table in the dining room, mind if I assume the lotus?"

"*I'll join you,*" the Crone said.

A moment after Wendy sat on the floor and folded her legs, the Crone, facing her, assumed the same position so they remained at eye level. "*Better?*" the Crone asked.

"Much," Wendy said, placing her hands on her knees. "So, I guess it's time we started our lessons?" The Crone nodded, so Wendy continued. "For the sake of argument, I'll assume that what you've told me is true. That Wither was not crushed at the old textile mill."

"*She was crushed,*" the Crone said. "*Defeated. But not destroyed.*"

"So this is all about revenge? I defeated her. Now she wants a rematch. What do they say in Hollywood? This time it's personal?"

"*That's part of her motivation to destroy you,*" the Crone said. "*But not the whole of it.*"

Wendy exhaled sharply. "Walk me through it."

"*Last year, Wither awakened from her century long hibernation.*"

"We covered that on the last exam," Wendy said. "Art noticed the pattern of destruction in Windale every hundred years: 1699, the year the Windale witches were hanged and thought dead, then in 1799, 1899, and 1999."

Although the creature, demon, whatever, that they thought of as *Wither* was thousands of years old, it had spent the last three hundred years in Elizabeth Wither's body, mutating it into monstrous proportions during the century-long periods of hibernation. Every hundred years Wither, along with the two Puritan women she had corrupted into her coven, had arisen, wreaking havoc on the small town and accounting for drastic spikes in the local mortality rates. These centennial rampages had become known as the Curse, with a capital C. Speculation on the causes of the Curse had run the gamut from paranormal hauntings to untenable scientific studies on the town's polluted water supply. Those who believed the Windale witches had been falsely accused, now advanced the notion that the witches' vengeful spirits returned on the hundred-year anniversaries of their unjust hanging to punish the town. Wendy suspected this line of reasoning had started out as a campfire tale, and had been gleefully adopted by the town's chamber of commerce as a way to boost tourist revenue. Despite the potential economic, albeit macabre, success of the "vengeful spirits" tourist campaign, and that it rightly attributed the centennial destruction to three witches the town believed long dead, it needlessly complicated their motive, which could be simply stated as this: after hibernating for one hundred years, the Windale witches awoke with a huge appetite for destruction and raw human flesh.

"*Soon after Wither awakened from hibernation, you also awakened.*"

"Say again?"

"I mentioned before that Wither tried to corrupt you. You were her choice before all others. Ever wonder why she chose you for her new body?"

Wendy shrugged. "Because I was dumb enough to be sitting sky-clad in a clearing in the woods at night, playing at white magic. Considering the power of her magic, she probably thought my harmless little ritual was a real knee-slapper. She really showed me."

"You never thought that maybe you showed her?"

"Showed her what? I was burning incense, writing, and chanting spells. My magic wouldn't pass muster as parlor tricks."

"You made it rain, Wendy. You were centered, you visualized it happening and it happened. You had power, even then."

Wendy shook her head, surprised by the surge of emotions, the grief and denial still connected to that night, to the magical rain, to Jack Carter's abduction and murder. Wendy still blamed herself for so many things, all of them out of her control. "No, you're wrong. That's what she wanted me to think. It was a trick, her little game. She was playing with me. But I know the truth now. I've known for a long time. It was her all the time. She's the one who made it happen. I had nothing to do with it. That was Wither's rain."

"You're wrong."

Wendy wiped at the tears she found streaming down her cheeks. "It wasn't me! It never was . . ."

"It was you, Wendy. The power awakened inside of you."

"No!" Then the painful admission, I don't have any power!

"How can you sit there looking at my astral image, speak to me telepathically, and still insist you have no power?"

"Maybe I'm delusional," Wendy said. "How do I know any of this is happening? *Really* happening?"

The Crone was silent for a moment. "You are right about one thing," she said. "She has tricked you."

"What?"

"She's made you believe you are powerless."

"I am powerless," Wendy said, stifling a sob. "At the mill, I was just lucky."

"Luck is often the result of preparation and taking advantage of opportunities. You weren't just lucky at the mill, Wendy. You were resourceful."

"What does it matter? Next time I may not be so . . . opportunistic."

"Preparation means training," the Crone said. "To begin your training, you must believe in yourself, in the power that resides within you. The power flows from visualization, just as you visualized the rain on that autumn night. You, Wendy, not Wither. That was never Wither's rain."

Wendy bit down on her trembling lower lip. For so long she had denied her role in the events of that night. Afraid of the guilt, even while she shouldered the responsibility.

"Without belief, without faith, you are helpless to visualize and the power lies dormant."

"What do I do?"

"Believe in yourself."

Wendy gave a wry chuckle. "That simple, huh?"

"That simple . . . and that difficult."

"You said before I was her natural adversary."

The Crone nodded. "And you are. The power intrinsic to your nature is what attracted her to you."

"Even if I believe I have this power—and I'm not sure I do—I still don't understand why I was chosen. Out of billions of people out there, why me?"

The Crone smiled. "Why not you?"

"That's not a good enough answer."

As the Crone thought about her reply, Wendy became aware of birdsong and the new sun, dawn's light evaporating the darkness around them. The Crone seemed to have come to her own realization. "Were you chosen as her adversary? Or is it simply that that is what you are? Perhaps the only reason is that you have the ability within you to defeat her. Have you not already defeated her once?"

"Defeated. But not destroyed," Wendy said, echoing the Crone's own words.

"Granted," the Crone said. "The truth is, I know not why you are the one, only that you are. But before our lessons may begin in earnest, you must learn to believe in yourself."

"I want to believe."

"That's the first step."

"I need to believe," Wendy said, sensing this statement as a deeper truth.

"I wonder," the Crone said with a mysterious smile. "Have you asked Alex about his health?"

"What?"

"Before, you said that you remembered your midsummer ritual up until I attempted the mental overlay." Wendy nodded. "So you remember your spells?"

"Two of them," Wendy said. "One for Hannah's protection and the other . . . for Alex's health!" The Crone smiled, nodded. "That—you mean, it worked? *Really* worked?"

"*Trust your eyes,*" the Crone said, her voice inside Wendy's mind growing faint. "*And maybe you should ask . . . about his limp.*" The morning sunshine spilled through the room and the Crone's ghostly image began to dissipate at last. "*Let the seed of belief . . . begin to grow anew inside you, Wendy.*"

In the last hour before dawn, Abby MacNeil's body temperature started to rise. As it passed one hundred degrees Fahrenheit, perspiration beaded her brow and matted her hair. She began to toss and turn in her sleep, sweeping away her bedcovers as her body contorted in her sweat-soaked nightgown. She whimpered in her sleep but the sound was too soft to wake Erica Nottingham, sleeping just eight feet away. At the foot of Erica's bed lay Rowdy, the Nottinghams' Labrador retriever. The dog's ears twitched once or twice, but then were still.

Abby's right arm twisted in its socket, shifting at the elbow and wrist, even as her fingers retracted into her palm, forming a paw. White fur raced down her shoulder across her forearm and flowed across her hand. When her right leg contorted and the knee shifted backward, Abby awoke with a gasp. For a moment, she was too stunned to cry for help. She stared at her body as the left arm began a transformation that mirrored the right. A sheen of sweat coated her face as she concentrated on stopping the progression, but it had gone too far. It was so much easier just to let the changes flow. Her body wanted to change, ached to change.

With a sudden flash of inspiration, she remembered how one time at the shopping mall she'd tried to run up the down escalator. When she ran as hard as she could she made progress but the effort exhausted her. The slightest hesitation before she reached the top and she would lose all the ground she'd gained. And that made her think of another time, when she'd gone camping with the Nottinghams, and Mr. Nottingham had instructed all the kids that if they ever fell into the stream they should swim with the current and work their way to the edge and safety. "Swimming against the current just exhausts you," he'd warned. Getting exhausted in deep water, Abby knew, meant you could drown.

So she tried a new approach. She swam with the current of the change. She concentrated on accelerating the change, willing the coating of fur to spread across her damp flesh, urging her left leg to twist and bend into its powerful wolf haunch. And giving in was like running downhill, as easy and as invigorating as letting nature run its course. She marveled as her body transformed from girl to she-wolf. When her spine bowed outward above the pelvis, she was struck breathless but, instead of pain, she experienced a thrill like the first drop on a roller coaster.

Across the bedroom, Rowdy stirred, making a chuffing sound as he kicked his hind legs. Abby wondered if he was dreaming of chasing rabbits. *Maybe he's dreaming of chasing me!* That thought steadied her, gave her the courage to finish her experiment, to see if she could come all the way back. If she became Abby the wolf, how could she blame Rowdy for attacking her? But could she ever forgive herself if she hurt Rowdy out of self-defense?

Last month, when she became full wolf for the first time, her identity, everything that made her Abby had slipped away. Those hours were a blank to her, a scary memory lapse, almost as if Abby MacNeil had winked out of existence. As she lay on her side, only her head remained completely human and with it her human mind, still in control. This time, before the change could flow up her neck, face, and head, before she lost herself to the change, she attempted to change herself back into a complete nine-year-old girl. The day before she had fought the change in her fingers, willed them back to human dimensions and the effort, even though success-ful, had exhausted her. That had been like running up the down escalator and would be futile to attempt so far along in the transformation. Instead, she rushed through the change back to girl as if she were racing downhill, surrendering to the pull of gravity, flying in long strides to the bottom. Instead of fighting the change into wolf, she willed the change back to girl. To her surprise, the bones began to flow back into human configurations and the breathless exhilaration was the same. Because of her altered nature, because the ancient witch had tampered with her body, Abby was neither wolf nor girl. Her nature was to be both and neither, something in between, something definitely not normal. By facing her new, changed nature instead of fighting it, she had at last gained some control over her body.

Within a minute or two, Abby had regained her girl form. Lying curled on her side, shivering as the sweat evaporated on her body, she explored her smooth, furless face with trembling, human fingers. Only when her fingertips trailed up her cheeks and she felt the moist tracks of recent tears did she realize she'd been crying. *I am a freak,* Abby thought, disconsolate. *I'll always be a freak.*

She let out a sob, a human sob, and the sound of it woke Rowdy, who jumped down from Erica's bed only to leap onto Abby's. His cold nose and wet muzzle nudged aside her hands and then his rough tongue licked away her tears. Abby sobbed again, but this time a laugh spilled out of her and, with it, a broad smile. She wrapped her little-girl arms around the big dog and hugged him tight. "Good dog," she whispered into his fur.

Across the room, Erica sat up and rubbed sleep from her eyes. "Whadizit?" she mumbled, slurring her words together. "What happened? Rowdy bothering you again, Abby?"

One arm around the panting dog's shoulder, Abby smiled and shook her head. "Not at all."

Wendy and Alex faced each other across the card table, eating Wheaties out of blue ceramic bowls decorated with hand-painted daisies. Wendy had purchased the pair of bowls at a local craft fair in the spring, after she and Frankie had talked about renting a place together for fall semester. Alex had banana slices mixed with his flakes, while Wendy ate hers straight up with skim milk. Between them was one plate stacked with bran muffins and another with sliced wedges of fresh melons—cantaloupe and honeydew. Wendy still wore her rose-patterned pajamas, though she'd threatened to throw on her flannel robe if Alex made one more bad pun about the magnificent view of the breakfast melons provided by her pajama top's peasant neckline.

Alex had put on his blue-and-white striped pajama bottoms, mostly because he was self-conscious about the deep scars that crisscrossed his legs. All she'd needed to hear was his casual comment about the scars being too frightening for the harsh light of day to know the truth. He considered the scars a disfigurement to be hidden. *Another ingredient to add to my kettle of guilt*, Wendy thought. She took a sip of orange juice and said, "You're walking much better."

He nodded and ate a spoonful of flakes with a banana slice. She noticed with a smile that he tried to take one banana slice with each spoonful of cereal, at least for as long as the banana lasted.

"So you're keeping up with the rehab?" Wendy said, going for casual. She speared a chunk of cantaloupe and popped it into her mouth.

"Every day," Alex said. "And the strength, the flexibility gets a little bit better every day, but . . . it was the weirdest thing. One day I woke up and it was really better, noticeably better. I don't know. Suppose recovery happens by leaps and bounds."

"Really? One day," Wendy said, sampling a slice of honeydew. "A memorable day."

"Actually, it was," Alex said. "Day before my sister's birthday. I had asked my mother to pick her up a present from me, but I felt so good that day I decided I was up for a little mall walking."

"Suzanne's birthday . . . ?"

"Twenty-third," Alex said. "Of June."

The fork slipped out of Wendy's hand. She covered by reaching for her napkin and wiping her mouth. "So your miracle day was the twenty-second."

Alex nodded. "It was a Thursday."

The day after my midsummer ritual, Wendy realized. *The day after I cast the health spell.*

The Crone's voice echoed inside her head. *"Let the seed of belief begin to grow anew inside you, Wendy."*

Abruptly, Wendy was too nervous to finish her breakfast. She dumped her cereal into the sink, turned on the hot water and began to wash her bowl. *Could it be true?* she wondered. *I cast a spell one day and Alex wakes up the next feeling a noticeable improvement. Do I really have the power inside me?*

Wicca had been a part of her life, something she practiced without demanding proof of its effectiveness. Only after Wither nearly destroyed her life had she begun to have doubts, question her adopted faith. Sometimes it was simpler just to attribute everything unusual that had happened to Wither, either her influence or interference. If Wendy believed she had power inside her, she also had to believe responsibility came along with it and that almost terrified her. Because that meant the Crone was right and Wendy was Wither's natural adversary.

Alex was beside her, his own empty bowl stacked on top of the two plates. "Let me help," he said.

"That's okay. I can handle this small load."

"Speaking of loads," Alex said, nodding toward the gap in her counter. "Looks like there should be a dishwasher there."

"There was," Wendy said. "Until I found the rotting pig's head inside."

"Pig's head? A real pig's head?"

"Leftovers from a Bloody Pus party," Wendy said. "Or possibly a satanic ritual, if they were into that kind of thing?"

"You think?"

"No," Wendy said. "At least I hope not. Still, as soon as I saw—and smelled!—that horrible thing, I slammed the door shut and begged my father to drag the whole unit outside. He said the dishwasher would probably still work but I said not under this roof. I'd rather buy a new one. And I will." Wendy shuddered. "I only had the dishwasher door open for a moment or two, but it took a long time for the stench to go away."

"I bet."

Wendy ran the disposal for a few seconds, then placed the dishes on the drainboard. "Fortunately, the door had been sealed, water-tight, so no maggot action. Just decay. Oodles and oodles of decay."

"Well, it's long gone now," Alex said. "This place smells brand-new."

Wendy smiled. "A little magical cleansing with my witch's broom."

"Really?"

"And a couple gallons of Lysol."

"All's fair in love and chemical warfare?"

"Sometimes you need heavy artillery," Wendy said. "But I finished the job without renting biohazard suits." She looked around the cottage. "Now I just need to furnish the place."

"I saw a secondhand furniture store in town once," Alex said. "Although, I'd say we've managed quite well with the card table and the one bed."

Wendy picked up a pencil and notepad from the countertop. "Ooh, that reminds me." Writing a note, she said, "Buy futon for Alex."

Alex wrapped his arms around her and wrestled for the pencil. "No, no. I don't mind sharing a bed."

He nuzzled her throat, kissing behind her ear. She shuddered and laughed, fighting for control of the pencil. "I bet you don't," she said, between laughing and squirming in his arms.

"Sharing is one of those important lessons we learn way back in kindergarten."

"I don't think they were talking about sharing beds and showers," Wendy said, giggling as she slipped from his grasp. She ran down the hall, unbuttoning her pajama top, then pausing to hop out of the bottoms. After tossing them through the bedroom door, she ducked into the bathroom, naked.

"Well," Alex said, following her. "We have to learn to

extrapolate from those early graham cracker and crayon lessons and apply them later in life."

Wendy peeked at him from behind the bathroom door. "How good are you at applying papaya extract and aloe vera shower gel?"

"I've always been a quick study."

When Sheriff Bill Nottingham arrived at Windale General, he found the daughter, Gina Thorne, just outside her stepbrother's room, sitting on a cushioned bench covered in hideous orange vinyl. Her eyes were closed, head back, resting against the wall as she let out a long sigh. She wore a sleeveless, turquoise angora sweater and a white denim miniskirt with silver buttons up the side. Her feet were bare in sandals with straps that matched the color of the sweater.

The sheriff stopped in front of her, Smokey the Bear hat held between his hands. He cleared his throat and said, "Hello, Miss Thorne. I'm Sheriff Nottingham. How is he?" The sheriff had stopped at the nurses' island long enough to find out from Jill Schuller that the boy was in critical but stable condition. Numerous broken bones, contusions, a concussion, internal bleeding, collapsed lung. The list was long and gruesome. Amazing enough that he'd survived the impact let alone stood a good chance of coming through the other side to tell the tale.

He hadn't been at the scene when the paramedics carted Todd Gallo off in the ambulance, but he'd heard the call on the police radio and he'd questioned the driver of the Yankee Silver Springs truck. Although the boy had been playing in the street on a skateboard, comments from the neighbors suggested the truck driver had a reputation for driving at unsafe speeds through the housing development. Todd Gallo had been at the wrong place at the wrong time, but the driver was far from blameless and would probably be facing charges.

Gina Thorne lifted her head away from the wall and looked at him for a long moment with weary eyes before answering. "It's a small town," she said. "I know who you are."

"Suspected you might," the sheriff said. "How's your brother?"

"Stepbrother," she corrected, almost reflexively. "All night they weren't sure if he'd live or die."

"But he's better now?"

"No guarantees from the doctors," she said. "But no, they don't seem as frantic anymore."

"That's good to hear."

"I suppose," Gina said. "If you trust doctors."

"Your folks in the room with the boy?"

She nodded. "All-night vigil."

A broad-shouldered young man about the girl's age, with a weight-lifter's build and gait approached with a black backpack slung over one shoulder. Took the sheriff a moment to realize he was Brett Marlin. The boy seemed to have aged and hardened in the last several months. No doubt the two were dating.

Brett sat down beside Gina, holding the backpack between them on the bench. Giving the sheriff a distracted look, he turned his full attention to Gina. "Came as soon as I could," he said. She patted his hand and gave the sheriff a meaningful look.

"Maybe I'll poke my head in before I get on about my business," the sheriff told her.

"Thanks, sheriff," she said, with a broad smile that seemed to fall short of reaching her weary eyes.

As soon as the sheriff approached the door, he heard whispering start between the teenagers, and supposed it was none of his business. Todd Gallo had a semiprivate room, but the other bed was unoccupied at the moment. Caitlin Gallo had fallen asleep by the window, her neck at an awkward angle. Dominick Gallo had pulled a chair up beside the boy's bed and had his hand over Todd's. The boy was unconscious or sleeping, his face and head swathed in white bandages. His right arm and leg were in fresh casts, while his left side trailed tubes from IV lines. One look at Dominick Gallo's grizzled face convinced the sheriff to pick a better time. "I'll come by later," he whispered.

Dominick gave a tired nod, accompanied by a slow blink.

When the sheriff left the room, he saw that the young couple had vacated the orange bench. *Probably went to the cafeteria for coffee*, he thought. *Especially if the girl had been up all night.* He made his way back through the pediatric ward and spotted Doctor Keya Khayatian walking in the opposite direction. "Excuse me, Doctor," he called.

Dr. Khayatian paused. "Sheriff?"

"I wonder if you could spare a moment of your time?"

"Quiet shift," the doctor said with an easy smile as he

checked his watch. "Maybe I can even spare two moments."

They sat opposite each other at a cafeteria table over large cups of coffee. Khayatian took a sip of his coffee, black with three sugars, and frowned. "What this place needs is a good barista." The sheriff managed a weak smile, his thoughts elsewhere. "What's on your mind, sheriff?"

"You treated Abby MacNeil last year."

"A strange case," Khayatian said. "And a complete recovery."

"Was it?" the sheriff asked. "Complete, I mean?"

"As far as I or medical science can determine, she's perfectly healthy."

"Were you ever sure, I mean completely sure, what caused her condition?"

A little guarded. "What do you mean?"

Abby's doctors never really knew about her connection to the Windale witches. How would a rational man of science and medicine treat an affliction derived from black magic, from pure evil? It just made no sense to even bring the issue into the equation. At least not with a doctor . . . maybe with a theologian. "You said yourself it was a strange case . . ."

"First of all, she came to us paralyzed from the neck down, the result of a terrible car accident. Next she experienced uncontrolled skeletal growth, like nothing I'd ever seen. Then, virtually overnight, she is completely cured. I'm sure there's a scientific explanation for it, but we haven't found it yet. I'd say that qualifies as strange."

"Was there any diagnosis you ruled out, maybe thought was just too far-fetched?"

"I'd really hate to speculate . . . but for a little while, I thought she might have FOP."

The sheriff smiled. "I'm guessing that has nothing to do with the Fraternal Order of Police."

"Fibrodysplasia ossificans progressiva," the doctor said. "An extremely rare genetic disorder that strikes in childhood, turning soft connective tissue into bone. Any injury, even surgery, results in swelling that triggers rapid, renegade bone growth. Joints can lock overnight and never move again. As the name suggests, it's a progressive condition."

"Sounds horrible."

"It is," Khayatian said. "And there's no cure as yet. Fortunately for Abby, she doesn't have the disorder."

"You're certain?"

The doctor nodded. "Of that, I am certain. While Abby was here I called in specialists, lots of specialists. FOP was definitely ruled out. I know you're concerned about Abby wandering off at night. She's been through a lot for someone her age, hell for someone of any age."

"You think it's psychological?"

"Medically, she passes all my tests with flying colors. I wish there was something I could do, but there's no condition for me to treat." The doctor stood. "I really should be getting back to my rounds."

"Thanks, Dr. Khayatian," the sheriff said, standing to shake the doctor's hand. "Thanks for your time."

After Khayatian had walked away, the sheriff looked

down at the table. His own coffee was untouched. He looked around at the few patients and family members scattered around the cafeteria and saw no sign of Brett Marlin or Gina Thorne. Couldn't blame them. He hated hospitals, too.

Gina sat beside Brett in his Ford F-150 pickup truck, the backpack in her lap. They'd slipped out of the hospital as soon as the sheriff walked into Todd's room. No way she wanted the sheriff to see or even ask what was in the backpack. Brett was staring at the main hospital entrance, as if expecting pursuit. "Worried about the sheriff?"

"Gotta admit, he spooked me," Brett said. "When I saw him standing there right in front of you, I thought, somehow, he knew something."

"He's clueless," Gina said. "Besides, there's no reason for him to suspect anything but a careless teenager and a reckless driver."

"Yeah, you're right."

"Can't believe I sat around all night waiting for little toad to give up the ghost. At first, I experienced this delicious anticipation. But after several hours it simply became tiresome. A couple hours after that and it was like an itch I couldn't scratch." She shook her head. Now that the wait was over she was able to laugh. "I wanted to scream, 'Die already, you annoying little son of a bitch!'"

"That's when you *called* me."

"I said you would know when I needed you."

Brett shook his head, a little in awe of his summons. "Wasn't like a voice in my head . . . I just had this feeling you needed me. And I knew you were at the hospital, but then I guess that was obvious, considering the seriousness of the accident."

Not so obvious, she thought. He had been drawn to her location, just as she knew he would. Excitement was building within her and part of it stemmed from the *other* living inside her, sensing Gina's growing power. Gina couldn't say how she knew, but she sensed the other's pleasure in her budding strength, knew as that *other* knew that Gina was becoming more powerful in her current form than the other had been when last it had appeared human. Something about the desperate way in which the other had been reborn inside Gina had changed the dark alchemy of its creation. While the other's memories remained in tatters, the flow of power seemed unfettered. Together, Gina and the presence within her needed to harness the power to best advantage. The time for caution was soon coming to an end.

Gina looked down at the backpack. "You disturb anything?" Brett shook his head. He was hers. She would know if he were lying, even through a mere gesture of denial. "Good." She unzipped the main compartment and removed the shoebox she'd had him retrieve from under her bed while she was stuck at the hospital. To keep the lid in place and the contents contained, she'd placed a fat rubber band around the shoebox. She removed the rubber band now, lifted the lid, and looked inside.

Since creating the rag dolls, she'd decided to avoid the potential for confusion by writing a single letter on each with dabs of her own blood: T, D, and C. Even without the "T" on Todd's little effigy, she would have had no trouble picking it out of the pile, since the legs were still entwined with black thread. She lifted the doll out of the box and looked at Brett again. "You brought the hanky?"

Brett nodded, reaching for his back pocket. "Swiped one from my dad's sock drawer."

"Cut it into quarters and give one of them to me."

Brett fished a red Swiss Army knife out of his front pocket and made quick work of cutting the wrinkled hanky into quarters. He handed one to Gina. "What's it for?"

"To finish what the truck started."

Gina draped the white cloth over the blindfolded head of the rag doll, forming a crude hood. Then she untangled the thread from around the legs of the doll and looped it several times around the base of the head. "Quiet," she said as she began to stoke her rage, her hatred of her whiny, meddlesome, lying stepbrother. Her forearms burned and she knew without checking that the tracery of veins beneath the pale skin was pulsing black. Even as she grew hot with the fires of rage, she felt Brett shiver beside her, his breath a frosty mist of condensation inside the truck. Her body was leaching the heat out of the air, out of his body, to fuel her power.

When she sensed the moment was right, she whispered, "Now!" Her fingers pulled the thread tight around the base of the white cloth and wove a simple knot with spidery grace. "Good-bye, Todd," she said with a malevolent grin, before dropping the rag doll into the shoebox. She replaced the lid, slipped the rubber band around the box, and returned it to the backpack.

Brett blew warm air into his cupped hands. "That's it?"

"We'll see," Gina said, without the slightest uncertainty in her voice. Her tone made Brett shudder again and this time, she knew, not from the cold alone. While Brett could only imagine what was happening on the fourth floor of Windale General, Gina saw stroboscopic images flashing in her mind as the events unfolded. The moment she tied the knot around the rag doll's head, Todd had stopped breathing. In five minutes, maybe a little more, Todd Gallo would suffer permanent brain damage and soon after that he would cease to exist. All the proud doctors and all the registered nurses would never put little toad together again. Gina chuckled at her private joke. *Humpty Dumpty was pushed.*

"Should we go back in?"

Gina shook her head. "I'm sick of keeping up pretenses." She rubbed the inside of her forearms, and as the swollen veins began to contract, the images faded and stopped. She nodded toward the exit of the visitors' parking lot. "I'm starving. Let's get some breakfast."

Wendy Ward's Mirror Book Entry
July 16, 2000, Moon: Full, day 14, (continued)

Late in the evening—but it's ESPN's SportsCenter, not all the music that's seepin' through. (Apologies to Paul Simon).

With a little assistance from the two guys in my life—Dad and Alex—I feel a little more connected with the outside world. Not that that's always a good thing.

But neither is isolation. This "continued" mirror book entry marks my techno plunge, at least as it relates to my practice of Wicca. Decided I needed to "walk the walk" if I'm ever going to convince Alissa that The Crystal Path really belongs on the Web. So ... I'm writing this entry on my portable computer on the card table—still the only table—in my new home. (Don't need to be psychic to know that a secondhand furniture store is in my future!) I'm even connected to the Internet through the splitter we put on the kitchen phone jack, with the help of a twenty-five-foot phone cable. Another splitter on the bedroom phone jack, even though it's the same phone line. Also brought my personal laser printer, which sits on a small printer stand with an ineffectual—considering the deep pile of the new carpeting—set of casters. Since my mirror book is just a journal of thoughts, feelings, and personal progress through Wicca, it seemed a natural candidate to get the digital makeover. Might have a little more trouble converting my Book of Shadows, since I have loads of diagrams in it, but I'm willing to bet there's software out there that will make it possible.

In a fit of parental charity, Mom and Dad gave me their old nineteen-inch color television. Of course they went on and on about how they had already decided to replace it with one of those fancy, wide-screen digital models and hated to see the old set going to waste. In what might be considered a bit of presumption, if not foresight, I had the cable company turn on basic cable long before I had any solid plans about getting a permanent television in the cottage. I knew I'd get one eventually, if only to play videos. Needless to write, Alex was thrilled when he hooked up the co-ax and discovered ESPN. That gave me some uninterrupted computer play time. Not only for the mirror book, but for The Crystal Path site development. True, Alissa said not to work on it during my "off" hours, but I thought it would be wise to have backups of everything on my laptop.

Haven't "heard" or "seen" the Crone at all since this morning. But I've been with Alex most of the day and maybe my mind hasn't been receptive enough. Still, I'm encouraged by the unlikely coincidence of Alex's condition improving the day following my midsummer ritual. Maybe my faith in myself and in my Wicca wasn't as misplaced and beyond reach as I had thought. Somehow, it just feels right to believe, as hard as that is to explain.

Received an E-mail message from Karen in which she states: "It would be easy to be proud of such a gifted child as Hannah, if her rapid development were limited to her advanced intelligence. That she, at eight months, is more physically developed than a two-year-old is what truly frightens me. My only comfort is that she is a loving child who is apparently, aside from her accelerated development, completely healthy. She's had all her shots, although who knows if we are on an accurate timetable! And she's never been sick a day in her life. I can be thankful for that. Last October was a nightmare for all of us, Wendy. I can only hope that the lingering effects of that night will fade and we will all be whole again."

I don't have the heart to tell her the nightmare may

not be over, at least not for all of us. Out there on the left coast, she, Art, and Hannah should be safe from whatever seems to be brewing again in Windale. And that's no small consolation.

It had been a long day.

Tie unknotted, shirt unbuttoned, and shoeless feet up on the coffee table, Sheriff Bill Nottingham sat on the blue-checkered sofa in the family room, staring at the thirty-two-inch flat screen in weary disbelief. Not sure why he had a hard time believing the eleven o'clock news report since he'd been at the hospital when young Todd Gallo had died.

Christina came into the family room and handed him a bottle of Coors Lite. She'd switched him to the watered down stuff right after Doc Jenkins told him he'd crept up the scale a notch or two since his last checkup. *Getting old*, he figured. *Metabolism ain't what it used to be.*

Christina settled down on the couch beside him, but not before giving his feet a gentle nudge off the edge of the table. She called it a bad habit, a hillbilly custom, even though neither of them had ever been south of Washington, D.C. He never argued with her, but still took his chances at this mildly boorish behavior whenever he was tired or alone. With the kids asleep, this was as close as he was likely to come to having the house all to himself. And he was so tired his whole body ached.

He had the remote control balanced on the arm of the sofa. When the news report switched back to the blond news reporter standing beside the emergency room entrance of the hospital in a live shot, microphone to her mouth, he tapped the volume up button twice.

"... in a near fatal accident, the thirteen-year-old boy was in critical but stable condition when he suddenly and mysteriously stopped breathing. An autopsy has been scheduled. Until then, Todd Gallo's family has only unanswered questions. This is Michelle Lundquist, reporting live for WTKN, News Nine."

Bill Nottingham sighed and turned off the television.

Christina leaned into his side, pressing the length of her body against his. "Strange," she said. "I guess when your time's up, your time's up."

He set his bottle down on a coaster, then fought and failed to stifle a yawn before curling his arm around his wife to hug her close. *Another unexplained death in Windale,* he thought. *Will it ever end?*

"Sad, though," Christina continued, softly against his chest. "A boy that age should have a full life in front of him."

Eyes heavy, he made a sound of agreement.

"Has to be rough on that poor family."

"Imagine so," he agreed. He wondered how close the girl, Gina Thorne, had become to her stepbrother. His last thought before drifting off to sleep was, *Would almost be a blessing if they hadn't become too attached.*

WINDALE, MASSACHUSETTS
JULY 17, 2000

Abby waited until everyone in the house was asleep. Long after Max and Ben became quiet, and Erica nodded off, Abby waited for the sounds of the sheriff and Mrs. Nottingham to stop. Even after the television was turned off, she had to wait an agonizing amount of time before she heard them troop upstairs to their room. She closed her eyes when Mrs. Nottingham peeked in on her and Erica. Fortunately, Rowdy took advantage of the interruption to jump down from Erica's bed and pad out into the hallway, no doubt looking for a warm spot at the foot of Max's or Ben's bed. It was well after midnight before she thought it safe to get out of bed.

She took off her nightgown and underwear and slipped on a fuzzy pink robe that fell all the way to her ankles. It was a warm night with little chance of rain, so the bedroom window was already open. Abby pressed her fingers against the screen locks and lifted the screen high enough for her to slip through and drop down to the backyard. This was her next big test. And she didn't want to botch it by ruining another set of pajamas. If she was successful, the Nottinghams need never know she had slipped out into the night. Buoyed by her ability the day before to switch almost all the way to wolf form and back, she crouched in the grass and gave into the metamorphic urge of her bones.

With the silvery weight of the full moon hanging

over her, only moments passed before she felt her skeleton begin to twist and bend, to lengthen in some places and shorten in others. As her fingers retracted and her hands turned into paws, she yanked her arms out of the sleeves of the robe.

The robe covering her like a shroud, she fell on her side, almost curled into a fetal ball, feeling the cool grass against her naked skin, at least as long as she had bare skin. With a shuddering spasm, fur rippled down her body. This time, she let the transformation flow across her face. Her head narrowed, eyes shifting back, her nose stretching forward becoming a snout as her teeth lengthened and formed points. In less than two minutes, she wriggled out from underneath the robe and padded across the yard toward the trees, a gleaming white wolf.

The wolf paused, turned its head back to gaze at the one-story house and the mound of pink cloth spread under the open window. Somehow, the wolf knew that it must return to this place before the end of night. Not why it must return, simply that it would.

And with the same sense of knowing a thing without completely understanding it, the wolf knew she had a name now . . . and her name was Abby.

CHAPTER SIX

Wendy dreamt she was running through a forest, darting between low-hanging branches of pines and spruces with an anticipatory sense of determination, the thrill of the hunt. Just ahead, a small bounding shape, covered in brown fur. But voices called to her, insistent distractions demanding her attention. She pulled up and ... away from the woodland hunter, a fleeting glimpse of white fur beneath her, with the sense she'd been a guest in another's dream. Into the night sky, wisps of clouds flashing by her until she returned to a deeper darkness ...

... and awoke at dawn, refreshed and alert, as if she'd somehow crammed ten hours sleep into the five that had passed since she'd put her laptop and herself to bed.

Reluctant to let a rare sense of morning invigoration go to waste, she decided to get her five miles in early. She ran a brush through her auburn hair to vanquish her morning fright-wig snarls and tangles, then slipped into a sleeveless sweatshirt and running shorts. So that Alex wouldn't wake up and worry that aliens had abducted her for a round of gruesome human experimentation, she left a brief note on the card table before slipping out the door.

Her run was uneventful, but reminded her of the dream she'd had just before waking and her glimpse of a white wolf. Instead of forest paths, she loped down suburban streets and for a brief while, the site of early morning pedestrians with newspapers folded under their arms and commuters sipping coffee at traffic lights seemed alien to her, as if she did not belong here, far from the rich scent of pines and animal musk.

An hour later she had showered and dressed in a jade green blouse—green was the color she'd recently chosen to augment her predominantly black wardrobe—with black denim shorts and running shoes. Alex was still out of it when she sensed the Crone's presence in the house, even before the Crone's voice called to her. She spread her meditation mat out in the backyard and waited for the phantom image to coalesce nearby.

"*You were expecting me?*"

"I had a feeling," Wendy said, smiling.

"*Good,*" the Crone said as she floated downward to sit opposite Wendy, no more than four feet separating them. "*I too have a feeling. That you are ready to believe again.*"

Wendy nodded. "Let's just say my faith, if not my confidence, has been restored. I still don't know what you expect me to do."

"*Only what you must do.*"

"That sounds scary."

"*As well it should, Wendy,*" the Crone said. "*You have much to learn. And at last you are ready.*"

"Let me have it," Wendy said, with a little more bravado than she actually felt. "Where do we start?"

"*With the protective power of the magic circle.*"

"I already know how to make a circle. Am I doing it wrong?"

"*No, but you limit yourself by thinking of it as a circle.*"

"Shouldn't I?"

"*No. While a circle exists in two dimensions, you exist in three. Four if you count time. Since magic is fueled by the potency of your visualization, you must not visualize your protective barrier as a circle, but as a sphere, enclosing you from all sides.*"

Wendy nodded. "Guess that makes sense. I never really thought of it that way before. I just got out my flour, funnel, and string and drew a circle on the ground."

"*There is no protection inherent in the tools, Wendy. However, your reliance upon them and the image you create with them limits you by placing two dimensional boundaries upon your visualization.*"

"Which is a nice way of saying I *am* doing it all wrong."

"*Incomplete, perhaps, but not wrong.*"

"So I need to imagine a sphere, not a circle . . ."

"*Yes. A sphere of protective energy, creating a dome above you and beneath you, passing through the earth.*"

"Like I'm trapped in a soap bubble?"

"*Enclosed and protected, not trapped,*" the Crone said. "*You create the sphere; you release the sphere. You remain in control at all times.*"

"Next question," Wendy said. "How do I draw this all-encompassing sphere with flour and my trusty old funnel? Even with a string circle, I don't see how . . ."

The Crone smiled. "*You are still limiting yourself, still thinking in terms of two dimensional representations, the circle and not the sphere.*"

Wendy returned the smile. "I'm confused, no question about it. Care to enlighten me?"

"*Compared to what you will someday become, now you are a mere apprentice in the magic of your Wicca.*"

"Wait a minute. How do you know what I *will* know?"

"*Because I have seen it,*" the Crone explained. After a moment of consideration, she added, "*You taught me so that I could teach you.*"

Wendy slapped a hand to the crown of her head. "Whoa! Was that a Zen koan that just ruffled my hair?"

"*If a sphere is a circle extended to three dimensions, what then is a sphere extended to four dimensions?*"

"Four dimensions? You mean, a sphere across time?" The Crone nodded. "I had astronomy fall semester last year, and we never got into the advanced theoretical stuff. But are you talking about a wormhole?"

The Crone shrugged with a wry smile. "*I wouldn't know.*"

"Then what . . . ?"

"*Perhaps it is merely advanced visualization,*" the Crone

said. *"For whatever reason, my visualization of the flow of time is not limited to a linear, forward progression."*

"You're saying, because I think tomorrow follows today as today follows yesterday, my visualization of time is limited?"

The Crone chuckled. *"The limitation is not yours alone, Wendy. Actually, I am the one who is alone in this . . . ability."*

"You can travel back in time?" Wendy asked, a little awed.

"However I appear here, it is not in a physical sense," the Crone said. *"I am a mental image, a projection of myself. Perhaps I am only something I created in your imagination."*

"But you are real to me."

"Yes, Wendy, I am real. If I exist only in your mind, it is because that is the only way for me to exist here."

"But how?"

"I look into portals, or windows to the past, if you will. Although, that may not be the truth of it. Maybe I only see memories, vivid memories that are not my own."

"But that would mean you can exist now because . . . you exist now." Wendy frowned. "My head is starting to hurt."

"I think, therefore I am," the Crone said, considering. *"Someday, maybe you will explain it all to me so that I in turn will be here now to explain it to you."*

"I'll work on it," Wendy said, massaging her forehead.

"Regardless of the method, I can neither explain the technique, nor teach it to you. Fortunately, advanced time visualization is an ability you don't need to know to defeat your adversary."

"Sounds like it could come in handy, though."

"It has its uses but many limitations as well."

"So, where were we? Oh, right, how to draw a sphere with flour."

"Let's begin with a question. What do you believe is the greatest limitation in your practice of Wicca?"

"If I had to guess," Wendy said with a wry grin, "I'd put all my blue chips on ignorance."

"Ignorance to a degree," the Crone admitted. "But more limiting is your need for ritual over visualization."

"I don't need to perform rituals?"

"As a mental focus, and as a precursor and aid to visualization, ritual is fine. That is its purpose. But where ritual limits visualization, you must leave ritual behind."

"Where would I begin without my rituals?"

"Rituals are a beginning," the Crone said. "They are part of your apprenticeship. Yet to cling to the stationary ritual is to cling to the circle when what you most need is a sphere. Consider this. In your rituals, you acknowledge and welcome each of the elements, but of air, fire, water, and earth, only earth might be considered stationary."

"But you haven't answered my question. If I believe in myself, that my magic is real, then I also have to believe the ritual enables me to invoke the magic."

"That is where you limit yourself. Your adversary is not bound to a ritual," the Crone said. "She is learning and practicing her dark magic even now without the constraints of a formal ritual. If you limit yourself, you grant her the advantage . . . and the eventual victory."

"But she is an . . . agent of chaos, maybe that's why she doesn't need ritual. There is order in ritual."

"The order of the ritual is merely an aid to concentration and visualization, to shift your mind into a receptive state."

"So how can I do this, any of this, without a ritual?"

"By remembering that the ritual is only an aid to visualization, not visualization itself. By recognizing that you draw the energy required for magic to you, wherever you are, and you can draw it whenever you need it."

"Don't my rituals sort of, I don't know, prime the pump for the magic?"

"Yes, but that is only one way of tapping into the energies around you. Don't forget that you, Wendy, are special. For want of a better phrase, you are one with nature. The elements will come readily to your aid."

"Since I'm so special, does that mean I get some sort of special shortcut? A password or code phrase or secret decoder ring?"

"You joke now, but that's not too far from the truth of your early technique in advanced magic."

"My early technique? You mean, that whole 'I taught you so you could teach me' mind-bender thing?"

The Crone nodded. "Do you know what a posthypnotic suggestion is?"

"Sure," Wendy said. "Like when a hypnotist puts somebody under and tells him to quack like a duck whenever someday says Pittsburgh."

"Exactly," the Crone said. "What you need is an aid to visualization, something to take the place of the formal ritual. Instead of a posthypnotic suggestion, think of it as a previsualization focus. Something to direct your mind and allow you to draw and wield the magical energy."

"A focus? Can I get a 'for instance'?"

The Crone laughed. "*For instance, in your rituals you commonly use a rose quartz in healing spells.*" Wendy nodded. "*Carry a rose quartz with you when you think you might need to use magical energy to heal. Since you are aware of the rose quartz's healing properties and have used it in your rituals, let it be a . . . shortcut for you.*"

"So far, so good. But how . . . ?"

"*That brings us to your earlier question.*"

"Drawing a sphere?"

"*By drawing the energy into you, then shaping it, molding it to your need. Symbolism is important to visualization. To create a sphere, you extend and open your receptive hand, to draw the energy into your body.*"

"Since I'm right-handed, my receptive hand is my left," Wendy said and the Crone nodded.

"*Once you feel the energy within you, extend your projective hand to wield it, to mold your sphere.*"

"Holding the athame in my projective hand?" In Wicca, the double-sided, black handled ritual knife directed the flow of power, while the white-handled bolline was reserved for cutting herbs, fruits, and whatnot.

"*If that helps you focus the energy.*"

"And where does the rose quartz come in?"

"*Grip the stone in your receptive hand as you draw in the energy, then extend your projective hand to unleash the healing power.*"

"Seems simple enough, in theory," Wendy said.

The Crone's phantom image was beginning to grow fuzzy around the edges. "*Realize two things. First, this* shortcut *only works as well as your ability to concentrate and to visualize. Second, the focus items are,* as your rituals have been, aids to visualization, not substitutes or prerequisites."

"It's a lot to think about."

"*It is not enough to consider these techniques. You must begin . . . practice them.*"

Wendy realized the Crone's mental voice had begun to fade as well. "Where should I start?"

"*With the sphere,*" the Crone said without hesitation. "*If . . . cannot protect yourself, nothing else will matter.*"

"That sounds ominous."

The Crone nodded. "*Then our time . . . not wasted. Nevertheless, I grow weary and, if I am not mistaken, your young man has awakened.*"

The Crone's phantom image at last fell prey to the gentle morning breeze and dissipated before Wendy's eyes. Only a moment or two after she was again alone in the backyard, she heard a gentle tapping on the sliding, glass patio door.

She looked over her shoulder and saw Alex standing barefoot in his pajama bottoms, sporting a worse case of bed-head than she'd had almost two hours ago and his sword-concealing cane, which he held high in his hand. With his free hand he pointed to himself then indicated the backyard, his eyebrow arched in a question. She beckoned him outside.

"You're up early," he commented.

"Already had my five-mile run."

"I saw the note, but then I noticed you sitting out here."

"Sorry. Meant to crumple and toss it when I got back, but forgot."

"What's shaking out here? Communing with Mother Nature?"

"Communing. Maybe a little meditating. And a little shifting of paradigms."

"Busy morning."

Wendy had an idea. "Care to help me out with something?"

Alex grinned. "If it involves another session of tantric sex magic, I'm your man."

"No such luck, cowboy." Almost in desperation, Wendy had enlisted Alex's help in her battle against Wither by performing a tantric sex magic ritual with him. Something she had never tried before or since. That night had ended with them making love for the first time. Actually, that was only partly true. The night had actually ended with Wither attacking and nearly killing Alex for daring to interfere in her plans to steal Wendy's life and take over her body. Wendy supposed she should be glad Alex saw the positive aspects of that fateful night. Instead, she felt a residual tinge of guilt for putting him in harm's way.

"What then?"

"Shower, get dressed, then come back. It'll be a surprise."

"Oh, goody," he said. "I love your surprises." He turned on his heel and made comical double-time with his cane in an approximation of Charlie Chaplin. Wendy laughed and couldn't help feeling a little lighthearted besides at seeing him walk without the grimacing pain of a couple months ago.

Minutes before dawn, Abby stumbled out of the tree line into the Nottinghams' backyard, her human legs weak and tentative so soon after her transformation from wolf to girl, as if she had to relearn two-legged coordination all over again. Without the pelt of white fur covering her naked body, she felt small and vulnerable. She hurried across the yard, falling once to hands and knees in the grass before pushing herself forward, to the fuzzy pink mound underneath the window to the bedroom she shared with Erica. Abby slipped into the robe, grateful for its warmth, then climbed through the window, slipping under the open screen and sliding down to the floor. Other than a graceless and hard landing on her rump, her return to the bedroom was quiet enough to avoid waking Erica.

Fearful that Rowdy or Mrs. Nottingham might open the bedroom door to check on her and Erica, Abby slipped into her underpants and nightgown and climbed into bed. Only then did she release a long-held breath and shudder with a feeling of uncontained excitement. I did it! she thought. I changed into the wolf and back again. I didn't lose myself like before.

The change was less frightening now that she knew she had some control over it. Fighting it had been her mistake. It was part of her now and to fight it was to fight her own nature. By letting the change flow through her she had retained some control and some of the memories,

memories of being a wolf, of hunting. Almost at the thought, she rubbed her cheek and her fingers came away bloody. Startled, she jumped out of bed and ran into the bathroom, only turning on the light when the door was closed behind her so as not to awaken anyone in the single-story house. Her ash blond hair was a mess, but no worse than after a normal night's sleep. That hardly concerned her, considering the smear of blood on her right cheek and under her chin. And not just blood. Bits of fur, brown fur. A vivid image of a bounding, brown-furred shape . . . *A rabbit?* she wondered. *I chased down a rabbit and ate it. Raw!* "Oh, that is so gross!" she whispered.

She turned on the tap, adjusted the water temperature until it was almost too hot, then lathered liquid soap on her face. Worried that the smeared blood and fur would stain one of Mrs. Nottingham's towels, she scrubbed at her cheek and chin with her fingernails. After a couple minutes, she rinsed the soap off her face, then repeated the whole process until she was satisfied that no bunny remains were stuck on her face anywhere. A few moments later, she rinsed out the sink until all the bloody evidence was gone.

She was about to leave the bathroom when another, even more disgusting thought occurred to her. If her wolf-self ate a raw rabbit, then her mouth . . .

She shuddered, ran back to the sink and opened her mouth wide, pulling her lips back to reveal her teeth. Even a brief glimpse was enough to make her gag. *Specks of blood, bits of fur . . .*

Gulping back an urge to vomit into the sink, she

opened the plastic bottle of blue Listerine on the sink and began to gargle with it, filling the lid over and over again, rinsing her mouth out until the tingling sensation almost numbed her gums and tongue. Still she wasn't finished.

As she uncapped the tube of triple protection Aquafresh toothpaste, Abby wondered if they sold a quadruple protection variety. *Freshens breath, whitens teeth, fights cavities* and *removes those stubborn bits of bunny guts.* She spat the messy gunk out and brushed three more times—*time for a new toothbrush!*—then dosed herself with another round of Listerine.

"Gross, gross, gross," she muttered as she slunk down the hall, back to her bedroom and climbed into her bed.

Across the room, Erica said something unintelligible in her sleep and flopped over on her other side, knocking her Suzy Superstar doll onto the floor with a loud plastic *thunk*. In an eerie, squeaky voice, the doll exclaimed, "Time for the show!"

Abby pulled the covers up to her chin and tried not to think about fluffy-tailed bunnies anymore. Yet, if she embraced her other nature, how could she ignore its needs. They were as valid as her own. *Okay, okay, but I don't have to think about it all the time.*

Abby yawned, stretching her mouth so wide, her jaw cracked. Even though it felt as if she'd been asleep all night, she had only been transformed into another waking state. No wonder exhaustion slipped over her as fast as the sky lightened from night to day.

She tried to remember other images from the night,

from her time in wolf form and beyond that fleeting moment of the thrill of the hunt and the sensation of pine needles crunching beneath her feet—her paws!—she remembered another person. No, not a person, a presence, somebody floating along beside her or within her, not someone she feared, rather someone she trusted, a welcome presence. Maybe even someone she had *called* to her.

While she grasped for a name, another yawn distracted her.

In moments she drifted off to sleep and dreamt little-girl dreams.

Wendy looked up from the meditation mat as Alex slid the patio door open. After his shower, he'd dressed in a banana-yellow, three-button knit top with Danfield College embroidered over the left breast in navy blue script. While Wendy had decided to add some color to her dark wardrobe, Alex had chosen to occasionally forgo his 'mind-over-cold-weather-matter' Hawaiian shirts. Either that or mid-July left him complacent and unwary of the rigors of the New England winter to come. He also had slipped on a pair of jeans that had seen better days and immaculate white running shoes with navy stripes. Months ago, in a game but futile attempt to be light-hearted and look on the *upside* of his serious injuries, he'd told her it would now take him much, much longer to wear out a pair of running shoes. "Ready for me?" he asked, then noticed the black-handled knife resting in her right hand. "Wait a sec, did I forget to mention I have this phobia about rituals involving daggers?"

"Then you're in luck," she said, grinning. "Technically, this is a nonritual and besides, this isn't my cutting dagger."

"Okay, now I'm worried that somewhere around here you actually *have* a cutting dagger?"

"Sure I do," she said mischievously. "Doesn't every Wicca?"

"I don't know," he said. "I mean, I don't want to know."

"Don't be such a wuss, Dunkirk," Wendy said with a teasing smirk. "I don't cut *people* with it." After a pause, "Well, not unless they really, really annoy me." Off his startled look, "I'm kidding, Alex! Get me some flour."

"No need to threaten me with a dagger to get flowers," Alex said with a wink. "Wait here ten minutes and I'll be back with a lovely mini-mart summer bouquet."

"Not flowers. Flour. There's a canister on the kitchen counter."

"Making pancakes out here in the backyard?"

"Just flour, no breakfast entrees."

"Damn," he said. "Now I have a craving for pancakes."

"Get me the flour and I'll give you directions to Denny's."

"Okay, okay. One canister of flour coming up." In a moment he was back at the door, the canister balanced on his free hand. "Now what?"

"Take a pinch in your fingers and throw it at me."

"Cool! Is this how witches make pixie dust?"

"Pixies make pixie dust, Alex," Wendy said. "Witches use magic wands to turn irritating young men into warty, smelly toads."

"You're joking, right? That's just fairy tales."

"Yes, I'm joking. Now, just give me a pinch already." She raised her left hand even as he opened his mouth again. "Sorry, that was an inexcusable straight line. I'll let you pinch me later, promise, but first the flour."

"Just . . . toss it?"

"Just like pixie dust," Wendy said and couldn't help smiling. "Pretend you're a little fairy, if that helps."

Alex frowned. "I don't see how it would." He leaned his cane against the doorframe so that he could open the canister and scoop out a bit of flour between his thumb, index, and middle fingers. "Here it comes. Close your eyes."

Wendy took a calm, measured breath. "I hope that won't be necessary. Fire away."

Alex flung the flour toward her head, creating a small cloud of powder that drizzled down above Wendy's head, without touching her. The small granules seemed to fall against an invisible barrier around her. Many simply hung in midair. Most drifted down into the grass in a smooth arc around her meditation mat.

"Again," Wendy said, excited. "More this time."

Confused by what he'd just witnessed, Alex nevertheless nodded and scooped out a handful of flour. He tossed it over her and watched as this thicker cloud fell, then slid down the curved side of an invisible barrier. A second handful followed and eventually an outline took shape around Wendy, formed by the falling flour. "It's some kind of a circle," he said softly.

"Not a circle," Wendy said, beaming. "A sphere."

"It's practically invisible. Is it plastic? Or glass?"

"Neither," Wendy said. "Let's try something else. Fill a pitcher with water."

Moments later, Alex returned with a stainless steel pitcher filled with so much water it sloshed over the edge and spattered his white sneakers. "You're sure about this?"

"I have to believe in myself," Wendy said, nodding. "Besides, it's only water."

"Cold water."

"Better than boiling water," Wendy said. "Although we should probably try that later."

"You're serious?"

"Yes, but for now, just toss the cold stuff at me."

Alex held the pitcher with one hand braced on the bottom, the other around the handle, then flung all the water at her expecting, no doubt, to thoroughly douse her. Instead, he stood there shaking his head in stunned silence, watching as the water cascaded down around her without a single drop touching her hair, skin, or clothes.

For a few brief moments, the sunlight glinting on the water revealed the perfect shape of the sphere. About six feet in diameter, she estimated. A bit smaller than her ritual circles, but somehow the size had felt right in her visualization. Since only half of the sphere was aboveground, anything smaller would not have protected her head. When she'd attempted to expand the sphere beyond six feet, she'd had the strange sensation that the energy forming the protective barrier was losing cohesion. She would have to ask the Crone about the limitation. For now, she gazed around her head as only twinkling droplets of water remained, suspended in midair.

"That's incredible," Alex whispered, voicing her own thought. He seemed unaware of his actions as he sat down in the doorway, dropping the stainless steel pitcher between his sneakers. "What is it?"

"Magic," Wendy said, a note of triumph in her voice.

"Incredible," Alex repeated. "Magic? I can't believe it really works."

"If you don't believe, it can't work."

"You're the expert."

"Actually, I'm probably still an apprentice, but I'm learning fast," she said. "And I'm ready for my pinch now."

A little bewildered. "What?"

"A pinch. You know, that painful little squeeze with the thumb and forefinger, usually administered to the fleshy part of a woman's buttocks in the crude yet ubiquitous expression of male lechery."

"Ah, the classic pinch," Alex said, waggling his eyebrows as he climbed to his feet. "How could I forget?"

"Beats me. I thought sex was all you guys ever thought about."

"Occasionally, we manage to squeeze another thought into our heads," Alex said, rubbing his chin pensively. "Sex . . . sports . . . sex . . . meals . . . sex. Yep, that just about covers it."

"You said sex three times."

He grinned. "What's your point?"

"Uh-huh," Wendy said. "Now get over here."

Alex took a step forward and Wendy glanced down at the grass. His next step would cross the arc of flour that the water had almost obliterated. Even without the visual aid, she could still sense the sphere surrounding her, a warm, tingling presence that lifted the tiny hairs along her arms and the back of her neck like a static charge.

When Alex took that next step toward her, he seemed to collide with an invisible wall and stumbled backward, falling on his rear, hands thrown back to catch himself. "What the hell . . . ?"

"It's the sphere," Wendy said, experiencing a slight tinge of guilt for not warning him. But overriding the guilt was a deeper sense of triumph. I *can protect myself,* she thought. I *really can.* But somehow she had known it was possible, she had had to know it was possible in order to believe it, for her belief created the reality. "The sphere protected me."

"Honest, I wasn't gonna pinch you that hard," Alex griped good-naturedly, while shaking his head in amazement.

Wendy held out her receptive hand, palm up, and visualized the protective energy of the sphere flowing back into her body through that hand. She trembled with the rush of power that washed over her and through her. Gooseflesh covered her exposed arms and legs and heat flushed her cheeks. Even her scalp tingled. After a few moments, she sensed that the sphere was gone, but even without that awareness, she would have known simply by noticing the suspended drops of water and granules of flour abruptly drop to the meditation mat and the grass around her.

Filled to bursting with a joyous sense of accomplishment as well as the magical energy she'd absorbed,

Wendy sprang from the mat and threw herself at Alex. He had no choice but to catch her in his arms, causing both of them to fall back on the damp grass. "That was exciting!" she said, her nose inches from his. "Wasn't that exciting?"

He nodded. "I'd say it qualifies."

She gave him a quick kiss. "I'm excited."

"You told me."

"I mean," she said, raising one eyebrow suggestively, "I'm *really* excited."

"Ah, you did promise me that pinch," Alex said, his hands sliding across the black denim of her shorts to cup her buttocks.

"Forget the pinch," she said. "I've got a better idea."

"Oh?" Alex said, playing along. "And what might that be?"

She leaned down and whispered in his ear, then laughed as he blushed. "Well?"

"No question," he said. "That's definitely a better idea."

Gina was responsible for making the liquor selections, Brett for lugging them around in the portable, plastic shopping cart. So far she had picked out an expensive bottle of red wine, a fifth of twelve-year-old scotch, a bottle of Bacardi rum and some peach schnapps. They strolled up and down the aisles of the liquor store while Gina sought some vodka and gin to add to her varied collection.

The little basket was so full, Brett had to lower the wire carry handles and support the load from underneath. "Sure you need all this?"

"It's my birthday," Gina said. "Not that Mother or Dominick care. All they talk about is Toad's funeral on Thursday, not that I turn eighteen today."

"Legal drinking age is twenty-one," Brett reminded her.

"Not a problem," Gina assured him. "Do you think they're planning a surprise party?"

"Wouldn't count on it."

"Neither would I," Gina said. "Which is why I've taken matters into my own hands. Champagne? Wait a minute. I don't see any Dom Perignon."

"They probably keep that behind the counter."

"Good thinking," Gina said. "I'm ready. Let's check out." She paused. "Should I wear this outfit to the little brat's funeral?" She was wearing a short, black sweater dress that buttoned down the front, although she'd neglected to fasten the top four buttons, and ankle-strap black high heels. When she spread her arms wide, as now, it was obvious she wasn't wearing a bra, black or otherwise. "If I decide to go, that is."

"Uh . . . maybe with black stockings," Brett suggested.

Her legs were bare now. "Ugh, I hate pantyhose. Ooh, maybe thigh-highs or a garter belt."

"Your decision."

"You're right. Maybe I'll just skip the whole dreary affair."

Brett placed the shopping basket on the checkout counter. Several bottles clinked together, which caught the attention of the cashier, who'd been distracted watching a Red Sox game on a thirteen-inch television.

The man was in his late fifties, gray, and balding with

bushy eyebrows and a thick mustache more salt than pepper. He had watery blue eyes, with bloodshot whites, and a bulbous, cratered nose. A soggy, unlit cigar poked out of his wide mouth and served as an exclamation point to the permanent scowl etched into the frown lines of his face. Gina thought his short-sleeved dress shirt might be his only one, considering the successive generations of yellow pit stains it bore. Not that his chocolate brown polyester pants were in much better condition. The seat was shiny as plastic and the knees had worn down to the translucency of wax paper.

After a good long look at Gina's daring neckline, he looked up and said, "Can I help you?"

"Do you carry Dom Perignon?" Gina asked sweetly.

He reached under the counter and placed the bottle in front of her. "That's a hundred and two dollars."

Gina slid the shopping basket toward him. "Add that to this other stuff."

The man rolled the moist stogie to the other side of his mouth with the dexterity of a street magician flipping a quarter across his knuckles. Bits of brown paper clung to the man's thin, purple lips. "Gotta see some ID, Miss."

"No problem," Gina said. "Today's my birthday."

"Happy birthday to you," the man said. "Still gotta see the ID."

Gina fished through her clutch purse and pulled out a laminated card calendar from the Windale Savings and Loan. It had come in the mail, along with a form letter invitation to open a free checking account.

The year 2000 was printed in red on the front, with 2001 in blue on the back. She stared at the man as she handed him the laminated card with her left hand. Behind her back, her right hand was clenched in a white-knuckled fist, even as she felt the black veins rise on the inside of her forearm. "See? Twenty-one today. Says so right there."

The man tilted the cigar upward in an apparent tobacco salute and nodded his head. "So it does."

"Can you double bag this stuff?" Gina asked. "Wouldn't want to drop anything."

"No problem," the man said, following her instructions. When he was finished he pushed the brown shopping bag across the counter. His eyes seemed a little vacant. "Feels like I'm forgetting something?"

"My change," Gina said. "I gave you three hundred dollar bills. My birthday money."

"Oh, right, that must be it," the man said, scratching his balding pate. He opened the register and counted out change for the three hundred dollars she'd never given him.

When they left the liquor store, the man was back on his stool, catching up with the Red Sox. They were losing. Brett turned to Gina as they walked along the sun-dappled sidewalk of Theurgy Avenue. "That's amazing. Like Obi-Wan Kenobi using the Force in *Star Wars*."

"It's illusion," Gina said. "A glamour. He sees what I want him to see. Remembers what I want him to remember. Lasts just long enough to win the moment. Later the whole transaction will seem ... fuzzy to him. He'll remember checking my ID, but won't be able to describe it. He'll recall taking three one hundred dollar bills from me, but not where he put them."

"Can you do that to anyone? Fool them like that?"

"I can usually sense when someone will be susceptible to . . . suggestion. Easily distracted minds make the best subjects. The strong-willed have some natural resistance to my glamour, but I sense my power growing stronger day by day. And if I get my hands on the materials to construct a personal effigy, as I have with my family, I believe I could control almost anyone."

"How do you know this stuff?" Brett asked. "Just by channeling that Windale witch, Elizabeth Wither?"

Gina had told Brett only that she was channeling the spirit of Wither, not that the ancient witch was also living under Gina's skin, inside her mind, a separate entity. "Her memories bubble up to the surface of my mind," Gina explained, her voice becoming softer to thwart any casual eavesdroppers. "When she died violently, her memories shattered, like glass, or maybe the correct analogy would be a jigsaw puzzle tossed in the air. As the pieces combine and make sense, forming partial pictures, I'm able to use the knowledge to access her abilities. It's thrilling to tap into so much power, but also frustrating."

"Why?"

"So many pieces are missing, some lost or simply hidden from me—from us—that it restricts my development. With all I am able to do, still I must be careful not to expose myself. The problem is, I don't know where my vulnerabilities are."

"Like a dragon unaware that its belly scales are soft?"

"Exactly," Gina said. "Take this Wendy Ward, for instance." Gina pointed. "She works on this street, in that store. I met her once . . . and it scared me. She killed me—Wither—once. Just last year."

"But Wither died three hundred years ago," Brett said, stopping at his pickup truck, parked at the curb.

Gina looked at him. "You're a fool to believe the history books. Wither never died. She went through long periods of hibernation with her coven, while they grew, became more powerful, evolving and rising every one hundred years in a glorious rebirth to wreak havoc on this shitty little town. But last time was different . . . The coven needed new bodies, to begin a new cycle of life—" Gina stopped herself. She'd come too close to the truth for Brett's ears. "Yet, somehow, an eighteen-year-old girl, a simple Wicca, was able to destroy her."

Gina shook her head as she climbed into the passenger seat. Brett twisted in the driver's seat to place the bag of liquor behind them. "This time will be different."

"What are you gonna do?"

"Kill her, obviously," Gina said. "But first I have to figure out how she defeated Wither. Can't make the same mistakes again. That's where I need your help."

Brett started the engine and let it idle, flicking on the air-conditioning system to cool off the cab. "Me? What can I do?"

"Watch her, learn her routine, see where she lives, where she hangs out, who her friends are."

"Anything else?"

"I need to test her, find out what her abilities are before I assault her directly."

Brett chuckled. "You want me to beat her?"

Gina shook her head. "I'd like someone more expendable for that kind of assignment. I'll need soldiers. Guys with questionable ethics, easily distracted minds."

"I know some guys who worked on my uncle's construction crew," Brett said. He currently worked for his uncle's construction business twenty to thirty hours per week, fewer when school was in session.

"How many?"

"Three guys, hung out together. Dropped out of Harrison this year. Bozos with more muscle than scruples, if I believe half the stories they tell. Always showed up drunk or late to work, so my uncle fired them. But I still have their numbers."

"Good. Bring them to me. Promise them money. Easy work."

"That should do it. What next?"

"The rest is up to me," Gina said. "I need to start thinking of my own recruitment campaign."

"What's that?"

"Building my own coven of three. There is more power to be had with a coven, the whole is greater than the sum of the parts. Another piece of the puzzle."

"How do you recruit a coven? An ad in the classifieds?"

"I've already sensed a presence here in Windale, someone possessing a . . . fragile mind, a mind I can mold into a receptive state and guide down the correct path.

Then one more besides and Wither will lead this new coven, through me."

"But first we have to get rid of this Wendy Ward?"

Gina nodded. "I've waited a long time for my revenge. Once I root out her strengths and weaknesses, I will know how to destroy her. But first I want her to suffer."

While she waited for her chicken-and-rice soup to cool, Wendy sat at the large oak kitchen table in the college president's mansion and flipped through the pile of mail, mostly junk, that her mother had set aside for her, along with a plate of Saltines. If she'd wanted to have her mail forwarded to her new cottage address, Wendy could have gone to the post office and filled out the requisite form. But she found she was in no hurry to cut off all ties to 100 College Way, her parents' campus home, and not just for its spacious accommodations. Stopping by to pick up her mail gave her an excuse, not that she needed one, to drop in on her parents on a regular basis. As an only child, she thought it her duty to delay the onset of empty-nest syndrome in her parents.

The pile of mail was largely catalogs, both clothing and New Age related, invitations to join various book, music, or DVD clubs, a few odd bills, and a rumpled postcard from Alissa, showing a gondolier in Venice, Italy. She was having a marvelous time, promised more postcards soon and hoped Wendy wasn't working herself too hard.

Sitting diagonally across from Wendy at a table large enough to accommodate ten people and two flower arrangements, Carol Ward took a tentative sip of soup and asked, "From Alissa?" She wore her gold real estate blazer with the royal blue piping over a white, ruffled blouse and a matching royal blue skirt. Since today was Alex's first day of his summer session, Wendy and her mother had arranged to meet at the mansion for a quick mother-daughter lunch.

Wendy nodded and handed her the card. "She's off to Greece after a couple weeks in Italy. Think she flies home from Athens."

"I'm jealous," Carol Ward said.

"I'm president of that club," Wendy said. "Maybe next summer you, Dad, and I could cross the Atlantic. Been a long time since our last Big Family Vacation."

"That would be nice, but remember your father hates flying. Especially across oceans."

"So we'll make it girls only," Wendy said. "A mother-daughter trip. Let Dad stay home and hunt, fish, or put the TV remote through its paces."

Carol Ward laughed. "Sounds like a plan." On top of the mail heap was a business-sized letter with Danfield College's official seal embossed in the upper left corner. She nodded toward it and said, "Bet that one's important."

Wendy held the closed envelope up to her forehead as if she were attempting to divine its contents through paranormal prognostication. "My schedule for the fall semester," she predicted, ripping the envelope open to examine the letter. "I am good."

"See Madame Wendy," her mother said in a hushed tone, "and have your future foretold."

Wendy grinned. "Let's hope my future doesn't involve a carnival tent."

"So, what've you got?"

"No surprises," Wendy said and read off the list of classes. "Zoology, Calculus, Organic Chemistry, and the Organic Chemistry lab sidecar. And, my elective, Italian."

"Italian?"

"Alex and I wanted to have at least one class together. I was leaning toward Latin and Alex was thinking Japanese, so we compromised."

"Well, that certainly seems like an interesting course load," Carol said noncommittally.

Wendy frowned. "It sounds demoralizing. I'm beginning to rethink this whole environmental sciences major. I mean, zoology is cool, but calculus and organic chemistry?" Wendy shuddered, reading the list again. "Oh—wait! It gets worse. I have Lutz for Chemistry. They say he's over ninety years old and falls asleep during his own lectures! I'm already anticipating massive boredom."

Her mother patted her hand. "I'm sure you'll excel. As always. Now finish your soup before it gets cold."

"Sure," Wendy muttered and tried a spoonful. It was good, even though it wasn't homemade. *Oh, well, nobody has free time these days.* "Just wish I could get back to biology, and what about botany? Or geology?"

"Give it time, dear. Danfield just wants to create a well-rounded college graduate out of you."

"Rounded? But I like my edges, Mother."

"I'm sure you'll still have a few when they release you into the wild."

"Grrr," Wendy said, raising one hand like a claw.

Her mother frowned at Wendy's unladylike display, sipped her iced tea and changed the topic. "How is Alex coming along?"

Wendy crushed some crackers into her broth, then began to scoop the soggy remnants onto her spoon. "Much better. Still has a slight limp but not much pain and he doesn't tire as easily."

"Are you two still . . . getting along?"

Was that supposed to be subtle? Wendy wondered. "Haven't managed to scare him off yet," she said. "So I must be doing something wrong."

"Just take care."

Wendy sighed. "News flash, Mother, I'm all grown-up now."

"Which reminds me, August first will be here before you know it. Anything special your father and I can get you for your nineteenth birthday?"

"A gift certificate to a secondhand furniture store."

"Your cottage is still a little Spartan?"

"Casa de Wendy, where every room has an echo."

"Sounds lonely."

"Little bit. But Alex drops by." Which was technically true. *No sense mentioning sleepovers at this point.* "And Frankie will be moving in at the start of fall semester."

"Why not have a little party in the meantime? Brighten the place up. Combination birthday party and housewarming?"

Wendy frowned. "Won't be much of a party before college starts."

"Once college starts you won't have much time to have parties."

"Yes, Mother. My nose will be pressed to the academic grindstone twenty-four-seven."

"That's not what I meant," her mother said. "You're still the president's daughter, even if you're not living in the president's mansion. Wouldn't want you to get a reputation for throwing wild parties."

"You mean you wouldn't want Dad to get a reputation for having a daughter who throws wild parties."

"Semantics, dear," Carol said as she carried her empty soup bowl to the sink. She took the empty pot off the stove, rinsed it out, and put it into the dishwasher with her bowl. "Are you finished with your soup? I need to skedaddle."

Wendy clamped a hand to stop herself from spraying her last spoonful of soup across the table. Laughing, she pressed a napkin to her face. "Mother, nobody says skedaddle."

"It's a perfectly legitimate word," her mother said, planting a kiss on the top of Wendy's head. "Now think about the party. I'll help you plan and prep, if you want. And feel free to leave any of those clothing catalogs you're not interested in."

Wendy grinned. "I could leave a few bills."

"Don't push your luck, dear."

Gina closed her bedroom door and sat cross-legged on the floor with her pouch of Scrabble tiles. After her liquor store run with Brett, she'd had an idea about the proper use of the tiles. Maybe they tapped into Wither's subconscious, the areas of her memories that were hidden or obstructed. If so, further experimentation was worth a shot.

Since the night she threw the board and tiles across the family room and they spelled out the name Wither, she'd had no success producing messages. She'd purchased another copy of the game, just to keep her own set of tiles in her room after the brief flirtation with buying a set of runes at The Crystal Path. The new tiles had proved to be duds, making her believe that maybe the original tiles had some special quality. But after a late-night session with the original game tiles produced zero results, she'd given up on receiving any further messages from beyond, wherever beyond actually might be, through the game pieces. Her new thought was that the tiles, both old and new, were valid tools; she just lacked the necessary trigger.

Rage had keyed Wither's powers before, and rage was an ingredient missing in her subsequent experiments. She needed to feel the flow of black in her veins to tap into the magical energy, Wither's powers. She gathered the tiles in her cupped hands and sought the rage, letting herself fill with the need for revenge, the need for blood. And her own blood, in turn, coursed black through the veins in her forearms. The wooden tiles felt like ice chips between her palms. *This time it will work,* she realized. *Start easy, just to open communication.* Through clenched teeth, she whispered a question, "What should I do about Wendy Ward?"

She cast the tiles.

They formed a circular pile, mostly facedown, with an open center. In the center were seven tiles, face up:

KILLHER

"Okay," she said, smiling. "So I know we're on the same page."

She gathered the tiles again, stoked the rage and asked her next question, "How did she defeat you?" She cast another circle and read the five face-up tiles in the center:

BLIND

Gina paused to consider the answer. Somehow Wendy had blinded Wither, but that failed to explain how she'd killed the witch. A third time she gathered the tiles. "How did blinding you destroy you?"

Nine tiles landed faceup in the center of the crude ring.

CRUSHMILL

"Crush," Gina whispered to herself. "Crushed at the old mill." Gina's sense of Wither in the witch's most recent incarnation was of a creature enormous and implacable, something not easily stopped. Wendy had first blinded Wither, then somehow tricked her or maneuvered her into the abandoned mill, crushing her under tons of rock. That explained Gina's feelings of fear and rage when she'd visited the mill with Brett. She hadn't understood at the time, but it made perfect sense now.

Gina wearied of the intensity needed to maintain the proper frame of mind for casting the tiles. Already her head was throbbing and white spots filled her vision, like retinal afterimages from hundreds of flashbulbs. *One more question. But enough of the past,* Gina thought. *Let's see if the tiles know the future.* After gathering the tiles, Gina asked, "Tell me of the one I have sensed, the one I seek to join my new coven?"

She cast the tiles.

Eight lay faceup, in a scattered, haphazard line.

BOSCHALL

"Boschall? Is that her last name?" She began to gather the tiles for another casting, a clarification, but a sharp pain shot like a spike through her skull. "Enough!" she whispered. "Enough for now."

Exhausted, she swept the tiles and the empty pouch under the bed, then climbed to her feet. She took an uncertain step and staggered with a wave of dizziness, grabbing the bed's brass headboard to steady herself. Chin pressed against her chest, she waited for the feeling to pass.

A moment later, blood poured from her nose.

CHAPTER SEVEN

Alex only noticed her after Professor Cermignano dismissed the summer session marketing class. Kapelski Business Center was about as far from his dorm room in Schongauer Hall as any two points on campus, so he'd allowed himself plenty of cane time to make it to the class. Consequently, he'd arrived early, taking a seat in the second row. In comparison, she must have arrived moments before the start of class, sitting in the back row and remaining quiet throughout, probably trying to avoid drawing attention to herself. As he scooped up his intro-to-marketing text, spiral-bound notebook, and cane, he glimpsed her out of the corner of his eye. Slender with long, straight black hair. *Almost sure it's her*, he thought, but ambled up the steps to the rear doors for a better look.

Out in the hallway, he looked left then right, just in time to see her step through the rear exit. He followed her across Parris Beach, the central lawn with its narrow reflecting pool, gaining ground despite his stiff-legged gait. She was dressed for the heat in a white, sleeveless cotton top, cutoff jean shorts, and white sneakers with pink stripes sans socks. "Jen?" he called. No reaction. "Jensen Hoyt?"

She stopped and turned to face him, books held in crossed arms, pressed to her chest. For a moment, she seemed puzzled, then recognition dawned. "Alex, right? You're in my marketing class?"

"Right," Alex said, closing the rest of the distance between them. "We had Glazer for comp lit last fall. I usually sat near Wendy Ward and Frankie Lenard."

Jen was nodding. "I remember."

Alex nodded toward Kapelski. "Guess we both have some catching up ahead of us."

"Yeah, last year was just crazy," Jen said, then looked away abruptly, as if embarrassed by her word choice. She'd been at the old mill when the flying monstrosity known as Wither plucked Jack Carter right off the covered bridge, and for a while nobody believed her story. She'd gone through a rough period. *Probably doubting her own sanity.* She'd missed most of the spring semester and rumor was she'd undergone some psychiatric counseling back home. When Wendy visited Jen's dorm room to find out what the creature looked like, she'd been disturbed to find not one, but hundreds of Jen's sketches of the creature, taped everywhere. Clearly she'd become obsessed. "You—you had that freak accident at the Marshall Field bleachers. Right?"

More like an attack by a freak of nature, Alex thought. But he'd noticed the haunted look in her eyes and thought maybe she wasn't ready to be reminded of the horrors many of them had faced last year. "Right. Never horse around under condemned bleachers."

Jen laughed, but with a brittle edge. "Guess not all good lessons come from textbooks."

"No."

"I had to take some time off," Jen said, avoiding eye contact. *Probably wondering what I might have heard. Worried I think she's some kind of nutcase.* "I wasn't exactly close to Jack or anything, but being right there, when he, you know, fell off the bridge. Freaked me out, I guess."

Alex nodded, he hoped sympathetically. "Would've freaked out anyone."

"Yeah," she said, nodding, reassured. "So, are you making up more than one class?"

"Two. Marketing along with Computers and Spreadsheets, but that one shouldn't be too bad. What about you?"

"Two also. Elementary Calc. Snorefest."

Alex made a sympathetic sound. "That where you're headed now?"

"No, I have a free period before that one," Jen said. "Heading over to my dorm to swap books."

"Me, too. I mean, I have a free period before Spreadsheets and I'm headed that way. Okay if I walk with you?"

"Sure, as long as you promise not to shove me into the reflecting pool."

"With my bad wheels? I'd probably fall in with you."

She laughed again, this time without the brittle edge.

Engaged in conversation, Alex almost forgot about the stiffness in his legs. Soon they passed Locke Science Center, crossed College Avenue and headed toward what was known as Dorm Row. Jen's dorm came before Schongauer, so Alex stopped to say good-bye and waited until the door closed behind her before continuing on his way. A glint of metal caught his eye. He looked back, then shrugged when he realized it had only been the sunlight reflecting off the metal letters of the nameplate mounted on the front of her building. Only parents, freshman or visitors needed the sign to know the dorm was called Bosch Hall.

Wendy Ward's Mirror Book Entry
July 19, 2000, Moon: waning gibbous, day 17

Alex officially moved into his dorm room on Monday and promptly started his two summer session classes. Each class has to cover a full semester's worth of material in less than six weeks, so the pace is frenetic. Surprised to learn that Jen Hoyt is in his marketing class. While I'm glad to hear that she seems better now, nine months after witnessing Jack's attack by Wither, I'm worried she might be in denial over what she actually saw that night. But what do I know? I don't have a degree in psychiatry. And I'd be the last one to blame her for not wanting to discuss the details with anyone who either wouldn't understand or would just assume she's crazy.

With Alex busy on campus, I've had more time to work on ritualless magic, namely generating protective spheres. My first successful sphere took over twenty minutes to build, erect, conjure? (Okay, let's go with *conjure*, it has the appropriate magical and paranormal flavor.) While pleased with my early success, the Crone keeps insisting I need to decrease the conjure time. Even though I've conjured these spheres without formally calling the elements or using the accouterments of a ritual, my problem—she says—is that I'm still relying on meditative thought to achieve results. My most recent sphere took less than ten minutes to conjure, better than half the time of my first sphere. "Still not quick enough," she declared. Frustrated, I finally asked her how quick is quick enough? Five minutes? Two minutes? She shook her head and said, "As quick as it takes to wave your hand." When I asked her how that was possible, her response, "It's all about focus. Focus and visualization."

Easy for her to say. She's a precognitive, telepathic astral projection. By comparison, I'm a Wicca bumpkin. Basically, my problem is I still have *apprentice mind*, meaning an undisciplined mind. No, I'm not stupid. Not even ignorant, well at least not completely ignorant. It's just that my approach to magic needs to undergo another paradigm shift. How? Here's her answer. The more powerful and immediate my power of visualization, the less I will need to rely on meditative thought to achieve focus. Put that in a fortune cookie, why dontcha?

Next problem? According to the Crone, size really does matter. The size of my protective sphere, that is. She rated my sphere diameter of six feet adequate. Adequate? I'm 5'8" in bare feet, so I figure I'm covered even standing in three-inch heels. Just adequate, she maintains. Adequate equates to what, a grade of C? That irks. I've never had below a B average in anything. Still, she insists improving my speed is more important than achieving a bigger diameter. She says, "The largest sphere in the world is useless if it takes ten minutes to conjure." Ouch! Anyway, my new mantra has to be, focus through visualization.

On the home front, Mother is forging ahead with plans for my birthday-cum-cottage-warming party. Since the student body is rather skeletal over the summer, it promises to be a short guest list. Although, the only person from Danfield I'll really miss is Frankie, but we can have our own house party when she arrives for fall semester. Of course, Alissa will still be in Italy on my birthday, August first, which also happens to be Lughnasadh, the celebration of the first harvest.

WINDALE, MASSACHUSETTS
JULY 20, 2000

A narrow asphalt lane meandered through the sprawling Harrison Cemetery, looping around the major sections to offer reasonable access to most of the family plots. The lane lacked a shoulder and was only wide enough for one car to pass at a time, so the grass on either side took a beating, especially on rainy days. Thursday, July 19, had delivered nothing but rain all morning. While storm clouds darkened the sky, the frequent rumble of thunder sounded as ominous as approaching warfare.

The right side of Sheriff Bill Nottingham's white Jetta had already sunk at least two inches in the mud on the side of the meager asphalt lane. Since he planned to leave before the graveside ceremony ended, he'd parked in front of the long line of cars making up the funeral procession for young Todd Gallo.

Hoping to remain somewhat unobtrusive, the sheriff observed the private moment from afar, at the bottom of the gentle hill, more than fifty yards away from the cluster of black umbrellas that had popped up like mushrooms as the mourners had climbed out of their cars.

He leaned against the front of his patrol car in a rain poncho, Smokey the Bear hat tilted forward to keep the rain out of his eyes, but still managed to become soaking wet. Todd Gallo's autopsy had found no evidence of foul play. No real surprise, he supposed. Even though Todd survived the initial impact, he'd still been in critical condition when he stopped breathing. No chemical or physical agents responsible. "Still too much we don't understand about the human mind," the medical examiner had told the sheriff.

"So this is it," the sheriff said to himself. Friends and family gathered to say their final good-byes to a boy who would never see his fourteenth birthday. The voice of the priest, standing over the coffin, was muffled by the approaching storm, but even if the sheriff had heard the words, he doubted they could make much sense out of a senseless tragedy.

Among the many mourners, the sheriff noticed the absence of Todd's stepsister, Gina, and thought maybe they had been close after all. *Kids and teenagers think they're indestructible,* he thought. *This kind of thing strikes too close to home. She's probably too distraught to say her last farewell in public.*

Dark clouds roiled across the sky, followed by a flash of lightning and a loud crack of thunder. *Summer storm,* the sheriff thought. *The steady rain is about to become a downpour.* He pushed himself off the fender of the patrol car, climbed inside, flicked the wipers on high, and drove away unnoticed.

Gina stared out her bedroom window at the gathering storm clouds, pleased with the result, and unwilling to let Brett's anger spoil her festive mood. The weather forecasters, who had unanimously predicted evening thunderstorms, could not have taken Gina's preternatural influence into account. With the storm system already approaching, Gina had discovered—or rather Wither had *recovered*—the ability to reach into all that natural chaos and violence and stroke it, accelerate it, intensify it. The least she could do to help set the appropriate mood for dear little Toad's funeral. With an exasperated sigh, she returned her attention to her offended keeper-in-training.

Brett was furious. "This wasn't part of our plan!"

"Our plan?" Gina asked, feeling the heat of her own anger, especially in her forearms. She smiled and took a slug from the green bottle of imported Tanqueray gin she was holding. She laughed. "Our plan. That's rich."

With a quick, sidelong glance at the three young men waiting outside Gina's bedroom, Brett whispered fiercely, "You said you'd pay them. You said I should offer them money."

"The promise of money brought them here," Gina said, now whispering also. "But money isn't strong enough. I need cat's-paws, not mercenaries. For that, I must blood them."

"There's gotta be another way . . ."

"Too bad, Brett. This is the only jigsaw-piece-way I know." She took another mouthful of gin. "If you'd rather not watch, step outside."

"Fine," Brett said, turning on his heel, fists clenched as he shoved past the three guys on the other side of the doorway.

With Brett gone, Gina could concentrate on the task at hand. In a way, she welcomed his objection. By ignoring his wishes, she reminded him of his place as her servant, not her partner. "Come in," she said, setting the bottle on her dresser. "Close the door behind you."

She observed their body language as they entered her room and walked past the dresser with the three burning black candles she'd prepared before their arrival. The tallest, Keith Hoagland, took the lead. Broad across the chest with muscular arms and big hands, he had close-cropped, dirty-blond hair, brown eyes, and a nose that looked as if it had been broken more than once. Confident, he looked around her room with open curiosity. Not that he'd find much to satisfy that curiosity, what with her walls stripped bare and all personal items long since trashed or tossed into the closet. Gina preferred not to be reminded of her life before Wither entered it. Nothing that had happened before Halloween 1999 seemed to matter anymore.

Following Hoagland was Val Misero, an inch or two shorter than Gina, with a wiry build, black hair pulled back in a ponytail, unlit Marlboro cigarette dangling between wide, thin lips. Last came Cecil Kerr, shaved head, wide silver loop earrings dangling from each ear, white-dyed goatee, stocky in a black mesh muscle T-shirt, serpent coils tattooed up one arm, across his shoulders, and down the other arm. Either two snakes were entwined or a single snake had two heads, since a pair of red eyes and extended fangs decorated the back of both hands. All three wore jeans, though Kerr's were black. Hoagland and Misero wore steel-toed boots, while Kerr sported black military boots, the kind that laced up to the knee.

Hoagland jerked a finger toward the closed door and sneered. "Pretty boy gotta problem?"

"Don't worry about him," Gina said.

"Said you got some work for us," Kerr said. "Requires our special talents."

Misero added, "Easy money, is what he said."

"This is one of those good news slash bad news scenarios," Gina said with a seductive smile. "Bad news? I lied about the money."

"Fuck you talkin' about?" Misero asked, stepping forward as if he'd like to backhand her.

"Cool it, Val," Hoagland said, his arm out to stop Misero in his tracks. He turned back to Gina. "If we don't get money, what's the good news?"

Gina reached back to tug down the zipper on her red summer dress. "You get me." She hunched her shoulders forward, letting the dress fall to her ankles. Once again she wasn't wearing any underclothes. It saved time.

"Fuck—" Kerr whispered appreciatively "—me."

Misero looked from Hoagland to Kerr, but his gaze never strayed far from Gina standing nude six feet in front of him. "I don't get it."

"With your shit-for-brains IQ, probably not," Hoagland said, flashing a wolfish grin for Gina.

"What?" Misero asked.

Kerr gave his shoulder a shove. "It's your lucky day, asshole."

"So who's first?" Hoagland asked Gina, trying for casual, as if this happened to him every Saturday night. Or Thursday afternoon, considering.

"I don't have that kind of time, boys," Gina said. Basically true. She'd begged off the funeral by claiming stomach flu. But her mother, stepfather, and their guests would return soon to eat all the food Sylvia, the house cleaner, had helped Gina's mother lay out on the kitchen table. Gina stepped forward to unbuckle Hoagland's belt. "Just consider me a full service station."

She needed to bind all three of them to her service and the quickest way to do that, the only reliable method known to her, was to blood them during sex. Hoagland was only too happy to have her tug him into the center of the room, duck-walking with his pants around his ankles. "On your back," she commanded.

The moment Hoagland plopped his bare ass down on the throw rug, the other two, as if freed from a trance, began yanking at the laces on their boots. Gina paid them little mind for the moment. She looked down below Hoagland's waist and was gratified to see she had his full attention. She stood over him, one leg on each side of his hips, and clenched her fists, until her fingernails bit into the flesh of her palms, until she felt the throb of black veins in her forearms. *Time to begin.* She kneeled astride his waist, then lowered herself, reaching back with one hand to guide him inside her.

"Oh, that's good," he moaned, placing his coarse hands on the outside of her thighs.

Gina, however, couldn't care less how good he felt about the arrangement. His pleasure was secondary to her purpose. She looked at the other two, both naked save for tube socks, which would have presented a thoroughly absurd picture had they not each been stroking their raging members. "Well?" she said. "C'mon!" Gina slapped her right buttock hard enough to raise a red imprint. "Kerr, back here already."

"What about me?" Misero asked.

"Come over here and I'll give you a long, deep kiss."

As Kerr and Misero moved into position, Gina leaned

forward and slid her hands up Hoagland's T-shirt. When her fingernails were over his chest, she dug them into his flesh and clawed downward, raking the flesh open.

"Shit!" Hoagland gasped, pushing himself up.

Gina shoved his shoulders back, banging his head on the floor. "Shut up," she said. "Be a man!"

Hoagland seemed a little dazed, unable to rip his gaze away from her eyes. Gina wondered what he saw in them. Perhaps some new power of compulsion. Not that it mattered, he'd been sex-blooded and he was hers now, for as long as she needed him and for whatever purpose. Hoagland nodded without further protest.

Kerr and Misero had all but ignored Hoagland's cry of pain. Nor did they seem to notice the blood now stippling his gray T-shirt. They only had eyes—and other things—for her.

Gina only had a moment's warning as Kerr dropped a meaty hand on her shoulder and moved close. Either he sensed that she enjoyed rough stuff or that was his own style, but she let out a sharp gasp of her own as he thrust deep into her ass. Seizing the moment, she reached back for the hand clamped over her shoulder and raked her nails across it, slicing the flesh in four, almost parallel lines. It was mark enough, and with his continued grunting she doubted he even noticed the wounds. *Two down*, she thought. *One to go . . . or come.*

She clamped her right hand over Misero's member and brought him closer, into her mouth. He stood with his hands curled in her strawberry blond hair, his head tilted back as he looked upward and moaned, unlit cigarette dangling from the corner of his mouth. Just to add a little variety to the proceedings, she blooded him with her teeth.

Brett Marlin waited outside Gina's bedroom for less than a minute before the need to put distance between himself and the rutting sounds coming out of her room became unbearable. He wandered into the sewing room, situated between her bedroom and that of her parents, but the walls weren't near thick enough. Next, he locked himself in the bathroom between her room and Todd's, but still he heard them. Even in the guest bedroom across the hall, he *imagined* he could hear them grunting and cursing. Although there was a storage room and an unused bedroom on the third floor, Brett decided on some fresh air. If he didn't get out of the house in the next minute or two, he thought he would puke all over the lovely blue carpeting.

He thundered down the stairs, banging into the wall at the middle landing, knocking a painting right off its wall hook. Rushing through the reception hall, he crashed through the vestibule and ran several steps down the walkway toward his pickup truck before stopping and coming back to the wraparound veranda. Inside his mind, in the place where she called to him, he knew she wanted him to stay, that he did not yet have her permission to leave. And so he had no choice but to stand around and suffer the indignity of waiting for her to finish fucking three complete strangers.

To the south, dark clouds rolled across the sky,

pulling a black shroud across the city, accompanied by the distant rumbling of thunder. The approaching storm suited his foul mood.

He stood on the veranda, knocking his head against one of the posts with the unflagging precision of a metronome. Each time his head struck the wood, he asked, "Why?" But the question was pointless. He could no more understand her than he could disobey her. Even this small measure of insubordination was making him queasy.

A sheet of rain sped across the street, raced across the lawn, and rattled the rain gutters. A driving wind whipped the rain around his legs, soaking his jeans. Dirty water spewed from the drain spouts.

"Fuck this!" Brett said, finally heeding his inner voice.

Leaving the relative shelter of the veranda, he strode into the heavy rain, determined to get away from the Gallo house, and away from Gina. With his third long stride along the cement walkway he felt a sudden pain in his abdomen. Two staggered steps farther, and he was gagging. One more and his legs trembled with devastating weakness. Falling to his knees, he bowed forward, palms slapping the wet cement as he retched. Dry heaves. The bitter taste of bile scalded his throat. Brett had sampled a few drugs over the years, but had never become addicted. Still, he could imagine *now* how withdrawal must feel. Like disobedience.

He glanced back at the Gallo house, almost glowing in stark relief against the backdrop of storm clouds. Even the thought of returning helped ease his nausea. Once more he looked toward the street, at his pickup parked at the curb, but something inside him, other than the now muted inner voice, warned him he would die before he could climb into the cab and drive away. Knowing he no longer had a choice, he returned to the veranda, and to the drug that was Gina.

After what seemed an eternity, he heard the rushed sound of footfalls from inside the house. *They're finished,* he thought immediately. And the sense of relief that swept over him made him aware of the cold sweat on his brow, the knots in his neck, shoulders, and arms.

Keith Hoagland came through the door first and Brett saw, true to her word, Gina had blooded him. Patches of blood stained his gray T-shirt from his chest almost down to his abdomen. Hoagland stopped when he saw Brett and clapped him on the shoulder. "She's a sweet piece, buddy."

Brett's jaw clenched.

Misero was close on Hoagland's heels, but not so jubilant. He had one hand pressed to his crotch and grimaced with each step. "Crazy bitch bit my cock!"

Wish she'd bit it off, asshole! Brett thought.

Kerr came out last, right hand rubbing his left until he glanced over at Brett and gave him a thumb's up. "Hey, Marlin, thanks for sharing!"

Brett took a step forward, fists clenched, ready to smash Kerr's nose and maybe relieve him of a few teeth, but as quick as the thought came, Gina pressed into his mind, calling him off. Brett stopped short, trembling with suppressed rage.

The three of them hurried down the walkway, heads

bowed against the steady rain. Kerr looked back, maybe sensing a threat, then shook his head. As they strolled down the walk together, Misero glanced over his shoulder and said to his two cohorts loud enough for Brett to hear, "What a fuckin' bozo." Hoagland and Kerr laughed.

Brett could have killed them all without a moment's regret.

Except for Gina in his mind, holding him back.

In silent fury, Brett watched them pile into Hoagland's old white Camaro, its body a mosaic of Bondo, rust, and primer. Hoagland whipped the car into the lane, missing the rear bumper of Brett's F-150 by the width of a court summons. Lightning flashed overhead, punctuated by a long peal of thunder.

With a bitter curse, Brett lashed out with his fist, slamming his knuckles into the nearest wooden post, splitting the wood in half . . . and breaking his hand in the process.

A flap of skin hung loose from his knuckles, revealing the white gleam of fractured bone and the scarlet of fresh blood. For a moment, Brett examined the wound with clinical detachment, aware of only the slightest pain. He had a strange urge to rip off the loose skin, to dig his fingers into the raw meat of his hand.

But Gina was calling him.

Anticipating the arrival of the funeral guests, Gina had slipped into a short black dress after putting her red number back into the closet. There would be many strangers in the house and she thought it prudent not to appear jubilant over Todd's permanent exit. If she wore the red dress, she might as well accessorize with a party hat and noisemaker. She had just snuffed the three black candles when Brett came through her bedroom door, broken hand pressed to his chest.

Lightning cracked, like the snapping of a whip, followed by a deep boom that shook the house. *Sounds like it took out a tree*, she thought, more amused by the storm brewing on Brett's face.

"Feel better now?" she asked sarcastically.

"They rubbed my face in it."

"Let them believe they're still in control of their lives," Gina said. *Do you still harbor those delusions, Brett?* "Stop pouting. It's done and they're mine now."

"Just the one time?"

"Once was enough," Gina said. *Not that I'm making any promises. Variety adds the spice, as it were, even if those three were simpletons.* "Now give me your hand. How can you serve as my keeper and commander of my soldiers if you're crippled?"

Brett extended his hand. Gina took it less than gingerly, flipping it back and forth, examining the split and bleeding skin, the shattered bones. "Hurt much?"

"Less than it should."

"That's my work," Gina said with a wry smile. "You're made of sterner stuff now. By no means indestructible, but I can't have you whimpering and helpless over a broken bone or three." She looked into his eyes. "What I'm about to do *will* hurt. Prepare yourself."

"No problem."

She grinned wickedly. *He has no idea. Well then, this will be another lesson.* With his broken hand in both of hers, Gina squeezed hard, clenching her own fingers around the pulped flesh until she could feel the heat rise in her arms. Brett gasped in pain, then gritted his teeth, determined not to cry out. Yet his pain had only just begun.

Gina concentrated on the shattered bones, crushed veins, torn capillaries. She needed to fix him, restore order in the crippled hand and it went against her destructive tendencies. Nevertheless, she began to make the repairs, forcing bones together, knitting them, tugging and pulling and patching blood vessels in a strange ballet of destruction and repair. Heat rose through her shoulders, crept up her neck.

Brett was shivering, teeth chattering. "So—so cold."

"Stay with me, Brett," Gina hissed, feeling the strain herself. Her power was sucking the heat right out of him to fuel itself.

Brett gasped, his eyes wide. "Your neck. Black . . ."

Gina looked beyond him and caught a glimpse of herself in her dresser mirror. The black veins had spread. No longer constrained to her forearms, they now etched a throbbing, branching path up her throat, creeping up to her jaw, like black ivy climbing beneath her skin.

Heat burned beneath her eyes.

Brett's bones crunched and cracked as she forced them back into place. Finally, he cried out and dropped to his knees. She went down beside him, determined to finish this task before she released the heat of her power.

Her hands trembled as she concentrated on the last few adjustments.

Releasing his hand, she fell sideways against the bed, exhausted, panting.

Brett was shaking, his skin bluish with cold. After a moment, he stared at his repaired hand. He turned it this way and that, flexing the fingers, making a fist. Though the outside of his fist and his knuckles were crisscrossed with a map of white scars, the hand appeared functional and pain free. That was all that mattered.

Over the insistent drumming of the rain, she heard the sound of car doors slamming. "The guests are here."

WINDALE, MASSACHUSETTS
JULY 28, 2000

Abby MacNeil and Erica Nottingham were parked on the family room sofa, laughing at CatDog, the strange cartoon on Nickelodeon. Cat-Dog was just as its name advertised, half cat and half dog: the front half of a dog attached to the front half of a cat. Two front halves, no rear ends. Abby guessed that meant no fighting over a litter box versus a fire hydrant. Cat and Dog had opposite personalities, as you might expect. But they were stuck together and had become best friends. Pulled between her human side and her wolf side, Abby found new sympathy in CatDog's predicament. And new hope in seeing that the two opposites could get along.

Bored with cartoons, Max and Ben had run out to the backyard. With the windows open, Abby could hear them outside with Rowdy, probably playing fetch with the tireless chocolate Lab.

In the kitchen, Mrs. Nottingham was preparing dinner. Although Mrs. Nottingham had let them have a bag of pretzels and a couple cookies since their peanut butter and jelly lunch, Abby was getting hungry again. She gnawed on her fingernails, watched the next couple shows on the Nickelodeon lineup and waited for Sheriff Nottingham to come home.

When Abby heard the door open, she jumped off the sofa and ran to greet him. "How was your day?" Abby asked.

"Oh, the usual," the sheriff said as he hung his jacket in the hall closet. "That pesky Robin Hood gave me the slip again." Abby laughed at the running joke they shared: sightings of the Merry Men; glimpses of Maid Marian; Little John breaking out of his jail cell. The sheriff dropped his hat over her ash blond hair and the brim fell down to her nose. She pushed it back on her head, so she could look at him when she asked her favor. "Everything okay, Abby?"

"Yes. Well . . . mostly."

"Mostly?" He kneeled down beside her so they were eye to eye. "You feeling okay, Little Lady?"

Whenever he called her that she felt like she was in an old cowboy movie, especially since he had the sheriff's badge and gun and stuff. "Feeling mighty spry, Marshall Bill," she said with a little salute.

"So what's up?"

"Could you take me to see Wendy again sometime?"

"Don't see why not."

Abby nodded. "Good."

"Anything you want to tell *me* about?"

Abby thought about it for only a moment and shook her head. "It's private."

"Private."

"Girl stuff," Abby added, knowing boys were never interested in girl stuff, even if they were too old to be real boys anymore.

"Okay, then," the sheriff said with a serious nod. "I'll see what I can do."

"Make it soon, though," Abby said, biting her lower lip. "It has to be soon."

"Should we call her then? I'm sure I can find her telephone—"

"No," Abby said quickly, squeezing her hands together. "Not on the phone. I have to see her. In person."

The sheriff strode across the kitchen, stepped up behind his wife, Christina, who was standing at the cupboard, and kissed her on the cheek. "What are you making?"

"Hot dogs for Max," she said. "Lasagna for the rest of us."

Max insisted he was allergic to tomato sauce. He would clutch his throat and pretend to choke after the smallest taste. When Erica reminded him that pizza, which Max loved, had tomato sauce in it, Max explained that the cheese kept the sauce hidden from his body, so it was safe for him to eat pizza, although not spaghetti and meatballs or tomato soup or, in this case, lasagna. The sheriff thought they were probably wrong to humor him, but he figured kids went through so many phases of likes and dislikes that it wouldn't matter in another year. *The kid loves broccoli, after all,* the sheriff thought. *Why not cut him some slack?*

"Talk to Abby much today?"

Christina turned from the cupboard and handed him plates to put on the table. "Just the usual. But then I think you're her confidant. Why?"

The sheriff set the plates around the oak table. "She wants to see Wendy again."

Christina started passing him drinking glasses. "Now that's a coincidence. We received a birthday house party invitation today from Wendy for August first."

"I knew some people gave their houses names," the sheriff said, smiling. "Are you telling me they have birthday parties for them too?"

"Two parties in one," Christina said. She walked around the table, laying a napkin and utensils at each place setting. "Apparently Wendy moved out of the president's mansion into a little cottage near campus. And it's her nineteenth birthday."

"Nineteen? Those were the days. Wake up every morning feeling invincible, no aches or pains. You know, days gone by, I could sneak up on the bad guys, get the drop on them. I was known for my stealthy approaches. Now I'm famous for the snap, crackle, and pop of my knees."

Christina slipped her arms around his waist and grinned. "You're telling me you weren't always a one-man percussion section?"

He shook his head, brushed back her blond hair. "Used to be a limber young fellow."

"You are still a young man, William Nottingham," Christina said. "And some mornings you are remarkably limber."

He nuzzled her neck, hands low on her back and drifting lower. "The best part of waking up."

She chuckled. "We have children scurrying about," she said. "Keep your hands in the PG-rated zones. Now, about this party . . . ?"

"What about it?" he asked, kissing behind her ear.

"Never mind, I'll just tell her to expect us."

WINDALE, MASSACHUSETTS
JULY 31, 2000

After a busy morning, The Crystal Path had become quiet enough for Wendy to slip into the back room and put some finishing touches on the store's Web site design. All the pages were in place and her database tests had completed, for once, without a bunch of cascading error messages popping up on the screen. Once she signed up the store for a secure server account, they could begin taking credit card orders over the Web. *That should impress Alissa,*

Wendy decided, then sighed with her subsequent thought. *But it will probably depress her, too. She disliked switching to an electronic cash register. And the first time she used the bar code wand it made her shudder.* "Oh, well, I'll handle this side of the e-business. Everything else is just packaging and mailing."

Wendy saved her work in progress, then checked her E-mail. Brief note from Alex telling her he was bored with all his textbook reading and was looking forward to seeing her tonight. She filed her New Age mailing list messages unread and skipped to a short note from Karen with a Hannah anecdote in it.

Karen wrote:

". . . I thought she was telling me she had a friend in Italy. Strange, I know, but of all the things to come out of her young mouth, definitely not the strangest. All I could think of was you telling me about your boss's trip and how she was in Italy now. Anyway, I asked Hannah who this friend was, her 'pal in Rome.' She kept shaking her head, repeating, 'Hannah is a pal in Rome.' Maybe it was just the different emphasis she placed on her name that time, but suddenly I realized what she meant. Not *Hannah has a pal in Rome* but *Hannah is a palindrome.* A palindrome! Like 'Madam, I'm Adam.' The same backward and forward. Nine months old and she knows what a palindrome is. Art says he keeps waiting for her to challenge him to a chess match. It's so crazy, Wendy, but sometimes I just have to laugh. BTW, I know it's a little early, but Happy Birthday!"

Someone knocked.

Wendy looked up from the computer screen to see Kayla poking her head into the back room. "What's up?"

"Tristan just showed," Kayla said. "Feel free to run over to the party supply store whenever."

"Oh, right. Thanks. Almost forgot."

Wendy saved her work, signed off her E-mail account and grabbed her purse from beside the desk.

After Wendy slipped out of the store, Kayla sliced open a carton filled with boxes of tarot cards. She handed them to Tristan, who was building an elaborate tarot pyramid within the display case under the cash register. Like the house of cards it resembled, Kayla expected the whole display to collapse the moment the first one sold. But only if Kayla made the sale. Tristan, with his long, spidery fingers wouldn't even need the tweezers to play the board game Operation. And Wendy just seemed naturally lucky. No, it would be Kayla of the Ten Thumbs who would be cleaning up that mess.

Feeling a sudden chill, even though the store's industrial-age air conditioner hadn't kicked in yet, Kayla felt compelled to glance up. A shadow caught her eye and pulled her gaze toward the middle of the store . . . and the young woman standing in front of the tiers of crystal balls. "Jesus," Kayla whispered, unnerved.

"What?" Tristan asked, nearly wrecking his elaborate tarot temple.

"When Wendy left, the store was empty, right?"

"Except for us. Sure."

"You hear any door chimes since then?" Tristan shook his head, pale blond eyebrows riding high like opposing question marks. Kayla nodded toward the woman. "So how the hell did she get in?"

"Who?" Tristan asked, rising from a crouch behind the display case.

With a nod of her head, Kayla said, "Gina Thorne. That's who."

CHAPTER EIGHT

"Maybe I should ask her," Tristan offered.

"Why you?" Kayla said, with a nervous glance at Gina Thorne's back. Wearing a white crop top and faded, cutoff jean shorts, the strawberry blond was running her lacquered nails over each crystal ball, as if feeling for imperfections. Yet Kayla had the strange impression she was aware of Kayla and Tristan watching her and was purposely ignoring them, at least for now.

"Because she freaks you out," Tristan said with a wry grin.

"She does not freak me out," Kayla said, unfortunately freaked out despite her protest. She gave Tristan a shove and whispered, "So go ahead. Find out what the bitch wants."

"My pleasure," Tristan said with a wink, enjoying her discomfiture. Usually, Tristan was the one squirming under Kayla's barbs, double entendres, and shocking confessions. Kayla frowned, pretending to look down at something on the countertop while all her attention was focused on Tristan's exchange with Gina.

"Help you find something?" Tristan asked Gina.

Gina smirked. "Doubt it."

Still ripe for abuse, Tristan spread his hands and said, "Answer a question, then?"

Gina looked him over, from his pale blond hair to his gray flannel shirt, gray pants, and black loafers. From the flat expression on her face, she'd found nothing interesting in her five-second appraisal. "You bore me, Tristan," Gina said, then raised her voice enough that she was sure to be overheard. "Send me the dyke, Kayla."

Kayla clenched her jaw so hard it ached. *Bitch called me a dyke!*

"I'll tell the d—uh, Kayla, that is, that you need some assistance," Tristan said, evincing a sense of caution in retreat. As he passed Kayla he said in a normal tone of voice. "The young lady prefers to speak to the assistant manager." Then, in a whisper, "She freaks me out, too."

When Kayla strode away from the cash register island, Tristan ducked down behind the display case, making himself look busy. Although her initial apprehension had been washed away in the sudden rush of anger, Kayla attempted to put on her customer-is-always-right face, but felt it go brittle and plastic around the edges before she even spoke. "Interested in purchasing a crystal ball today?"

"Maybe," Gina said. "These are more expensive than others I've seen."

"Those were probably leaded glass, not genuine crystal."

"And these are?" Gina asked. "Genuine?"

Kayla nodded, enjoying a mental image of shattering one of the larger crystal balls over Gina's smug head. The fantasy made her smile almost natural. *Wendy would be proud.* "Yes, they are. Can I wrap one up for you?"

"Not so fast."

"Take your time," Kayla said and started to turn away.

A hand carved from ice gripped her upper arm. Kayla shuddered and shot a glance at Gina. "What?" she asked, her voice faint.

"If these are genuine, I should be able to gaze into them and see my future, right?"

Kayla nodded, swallowed hard, and forced herself to speak. "Some people believe that."

"Could I see your future as well?"

"I—I don't know. Maybe."

"Let's test that theory."

With her free hand, the hand not clutching Kayla's arm, Gina reached toward the nearest crystal ball, nearly six inches in diameter, resting atop three crouching, pewter dragons. Her palm stroked the surface, left to right in a slight arc. Stunned, Kayla watched as the interior of the crystal ball began to darken, as if tiny storm clouds swirled within. An image resolved out of the gloom, a woman's face—Kayla's face—and, within the murky depths of the crystal orb, Kayla's face was silently screaming.

"Nothing," Gina said, releasing Kayla's arm and pretending not to notice as Kayla staggered a step away.

The crystal ball was clear again, only reflecting the overhead lights.

Kayla was trembling.

Gina looked at her with a chuckle and a brief shake of her head. "Guess only fools believe that nonsense." Kayla was nodding. "But you're not a fool, are you?"

Kayla shook her head, her voice still eluded her. She wanted nothing more than to be out of this woman's sight, yet her legs felt too weak to carry her anywhere, felt barely strong enough to continue supporting her weight. Only by sheer force of will did she manage to remain standing.

Almost as an afterthought, "What about your boss?"

"What—what about her?"

"Wendy Ward," Gina said. "She is your boss, right?"

"She's the manager, yes."

"And is she a believer? A fool?"

"She's a believer," Kayla said, feeling defensive. "Not a fool."

"You've witnessed her practice magic?"

"Her practices are private."

"Convenient," Gina said, smirking. Then she took a step forward.

Kayla fought the urge to back away. *Forget pride,* she thought to herself. *Just run. Get the hell out of here!* Instead she felt pinned to the spot. *Deer in the headlights,* she thought. *Big time.*

"What about you, Kayla? Do you believe?"

"I—I keep an open mind."

"Good," Gina said. "I'm glad. Your coworker bores me, but you . . . I'm glad you're open to new . . . experiences." Gina reached toward Kayla's face, a red lacquered fingernail touching the stainless steel post piercing the outside corner of Kayla's right eyebrow. "You enjoy pain, Kayla. I find that attractive in a person."

"I don't *enjoy* pain."

Gina flashed a wry grin. "Oh, really?"

"I don't let pain—the fear of pain—control me."

Gina shook her head. "That's only part of it. Another part of you relishes the pain."

"That's a lie!"

"Is it?" Gina asked. "You have a defiant streak. That too will serve me well."

"What are you talking about?"

"Never mind," Gina said, a mischievous light in her pale eyes. "Wouldn't want to spoil the surprise."

With those words she turned on her heel and walked toward the door.

Kayla stood there, staring after her with a wave of revulsion that danced along her spine. She wrapped her arms around her chest, fighting the remembered chill of those so-cold fingers that had clutched her arm. Finally, she was simply relieved Gina Thorne had left the store. This time, her passage was heralded by the clinking of the door chimes.

Tristan hurried to Kayla's side as she walked over to the tiered shelves of crystal balls. She reached out for the one that had shown her own face screaming, and her fingers began to tremble. She forced herself to touch the cool surface, but the moment she made contact with the clear surface, she heard a muffled crunch. Cracks sped through the center of the sphere like a complex tracery of milky white veins.

"Whoa . . ." Tristan said. "What just happened?"

"She made . . . did you see . . . ?"

"What?"

"I was inside," Kayla said. "My face. I was screaming."

"You basically admitted she freaked you out. Maybe you just imagined it."

"Did I imagine what just happened?"

"Must be some sort of internal flaw . . ."

"Keep telling yourself that, Tristan," Kayla said. "It's called denial."

Lugging a large shopping bag filled with party store supplies, Wendy paused at a busy intersection on Theurgy Avenue and waited for the light to turn green. She'd walked the entire half mile to the store before realizing she'd left her shopping list at The Crystal Path. Ignoring an illogical urge to walk all the way back for the list, Wendy had decided to shop from memory. Now, with a nagging sense of unease, she wondered if she might have forgotten something. But not for long.

As she stood by the traffic light, between the hurried passage of foot traffic and the darting rush of cars, Wendy had the disturbing sensation that someone was watching her. An atavistic prickling of the hairs on the nape of her neck. She glanced left, right, then back over her shoulder, but nobody seemed to be paying any special attention to her.

A taxicab braked right in front of Wendy, an abrupt stop to pick up a fare, which caused her to look forward again, and across the intersection. First thing she noticed was strawberry-blond hair, blowing in the hot July breeze.

Wendy's breath caught in her throat.

Gina Thorne—on the other side of Theurgy Avenue—staring at her.

For one long hypnotic moment, separated by the river of speeding cars, they watched each other, recognition without the slightest physical gesture of acknowledgment. Then Gina winked, breaking the spell. A sly smile curved her wide lips before she turned her back to the intersection, and to Wendy, and strode away.

As the taxicab sped off, Wendy succumbed to an unbidden urge to follow Gina. With her gaze locked on the young woman's retreating back, Wendy stepped off the curb. Toward a glaring red traffic light. A car horn blared, startling Wendy. She took an ungraceful step or two back to the curb, just as a dingy yellow rental truck barreled through the intersection, momentarily interrupting Wendy's line of sight. A split second later the truck was gone—and so was Gina!

Green light! Wendy rushed across the street, looking left and right along the far sidewalk. Gina had been walking with the flow of pedestrians, and then, a moment later, she'd vanished. Wendy shook her head. *I was zoning out back there*, she thought. *Is it possible I imagined her?*

No other explanation seemed plausible. But her intuition had another idea. It's *happening again*, Wendy realized. *And somehow, Gina's involved.*

WINDALE, MASSACHUSETTS
AUGUST 1, 2000

Wendy drove through Eden's Crossing twice, slowing to a crawl both times she passed Gina Thorne's house. Painted on the curbside mailbox was the name Gallo, but Wendy knew that was Gina's mother's married name. She had the right house. A large, sprawling executive home. One of dozens scattered along the winding road of the upscale development. Now that she'd found it, she wasn't sure what she'd been expecting. *Maybe vultures circling overhead*, she thought with a bit of gallows humor.

She'd been returning from the supermarket with chips, pretzels, and soda for her party, when the sudden urge to locate Gina overwhelmed her. Wendy's unease had been growing since she learned about Gina's visit to The Crystal Path the previous afternoon. A visit that had rattled Kayla and Tristan enough to worry Wendy, even without Gina's Theurgy Avenue vanishing act thrown into the mix.

Staring at the unremarkable house, Wendy sensed no threat emanating from it. *She's not there*, Wendy realized with a profound sense of relief. But guilt followed that relief. She should do something. But she wasn't sure what she *could* do. As she returned to her cottage, Wendy still had to wonder how much of a threat Gina posed. *And if Gina really is in league with Wither, I can only hope she has no idea how limited my magical power is right now. I need more time to prepare, to train myself. When Wither finally comes for me, I won't get a second chance. I can't afford to fail. I can't . . .*

"She knew my name, and Tristan's," Kayla told Wendy, then sipped her glass of Pepsi One. "How could she know that?" Even though they were standing in the kitchen, the cottage was small and open enough that the music from Alex's party mix CD acted as a privacy screen. Nobody else at the party would overhear them unless they stepped within arm's length.

Wendy frowned, taking a moment to refill a wicker basket from a twenty-ounce bag of pretzels. "Knowing your names isn't the weirdest part of her little visit."

"We don't wear nametags."

"No, but she might have overhead us talking to each other," Wendy reasoned. "What about the whole deal with the crystal ball?"

"Maybe I just imagined seeing myself," Kayla said, shrugging. She plucked a pretzel from the brimming basket and took a bite out of it. "She didn't seem to notice."

"Now you sound like Tristan," Wendy accused, topping off the Tostitos basket. Magic had been involved in the confrontation, Wendy was certain of that. Gina had used magic powers against Kayla and Tristan. During that first encounter with Gina, Wendy had sensed something . . . odd about her, maybe something dangerous. "I think she destroyed that crystal ball."

"Wendy, she wasn't even in the store when that happened," Kayla said. "I'm the one who touched it . . . not that you should dock my pay or anything."

"Okay, on Tristan's advice, we'll continue to call it a manufacturing defect," Wendy said. "Still . . ." Why had Gina come to the store this last time, just moments after Wendy left? Obviously not to confront Wendy. More likely, she had been lurking nearby, outside the store, waiting for Wendy to leave. "What do you think she found out?"

"What do you mean?"

Wendy's mom swooped in like a hungry seagull and plucked the Tostitos basket off the counter. "Your father's waiting for these," she said. "And he wants to know if you have any more salsa."

"One jar left," Wendy commented. "Is that all Dad's eating?"

Carol Ward nodded, frowning. "Chips and salsa. And he's washing it all down with beer."

"Maybe we should introduce him to the tray of baby carrots, cucumbers, and vegetable dip," Wendy said.

"What? And ruin all his fun?" her mother laughed. "Wendy, remember this is your party. Mingle, mingle, mingle."

Wendy rolled her eyes. "Yes, Mother." She noticed Kayla was employing a pretzel to camouflage her own smile. After Carol Ward wandered off with the nacho basket, Wendy said, "She so wants me to be a debutante."

"Mothers," Kayla said knowingly.

"Besides, I already know everyone here." The party might charitably be described as intimate. Aside from her parents, Alex, Tristan, Kayla, the sheriff, his wife, and Abby, there were only a few surprising faces, one of them belonging to Jensen Hoyt, the others to some of the students in Alex's summer courses. The conversational clusters had developed along generational lines, although Jen tended to drift away from everyone and managed to look lost and uncomfortable at the same time. The television was tuned to ESPN, but the sound was off, making it seem as if the sports highlights had been edited to Alex's eclectic party mix. Abby sat on the floor with her back against the wall, her attention focused on a lime green Game Boy clutched in both hands. Occasionally, she would look up and scan the cottage, only returning to her game display after she located Wendy. At the door, the sheriff had mentioned that Abby specifically requested to see Wendy in person. A sudden thought came to Wendy. *She wants to talk to me alone.*

"What did you mean?" Kayla asked her.

"What?"

"You asked what I thought Gina found out during her little visit."

"Oh, Gina, right," Wendy said. "I'm just wondering why she bothered to come there, when she knew I was away."

"You don't think she was there shopping for crystal balls?"

"Nope."

"She ignored Tristan," Kayla said. "She specifically asked for me."

"And what did she want to know?"

"You mean, besides whether or not I enjoyed pain?" Wendy nodded. "Only what I already told you. She asked if you were a true believer." Kayla frowned, causing the steel posts in her eyebrows to bow toward each other. Whenever Kayla was in deep thought, she had a habit of clicking her tongue stud against the back of her teeth. Wendy heard clicking now. "No, that's not quite right. She wanted to know if I had ever witnessed your magic."

"What did you tell her?"

"What could I tell her? You do your own thing in private."

"Right," Wendy said. Wendy recalled the unaccountable revulsion she'd felt in the young woman's presence, and Gina's own apparent fear—or loathing—of Wendy, her rush to leave the store. *Could she be worried about me, about what I could do against her?* Wendy felt a chill in her bones. *What if she's the one? What if she's Wither reborn? But . . . if she is and she's worried about me, she must not remember everything that happened last Halloween, how she nearly killed me, would have killed me if I hadn't tricked her into bringing the old factory down on her head. I haven't changed enough since then to pose much more of a threat to her, have I? . . . No, but she's changed. She's no longer a brutal animal, driven by rage and hunger, fueled by immense power. She's either worried or plotting something. And she might be close to making a move against me. If that's true, the real ques-*

tion isn't what can I do against her, but what can she do to me?

If Gina was Wither in a new body, Wendy was convinced Kayla had witnessed a small demonstration of this new Wither's powers: slipping into the store without sounding the chimes, the image in the crystal ball, and its destruction minutes later. Kayla had even mentioned an icy grip, and a feeling of being mesmerized by the young woman. Less than a half hour later, Wendy had witnessed Gina's disappearing act on Theurgy Avenue. Imagine that young woman hosting an ancient evil in her mind and body . . .

Wendy felt a light touch on her arm, looked down and saw Abby staring up at her with those big blue eyes. "Hey, Abby, what's up?"

Abby cast a quick glance at Kayla before returning her gaze to Wendy. "Could you show me your room?"

"My room," Wendy said, catching Kayla's eye and quirking an eyebrow in what amounted to a shrug. "Sure, Abby."

Good soldier that he was, Alex had renounced any claims to one of the few available folding chairs and sat on the floor, cane balanced across his knees, in an animated discussion with two of his classmates regarding the performance of the Red Sox. He winked at her as she passed and mouthed the words "Happy Birthday" for about the hundredth time. She mouthed back "Thank you" before leading towheaded Abby down the short hall to her bedroom.

* * *

Abby had decided she couldn't wait any longer to catch Wendy alone. It was Wendy's party so she wasn't likely to wander off . . . unless Abby asked her. So she had.

"Standard issue girl's bedroom," Wendy was saying. "Well, except for the incense, the pentacle, and the Witch's calendar, I suppose." But knowing Wendy, she wouldn't think Abby had come for the quick tour. "What did you want to ask me, Abby?"

"Nothing, really," Abby murmured, distracted as she wandered around the room.

"Tell me, then?"

Abby's eyes darted from one object to the next—frosted glass candleholder on the bedside table, black Sony radio alarm clock, glossy cedar chest at the foot of the bed—but she was taking in the forest-themed bedroom with more than just her eyes. Because she knew it would be important, she was creating a sense memory of these surroundings.

Finally, Abby returned to Wendy's side and felt a collection of butterflies begin a hectic dance in her stomach. What she was about to do might be dangerous, if she could do it at all. She stretched up on tiptoe. Obligingly, Wendy leaned down a bit to put them at eye level. Abby wrapped her arms around Wendy's neck. Misinterpreting the gesture, as Abby knew Wendy would, Wendy encircled Abby in her arms and gave her a hug. Abby pressed her face into Wendy's auburn hair, nuzzling her neck . . . and starting the change.

Abby wasn't quite ready to tell Wendy what she had become, or to demonstrate the change in front of her, especially not with a party just down the hall. Yet this might be Abby's only chance. She had to risk a partial change so her other self could learn Wendy's scent. In the remembered pieces of Abby's dream, Wendy was outside at night, in great danger, and only Abby's wolf form could save her. To reach Wendy in time, the wolf had to track her by scent. Without that scent to guide the wolf, Wendy would die.

Letting her other self peek out, Abby felt the skin and bones along her face protrude, forming a fur-covered snout. She only had a moment before Wendy would sense something was wrong, so she inhaled deeply, filling her lungs with Wendy's scent. Beneath the flowery bouquet of shampoo and the intermingled layers of body lotion, shower gel and deodorant, was the primal smell, the human musk that separated Wendy from all others and made her unique. In her slightly altered state, wearing a wolfish snout, Abby learned the scent in the span of a heartbeat. Long before she felt Wendy's arms stiffen and start to push her away, alarmed.

Rather than shoving aside the wolf, Abby flowed back into her human self, feeling the flesh slide back across receding bones. By the time Wendy held her at arm's length, staring into her eyes, Abby looked completely human again.

"What just happened?" Wendy asked, eyes wide.

Abby just looked at her, not trusting her voice yet.

"Did you feel that? Something just happened. I thought—" Wendy shook her head, perplexed. "The air felt charged. Like electricity . . . or magic."

"I didn't notice anything," Abby said quickly.

Wendy searched Abby's eyes, a probing gaze, unnerving her, but Abby was sure all traces of the wolf were gone. Certain she appeared completely human again. "I look at you and I think of trees," Wendy said softly. "The forest."

"Because I'm always wandering off into the woods," Abby suggested, forcing a little smile.

"Abby, do you know what's been happening to you?" Wendy asked. "Something you're not telling me?"

Abby swallowed, fidgeting under the weight of Wendy's hands on her shoulders. Abby had to tell her something. "I feel . . . different from everybody else." *Too close to the truth!* "Sometimes, I forget what it was like to be normal."

With a resigned sigh, Wendy said, "Me too, Abby."

"I'm sorry," Abby said. *Sorry for frightening you. But it's the only way. At least for now.*

"Not your fault," Wendy said, looking around the room as if she expected to find an intruder lurking there. "Wait a minute. You wanted to tell me something? What?"

Abby chewed on her lower lip. "You have to trust yourself."

"What do you mean?"

How can I explain something I don't even understand myself? It's something the wolf knows. "Just be careful, Wendy. Okay?"

Wendy looked into her eyes again. "I'm always careful, Abby."

"Be *extra* careful, then," Abby said. "Something bad is coming."

Wendy frowned. "You feel it too, huh?"

Abby nodded. "Like an itch under my skin." *Maybe it goes all the way down to my bones, my changing bones.*

"We're quite a pair, aren't we?" Wendy said. "A couple of long-tailed cats in a room full of rocking chairs."

Abby nodded, the image capturing her unease exactly. "We have to save each other."

"How?"

Abby shrugged. "I'm not sure . . . I just know that if we don't save each other, we both die."

"You mentioned something about that in the hospital," Wendy said. "Do you remember?" Abby nodded. "Isn't there anything else you can tell me? To help me? Us?"

Not yet, Abby thought. *It's too early. That's all I know.* "I'm sorry."

"But there's danger? Coming for us?"

"Soon," Abby told her again.

Val Misero sat alone on a threadbare, cat-clawed sofa in the darkness of his parent's finished basement. An old console television set broadcasting yet another MTV beach party cast ghostly light across his face, bare chest, and arms. Between the sofa and the stairs was the oblong darkness of a pool table whose felt had seen better days. Lined up along the near wall were an old pinball machine, an air hockey table with a damaged leg, and a broken karaoke machine. All junk that should have been put curbside long ago. Castoffs not yet cast aside. For lack of a sledgehammer, he managed to suppress the seductive urge to smash all the junk into tiny shards of plastic and metal.

Instead he flicked the igniter wheel on the cigarette lighter in his hand again. Must have been the twentieth time. The metal cap and blue plastic housing had grown warm in his palm while he worked up his nerve.

Flickering under the minor assault of his steady breathing, the flame was a long orange tongue, tasting the air, expectant . . .

Lifting his left forearm, he held it inches above the flame and nodded as heat spread across his flesh. Warmth soon became discomfort.

A voice, a woman's voice, whispered in his mind, *Not enough.*

So he moved his arm closer to the flame, close enough for it to brush his skin, scorching it red in a moment. He gritted his teeth, balled his fist until the knuckles turned white and his fingernails summoned crescents of blood from his sweaty palm. But he didn't pull away.

Not enough.

Into the flame now and his skin began to hiss and darken.

He panted, fighting the urge to pull away. And the rising urge to vomit.

The stink of cooked flesh filled his nostrils. Black smoke wafted around his trembling arm. Agony flared inside his skull, a white nova of pain that shattered coherent thought.

Not enough.

. . . charred flesh split open, fat sizzled, and droplets of hot blood began to spatter his pants . . .

Sweat rolled down his face, dripped down his chest.

Knees bounced up and down—a little jig—as his body began to spasm.

Eyes rolled back in his head, flashing whites.

Slipped toward shock and unconscious . . . and still he refused to pull away.

Enough . . .

He dropped the hot lighter on the floor, its hungry orange fire winking out before it struck the carpet.

Breathing raggedly, he explored the charred flesh with his right thumb and index finger, slipping both digits into the blackened cracks in his flesh, touching ruined muscle and deeper, scraping his fingernails against warm bone. He gasped . . . then a slow smile spread across his face.

Doesn't matter, he thought. *The pain, the damage—none of it matters. I'm fire-hardened, baby. Proved myself. Fucking right, I proved myself. I'm ready now. Oh, man, am I ready.*

To celebrate the first harvest, Lughnasadh, which fell on her birthday, Wendy had placed in the center of the card table a bowl filled with sheaves of wheat, a homemade loaf of bread and several apples and oranges. As Wendy sat down across from Jensen Hoyt, the apples and all but one of the oranges were gone. Judging by the thumb hole gouged in the side of the loaf of bread, somebody at the party had doubted its authenticity. And although Jen's pale face seemed particularly forlorn, framed by her straight dark hair as she looked down at the piece of birthday cake Carol Ward had set before her, Wendy doubted she was the guilty party. Had to have been one of Alex's friends, Wendy decided. Maybe even Alex himself.

Wendy was more concerned with Jen's case of nerves, demonstrated by her fidgety hands. One minute her palms were flat against the edge of the table, then she would drum her fingers on the padded surface for a bit before noticing this bout of nervous energy, at which point she would clasp her hands together. A minute or two would pass before she began the whole cycle over again. Never touching the cake. Maybe I'm overanalyzing, Wendy thought. Maybe it's just a diet and temptation tug of war. "You know, that cake was made to my specifications."

"What?"

"Chocolate icing over vanilla cake," Wendy explained. "As opposed to the other way around."

"Ah."

It wasn't as if Wendy felt compelled to make sure everyone had a good time at her birthday-slash-housewarming party, but after her encounter with Abby, she needed something ... ordinary to take her mind off the weird sensation that Abby had changed somehow, the sense Wendy had that Abby had growled deep in her throat, a bass rumble, and also the brief, visual echo of yellow light Wendy had seen in the young girl's eyes. Wendy trusted Abby, but something unexplained had occurred in Wendy's bedroom and she wasn't quite sure what to make of it. Mingling with party guests seemed simple in comparison.

"You know what the problem is?" Wendy asked her.

"No." Jen brushed her hair back, tucking it behind

her right ear, another nervous gesture, something for one fidgety hand to do, if only for a moment.

"This party lacks . . . critical mass."

"Critical mass?"

"Yep. You need a certain number of bodies for a gathering to become a true party. We're about a half dozen short."

Jen quirked a minor league smile. Still, an improvement. "Think so?"

"Oh, definitely," Wendy said. "More bodies equal more conversations. Each conversation gets louder to be heard over the others, which forces you to turn up the music . . ."

Jen nodded. "Which requires everyone to talk louder."

"Right, it's a cycle of loudness," Wendy said. "We can't get beyond that quiet conversational stage."

"Couldn't we just turn up the music? Force people to talk louder?"

Wendy shook her head. "No, it's gotta be people first, pushing up the dBs. Otherwise it all seems forced."

"You may be on to something."

Wendy shrugged. "The only alternative is for someone to spike the punch bowl. Think Danfield is ready to offer Party Theory 101?"

Jen laughed. "Maybe not by fall semester."

While Jen's hands were clasped together one more time, Wendy reached beyond the Lughnasadh basket and placed one of her hands over Jen's, and was startled when Jen flinched and pulled away. "Jen? You okay?"

Wendy scratched her palm under the table and resisted the urge to jump up and scrub it with hot water and cleanser. Jen's hand had been cold and clammy to the touch, but nothing more than that. Wendy guessed she was still reacting to the weird vibes she'd experienced while alone with Abby.

Jen sighed, looked away. "I'm f—fine. Why do you ask?"

"It's just that, after last year," Wendy began. "I mean, with everything . . . Jack's murder, nobody believing your story . . ." Wendy shook her head. "It's amazing anyone could come through that."

Jen dropped her hands to her lap. "Look, Wendy, I just want to move on, you know?"

"Sure," Wendy said. "Sure, I can appreciate that. Just . . . if you ever feel you need to talk to someone, someone who will listen, who understands . . ."

With a wry smile, "I'll talk to my therapist."

"Right. Therapist," Wendy said. *Serves me right for acting like a psych major.* "That's what they're there for."

Jen pressed fingertips to her temples with a slight grimace. "Wendy, thanks for inviting me to your party. Appreciate the gesture. It's just—I've had this *extreme* headache all day and, if you really want to help me out, you'll find me a ride back to my dorm."

"Not a problem," Wendy said. "Another of my party theories states that it's all downhill after the cutting of the cake. And, of course, the unwrapping of the ceremonial offerings." Wendy had received silver earrings with a dangling goddess symbol—the waxing-full-waning moon phases—from Tristan and Kayla; a black cable knit sweater from the Nottingham contingent; a furniture store gift certificate from Mom and Dad and a heart-shaped gold pendant from Alex. The official Danfield College pewter beer stein was a gift from Alex's assembled classmates, and had drawn a pair of disapproving frowns from her parents. An odd gift from Jen: a wall clock with hopelessly jumbled black numbers. Overall, Wendy had made out better than her cottage had in the gift department.

At that moment, Alex passed the table, his limp barely noticeable as he balanced three soda cans, a basket of potato chips, and his cane, dangling from the crook of his elbow at the moment. Wendy reached out and snagged one of his belt loops with her index finger. "Yes, birthday girl?" he said. "Excuse me, birthday lady?"

"Nice recovery," Wendy said. "A favor, please?"

"Name the deed and it shall be done, milady."

"Jen's gotta bail. Wanna borrow my car and escort her back to her dorm?"

"Wanna tell me your candle-blowing wish?"

"The wish kiss of death? Never."

"Just checking." He looked over at Jen. "Give me a sec to unburden myself, and we're off."

Wendy blew him a kiss. "Thanks."

By the time Alex had driven half the distance to Bosch Hall in Wendy's Civic, a persistent drizzle became a steady rain. Successive flashes of distant lightning backlit the stacked clumps of racing clouds. Alex flipped the wipers from the intermittent setting to low. *Thrump* . . .

squeak, *thrump* . . . squeak replaced by the more up-tempo, *thrump-wush, thrump-wush*. So far neither he nor Jen had said a word. Rubber scraping wet safety glass was the only sound in the compact car.

Resisting the urge to turn on the radio, Alex cleared his throat and said, "TV weather guys botched another one. Satellite imagery, barometers, weather balloons, Doppler radar . . ." He shook his head. "About time they admitted they have no clue."

Distracted, Jen looked over at him from the passenger's seat in Wendy's Civic and asked, "Could I borrow your notes from Cermignano's class?"

Okay, so she takes a pass on weather humor. "Yesterday, right? I thought you were missing."

Jen nodded. "A flopsy stomach day. Listen, I wouldn't ask, but it was the exam review . . ."

"No, that's fine."

"I'll copy them first thing tomorrow and get them right back to you."

"I trust you," Alex said. "Besides, my dorm's not that far from Bosch. No biggie."

"Thanks."

Although she was quiet the rest of the way, when Alex parked the car and reached behind the driver's seat for Wendy's white umbrella with the black cat silhouettes, Jen said, "Could I come up and use the bathroom?"

"Suppose so," Alex said. "If you don't mind getting a little wet."

"I've been through worse."

They raced across the nearly empty parking lot at

Alex's pace, which was a stiff-legged gait, with Jen huddled over to get under as much of the umbrella as she could, pocketbook clutched at her side. By the time they made it inside and took the stairs, they were both laughing at their sodden, squeaky condition. "The worst part of this is I take horrible notes," Alex admitted.

Jen glared at him good-naturedly and jabbed him in the ribs.

Alex unlocked the dorm room and pointed Jen toward the bathroom. After she closed the door, he took his three-ring binder off the shelf above his small student desk and turned to the marketing tab. Then he flipped to the most recent pages, popped open the rings and removed the seven pages of notes he'd taken the previous day.

The bathroom door opened. Jen stepped out, her straight hair still wet, but presentably combed, her hand clamped over her pocketbook hanging by its shoulder strap. "Find your notes?" she asked.

"Right here," he said, holding up the loose pages. "Hope you can read my chicken scratch."

"I'll manage."

"I'll shove them in a folder and hope that keeps them dry."

"Shove me in too and we'll be all set."

Alex grinned. "Times like this make you wish you'd bought that pocket Danfield rain poncho."

Wither sits at the widow's gateleg table, the keeping room lit by three black candles forming the points of a triangle on the table. Centered within them is a divining glass on a silver stand. Wither stares into its murky depths.

Rebecca Cole, dressed only in her shift, dances airily around the table, her hair uncovered and unbound. She is radiant in the candlelight . . . and well on the way to madness. Her arms flutter up and down gracefully, as if she were launching doves from her fingertips. Yet it is that very touch of madness that unlocked her mind to Wither, brought her into the three. "What see you, dear Elizabeth?"

"Trouble."

"Why fear trouble?" Rebecca says with a confidence Wither does not share. "With Sarah, we have the strength of the coven now. Have you not said so?"

"Still too soon to protect us from foolishness." Wither adjusts the divining glass and its depths become shadowy and quick. Currents and eddies that are a second language to her. Glimpses of possibilities. The glass often spoke half-truths or near-truths, never quite revealing all, as nothing could ever be completely, utterly known before its time. To see into the future was, by nature, to change it, for awareness was a living thing. Still, she must take from the glass what is revealed or mayhap suffer a terrible price.

Without Alex slowing her down, Jen jumped out of the Civic, held the folder over her head like a mortarboard and raced with the grace of a gazelle across the lawn to Bosch Hall. Alex waited until she slipped inside the door before driving away.

Sometimes he saw Jen as an expensive, porcelain doll marred with fine cracks, distant and solitary, as she'd been at Wendy's party. Other times, she seemed to have put the tragedy of Jack Carter's murder squarely behind her. He supposed recovery worked that way sometimes. No overnight remedies or quick fixes. Just coping one day at a time.

Jen fumbled for the key to her dorm room, but when she pushed it into the slot, the door swung inward on whispering hinges. With a startled gasp, she balked on the threshold between the light of the hallway and the utter darkness enveloping her small dorm room.

The light out here doesn't seem to penetrate at all.

Locking her door behind her had become an obsessive-compulsive problem for her. Sure that she'd forgotten to engage the lock, she would return three or four times just to be absolutely certain, often arriving late for classes. And because of her dread of returning home to darkness, she'd gotten in the habit of leaving a light on, even if she was sure she'd return before nightfall.

So why is the door unlocked and the room totally black?

From within, a teasing whisper. "Have fun at the party?"

"Is that . . . is that you?" Jen asked, her voice timid.

"Of course, it's me," the voice whispered. "Come in. Close the door. And tell me what you've done."

Jen stepped into her room, closed the door and the utter darkness seemed to lighten. Before moving deeper into the room, Jen fumbled for the light switch and flicked it on. For a moment, the light dazzled her eyes, nearly blinding her, but not enough for Jen to miss the strawberry blond woman sitting on her bed with a cat-noshing-canary grin on her face.

Scattered across the bedspread were at least two dozen pictures Jen had drawn months ago, before the endless hours of therapy, pictures of a single, leering, gargoylelike visage. Two dozen identical images out of the hundreds she had sketched. Jen had told her therapist she'd thrown them all out. A lie, of course. By then she always knew which lies the therapist wanted to hear. After that revelation, her treatment had gone much smoother.

Gina sat with her back against the plain headboard, braced on her elbows, legs straight out, crossed at the ankles. Picking up several of the pages, she fanned them out like an oversized hand of playing cards. "This is one ugly fucker," she said, chuckling before she tossed the sketches toward the trash can. "I really looked that . . . nasty?"

Jen nodded meekly.

"Makes liver spots and varicose veins look like dimples and beauty marks. But . . . I suppose I won't mind patches of rough skin when I'm three hundred years old and nine feet tall."

Jen stepped sideways and sat on a folding chair. Sometimes Gina started off in a jovial mood before flying off into a frightening rage. And the evening hadn't gone quite as they'd planned. Wendy had unnerved her.

Gina patted the bed at her side. "Don't be a stranger. Join me."

With a slight nod, Jen crossed to the bed and sat

down beside Gina, who immediately looped an arm around her shoulder. "You're all wet, girlfriend."

Jen glanced toward the tall window, a gap exposed between beige curtains, streaked with rain. "It's raining."

"No shit," Gina said. "Must admit, I'm getting better at that."

"You?"

"Why not? I was bored. You were the one having all the fun at Ms. Ward's soiree." Gina patted Jen's knee. "So how'd it go?"

Jen stammered. "I was . . . I couldn't—I mean, I was getting physically ill. Like some kind of allergic reaction."

"We have that effect on each other, Wendy and I," Gina said. "Hope it wasn't strong enough for her to notice."

"So that's why I . . ."

"Are you trying to tell me you have no little Wendy treats for me?"

"Not hers," Jen said. "But I got his."

"His? You mean her boy toy? Alex, isn't it?"

Jen nodded, unsnapped her pocketbook. "He drove me here from the party. I asked to use his bathroom."

"Ooh, goody! I like this even better. What did you get?"

"Nothing he'll miss," Jen said. "From his hamper . . ." She pulled out a balled up pair of white tube socks, soiled with grass stains. "And . . ." She removed a baggie filled with strands of brown hair. "This from his hairbrush."

"Perfect," Gina said. "I can work with this." Gina shot her a concerned glance. "You're sure he doesn't suspect anything?"

Jen forced a confident grin, but the expression felt

wrong on her face somehow, like a wall hanging that's not quite level. "Positive."

"Excellent."

"So . . . you're not mad at me?"

"No, no, Jen. Not mad at all. True, I was expecting Wendy's stuff, but I'm not sure that little trick would work on her. And, at this stage, it might have been dangerous to try and fail." She pursed her lips thoughtfully. "I haven't really tested her yet, although I have an idea on that end. No, this is probably better for now. I want her totally outflanked and vulnerable when the time comes . . ."

"What time?"

Gina's generous lips slipped into a broad, easy smile. "When I kill her, of course."

"So . . . what now?"

"I feel like celebrating," Gina said. "I've been having these strange dreams . . ." She raised her forearm, and Jen saw that where Gina should have had blue veins under her pale skin, the vessels seemed much darker. First Gina examined the long fingernail of her index finger, as if it were a medical instrument, then she flashed a mischievous grin at Jen when she said, "Are you in the mood for some experimentation?"

"Um . . . what did you have in mind?"

"Oh, just a little blood bonding," Gina said and opened a vein.

CHAPTER NINE

Sitting in lotus position, a quartz crystal digging into her now sweaty palm, Wendy opened her eyes and looked at the opaque image of the crone standing before her. "Done!"

"*Better,*" the Crone said in that tone that meant *still not good enough.*

Wendy sighed. "How long?"

"*One minute, fifteen seconds.*"

"New personal best," Wendy reminded her.

"*Yes.*"

"By at least thirty seconds."

"*Thirty-two.*"

"Size?" Even though it was invisible, Wendy could

feel the sphere surrounding her, almost as if it were glowing but just outside the visible spectrum. From the way the Crone glanced left to right, then top to bottom, Wendy guessed that on whatever astral plane the Crone hailed from, magical spheres *were* visible.

"*Seven feet, six inches in diameter.*"

"That's a five inch improvement! You have to admit, my circle—excuse me—*sphere* conjuring time and size is much improved since I started holding the quartz."

"*The quartz crystal helps you focus on the task,* the Crone said. *The crystal is what first gave you the idea for the bead bracelet.*"

"Bracelet? Power beads?"

"*You put a new spin on power beads by mixing over a dozen different beads on one bracelet. Many focal points for various magic spells in one piece of jewelry.*"

"That was a good idea," Wendy said. "Um, *will* be a good idea."

"*That's nothing compared to some of the protective sphere innovations.*"

Wendy shook her head. "You know, it's really weird when you talk about the future as if it's already happened."

"It *has,*" the Crone said. "For me. But *there is no guarantee that same future will happen for you.*"

"And this whole time logic is even weirder," Wendy said, waving her hands in front of her face. "Let's take a break from spheres and try something else." Wendy promised herself she'd start consecrating beads for the multibead bracelet as soon as tomorrow.

"*Release your sphere, grab an agate geode and follow me to your bedroom.*"

"What is so damned fascinating about my bedroom lately," Wendy mumbled. With a sharp exhale, Wendy began to dissolve the sphere by absorbing its energies back into her body through the black-handled athame. That task completed, she sorted through the stones she'd laid on the counter and scooped up the rough-textured agate geode.

The Crone had already glided down the short hallway to Wendy's bedroom. As Wendy approached the doorway, she caught a glimpse of the Crone before the door slammed in her face and the lock clicked. "Okay, what's up with the poltergeist attitude?" Wendy called through the door. She looked down at the stone. "Something psychic."

"*Something simple,*" the Crone called through the door. "*Open the door.*"

"This door doesn't take a key," Wendy said. "It's one of those push button locks."

"*As I said, simple.*"

"Where's a paper clip or a hairpin when you need it?" Wendy muttered.

Still the Crone heard. "*No paper clip. Use your mind.*"

"My mind? You mean, telekinesis?"

"*That's one word for it.*"

"Does this mean I have a future in breaking and entering?" Wendy said with a sigh before setting her mind on the task. After about ten seconds, she realized she had no clue how to begin. "Pointers?" she called through the door, though the Crone obviously could read her mind.

"*This is simply a crude test of will.*"

"Crude, huh?"

"*There are two physical ways to disengage the lock,*" the Crone explained. "*Name them.*"

"Shoving a paper clip through the little hole pops the lock mechanism and . . . well, turning the knob on that side of the door."

"*Correct. Now you must focus your will alone on either task. Use the agate geode to focus if you must. Remember, Wendy, you can do this. I've seen you do it dozens of times.*"

"Yeah, yeah, Future Girl," Wendy said. *Focus my will, huh? Well, of the two methods, turning the knob would seem to involve more force—torque?—although I'm not sure that matters to my will. Does my—will my will have the same limitations as my physical strength? Could I move more with my mind than I could move with my muscles? Question for later, I suppose. Back to the task at hand. The short and sweet way to unlock the door would be to pop that little trigger doohickey.*

Gripping the agate geode in one hand and the quartz crystal in the other, Wendy crouched before the closed door and stared into the pinhole opening. Two minutes passed and the only result was trembling thighs, a sheen of sweat on her forehead, and the beginning of a headache.

"*Visualize,*" the Crone whispered to her mind.

To make herself more comfortable, Wendy kneeled before the door, butt resting on her heels, curled hands on her thighs. She took one deep breath, then began a

series of even breaths designed to ease the tension building behind her forehead. *Visualize*, she thought and
closed her eyes. *See with my mind . . . act with my mind.*
She waited, imagined herself gathering energy, shaping
it as a tiny sphere of will—of power—until it seemed to
pulse within her chest. Then she visualized compressing
that pulsing orb, streamlining it into a coherent, glittering sliver of energy. With a sharp exhalation, she visualized this sliver flying out of her, a burst of golden energy,
aimed unerringly for the pinpoint of darkness pictured
in her mind.

CLICK!

In her focused state, the sound was like an
explosion.

Her eyes flew wide and she reached for the door
handle, dropping the agate geode in the process. With a
twist, she pushed the door open. On the other side, the
Crone was smiling.

Wendy climbed to her feet, completely invigorated
by something that felt as if it should have drained her
last ounce of energy. Her voice low with awe, she said,
"That was incredible!"

"*Just wait till you pop your first dead bolt.*"

"Dead bolt?"

The Crone nodded. "*However, forming a mental key is
the real challenge. All those tiny grooves and ridges.*"

Wendy plopped down on her unmade bed. "I'll take
your word for it." She heaved a sigh. "What next?"

"*Let's try that one again,*" the Crone said. "*But this time,
try to pop the lock in less than ten minutes.*"

"I—that took ten minutes?"

"*Eleven minutes, forty seconds. But it's a good start.*"

Gina stood barefoot in front of her dresser mirror wearing a spaghetti-strap, red slipdress, fingers spread at the sides of her throat as she swept her hair back over her shoulders. Not really watching her own reflection anymore as much as listening to the staccato burst of footfalls racing up the stairs. First Thursday of the month meant Mother was at her planning-board meeting. Although Caitlin had almost passed, would have passed, if not for a little mental prodding from her daughter. *Like I need her moping around the house,* Gina had thought. And the regularly scheduled meeting had given Gina the germ of an idea.

She was alone in the house with her stepdud, Dom. And, right that moment, he seemed to be out of his grief-stricken funk. *Things could get interesting.*

From Todd's bedroom—*correction, Todd's frozen-in-time memorial shrine*—she heard a heavy crash. If she had to guess, she'd say it was the sound of Todd's fried computer monitor taking the express route to the floor.

A moment later, her bedroom door burst open, revealing a wild-eyed Dominick Gallo. "You're responsible," he said, his voice harsh, almost a croak. "You killed him!"

"Forget to knock, Dom?"

"I don't know how . . . but you killed my son!"

"A big truck killed your son, Dom," Gina said, returning her attention to the mirror. "A truck and his own clumsiness."

Dom was on her in a flash, grabbing an impressive

hunk of her hair in his fist and pulling her head back. The pain was so sudden and intense, the periphery of her vision danced with white spots. She staggered backward, pressing a hand against his to stop him from tearing her scalp. His rage swirled around him, a white hot aura. "You killed him, bitch! Just like you tricked us into believing you replaced his computer."

"You're—delirious, Dominick!" she gasped. "You've been drinking!"

He struck her with a strong backhand, buckling her knees, then shoved her away, toward the bed, releasing her hair a moment later so that, off balance, she stumbled and fell. Fists clenched at his sides, he looked down on her, his rage simmering beneath the surface of his skin, thrumming the tendons in his neck, working the muscles in his jaw.

Sensing his volatility, Gina sat perfectly still, her back against the side of the bed, her legs a helpless tangle before her. She glanced at her dresser, behind him, saw the overstuffed top drawer, where several pairs of nylons hung like garlands. Her gaze meeting his once again, she said in a soft voice, "Don't, Dom . . ."

He glanced back and saw what she had seen. The idea blossomed in his head, just as she thought it might. Tugging the snarl of nylons free, he proceeded to knot the taupe end of one around her right wrist. "Stop it," she cried, glancing at the brass headboard rails, anticipating his next action. "You don't know what you're doing!"

"Oh, yes I do," he said harshly, looping the other end of the nylon around one of the far-side footboard rails, pulling her arm back painfully and lifting her butt clear of the floor. "For the first time, I see everything clearly!" He grabbed her around the waist and twisted her over, so her back was to him. "Know exactly what I have to do . . ." A black nylon encircled her left wrist in a flurry of movement and, a moment later, that arm was tugged up to a far rail on the headboard. She was bent almost double over the side of the bed and now had a good idea where Dom's rage was leading him.

"Dom—stop! Don't do this," she cried, looking back over her shoulder. "Not again—please not again!" But she doubted he heard her protests. He was beyond listening, beyond reason by this point. All too soon she felt his hands on her thighs, shoving the slipdress up over her hips so he could rape her from behind. She wore white cotton panties under the short dress and that, more than anything, seemed to break his rhythm.

Dom just stared down at her as if he couldn't remember where he was or what he was about.

"Dom?"

Labored breathing.

"What are you doing . . . ?"

He was pushing away from her, away from the bed, backing up across the bedroom. As she glanced over her shoulder, she saw the lost look in his eyes. He shook his head and ran from her bedroom.

With a heavy sigh, she said, "Shit." After a moment, she looked to the left, at the two-inch gap in her closet doors and the blinking red light at eye level. "Show's over, tiger. Stop fucking around in the closet."

The vented doors rasped along their metal track, creating accordion folds as they opened. Brett stepped out, the family camcorder balanced on his shoulder, its red eye no longer winking at her.

Gina swiveled her wrists to grip the stretched nylons in her palms. Letting the rage spark through her was no more than an afterthought. The nylons sizzled, burned and, as she tugged on them, ripped in half.

"Think we have enough on tape?" Brett asked. By his wide-eyed look, she could tell he was hoping they wouldn't need an encore performance.

"A good start, wouldn't you say?" Gina said with a teasing grin. She walked over to her mirrored dresser, snuffed out the single black candle, and picked up the cloth Dom doll. She'd removed the tiny black ribbon blindfold less than an hour ago, enough time for Dom to shake off the mental fog and start to question the glamours, the daily illusions, she'd draped over his life. "But I'm afraid I went overboard on the white cotton undies. Tried to play the part of the innocent for our little feature and it turned into a cold shower for Dom. So, we probably don't have quite enough to twist Dom around my little finger. Plain old extortion would have been so much more wicked and fun than playing with illusions, but . . ."

"What now?"

Gina picked up the short length of black ribbon and knotted it around the Dom doll's head again. "We forget the fun and games with Dom. Necessity being the mother of invention, I believe it's best to simply remove

Dom from the familial equation. Involves a bit of house-cleaning. Figuratively . . . and literally."

"Want me to push his head through a brick wall?" Brett said, nodding slowly as if relishing the mental image. "Or—I've got a rusty old crowbar—I could shove it up his ass."

"That's jealousy talking, Brett," Gina said. "Drop it. Besides, I have no desire to clean up your mess and you're no good to me rotting in jail."

"What, then?"

"We'll let Dom make his own mess," Gina said, toss-ing the doll from one hand to the other. Her eyes took on a faraway look, her focus somewhere beyond her bed-room. "He's distraught right now. Can't believe what he's done. Worried about Caitlin's reaction. Still wants to hurt me in a big way. And he's torn up about little Toad. Oh, yes, Dom is one big sopping mess right now. In fact, I'd say he's borderline suicidal." Gina held the Dom doll with the flat head pinched between her thumb and index fin-ger. "All he needs is a little *shove*. Oops—now I've done it!"

Brett stared at her face, as if trying to see what she was seeing. "Where is he?"

"Master bedroom. Pacing . . . now he's looking for something, bedside table, revolver—ooh, good Dom! Don't know much about guns, but that looks nasty enough to get the job done. Oh, but let's not be too hasty. That's it, note and paper. Let's record this moment for posterity. Hmm, what should we say, Dom . . . How about this, 'Todd's gone. Life has become hollow. Can't go on. Don't want to live anymore.' Oh, Dom, I know, it's trite, clichéd, hackneyed, but what the hell, inspiration is always darkest before the brain matter splats against the wall. Now let's put in some stuff about poor little Gina. 'Unhealthy fascination with my stepdaughter. Afraid I'll abuse her again. I blame myself for her mood swings.' Yada, yada, blah, blah. 'Please forgive me, dearest Caitlin.' Enough already, Dom, you're really starting to make me yak here. Let's summarize and conclude.

"Cool, he's got the barrel in his mouth! Hard to botch the assignment that way. Oh, wait . . . Shit, he forgot to load it. What an incompetent! Okay, okay, bullets in the closet, on the shelf . . . all the way in back. Got 'em! And— spilled 'em! He's a fucking klutz! Here's a tip, Dom: you only need one to puree the gray. Fine, ignore me, load every damn chamber. Now he's back at the foot of the bed, sitting down. Barrel in the mouth, pressing against the upper teeth. We'll be kissing that comforter good-bye." Gina sighed. "Come on, Dom. Second thoughts are for losers. True, you are a loser, but here's your chance to go out with a bang. Stop it! Stop crying, Dom. That's not very manly, you know." Gina sighed. "Guess you need a little more help, after all. Don't worry, it's my pleasure . . ." She crushed the cloth doll in both hands. Her eyes fluttered back in her head, exposing the whites. She began to tremble, and the network of black veins pulsed along her forearms and crawled up her neck. "All we need to do is . . . squeeeezzze . . ."

BOOOM!

Even though he should have expected the shot, Brett flinched at the sudden explosive sound. A moment later they heard a muffled thump. Softly, Brett said, "He really did it?"

"Sure did," Gina said, nodding. She patted a hand just behind the crown of her head and added, "Installed a skull skylight right about here."

"What do we do now?"

"Well, as much as I'd love to abuse his corpse . . ." Gina began. "I suppose I should call nine-one-one. You parked the truck several blocks away, as instructed, right?" Brett nodded. "Good. Lose the tape for now. Go out the back way and make yourself scarce. No need to complicate the scenario for our local law enforcement."

"What if they're suspicious? Dom killing himself so soon after Todd's death."

Awash with the afterglow of her tide of black blood, an intoxicating confidence, Gina shuddered pleasantly. "At this point, I'm almost beyond caring . . ."

Jen Hoyt writhed in sweat-soaked sheets, her limbs thrashing against the cloth, as if she were a bug snared in a web. Deep in her fevered sleep, her left hand drifted to her right forearm and scratched the inflamed wound that stretched from wrist to elbow. A narrow black scab had begun to form over the uneven incision.

BOOOM!

Jen sat upright in bed and flung the damp covers aside. A sheen of sweat coated her nude body. Her heart was pounding, her mouth dry. In her mind, she still heard the echo of a gunshot, and doubted the sound had been part of her own dreams.

For the last two nights, since her blood bonding with Gina Thorne, who sometimes referred to herself as Wither, Jen had been running a fever, around 101 degrees, had craved sleep and had dreamt of nothing but the blood ritual.

She climbed out of bed, flicked off the forty-watt desk lamp and padded over to the window, peering through the gap in the curtains, expecting to see flashing red lights, hear the wail of police sirens. Soon, she began to realize the gunshot had come to her with a sense other than hearing, a gift of the new blood, a product of her bond with Gina. A *mental telegram*, Jen thought and chuckled softly in the dark. *Telepathic E-mail . . . or should that be t-mail?*

Because she found the idea of the gunshot and the method of its transmission so amusing, Jen understood that it was a good thing, part of Gina's plan. When Jen glanced at the phone, she had a nonimpulse to call Gina, sort of a negative vibe, almost a whispered command to leave it alone for now. Gina would be in touch when it suited her.

With no thought of disobeying her mistress, Jen turned back to the streetlights and tried to remember how terrified she'd been the first time she'd found Gina Thorne waiting in her dorm room. An attractive, college-aged blond woman sitting at the foot of Jen's bed should not have been enough to weaken Jen's knees with fear. But somehow, she had known even then . . . something about the eyes looking back at her, as if they'd seen her before. Gina had said, "I haven't forgotten you, Jensen Hoyt."

"What are you talking—who are you?" Jen had stammered.

"I seem to recall we dated the same guy," Gina had said. "Well, actually, you dated him. I *ate* him." Gina had shrugged. "But I was much bigger then, with a mondo appetite."

Jen had stared in dawning horror at the smiling woman.

"Surprised you don't recognize me, considering all those less than flattering portraits you sketched. Of course, I had the whole, dark leathery hide back then. And I could fly . . . a little trick I haven't quite been able to master yet, but give me time."

A dreadful certainty had begun to fill Jen, to sap all the strength from her muscles. An image of the monster had flashed in her mind, an image she had trouble reconciling with the woman standing before her. The monster had plucked Jack Carter off the covered bridge by the abandoned textile mill last year while Jen had stood by, helpless and terrified.

The months in therapy had evaporated, giving free rein to the sense of doom that had pervaded her every waking and sleeping moment. The monster had not forgotten her. The monster had come back . . . in an attractive, seductive form, but no less evil than before.

Only this time, the monster had fed her victim . . .

Standing naked by the window, Jen shuddered at the memory of that first meeting, of Gina's blood in her mouth, oozing down her throat, creating luscious tremors in her body. That first time, Gina had sliced open her index finger, from tip to palm, instructing—commanding—Jen to suckle on the black blood that ran free and swirled off the fingernail with a life of its own. At nineteen, Jen had done little experimenting with legal or illegal substances. Wine, black Russians, and beer, a little weed on several occasions . . . none of it compared to the thrill of Gina's blood. Better than any sex Jen had ever had or could imagine having, because it was so effortless and all-consuming, like drowning in pleasure.

As sudden and powerful as that rush had been, Jen had known she was lost. Her will had caved immediately. But if her desire to resist had fled, so too had her fear of what she'd once thought of as a monster.

In their first two meetings, Jen had consumed a little bit of Gina's blood. This last time had been different and significant in another way. On the night of Wendy's party, Gina had sliced open both of their forearms with a razorlike fingernail and had pressed their flesh together, red blood to black. Gina had made a promise that night, that Jen would never be the same frightened little girl again. And the outward signs had been quick to manifest: the need for long, almost drugged sleep, the steady fever, both tortured and delicious dreams, and a craving for rare, blood-dripping meat. She could only imagine the glorious changes going on beneath the surface.

In surrendering to Gina Thorne, to the creature that called itself Wither, Jensen Hoyt had found peace at last.

Gina had already been over her story twice with Sheriff Nottingham before Mother Caitlin had rushed home from her planning-board meeting. At first Gina had been undecided about how to play her part, weepy witness to a messy family suicide or sullen victim of an abuser, still in a state of shock from the recent abuse and its unforeseen consequences. In the end, she'd gone for sullen. She could play sullen much better than weepy. Besides, Caitlin was weepy enough for both of them.

Gina sat at the kitchen table next to her mother, opposite the sheriff, with her arm looped around her mother's quaking shoulders in a daughterly show of support. In what passed for a vacant look of shock, Gina stared at the summery flower arrangement in the center of the table, the bouquet she had wilted—withered—with a parasitic touch of her hand while waiting for the damn paramedics to arrive. Sucking the life out of the fresh flowers had actually given her a giggling little buzz. *You learn something new every day,* she thought, fighting off an inappropriate smile.

Caitlin's looking a little wilted herself, Gina decided. *Pale, distraught, haggard, you name it . . . and not simply because I've been siphoning a little life juice off the top of her tank these past nine months. A big bad day in the life of Mrs. Caitlin Thorne-Gallo. Finding out her husband's killed himself the same day she finds out said husband had been abusing her firstborn. If nothing else, the fiction of abuse might help take the edge off Caitlin's grief.*

"Of course, he's been depressed since Todd died," Caitlin said to the sheriff, as she wiped away brimming tears with the knuckle of her index finger. "We all have. It was a horrible accident. I just had no idea . . ."

"That he was abusing Gina," the sheriff finished for her, grasping between steepled fingers the mug of coffee Caitlin had insisted on making for him.

Caitlin shook her head. "Gina's been so angry lately, but I just thought . . . you know, teen rebellion. I never dreamed Dom would . . ."

The sheriff directed his next question to Gina. "How long has this been going on?"

Sullen, "Since late last year."

"How often?"

"Only a couple times . . ." Gina said. "I just wanted to . . . pretend it never happened." To emphasize the tragic futility of that course of action, she let her free hand drift up to touch her swollen cheek, the angry red welt she'd received courtesy of Dom's impressive backhand. For the added credence the wound lent her story, she'd thought it best not to heal prematurely, neither had she made any attempt to repair the abrasions on her wrists, friction burns from the nylons Dom had used to bind her to the bed. "I never thought he'd shoot . . ." Gina shook her head. "I guess the guilt finally overwhelmed him."

Caitlin directed a watery, concerned gaze at her daughter and grabbed Gina's hand, squeezing it between both of hers. "Why didn't you tell me?"

"My word against his, he said. Nobody would believe me. Said he'd twist it all around so it was my fault, that I seduced him to try to ruin your marriage. That you would call me a slut, disown me, kick me out on the street."

The sheriff cleared his throat and said, "Gina, I'd like to take you to Windale General."

"Why?" Gina asked the question the same moment as her mother.

The sheriff looked back and forth between them. "Just some tests. To have you exam—"

Gina's look of shock was genuine. She had no desire to be poked and prodded by a member of the medical establishment. Fortunately, Caitlin caught the look in Gina's eyes, misinterpreted its cause, but came to her rescue. "No," Caitlin said. "I forbid it."

"Why? I just want to clear up—"

"What's the point, Sheriff?" Caitlin said, a harder edge to her voice. Gina was grateful to see some spunk left in her mother, no matter that it would never be enough to save her from Gina. "Dom's dead. Whatever he . . . did to Gina, it's over. She can't press charges. He can't be tried or punished. The only one who will get hurt here—by exposing all of this—is Gina, and God knows she's been through enough already." Caitlin took a deep breath. "Dom killed himself in grief over the loss of his son. That's all anybody needs to know. Let's leave it at that, sheriff . . . for all our sakes."

The sheriff looked down at the lukewarm mug of coffee in his hands. Gina hadn't seen him take one sip yet. He turned the mug in a slow circle once, twice, then looked up at them, his gaze settling on Gina. "Is that all right with you, Gina? Forgetting about it?"

Gina nodded. *Hell, yeah!* she thought.

"Well, there's the matter of the suicide note," the sheriff continued.

"I'll burn it."

"That would be destroying evidence, Mrs. Thorne."

"Then arrest me."

"Don't do it," the sheriff said. "We'll keep this private. I promise."

"Thank you, Sheriff."

The sheriff stood, picked his hat up from the seat next to him and walked to the door. Caitlin followed close behind him, Gina trailing her. "We're finished here. Upstairs, that is. I can send someone to come in and take care of the ... cleaning."

"I have someone who can help."

And won't Sylvia be pleased with that little chore, Gina thought.

"Anyone you can stay with?"

"Don't worry about us, Sheriff," Caitlin said. "We'll be okay."

The sheriff stopped at the front door and turned back to face them. "You should consider therapy," he said. "For Gina, I mean. She's a victim here. Keeping this private is one thing, but pretending this never happened won't do her any good. Trust me."

"I'll take care of it, Sheriff," Caitlin assured him, wrapping her arm around Gina's waist and hugging her close. "Gina's in good hands now." She shook her head, followed by another chest-heaving sigh. "We can begin to heal now. This ... nightmare is finally over."

And Gina thought, *Depends on how you define nightmare ...*

Wendy Ward's Mirror Book Entry
August 5, 2000, Moon: waxing crescent, day 5

I've gotten better at popping locks. Takes me less than a minute now. Still long by the Crone's standards, but she already has me working on deadbolts. That and my sphere conjuring, which has also improved. What's helped me most during these past couple days is Alex. Or rather, lack of Alex. He's been a busy boy, cramming for today's marketing exam.

For several reasons, I haven't told him about my suspicions that Gina Thorne is Wither reborn. First: bad timing. He's studying like crazy to make up for ground lost spring semester recuperating from the injuries Wither inflicted. Emotionally, physically, and psychically, he's still not over that last encounter. He's certainly not ready to deal with this yet. I blame myself for involving him in my magic rituals, for putting a bull's-eye on his back. I won't make the same mistake again! This is something I have to fix alone. He's better off at college, where his only worry is his next exam, maintaining his GPA . . . If I told him, he would worry about me or try to help me, and I won't let him get involved in this again. Last thing he needs are my issues ruining his life all over again.

Anyway, I've taken advantage of the solo time to cram as well. No TV or tunes for this gal. The Crone has become my personal trainer in more ways than magical. She insists I get regular exercise, sleep, and meals to keep my mind rested and focused. When I'm not manning— *womaning?* Nah, staffing—the counter at work, or putting the finishing touches on The Crystal Path's Web site, I'm practicing my magic, with time off only for jogging, cat-napping and partaking of the occasional meal. Can't argue with the results. Make that *progress* since, as the Crone says, the word *results* connotes achieved goals and I've still got a ways to go. Spoilsport, that Crone, if you ask me.

Oh, I now have a rainbow on my wrist. Well, a rainbow of polished stone beads, anyway. (Better than power beads, the Crone tells me. So does that make them *super* power beads?) More and different colors than good old Roy G. Biv, certainly, but a colorful accessory nonetheless. Best of all, it's not likely to draw too much unwanted attention.

Latest trick the Crone has me working on is creating a flame in my palm by drawing heat from the surrounding air. So far, no success. The heat-drawing doesn't freak me out so much as the "in the palm" part. Flame needs fuel, right? And I'm not in a great big hurry to roast my palm. The Crone insists paranormal flame works differently, tells me I just have a mental block on this one. I, on the other hand, insist it's my survival instinct kicking in. Guess who's right? Yeah, yeah, take her side! See if I care.

Oops, it's getting late. If I hurry, I have time for a jog and a quick shower before Alex comes over. We're gonna catch one of the late shows at the multiplex over in Peabody. He's leaning toward the new supernatural thriller, but I'm thinking romantic comedy. Guess who'll win that debate? Forgive me, but I could use a nice, relaxing Saturday evening.

• • •

A muggy August night. Wendy dressed light in a loose gray tank over a black jogging bra, gray shorts with parallel white stripes down the sides, and white socklets that barely cleared the top of her running shoes. Even so, she'd worked up a healthy sheen of sweat before she was halfway through her warm-ups. The kind of night that seemed robbed of oxygen, where the slightest exertion panicked the lungs and the deepest breath seemed no more than a shallow and futile gasp for air. *Street's practically deserted. Everyone's best friend tonight is their air conditioner.* Oh, yes, Wendy thought as she began her five-mile run, *we joggers are gluttons for punishment.*

He was watching her.

Across the street, leaning against the bus stop sign, newspaper folded under his sore left arm to hide the hunting knife, he watched her run, lean thighs flashing beneath the baggy, striped shorts. Made him think about sliding his hands under those shorts, see what she was wearing—if anything—underneath. *Most definitely,* he thought. *You'll want a piece of me, baby. I'm fire-hardened. One night with me and you'll forget all about that gimp you're dating. Just be patient, sweetness . . . I'll catch you on the flip side.*

He'd been watching her for days now. The recent heat wave had changed her routine a bit. Spending a lot of time indoors. Switched her daily run to evenings, just after sundown, when there was still a purple hint of twilight in the sky.

When she ran out of sight, his mind started to drift, but now, just as whenever his attention wandered, the unhealed burn on his forearm flared up with a fresh agony. That helped him focus on his mission. The pain reminded him of his purpose. He stopped thinking about how hot he was in his black leather jacket, even if he only wore a muscle T-shirt underneath, stopped mentally bitching about his grimy jeans chafing his thighs. *Just stay focused, man,* he told himself. All he had to do was wait for her to make her way back. She'd be near the end of her run, heart racing, lungs sucking air, and those long shapely legs quivering with exhaustion. *Time for a little slam dancing, then, baby,* he thought. *Oh, yeah.*

He was fire-hardened.

He wouldn't fail.

Wendy's legs felt like unwieldy blocks of wood dragging beneath her. After just fifty yards, her five-mile run had become brutal, and then it had gotten worse. She felt oxygen-starved the whole way and never got the kick of a second wind. At the intersection of Mage and Ash, where Spellcaster Video Rentals faced Mike's Sandwich Shop, she hadn't even bothered to touch the traffic pole for luck. *No sense timing this run,* she'd thought. *Save the record breaking for another day.*

Now all she wanted was to get the run over with and hit the shower, the cool, relaxing, refreshing shower. And so she was careless, her attention narrowing to a tunnel focused straight ahead, one plodding foot in front of the other, almost in a trance, balanced between discomfort and determination. *No runner's high tonight*, she thought. *Just pain with minimal gain. Never mind, just make that pain, pain, pain—*

Air exploded from her lungs as someone slammed into her from behind, propelling her away from the street and the security of the streetlights.

Wrapped in a bear hug, struggling for breath with her arms pinned at her sides, Wendy was forced into the darkness beyond a closed dry-cleaner's rear parking lot. A quick glance revealed a battered, one lane asphalt road running behind the row of small shops and, beyond that, a gloomy tree line separating the commercial district from the nearest housing development. Flashing in her mind was an image of a shallow grave in that anemic patch of woods, and that mental picture gave her more than enough incentive, in a quicksilver adrenaline boost, to break free of her attacker's arms. At least long enough to land a lame kick at his shins. He made a grab for her hair, which she jerked away from, but her left foot slipped into a rubble-strewn pothole, tripping her. She collapsed in an awkward jumble, palms slapping the asphalt painfully in an effort to break her fall.

A strong hand clamped in her hair and pulled her back. Using her head as a pivot point, he spun her around and threw her to the ground. The back of Wendy's head clapped against the asphalt, stunning her. Before she could shake off the fog, the man had straddled her waist and was holding a gleaming hunting knife in front of her face.

She saw now that he was small, shorter than she was,

but lean and wiry, black hair pulled back in a greasy ponytail, a crooked nose, and a thin-lipped sneer twisting his pale face. Something about him seemed vaguely familiar, as if she'd seen him in a crowd and more than once.

Wendy opened her mouth and the point of his knife jabbed under her chin. "Scream and I slice you from ear to ear."

Wendy shook her head, silently promising she wouldn't scream . . . at least not until she had nothing to lose.

"Supposed to be hot shit, aren't you," he said, voice breathless from exertion. "But you're nothing." He waved the knife in front of her face. "You're less than nothing, freak."

Wendy gulped air, all too aware that her limbs were trembling. Weak and almost too afraid to think, she desperately sought an advantage, any advantage. If he thought she could identify him, he would probably kill her for sure. *Okay, don't play that card. What, then—magic! How? If I conjure a protective sphere, we'll both be inside it. Damn, what else can I do? Pick a lock—sure, maybe he needs a partner in crime. Just—just stall him!* "I—I don't have any money."

"Don't want your money, bitch." Sneering again, "Maybe you got something else for me." He slid the back of the blade along the center of her heaving chest.

"Please . . . don't . . ." she whispered. *Think, damnit!*

"Shut up!" he said, raising a fist. "You're not the one gives me orders."

"What do—why are you doing this?"

He shrugged. "Why not?" He laughed at his own joke. "Supposed to try to kill you, but that don't seem like much of a challenge anymore. Might as well sample the wares first."

"Let me go and you have my word this never happened," Wendy promised, hoping he'd have second thoughts.

"Oh, it's gonna happen all right," he said. "Just the way I want." He leaned back and ran the point of the knife along her bare thighs. "Like flashing these legs, don't you?" Then the knife gleamed above her again, a moment before he slipped it under her top and cut it down the middle, revealing her black jogging bra. "Maybe you won't mind flashing a little more for me before we're all done."

"No . . ." Wendy said, ashamed at how faint and help-less she sounded. She tried to convince herself that everything would be different if he wasn't holding the knife against her, that she'd beat the shit out of him, claw his eyes right out of his face. And she felt herself reaching a level of desperation where that might be her only course of action.

He pressed the flat of the blade against her bare midriff, slipped the point under the bottom edge of her jogging bra and twisted the cutting edge up, tearing the cloth and exposing her breasts. "Nice tits," he said, chuckling. "Maybe I'll cut one off. Take it home as a memento."

Tears stung Wendy's eyes.

She had no hope left . . . finally nothing left to lose.

He might kill me, but I'll gouge his fucking eyes out first. No— not gouge. Burn! My mental block. Nothing left to lose. She held her palm out, open and, as far as he was concerned, harmless. A hot, muggy night. Plenty of heat to draw upon, draw to her, stoke in her hand, feeling the flame coalesce above her flesh . . .

In an astounding display of grace under pressure, Wendy concentrated her magical energies and brought a flickering tongue of flame to life above her palm in under five seconds. As miraculous as this feat seemed to her, still it seemed futile. No brighter or larger than a single candle flame, what damage could she hope to inflict with so small a fire?

Set his clothes on fire . . .

A flash of white streaked over Wendy's head, striking her attacker with a deep-throated growl and enough force to knock him off her. Her flame flickered out, and Wendy scrambled backward on elbows, butt and heels, staring at the large white dog whose jaws were latched onto the man's knife hand. *Not a dog,* she realized. *A wolf! A white wolf. Must have come out of the trees.*

Wendy climbed to her feet, her gray tank top and black jogging bra hanging in rags around her exposed chest. *Wolves are wild,* she thought. *Just dumb luck it attacked him instead of me. Better get the hell out of here before it turns on me.*

Giving them a wide berth, Wendy began to distance herself from the wolf and her attacker, hobbling along on her sore ankle, but stopped as a thought occurred to her. *I dreamed of running with a white wolf. What if it's more than dumb luck?* She glanced back at the struggling pair, circling each other. Hackles up, the wolf snarled continually, pausing only to snap a vicious set of jaws at the man's arms and legs, but looking ready to pounce on his throat at the first opening. Wendy's attacker brandished the knife in front of the wolf's face, kicked stones, and hurled curses. Each time the wolf leapt into an opening, the man thrust his leather-jacketed arm into the gaping maw and tried to stab the wolf's side with the long hunting knife. So far the wolf was quick enough to avoid the knife, but was no closer to a fatal throat hold. *Just get away*, a rational voice inside her warned. *Call the police. Let them handle this.*

Once again Wendy turned away, but had no sooner made the decision to flee when she heard the man grunt and the wolf's sharp squeal of pain. A glance back revealed the man running away, down the back street, limping, with the wolf bounding after him, relentless, yet favoring its left front paw. They looped around another building, almost a block away, and were lost to her view. A moment later she heard the man's wild yell, followed by another squeal and tormented whimpering from the wolf. Then silence.

Guessing the wolf had died in her stead, Wendy began to run toward home with long, ground-eating strides, whimpering herself each time her bum left foot struck the pavement and sent shockwaves up her inflamed ankle. The wolf had saved her, but the man might return and try to finish what he'd started.

The image of his sneering face flashed in her mind

again, but this time she remembered where she'd seen him. The last time had to have been almost two years ago. She associated his face with crowded hallways, the noisy cafeteria, packed auditorium . . . He'd been a student at Harrison High. Maybe not a stoner or a troublemaker, but definitely one of the bunch she always thought of as marking time. *Mizelli, maybe . . . ?* she thought. Regardless, she was sure she could ID him from a yearbook photo, assuming she survived the night.

Sitting on her bed wearing only a red silk bra and jean shorts, Gina rocked back and forth, fingertips pressed to her temples, concentrating on Val Misero's assault on Little Miss Wicca. Her sex-blooded soldier's mind was simple, but undisciplined. Thanks to Gina's experimental tampering, he was also more than a little psychotic. His fractured mind made him the perfect tool to test Wendy's defensive magic, but the mental mess was hard to control and hard to channel. Gina received only fleeting, infuriating images of the struggle.

"Come on, Val!" Gina whispered harshly. "I wanna see what she's got up her magical sleeve. C'mon girl, show me something. Don't fuck around, Val, you're just supposed to kill her. Hear me? Kill her. Kill her. Come on, you worthless piece of shit! You can rape her corpse *after* you slit her damn throat. You're on the clock now, moron. Do it!"

So far, Wendy seemed helpless against Misero, but he was enjoying himself too much to get the job done. Gawking at her tits, taunting her . . .

Gina sat perfectly still. "Fuck—was that a fire? How about that! Bitch just conjured fire. So, she's not a complete fraud—

A blur of white filled Misero's vision and Gina's mind. Next moment she was looking up into the hazy night sky with him, as a snarling dog—no, not a dog, a fucking wolf!—was trying to rip his throat out.

A sound intruded, but Gina ignored it.

"What the fuck—! She can summon wild animals? Val, you worthless son of a bitch! Should have killed the cunt when you had the chance." She clenched her teeth, then shouted. "You dumb bastard! I'll gut you with your own fucking knife!" *If the wolf doesn't take care of that little chore before me.*

Then she remembered the sound. Knocking.

Gina looked up, her eyes wild. *Who—?* "Sylvia?" The stout, fifty-year-old housekeeper, hair dyed an improbable rust orange and pulled into a severe bun, standing in the doorway, staring at Gina open-mouthed in shock. To Gina's irritation, the lonely old woman had practically moved in with them after Dom's suicide, taking care of Mrs. Caitlin, cooking meals, washing clothes, running errands, managing the funeral arrangements, and, no doubt, well on her way to earning a big fat bonus. "It's okay, Sylvia," Gina said, smiling as she hopped off the bed.

"Sorry," Sylvia said, backing away and shaking her head, suspicious, frightened. "So, sorry. Just—Mrs. Caitlin wondered if you would be joining us for tea. I'll tell her—tell her you're busy, Miss Gina."

"Sylvia, there's a perfectly good explanation," Gina called, following the woman out into the hall. "I was practicing—auditioning for a part in a play."

Sylvia gave her a distrustful look. "It's summer, Miss Gina. No school."

"What? You've never heard of community theater?"

"What is the name of this . . . filthy play where you curse so much?"

Gina shrugged. "Oh, I don't know, Sylvia. It's . . . experimental theater. The working title is *Wither's Revenge*." *Shit, the woman's crossing herself. Probably thinks I'm possessed . . . which is not that far off.* Gina sighed. Sylvia was already hurrying down the stairs. *Great, now I have to kill the housekeeper.*

Gina stood at the top of the stairs, and made a mental *call* while she listened to the hubbub below. Sylvia yelling at Caitlin, "I can't work in this house no more." Caitlin asking over and over again what was wrong until Sylvia screamed some nonsense about a devil child and exorcisms, grabbed her coat from the hall closet and headed for the front door. Brett hadn't been far away. Gina walked down to the landing just as Sylvia pulled open the door and saw Brett standing in the doorway with a cold smile on his face and his rusty old crowbar clutched in both hands.

Brett stepped into the foyer, backing up the terrified housekeeper far enough for him to close the door. "Hi, Sylvia," he said pleasantly. Then a blur of motion as he shoved the steel bar right through her flabby neck, shattering her spine.

Sylvia slumped to the floor, probably dead before her rolls of fat stopped jiggling. Brett pressed the heel of a work boot to her collarbone and tugged the rod free. A *nice silent kill, at least,* Gina thought, pleased.

Then Caitlin screamed.

All the way home, Wendy debated stopping to pound on the door of one of her neighbors, any of her neighbors, but three factors postponed her decision until it was moot. Having worked the stiffness out of her twisted ankle, she was able to increase her pace to a brisk, if painful jog, during which she noticed no signs of pursuit, by the wolf or her knife-wielding assailant. Finally, the mortifying thought of one of her neighbors seeing her practically topless convinced her to go a little farther, just a little bit farther, until she saw her cottage at the end of the cul-de-sac and that settled the matter. She succumbed to the intense desire to be home, sheltered and safe in familiar surroundings.

Sensing movement in the darkness near her front door, Wendy froze midstride. "Who's there?" For a moment, she thought it might be Alex, clowning around, trying to scare her on the worst possible night of her life. But the figure was too small, huddled over, whimpering and . . . naked. Wendy took another step closer, into the shadows, letting her eyes adjust. A young, towheaded girl. "Abby . . . ?"

The girl leapt to her, wrapping her arms around Wendy, her body wracked with sobs. "Wendy . . . I'm so glad . . . I made it in time."

"My God, you're bleeding!"

Abby's mouth, neck, and left arm were smeared with blood. Fresh blood was running down her left side, staining her hip and thigh. "Let's get you inside and call an ambulance."

With all of Abby's weight leaning against her, Wendy fumbled with her keys for a moment before turning the deadbolt and unlatching the lock. *Still quicker than I could have popped it with my magic*, she observed with painful irony.

She helped Abby into the kitchen, sat her on one of the folding chairs, made sure she was secure there, then hurried down the hall to the linen closet for a spare blanket. When she returned to the kitchen, Abby was shivering—*probably going into shock*—and, beneath her chair, there was a spreading pool of blood on the tile floor.

As Wendy wrapped the blanket around the young girl's shoulders, Abby started to swoon. Wendy caught her under her arms and laid her gently on the floor and wrapped her in the blanket to keep her warm. The young girl was trying to speak, her lips pale and waxy, forcing Wendy to lean close. ". . . stop bleeding . . . my side—" was all Abby managed before a sharp gasp stiffened her body.

Have to call nine-one-one, Wendy thought and started to rise.

Abby's right hand caught Wendy's wrist. ". . . no time . . . *you* stop it . . . for me . . ."

"What?"

"We save . . . each other . . ."

She's delirious, Wendy thought, rising. *Grab the damn phone already!*

"*She's right, Wendy.*"

The sudden voice in Wendy's mind almost made her jump out of her skin—for the second time that night. The Crone was standing behind her. "What are you talking about? She needs medical help now!"

"*Yes, she does. But the paramedics won't arrive in time. You must save her.*"

"I don't know what—how can I help her?"

"*The rose quartz bead on your new bracelet,*" the Crone said. "*A focus for healing magic.*"

Wendy was near panic and that wouldn't do any of them any good. "But how? Tell me how!"

"*First, stop the bleeding.*"

Wendy nodded and took a deep cleansing breath. Pulling off the bracelet, she gripped the rose quartz bead between her left thumb and index finger. Then she peeled back the blood-soaked flap of blanket covering the wound in Abby's side, gasping when she saw the steady flow of crimson pulsing out of Abby's pale flesh. Wendy cursed herself for never having taken a first-aid class and made a silent promise to remedy that oversight as soon as possible. All she could remember was to compress a wound, slow the bleeding and give the body time and opportunity for the blood to clot. Somehow she knew that wouldn't be enough here. The Crone was convinced healing magic would save Abby and the Crone had a whole different time perspective. Wendy had to trust that.

She pressed her right hand, her projective hand, against the wound, hot and slippery with fresh blood, while rolling the rose quartz bead in the fingers of her receptive left hand, drawing upon the energy she would need to heal the young girl. She imagined the energy, raw and shapeless but infinitely malleable, flowing into her, charging her like a battery. Through the power of her focus and the specificity of her visualization, Wendy could channel that raw power into anything she needed. And now what she needed was to heal Abby.

Eyes closed, Wendy began to sway to the rhythms of Abby's weakening circulatory system, her slowing pulse, attuning herself to the girl's body as it attempted and failed to heal itself. The light of her vitality dimming as she fought a losing battle second by second. But the healing knowledge was there within Abby, down to the molecules of her body. What the body lacked was time and energy. Wendy couldn't circumvent the implacable march of time, but she could add her energy to the cause.

"Wendy. She's dying. You must hurry!"

Wendy visualized herself drawing vast flows of energy into her body, up through her receptive hand, letting it build within her, a pulsing sphere of golden power waiting to be shaped and released, holding it inside as long as possible, until she imagined her skin must be glowing with her effort to contain it. Gooseflesh raced along her arms and legs, but she waited, focusing on her projective hand, pressed now against Abby's body, directing the energy, now healing energy, along that arm, and finally releasing it with a shuddering rush—

—into Abby's wound, employing the girl's own racing blood as a conductor.

Abby sucked in a great gulp of air, her back arching, rising off the tile floor. Her arms and legs went rigid, trembling with the vast influx of energy. Her body seemed to flare with golden light. As Wendy watched, fascinated, the periphery of her own vision became dim and gray, while the room began to tilt at a funhouse angle...

... just before everything went black.

Caitlin Thorne was brain damaged beyond repair.

Gina just had to accept that.

As incestuous as it had sometimes seemed, or maybe even because of the sheer perversity of it, Gina had toyed with the idea of seducing her own mother into her coven. Now that was simply impossible. A large portion of Caitlin's brain was about as cognitively effective as warm bread dough. *So, back to Plan B,* she thought.

Brett and Gina shared equal responsibility for the fuckup. When Caitlin rushed for the phone, Brett had swung the crowbar like a baseball bat, catching Caitlin across the back of the skull before Gina could call him off or still his hand. *Water under the bridge at this point,* she thought. Gina's power had been sufficient to close the wound and revive Caitlin but not much more. Her power was intrinsically destructive and the type of crude healing she'd performed on Brett's busted hand just wasn't good enough to put a brain back in working order. *Well, at least this way, Zombie Caitlin won't be much of a bother. Can't seem to stop drooling but, on the plus side, she's quiet and obeys simple instructions.*

"Caitlin, you're distracting me," Gina said. "Wait in the kitchen." Without even a nod, her mother turned and plodded down the hall, making the turn into the kitchen after bumping into the archway. Gina shook her head in disgust.

"What now?" Brett asked, the bloody crowbar dangling from his right hand.

"I've lost my connection to Misero."

"She killed him?"

"Nothing of the sort," she said. "Well, the fool may be dead, but she wasn't responsible." Gina sighed. *A wolf of all things?* "If he hadn't stopped to mix his pleasure with my business, the meddling bitch would be dead now, and I'd be moving on to bigger and better things. Should have castrated him when I had the chance. But . . . his little wrestling match proved one thing, if nothing else. I have been overestimating the prissy little Wicca all along. She may have potential, but her magic is too raw and weak to matter."

"You're gonna kill her now?"

"She almost killed *me* once," Gina said. "So don't worry, I will put her out of my misery and soon. But now that I know how helpless she truly is, I want one more taste of sweet revenge out of this. Before I kill the little bitch, I will make her suffer."

PART THREE:

COVEN

CHAPTER TEN

The ground had crumbled beneath her and she was falling into unending darkness, falling for the longest time until . . .

. . . a male voice spoke. "Wendy . . . Wendy, wake up."

Feeling weak as a kitten, Wendy opened her eyes and tried to shake off the lethargy, but succeeded only in making her temples throb. Her head felt as if it were being squashed in a vice. *Where am I?* she thought, trying to sit up. *The cottage . . . on the living room floor.* A fresh blanket fell away from her as she tried to rise. A slight draft reminded her that her tank top and bra were a slashed peepshow underneath. With a deft grab, she pulled the blanket up to her throat and tried to talk. "What happ—?" She coughed. Her mouth was dry as cotton.

Sheriff Nottingham was kneeling on her left side, while Abby was on her right, now wrapped in a ratty beach towel, a few specks of dried blood dappled her pink, scrubbed cheeks. *How long have I been out?* The sheriff offered Wendy a glass of water. She nodded her thanks and gulped down half the glass before coming up for air. "Abby? You're okay?"

Abby smiled and gave her a big nod.

I did it, Wendy thought. *I healed her. Thank God—and the Goddess—I healed her!*

"Once you're finished with the water, there's a can of chicken noodle soup simmering on the stove."

"Soup?"

After a quick glance at Abby, the sheriff nodded. "Abby tells me you need soup."

Wendy looked at Abby. "I do?" Again Abby nodded, her smile more secretive this time. *She's talked to the Crone!*

Sparing a quick glance at the pool of congealing blood on the kitchen floor, the sheriff added, "She also tells me you saved her life."

No point denying it. But not quite sure how to explain what had happened, Wendy just nodded.

The sheriff frowned. "After the soup, I expect you— *both of you*—to tell me exactly what the hell is going on."

I wish I knew, Wendy thought. "Right . . . but first, I need a shower."

"Can it wait?" the sheriff said. "I need to explain the dead body outside, a body with its throat torn out. According to Abby, you're both involved."

"I—he's dead, then . . ."

"Head's barely attached," the sheriff said. "Qualifies as dead in my book."

"He—he attacked me"—*was about to rape me*—"and would've killed me if the—the white wolf hadn't . . ." Wendy glanced at Abby, at the girl's fine, almost white hair . . . Abby had suffered what appeared to be stab wounds, in her side and her left arm . . . and the wolf had favored its left front paw as it pursued Wendy's attacker. *My party,* Wendy recalled. *When she hugged me, I thought she growled* . . . As her mind tried to close the fantastic gap in her speculation, Wendy's eyebrows rose, staring an unformed question at Abby, who shook her head just enough to still Wendy's tongue without drawing the sheriff's attention to the silencing gesture.

"Ten minutes, sheriff," Wendy said. "Give me ten minutes to freshen up. Then I'll explain . . . whatever I can."

The sheriff looked to the blanket Wendy was clutching to her chest, cleared his throat and said, "Wendy, if he . . . if Misero attacked you, there might be evidence on your person—"

"Dirt, sheriff," Wendy said abruptly. "Dirt is the only evidence on my person . . . aside from some scrapes and bruises, and a slashed up jogging outfit, and you're welcome to the scraps after I change. So the answer to your question is, no he didn't rape me."

The sheriff met her gaze for a long moment, then nodded. "Fine. Take your shower. Then I want some answers."

"Fair enough," Wendy said, climbing to her feet slowly. Her legs were trembling and she half expected the room to start spinning again.

As she walked down the hall to the bathroom with mincing steps, Wendy heard the sheriff say to Abby, "I brought fresh clothes for you. In that duffel bag by the door. Why don't you get dressed while we're waiting for Wendy?"

Wendy expected her left ankle to be stiff and sore, but it was flexible and pain-free. And her palms—she'd scraped them on the street when she fell—were healed. As she closed the bathroom door, she explored the back of her head, where it had struck the asphalt, searching for the lump, the tender spot that must be there . . . but wasn't. Sagging against the door, Wendy closed her eyes and released a long sigh. "I healed Abby . . . but who healed me?"

"*So much healing energy flowed through you into Abby that it repaired your injuries along the way.*"

Wendy's eyes fluttered open. The Crone was standing, rather floating, in the bathtub. "Wasn't really expecting an answer," Wendy said, "but thanks. I'm glad you're back. Now maybe you can tell me why I passed out."

"*When you channeled the energy into Abby, you poured more into her than was strictly necessary.*"

"I emptied some of my own . . . personal energy into her?"

"*Not enough to permanently harm you . . .*"

Wendy rolled up the blanket and tossed it on the floor near the sink, then shrugged out of her torn top and bra, dropping them on the closed toilet seat lid. "Just enough to turn out my lights?"

The Crone nodded. *"Remember to eat your soup. And a sports drink might be called for, if you have one."*

Wendy kicked off her running shoes, peeled off her socklets. "Ah, the soup," she said as she skimmed off her jogging shorts and panties and tossed them toward the wicker hamper. "Let's use this time productively and have a little impromptu debriefing." Wendy waved the Crone out of the bathtub. "Switch places with me."

The Crone drifted sideways out of the tub, her lower legs passing ghostlike through the porcelain. Wendy turned on the spigot and adjusted the flow to just short of scalding before stepping in and pulling the curtain closed.

As Wendy lathered her hair, she said, "You can speak to Abby."

"While she's in your presence."

"Bring me up to date," Wendy said, scrubbing her face with liquid soap and a washcloth. "What happened after I took a nosedive?"

"Abby's wounds were healed. She tried to wake you. I'm afraid I might have . . . startled her, making my presence felt. But she acted almost as if she expected me to contact her. I told her to call for help. She called her adoptive father, the sheriff." Apparently Abby had given Sheriff Nottingham very specific instructions, telling him she and Wendy needed help at Wendy's house, to

bring Abby a change of clothes and that there was a dead man lying in the street about a half mile from the cottage, a man who had tried to kill both of them.

"That's not right," Wendy said, rinsing off the accumulation of lather. "This Misero creep tried to kill me and the wolf—the wolf saved me and . . ." Wendy blinked at the water coursing over her face. "Are Abby and the white wolf one and the same?"

"Yes, I believe they are the same . . . entity."

"So Abby's some kind of werewolf? But, wait—she almost died from stab wounds. I thought you need silver bullets to kill a werewolf."

"What can I tell you? Her entire skeletal structure was altered by one of the Windale witches. Somehow that experience has given her the ability to shape-shift into a wolf, but she hasn't been bitten, as far as we know, by an actual werewolf."

"Oh," Wendy said, not at all sure she understood the distinction. "So she just becomes a regular wolf, no special powers or immunities?" Not even a full moon tonight. Still . . . If it walks like a duck and quacks like a duck . . . Wendy turned off the water, pulled a fresh towel off the rack and began patting herself dry. "You're from the future and you didn't know about this? About Abby?"

"I'm from a future . . . I suspected something like this . . . but I haven't known Abby MacNeil in many, many years. Obviously, this shape-shifting ability is something she wished kept secret."

"If you didn't know and I know now, then you can't be me," Wendy said, stepping out of the tub. She wrapped the towel around her, tucking the flap in next to her left arm to keep it from falling while she ran a brush through her hair. She shrugged. "I had this idea, in the back of my mind that somehow, you might be a future version of me."

"*Eye color alone should have convinced you of that,*" the Crone said, smiling. "*Yours are green, mine blue.*"

"I suppose . . . Still, it sort of made sense." Wendy pointed at the wall. "Take the shortcut and meet me in my bedroom." A few quick strides covered the distance to her bedroom, but her legs felt wobbly and weak. Wendy slipped inside and closed the door, ignoring the urge to sit down and rest. The Crone emerged from the wall and floated before her.

Wendy pulled a fresh set of clothes out of her dresser, tossing the items over her shoulder, on the bed: gray bra and panties, hunter green cropped fleece pullover with a V-neck, black jeans, and fresh, gray socks. "Forgot to tell you. I overcame my mental block, when Misero attacked me," Wendy said. "Conjured fire. Without a focus, no less."

"*I know, now,*" the Crone said, sadness in her tone, "*Certain memories of past . . . events only become clear to me here after they have happened in your timeframe. There is a . . . persistence to the timeline, that resists attempts at alteration. While I knew fire conjuring was important, I could not remember why or even when.*"

"Well, that little flame amounted to no more than a neat parlor trick," Wendy said bitterly. "What good is any of this? Your foreknowledge, all my magic training? One deranged guy with a knife and none of it mattered. There was nothing I could do to stop him from killing me . . ."

Wendy realized her body was shaking and she pressed her hand to her mouth to cover a sob.

"*If none of it really mattered, Wendy, both you and Abby would be dead right now.*"

"She knew," Wendy said, remembering Abby's premonition, or whatever it had been. "Abby knew he was going to attack me."

"*We have been changed by past events, Wendy, although maybe you least of all. You have always had this destiny.*"

And maybe it's time to stop feeling sorry for myself, Wendy thought, slipping into her clothes in record time. "For whatever reason, it seems certain events are just meant to happen . . . which reminds me, Alex and I had a date tonight. How long was I out cold?"

"*Nearly an hour.*"

Wendy frowned. "He should be here by now." She picked up the bedside phone and called his dorm, hanging up after ten rings. "He's left," she said. "Probably running late." With a sigh, she finger-combed her wet hair, casting one last look at the Crone before she left the privacy of her bedroom. *So many unanswered questions. And I promised Sheriff Nottingham answers.*

Alex had just finished shaving, was slapping aftershave on his cheeks when the telephone rang. *Gotta be Wendy,* he thought. *Wondering why I'm late. So how do I explain to my young, nubile Wicca princess that I was so incredibly psyched for our big Saturday evening date that I dozed off mere hours beforehand? All night cramming for that marketing exam and one major sleep debt. Oh, yeah, she'll understand. No problem.*

Grabbing his dragon-head cane from where it leaned against the sink, he hurried to the telephone and scooped up the receiver on the third ring. He decided his best course of action was to lead off with the apology. "Hi, Wendy! Look, I'm really sorry about—"

All trace of animation drained from his features. His eyes became slightly unfocused and his jaw sagged a bit. "Yes, I know who this is," he said, his voice emotionless. He listened for a while. "Yes, I understand completely . . ."

He dropped the receiver onto the cradle, made his way to the student desk, scribbled a note on a sheet of looseleaf paper and taped it to the computer monitor. Taking his cane and nothing else, he left the dorm room without switching off the lights and closed the door without bothering to engage the lock. As he made his way down the hall, he could hear his telephone ring again, but never considered returning to answer it. After ten rings, it fell silent, and Alex had already stepped out into the night.

"I want to believe what you're telling me, Wendy," the sheriff said, "but your story is full of holes. You went jogging, this creep Misero sneaked up on you, attacked you and would have killed you if this mysterious white wolf hadn't decided to tear his throat out. Is that about it?"

Casting a furtive glance at Abby, Wendy nodded. "You said yourself, his throat was torn out by an animal." She finished the last spoonful of soup and pushed the bowl aside. Had to admit she felt better after some hot nourishment, but she still felt as if she had newborn fawn legs. Not injured . . . just weak and drained.

"Coroner's preliminary guess is a big dog or, yes, a wolf."

"So why don't you believe me."

"Oh, I believe that, but what about the rest of it? How exactly did you save Abby's life?"

"I stopped her bleeding," Wendy said, pointing at the congealing mess on the kitchen floor, beneath a spread of ratty old towels. "She was severely injured," Wendy continued, then sighed. *He's right. Too many holes.*

"Maybe you haven't noticed, but Abby doesn't have a scratch on her. How she ended up miles from home, naked on your doorstep is a whole other problem."

And Wendy realized they would have to tell him the truth. *But how much?* "She *was* injured. Until I healed her . . . with magic."

"Magic?"

"Sheriff, you were there last year. You saw those monsters, saw what they could do, what they were capable of."

Sheriff Nottingham scrubbed his face with his hands. When he spoke again, his voice was softer, tired, "I've tried like hell to forget that night."

"You think I haven't?"

"Just tell me how Abby is involved in this? For God's sake, she's only nine years old."

"Abby should be the one to tell you."

Abby's eyes became big and round. "No!"

"Abby, he deserves to know the truth."

She shook her head vigorously and wailed, "I can't—I won't! Don't make me . . . please don't make me." Tears ran down her cheeks. "He'll hate me. I know he'll hate me. They all will."

Alarmed, the sheriff looked at her and clasped her hands in his, "Abby, I won't hate you, no matter what."

"You will, I know you will. You say you won't, but you can't understand. Nobody could . . ."

"Abby, it's not your fault," Wendy said. "Sarah Hutchins is to blame, not you. You've made the best you could out of it. Listen, Abby, you saved my life tonight. Don't you know how grateful I am?"

"Sarah Hutchins," the sheriff said, looking at Wendy. "Abby's bones . . . this has something to do with her bones, doesn't it."

Abby sat with her head down, chin against her chest. Her voice was a whisper, barely audible. "They change," she said. "My bones change . . ."

"What are you saying?" the sheriff asked her.

"I can't stop it . . . all I can do is let it happen. That's the only way I can control it."

The sheriff looked to Wendy, "Do you understand?"

But Abby answered, admitting the truth at last, "I was the wolf. I mean, sometimes the wolf replaces me, and other times I replace the wolf."

Wendy added, "Because of how Sarah Hutchins altered Abby's bones last year, Abby has become a shape-shifter."

Abby looked at the sheriff, her eyes red-rimmed but defiant, daring him to call her a liar . . . or maybe daring him not to look away in disgust. "It's true. That's why I had you bring me here for Wendy's party, so that I—so the wolf—could learn Wendy's scent, so that it could track her and save her life."

Wendy's turn to ask a question. "How could you know?"

Abby shrugged. "Just a feeling," she said. "The wolf has different . . . instincts. Is that the right word?" Wendy nodded. "Different from other wolves, even. Because of what I've become, the wolf knew *she* was responsible for this."

"Who?" the sheriff asked. "Who's responsible?"

"The evil one."

The matter-of-fact quality of Abby's statement chilled Wendy to the bone. She hugged herself and said to the sheriff, "She means Wither."

"Wither's dead, Wendy. No matter what kind of monster she was, you killed her."

"That's what I thought," Wendy said. "But somehow she survived. Or rather, her blood survived. And that was enough. Still, that doesn't explain why Misero attacked me." *Unless she'd been using Misero as an attack dog. But why?*

Wendy recalled Misero's words, *"Supposed to be hot shit, aren't you? But you're nothing. You're less than nothing, freak."*

"He said something," Wendy told them. "Something I thought odd at the time. He said, 'You're not the one gives me orders.' Not, 'You don't give me orders.' Or, 'You're in no position to give me orders.' He specifically said, 'You're not the one gives me orders.'"

The sheriff reached the obvious conclusion. "Meaning somebody else *was* giving him orders. Orders to kill you. But why? Revenge?"

"More than that."

Abby nodded. "She was testing you. To see how powerful you are."

"You'd think she'd remember," Wendy said, then recalled an idea she'd had earlier, a bit of magical intuition. "But she *doesn't* remember. That's it . . . she knows I almost killed her but not how. She's been circling me like a shark, cautious, waiting to see if I might somehow be dangerous before she comes in for the kill." Wendy took a deep breath. "If that was her test tonight, I'm afraid I failed with flying colors."

"If she thinks you're helpless, what's to stop her from . . ."

Wendy nodded grimly. "Open season on Wiccas. At least this Wicca."

"Best defense is a good offense. I say we take the battle to her . . . assuming we can find her. With that old barn burned to the ground, where's a nine-foot-tall, leathery skinned monster likely to be hiding?"

Wendy shook her head. "Her black blood has corrupted a human," Wendy said. "Wither's in human form now. She's returned to the first stage of her three-hundred-year growth cycle."

"Human? Well, that's better—for us, I mean. Right?"

"Not necessarily," Wendy said. "I have a bad feeling that as the witches became more monstrous, more physically imposing, they lost most of their magical abilities, simply through atrophy. They survived through brute strength alone. The ability to fly was the last of their active magic and even that served only to increase their physical threat."

"Meaning, the human-sized witch probably has more and nastier tricks up her sleeve than the super-sized, monster witch."

"In a nutshell."

"Don't suppose you know who this human is."

"Actually, I do—"

Knuckles rapped on the door.

Hanging on Wendy's every word, the sheriff was startled by the sudden knocking at the door. Made him feel a bit unprofessional, like a kid spooked by ghost stories around a campfire. But he thought he covered his reaction well.

"That's probably Alex," Wendy said.

"Even so, maybe I should get it," the sheriff said, rising from his chair, his hand falling to the .357 Magnum holstered on his hip. "If you don't mind."

Wendy shrugged. "Sure. Just don't shoot my boyfriend."

But it was Jeff Schaeffer, the sheriff's senior deputy, at the door, not Alex Dunkirk. Too polite to invite himself in, Schaeffer stood at the doorway. Nor was the sheriff about to invite him to the bizarre party of paranormal revelations Wendy was hosting. "What is it, Jeff?"

"Just wanted to let you know everyone is finished at the crime scene." Schaeffer nodded toward the kitchen. "They witnesses?"

The sheriff glanced over his shoulder and frowned. "Something like that."

"Abby too?"

"That's what I'm trying to figure out."

"You want I should call the animal control people, sheriff?"

"I'll take care of that," the sheriff said quickly, since Abby was apparently the animal they would try to *control.* "Hank report in yet?" Jeff nodded. "Good. Then why don't you call it a night, Jeff. Paperwork can wait till morning." Jeff smiled, thanked him and left.

The sheriff closed the door and walked back to the kitchen, trying to piece together everything he'd heard. To a rational man, none of it made any kind of sense at all. But that rational man hadn't stared into the evil eyes of a nine-foot-tall creature that could fly and feasted on human flesh. As the presiding sheriff of Windale, ancestral home of the Windale witches, Bill Nottingham had to take a lot on faith. Still . . .

He sat down at the card table and took Abby's left hand in his, "Abby, does this . . . changing hurt you in any way."

"Not since I stopped fighting it."

"Could you . . . ?"

"Show you?"

"It's not that I don't believe you," he said, sounding as if he thought she was telling some mighty big whoppers. "It's just . . . sometimes . . ."

Wendy flashed a wry grin. "One demonstration is worth a written deposition?"

"Sometimes the human mind refuses to . . . wrap itself around an idea." He shook his head, not sure what he wanted to say. "This would really help me."

"Promise you won't hate me?"

"Of course," he assured her, bringing her head against his chest. "I love you, Abby. Like a daughter. You *are* my daughter now."

She pulled away, and looked down at her hand still in his. "Don't touch me," she said.

"Abby . . . ?"

"I mean, don't touch me while I'm changing," she said, looking embarrassed. "I think it might be gross."

He nodded, releasing her hand. She was staring at it, so he followed her gaze. Even Wendy leaned forward and the sheriff realized Wendy had yet to witness Abby's transformation. Yet she had no trouble believing it. Points for her. The sheriff returned his attention to Abby's left hand and, for a moment, he thought his eyes had begun to water, distorting his vision. Abby's wrist and the back of her hand blurred before him. First the hand narrowed, then, as the fingers shortened, becoming stubby, the fine down on her arm thickened and spread across her skin, a wave of white fur flowing down to the . . . paw—a paw, because she no longer had a hand at the end of her forearm. "Sweet Jesus," he whispered.

Abby gave a mortified cry and yanked her hand—her paw—under the table, tears brimming in her eyes. "You think I'm a freak!"

"I—no, Abby, it's just—that's, that's . . . remarkable," the sheriff said, his heart racing, mouth suddenly dry. *Have to reassure her. God, how must my face look? She probably thinks I see her as a monster.* Without thinking about it, he reached under the table and grabbed her paw before she could pull away, but she was already changing back, her fingers flowing outward, elongating in his palm.

"Incredible," Wendy whispered from her side of the table, a look of awe on her face. "Abby, that is so awesome!"

Abby smiled, forgetting for the moment that he'd been holding her paw when it reverted to a human hand. "I was scared the first couple times," she admitted.

"I bet you were," Wendy said. "Would've scared anyone."

"But now it just feels like . . . being free."

Thank you, Wendy, the sheriff thought. Thank you for being the type of person who can immediately see the beauty in Abby's affliction. And maybe that's my problem. I have a hard time seeing this as a gift . . . He took a deep breath. "Okay, so there's no denying Abby was—is this white wolf that saved you, Wendy. But her other self, the wolf self, killed a man."

"In self-defense," Wendy said. "Misero was trying to kill me. And her."

The sheriff shook his head. "Look at you two," he said. "Fresh scrubbed, rosy cheeks. Like an ad for a health spa. How will we convince anyone you were both in a fight for your lives . . ." The sheriff's voice abandoned him, replaced by a huge lump in his throat. He leaned across the table and gave Abby the biggest bear hug he could manage without cracking a few of her ribs.

Startled, Abby was giggling, "What—what did I do?"

He stared at her, tears in his eyes. "My God," he said, his voice hushed. "It's just—I've been so caught up in this incredible story, and it just hit me . . . if you were that wolf, then all that blood on the floor . . . that creep stabbed you! And you would have died if not for Wendy . . ." He looped an arm around Wendy's shoulders, pulling her into his embrace, resting his chin on her head. "Thank you, for whatever you did—however you did what you—well, you know what I mean."

Wendy patted him on the back before slipping from his grasp. "I've come to find out Abby and I are a team."

The sheriff sat back in his chair. "Wait a minute," he said to Wendy. "The witch in human form. You never told me who you think Wither is."

"I believe the entity that corrupted the body of Elizabeth Wither three hundred years ago now lives again inside Gina Thorne."

"Gina Thorne?" the sheriff asked, picturing the strawberry blond teenager and trying to reconcile the image with the monster witch he'd seen in Matthias Stone's barn last Halloween. Technically, that fearsome creature had once been human, too, Sarah Hutchins, still . . . "Gina Thorne's a seventeen, maybe eighteen-year-old girl."

"Abby was only eight when Sarah picked her," Wendy said. "Hannah hadn't even been born yet. The only prerequisite for demon-witch hosting seems to be two X chromosomes."

"Ohhh, shit!" the sheriff whispered, his voice harsh. "Forgive my language, Abby."

"What?" Wendy asked. "What is it?"

"A few days ago, Gina Thorne's stepfather, Dominick Gallo, killed himself," the sheriff said, reviewing the open-and-shut suicide case in his mind. "And last month, Todd Gallo, Gina's stepbrother, was struck and killed by a speeding truck, right outside the Gallo residence."

Wendy looked ashen. "Was Gina a suspect in either case?"

The sheriff shook his head. "No. How could she be? She was inside the house when Todd was hit. And Dominick Gallo was depressed and there was evidence he—he left a suicide note. Handwriting matched. His were the only prints on the gun, and he had gunpowder residue on his hands. No doubt he fired that gun."

Wendy was shaking her head. "She's responsible. I know it."

"How can you know that?"

"It's too big of a coincidence," Wendy said, her voice unsteady. "Either they found out what she was or they got in her way. This is all my fault."

"What's your fault? Wendy, you haven't done anything."

"Exactly!" Wendy yelled, losing her composure. "I didn't do *anything*."

"Then why blame—"

"Because, I've suspected Gina Thorne was Wither reborn for a while now and I never . . ." She wiped a tear away with the back of her hand. "Don't you see? I've been acting as if it's her versus me in some sort of magical . . . vacuum. But if I had done something, anything, Todd and Dominick Gallo might still be alive."

The sheriff laid a hand on her shoulder. "More likely, you would be dead right alongside them."

Wendy looked at him, bit her lip as if fighting off a sob and shook her head, but not as vigorously this time. The sheriff thought, *Maybe she's remembering how defenseless she'd been, how ineffectual her magic had been, against Val Misero, a mere mortal.* "I should have done something . . ."

"The question is, what do we do now?"

"Destroy her," Abby said.

The sheriff put his hands up, palms out in a braking gesture. "We'll get to that. First, we need a plan of action."

Taking control of her emotions again, Wendy said, "If she killed Todd and her stepfather—and I'm sure she's somehow responsible—she's covering her tracks well."

"First problem: if she's human, even if she only appears human, the law is on her side. There's not a shred of evidence against her in any of these crimes. Not even Misero's attack on you, Wendy. You can't make the legal connection between them. And since he's dead, he can't testify against her. All Abby had is a *feeling* that Gina—that Wither—was orchestrating the attack, and we certainly can't have Abby morph into a wolf on the witness stand, even if that would help us prove anything."

Wendy said, "So we expose her first, then destroy her."

"No way in hell I could get a judge to issue a search warrant, even if I thought it would turn up any evidence and I'm not sure it would. But I can watch the house, maybe get myself invited in by the mother."

Abby grabbed his forearm on the table. "No. You can't stop her."

"Don't worry about me, Abby," he said. "I can take care of myself."

"Don't count on it," Wendy said. "Not where Gina is concerned."

The sheriff looked at Wendy, "Please don't tell me she's immune to bullets."

Wendy pursed her lips. "I crushed her under tons of rock and torched the corpse and all that did was make her very unhappy." Wendy shook her head. "You could probably slow her down with bullets—if they actually make contact—but fire is the only sure way. My mistake was taking too long to start the fire. Her blood escaped the trapped corpse."

"You've made your point," the sheriff said grimly. "Do you have any idea how powerful she might be? Her magic?"

Wendy shook her head. "Only that it's much stronger than mine."

"All we know for certain is she'll come after you," the sheriff said. "If this were a much simpler time, I might get away with putting a bullet between her eyes and cremating the body. Thing is, I do that now, I'm looking at life with no parole up at Gander Hill. So this is the plan, ladies."

The sheriff's plan sucks, Wendy thought as she parked the Civic in the lot behind Schongauer Hall. *Sucks big time.*

Before leaving the safety of her locked car, she searched through her clutch purse for the spare set of keys Alex had given her. He'd looped them through a large paperclip, where a bright, fluffy key fob would have jumped out at her. Keys in hand, she climbed out of the

Civic and locked the doors behind her. With a quick glance around the deserted lot, she hurried to the back entrance of the dorm and slipped inside.

As she climbed the stairs, she began talking to herself. "Expects me to sit in the cottage until he can pin something on Gina. What he really means is, he'll try to find some legal excuse to take her out, preferably with a lot of unbiased witnesses around to say he acted in self-defense. Meanwhile, I'm a sitting duck in my own home."

Ten minutes after the sheriff left to drive Abby home, Wendy made up her mind to take off. Specifically, to drive over to Schongauer Hall and find out what had happened to Alex. He still hadn't answered his dorm room telephone.

Oh, sure, the sheriff promises his deputies will make regular patrol car sweeps of my street, for all the good that will do against Gina—Wither!—whatever the hell she is.

Wendy was about to knock on Alex's door, then paused, her knuckles poised beside the dry-erase message board. *Maybe he's sleeping or sick.* Compromise: she knocked softly. "Alex?" she called. "Alex, you in there? Think maybe you forgot something?" *Namely, me.*

So who am I really mad at? The sheriff . . . or Alex?

Admittedly, Wendy agreed with the sheriff on one count, keeping Abby out of harm's way. True, she had saved Wendy's life, but she had almost died herself. While she was much stronger as her wolf-self than as her girl-self, the wolf offered her no special protection against magic or knives. *Yes, the sheriff was right about Abby. No sense tempting fate a second time.*

Wendy decided to wait another moment or two before breaking and entering. *Technically, is it breaking and entering if you have a key? Or just entering . . . which doesn't sound all that bad.* "Time's up, buddy," she said, if only to the door, and inserted the key into the deadbolt lock.

She felt no resistance. On impulse, she turned the knob and the door opened. Not only had Alex forgotten to lock the door, he'd also left his lights on. *I have a bad feeling about this,* Wendy thought, walking slowly through the small room. She peeked into the bathroom just to be sure it was empty, then turned around . . . and saw the note taped to the computer monitor.

Definitely Alex's scrawl, she could tell, even before plucking the note off the dark screen. She frowned as she read it, her frown deepening on the second pass. "Wendy, please forgive me . . . forgot I had plans to hit Cambridge with Jen and others in study group—post-exam—to blow off steam. An 'ALL-4-1, 1-4-ALL' thing. Can't bail. Tried 2 call U: no answer. Don't worry. Be in touch after we stagger home. XX&OO . . . ALEX"

"You've gotta be kidding me," she said aloud, annoyed. Had he called while she was out jogging? While she was being attacked?

No excuses or bouquets or boxes of chocolate are gonna help you this time, party boy! She couldn't believe he'd just run off, without a moment's notice, to party with Jen and his buddies. *Jen, huh? What's that all about? And me, the dope—jeez, I asked him to drive her to her dorm. Maybe she put a move . . .* Wendy heaved a weary sigh, shook her head. *I can't dwell on this now. I need to focus. More important things* to worry about than . . . *just deal with him later,* she told herself. *Maybe it's better this way, him out of town, out of harm's way.* Wither had almost killed Alex once because of her. Besides, *what was good for Abby, was good for Alex. Better not to tempt fate twice.*

She balled up his note and tossed it into the trash can. *Still . . .* "I thought you were different, Alex," she said as she left his dorm room and locked the door.

On the drive back to her cottage, she had the strange feeling she was missing something important, something the Crone had said recently. And she had no idea what it could be.

CHAPTER ELEVEN

Menlo Park, California
August 6, 2000

"Anything wrong, Hannah?" Karen Glazer asked her nine-month-old daughter. A nine-month-old who looked and acted as if she were over three years old. *At this rate she'll be ready for kindergarten next month. Seriously doubt they'll let me enroll a ten-month-old in kindergarten. We'll probably have to arrange for special tutors.*

Eschewing milk this morning, Hannah had been eating dry Cheerios from a bowl, scooping them up with her Nala spoon—Nala being the spunky, young lioness from Disney's *The Lion King*—and crunching away while Karen read term papers from her summer session class, Literature of the Fantastic. *Since the Cheerios aren't swim-*

ming in milk, Hannah had reasoned, *they won't get all soggy.* This morning Hannah had asked for milk in a glass. *As a chaser*, Karen had thought, smiling. Hannah was now on her third bowl of Cheerios, which had followed scrambled eggs, two pieces of buttered whole wheat toast, and a banana. Her body had developed so fast since birth, her metabolism was always playing catch-up with the growth spurts.

With the cessation of Hannah's steady crunching, Karen had looked up from the term papers and her own half-eaten toast and scrambled eggs. Admittedly, she was on her second cup of coffee. *So easy when the full pot's just sitting there, almost within arm's reach.*

Hannah held her glass of milk in both hands as she drained the last of it, freshening her milk mustache, before setting the empty glass on her placemat. "I have to go now, Mama."

As part of his new "fit by forty" health regimen, Art had already left for his brisk morning campus walk, leaving the "two ladies of the house" to themselves. At least until the baby-sitter showed up, freeing Karen to go grocery shopping.

Taking Hannah to the grocery store was out of the question. All that food in one place seemed to send an *all you can eat buffet* message to Hannah's racing metabolism. The little girl filled the shopping cart faster than Karen could return all the Oreos, Pop Tarts and Fruit Rollups to their shelves. Karen avoided telling Hannah when she was making a trip to the grocery store, because Hannah would cry and demand to be taken along. Instead, Karen used the euphemism, "I have some errands to run," wondering when the shelf life on that little bit of misdirection would come to an end.

Karen reached for Hannah's napkin to wipe her mouth, but her daughter beat her to it. "Is Miss Kim taking you somewhere while I run some errands, honey?"

Hannah shook her head.

The doorbell rung.

"That must be her now," Karen said, dropping her own napkin on her chair as she went to answer the door.

"Don't worry, Mama," Hannah yelled after her. "I'll take extra clothes and underwear."

"Stay put, young lady," Karen called back, frowning as she walked to the front door. Raising her accelerated child had provided no end of strange moments, not the least of which was Hannah potty training herself before she was seven months old. Any money Art and Karen saved on diapers was more than absorbed by all the extra food Hannah consumed and the clothes she outgrew after two or three washings. *Wearing 3T and 4T now,* Karen thought. *Technically she shouldn't even be walking yet.*

Kim Laird, a local undergrad at Stanford pursuing a degree in childhood development, was a tall, natural redhead with fair skin and a wide, easy smile. Once Karen had gotten over her initial fear that Kim would treat Hannah like some lab specimen, Karen was delighted to have her as a part-time baby-sitter. That Kim and Hannah enjoyed each other's company so much helped alleviate Karen's maternal guilt over abandoning her child five days a week to walk the halls of academia, even during the summer. She and Art could certainly use the extra money to get ahead on the mortgage, which provided a good home for Hannah. But sometimes—too often—that easy rationalization was laid bare and wanting by her demanding conscience.

"How's the little princess today?" Kim asked, a black beret perched at a jaunty angle atop her red, shoulder-length mane.

"You two planning a trip to Paris this morning?" Karen asked.

Kim minored in French and usually, when she wore the beret, she and Hannah would role-play characters in some French setting, a Parisian restaurant or museum, giggling all the while. Hannah's French, Kim informed Karen, was almost as good as her English. "Trip? Oh, the beret! No, nothing planned. Why?"

"Hannah just mentioned taking a trip . . ." Karen said, frowning again.

Her frown deepened when she found the kitchen deserted.

Karen ran upstairs, with Kim right behind her.

Hannah was in her bedroom, all the drawers of her dresser open, tossing clothes into a pile in the center of the room, atop her Winnie the Pooh backpack. More clothing than would ever fit within the confines of the junior backpack, if Karen was any judge. She kneeled beside Hannah as the little girl began to cram her clothing inside Pooh's vinyl belly. Looking at her daughter's midnight black hair, Karen couldn't help think how telling the thin streak of gray hair was. Hannah had been born with that streak in her hair, and while Karen had thought it would go away eventually, she now saw it as another symptom, a benign symptom at least, of Hannah's rapid development. Karen stroked her daughter's hair, letting the gray run between her fingers. "Hannah?"

"How far is it to the airplanes, Mama?"

Karen shot Kim a quizzical look, but the undergrad, leaning against the doorframe, merely shrugged and raised an eyebrow. *So this isn't part of their fantasy games.* Returning her attention to Hannah, Karen asked, "Do you have to fly in an airplane, sweetie?"

"Don't be silly, Mama," Hannah said, smiling indulgently, as if her mother should know better. "Windale's too far to walk!"

Karen's breath caught in her throat. "Win—Windale?"

"Yes," Hannah said, compromising on some of her favorite outfits so she could close Pooh's zipper. "We have to help her."

Karen caught Hannah's shoulders in her hands, forcing the young girl to concentrate on her mother and not the size of the backpack. "Hannah? What's wrong? Do you miss Wendy?"

"All the time, Mama."

"We can visit her sometime during Christmas break," Karen promised, not at all sure it would be possible. "Would you like that?"

"Yes, Mama."

"So it's settled? You'll stay here and have fun with Miss Kim?"

Hannah shook her head. "No, Mama. I have to leave. Before it's too late." Hannah took her mother's hand, a look of disconcerting seriousness on her young, innocent face. "If you come with me, you won't be lonely, Mama. Would that be okay?"

Karen smiled, despite herself. "Hannah, I don't understand. Why is this so important?"

"It's the bad things, Mama. The bad things are coming again."

"Has she been having nightmares?" Kim asked.

Karen shook her head. *No, but I have. Does that count?* "Let me call Wendy. Okay, Hannah? To see if everything's okay."

Karen made the call, only to learn everything was definitely not okay. On the phone, Wendy seemed tired and tense, but more than anything, frightened. When Karen suggested she and Hannah fly back east, Wendy almost panicked, insisting they stay on the west coast, as far from Windale as possible. When pressed for details, Wendy deflected the question, telling Karen not to worry about anything, promising she would take care of everything in Windale, and that Karen and Hannah were safest on the other side of the country.

Karen's hand, as she hung up the telephone receiver, trembled. Hurrying down the hall from the master bedroom, all she could think was, *Hannah knows. Hannah knows something's wrong.*

"Here's your mother, princess," Kim said in soothing tones as Karen returned. "I was just telling Hannah everything's fine. Isn't that so, Ms. Glazer?"

"No," Karen said, kneeling to finish zipping Hannah's backpack, "it's not."

Kim, wide-eyed, said, "What?"

"Do me a favor, Kim," Karen said. "While I pack an overnight bag, call the airline, book two tickets to Logan International. Then call me a cab or a shuttle or something for the airport."

"You're leaving? Just like that? What did Wendy say?"

Karen nodded. "She told me under no circumstances should Hannah and I come to Windale." Ignoring Kim's puzzled expression, she rattled off more instructions, "Leave a message with the dean's office, tell them I had a family emergency and have to cancel Monday's classes. Don't worry about Art, I'll call him from the cab or the airport, tell him we had to leave."

Karen took Hannah's hand, led her down the hall, the Pooh backpack slung over her shoulder. Kim trailed behind them, at something of a loss. "Sure—but if Wendy said . . . I mean why—"

"Hannah's involved in this," Karen said.

Hannah ran and jumped on the bed, swinging her feet in an alternating pattern, probably happy her mother wouldn't be lonely after all.

Karen whispered to Kim, "Even before she was born, Hannah was involved. I tried to take us away, to run away from it, but . . ." She shook her head, wiping away tears as they came to her eyes. "I can't run away from Hannah, from what she is. She's my daughter. And this is something inside her."

Kim crossed her arms over her chest, and Karen

knew enough about body language to know she was unconvinced by Karen's reasoning. "And that means you just fly back to Win—"

"Hannah knowing about this . . . situation." Karen took a deep, trembling breath. "I don't know—but you've seen some of what we've been through. I think it means she has to be there, for this to end, for her to ever have a normal life. I thought it was over, prayed it was over. But I was wrong. Everything has been leading us to this minute."

"What if you're wrong? What if you're just exposing her to danger?"

"Then God forgive me."

WINDALE, MASSACHUSETTS

Wendy spent most of the night alternately wondering about Alex's odd behavior and worrying about when and how Gina would strike next. No big surprise she spent little time actually asleep. Even the idea of a relaxing, lavender petal bath lacked its usual appeal. Lounging in a bathtub would have made her feel too vulnerable, and her anxiety would have nullified the soothing effects of a hot bath. Whenever she managed to doze off, strange sounds woke her but, try as she might, she couldn't locate their source. Several times she crossed over to the empty room—Frankie's bedroom-to-be—to peer through the mini-blinds at the deserted street. One time, she spotted the black-and-white squad car gliding along the cul-de-sac, headlights slicing the darkness, Deputy Hank Rossi behind the wheel, looking confident in his environment. *Just proves how wrong appearances can be,* Wendy had thought as she attempted to stifle another yawn.

Early in the morning she called Sheriff Nottingham at home, and he assured her Abby was safely tucked in her bed. He'd spent a sleepless night checking on her, making sure she hadn't wandered off. Wendy neglected to tell the sheriff about her visit to Alex's dorm, but did inform him she would be heading out to work before noon. She overcame his quick protest by pointing out, with unassailable logic, "Am I safer in a crowded store or home alone ... all alone?" Besides, she'd go stir crazy locked in the cottage all day, just waiting for the other shoe to drop.

Wendy ended her brief shower with a blast of cold water to knock loose the mental cobwebs. Since the weatherman warned of a hot, humid day, she put on her lime green, sleeveless top with its daring V-neck. And because the ribbed top was clingier than her personal modesty usually allowed, she contrasted the look with a pair of her baggier jeans.

Karen called just as she was heading out the door to work and said that Hannah was insisting she and Karen come back to Windale. The last thing Wendy wanted was for Hannah to be at risk in Windale. Let her stay out in California, a whole continent away from Gina's evil. Wendy could only hope she'd scared Karen enough to keep her and Hannah safe out there in Menlo Park.

Wendy arrived at the store a half hour early, decided to skip her usual morning tea and instead put on a pot of coffee with one of Kayla's jump-starter tricks, two measures of coffee in one filter. Tasted like battery acid, but as long as she kept sipping the foul brew, she doubted she'd be in danger of dozing off.

"*Wennndyyyy.*"

The voice, behind her, was faint and ghostly, or as Wendy imagined a real ghost might sound like.

Startled, Wendy spun around and sloshed hot coffee over her hand, cursing at her clumsiness and simultaneously wondering if Kayla might have slipped a controlled substance or two into the ground coffee bean tin. But it was only a passing thought, for the voice belonged to the Crone, who was wavering before her, no more than a smoky apparition. "Oh, it's you," Wendy said, willing her heart rate to drop back below triple digits. "You don't look so good."

"*Pressing against . . . temporal persistence . . . great resistance,*" the Crone shook her head, frustrated. "*Won't be . . . to help . . . can't communicate.*"

"Temporal persistence? You mentioned that before. The tendency for the timeline to maintain a particular course."

The Crone spread her wispy arms and the left one vanished briefly. "*Major event approaches . . . if change . . . course . . . our timelines . . . not coincide.*"

Wendy tried to get the gist of the message before the paranormal transmission blinked out on her. "Something big is coming?" The Crone nodded. "And your ability to influence the outcome is weakening against this . . . force? The temporal persistence?" Again, a nod. "It wants things to stay as they should be. But if you come from a time where I triumphed over Gina Thorne, or Wither, whatever, then doesn't that mean everything will work out?"

The Crone shook her head, looking too solemn for Wendy's liking. ". . . *my time, events occurred as . . . would hope. This . . . turning point . . . steer you . . . different timeline.*"

This timeline stuff really makes my head hurt, Wendy thought. But she also knew that it was important for her to understand what was happening. "You're saying your timeline may not be the same as mine? Because, from your future vantage point, you obviously survived these events. So, even though I'm heading down the same . . . time track right now, I could get switched onto a different path, like a train that's diverted to a different track at a switching point."

"*Essentially,*" the Crone said nodding. One side of her head fluttered away like a dissolving smoke ring. After a moment, the Crone seemed to will it back into existence. "*We should meet . . . but Wither and now . . . na Thorne corrupt nature . . . may . . . power . . . corrupt timelines . . . eliminating my . . .*"

Again, Wendy attempted to fill in the blanks. "It's possible they—she—could be blocking you from me, to increase the chances of her winning this battle?" The Crone nodded. "She can really do that?"

"*A possibility . . . aybe not even consciously,*" the Crone said. "*Beware . . . her powers . . . too fast . . . oss of control, like a dam bursti—incredibly destructive.*"

Wendy felt weak in the knees. While Gina Thorne's powers were bursting out of control, Wendy could barely pick a cheap lock. "Okay, so what's the good news? There's gotta be good news. First the bad news, then the good news."

The Crone shook her head, and this time it began to dissipate for the last time. "... if I leave ... you ... alone ..."

"That's it? That's the message? She's supercharged and I'm all alone?"

"I ... try, perhaps already ha ... near you ... coven."

"Wait! Don't go! I don't understand. If you're from the future, how can you be near me? And what about a coven? Does Gina have a new coven already? Because, right up until this second, I was thinking no way in hell this could get any worse." But it was too late for more answers. The Crone's insubstantial body had become nothing more than thin tendrils of vapor and, as she lost what little remained of her fragile consistency on the astral plane, so too did she lose her voice.

Wendy only had a few minutes to think over the implications of the Crone's warning before Kayla, wearing a white, sequined Betty Boop tank top and black jeans, and Tristan, a study in grays, arrived for work. She attempted to bring them up to speed, out of earshot of their occasional customers. If Gina showed up at the store Wendy wanted both of them out of the magical line of fire. "I know this is a lot to process," Wendy said. "And I won't blame you if you think I'm stark raving loony tunes. But humor me on Gina Thorne. Believe me when I tell you she's dangerous. Do *not* mess with her. "

Kayla glanced at Tristan, unconsciously hugging herself. "Don't worry. That chick gives us both the heebie-jeebies."

"If she shows up here, don't talk to her unless she talks first. Don't antagonize her. If she asks where I am, tell her. And as soon as she leaves, call nine-one-one. Then call this number." She handed them a card. "The sheriff's home number."

"You want us to tell her where to find you?" Kayla asked. "Just like that?"

Wendy forced a smile. "Only if she asks."

"Why not lie?" Tristan asked. "Just tell her we have no idea?"

"She might be able to tell you're lying. She might get mad. And you don't want her mad at you."

With all her frowns, Kayla's steel eyebrow posts were getting an aerobic workout. "And what are you gonna do?"

A little voice nagged at Wendy, *Your magic's not good enough to beat her, and you don't have time to get much better.* Wendy had practiced her training exercises off and on throughout the night, but she'd been too jumpy and tired to focus. Sounding more confident than she felt, Wendy said, "I'll think of something."

Kayla sighed, shook her head at Wendy. "You realize this is major trippy shit, don't you?"

"Oh, yeah."

An hour later, Kayla came out of the back room and found Wendy at the cash register island staring down at a tiny, laminated card in her palm, working the phone. Kayla nodded toward the back. "Holding out on us."

Distracted, "What?"

"You never told us we went live," Kayla said. "You know, the Internet incarnation of The Crystal Path."

"Oops," Wendy said. "Couple days now. I forgot to check on it. Is something broken?"

"No, but we have about two dozen orders logged already," Kayla said, grinning. "Suppose it's too soon for E-mail complaints about slow service."

"Could you . . . ?"

"Yes, yes, I'll take care of it before our online rep goes down the virtual toilet. What's with the wee little card?"

"Something I plucked out of a pewter beer stein," Wendy said. "Gift from Alex's friends, remember?"

"Ah, yes, his Cambridge road crew," Kayla said. "Gonna put a hex on them?"

"Even if I was into that sort of thing, all these guys would be safe. I just contacted the last one. They're still in Windale. And none of them have any idea who Alex might have been talking about in his note."

"What about the tramp—I mean, Jen?"

"No answer," Wendy said. "No one has seen her since yesterday."

Kayla's expression was pained. "Oh, Wendy, I'm not thinking good thoughts right now, sugar."

"You and me both."

With an hour left till closing, all three of them finished boxing up the rest of the Internet orders, including a few that trickled in during the day. A slow day in the real world, but the e-world helped pass the time. Despite the lack of any new developments, Wendy's anxiety remained high. She couldn't shake the feeling that she was in the calm before the storm, a storm brewing in the foulest pits of hell.

The sheriff had parked his white Jetta half a block away from the Gallo residence and sat in the car, listening to the chatter on the police radio as he watched the front of the house. The only problem of the day had been a three-car pileup at the intersection of Main and Enchantment, but Jeff assured him it was nothing more than a fender bender, no apparent injuries. The town was almost too quiet . . . and that bothered him.

While he considered himself fortunate to have escaped the battle in Matthias Stone's old barn with only a compound fracture, he could have done without the dull ache in his thighbone that forecast every thunderstorm. Intent as he was on watching the Gallo place, half a minute passed before he noticed he was massaging his thigh with the heel of his left hand.

Physical discomfort, impatience, or the simple acknowledgment that he couldn't remain inconspicuous in a white car with the silhouette of a broom-riding witch painted on the doors, prompted him to get out and approach the Gallo residence. Recalling the terrifying image of the *monster* witch, Sarah Hutchins, the sheriff suddenly felt naked without his shotgun. The Remington would have been a little extra comfort, especially since he'd switched from buckshot to flechette rounds first thing in the morning. *Problem is*, he thought, *just as hard to look inconspicuous toting a shotgun in the crook of your arm.* For now, he'd have faith in his trusty old .357 Magnum.

Located near the entrance to Eden's Crossing, what was billed as "a community of executive homes," the Gallo residence was three stories, built in the Gothic Victorian style, with a wraparound veranda and a two-car garage attached to the right. The sales brochure had probably touted a "modern conveniences interior with an Old World charm exterior." The house seemed quiet, shades drawn against the hot August sun, but something about it made his hackles rise, almost as if it were vibrating beneath the surface.

Just my imagination, he told himself. *Even if Gina Thorne is somehow Wither reincarnated, the Windale witch took over three hundred years to become a nine-foot-tall flying monster. Gina Thorne's all of eighteen years old, at—what?—five-seven, weighs maybe a buck-and-a-quarter sopping wet.*

Almost a full minute after he rapped his knuckles on the front door, it opened a crack and Gina Thorne herself peered out at him, her face pinched with irritation. "Yes, sheriff?"

"Hello, Ms. Thorne," he said. "May I come in?"

"Why?"

"Just to speak with your mother. Won't take long."

"She's doesn't want any visitors. Now, if you'll just—"

"May I ask why?"

Gina rolled her eyes, sighed. "Migraine, if you must know." She looked over her shoulder, as if taking or giving silent instruction, then back to the sheriff. "Dom's funeral is tomorrow. She's a real mess." Gina shook her head, resigned. "Look, if you want, I'll give her a message. Fair enough?"

"Better I tell her personally. It concern's your stepfather's death."

"Dom's suicide? What about it?"

Here goes, he thought. *Bluster.* "Ms. Thorne, I am fully prepared to get a search warrant. However, in light of recent tragedies your family has suffered, I thought I would take the more . . . civilized approach." He pushed back his hat about five degrees, hoping his casual body language told her his ability to obtain a search warrant was all but assured—when in truth it would be damn near impossible—and the end result would not be pleasant for her family. "Polite or nasty, Ms. Thorne. You're choice. Of course, if you're really concerned about your mother's welfare . . ."

"If it means that much to you, sheriff," Gina said, her tone less irritated than confident. "Step right in."

As Gina swung the door open, he saw she wore a black slipdress, was barefoot with toenails painted cherry red. *Nothing inhuman about her . . . yet something was making his skin itch.* Although he fought the impulse, he desperately wanted to unsnap his holster flap and rest his palm on the grip of his .357 Magnum. As he stepped into the house, he covered the nervous gesture with a courteous one, removing his hat.

Despite the brutal August heat and humidity, a blast of cold air chilled him the moment he was inside. *Like a meat locker in here.*

"Let me take that for you, sheriff," Gina said, reaching

for the hat in his left hand. Her palm brushed over his fingers and lingered there, her flesh unnaturally warm and sweaty against his, considering the ambient temperature in the house seemed at least forty degrees below human body temperature.

"S—sure," he said, voice thick.

Though there was a coat rack inside the vestibule, she held on to his hat, running her index finger along the inside brim as she stepped into the reception hall and waited, standing on a throw rug he didn't remember from his last visit. When she noticed him staring at her, she smiled and said, "Mother's in the kitchen. Talking pains her. Keep your voice low." She nodded in the direction of the kitchen. "After you."

Last thing he wanted was to have her behind him, but he'd bluffed his way into the house and had to maintain the show of bravado. At least he needn't be concerned about her carrying a concealed weapon. *Her dress barely conceals her.* Turning his attention away from Gina, he noticed all the surfaces in the house seemed moist with dewy condensation, the walls, the wood trim, the banister railing. He had the odd conviction that anything he touched would be spongy, in the early stages of some kind of liquefying decay or putrefaction. But something held him back from putting that conviction to the test, something primitive in his mind that he couldn't explain but trusted nonetheless. Even the flow of cold air brought the pungent scent of fermentation to his nose, inducing a slight queasiness, like the onset of motion sickness.

As he glanced back with a polite nod, he couldn't help but notice she wasn't wearing a bra under her flimsy dress. A strange little voice inside his head provided its own bit of lecherous speculation, *Not wearing panties either.*

That thought, so abrupt and foreign, caused him to stumble a bit in confusion, as if a dirty old man had snuck up behind him and whispered that assertion in his ear. He smiled at Gina, shaking off his embarrassment.

Don't believe me? Run your hand up her thigh and see if I'm wrong. Don't worry, she won't mind a bit. Not that one.

This time the sheriff stopped short and looked back at her. "You hear something?" He looked toward the family room. "Television on, radio maybe?"

"Nothing's turned on in here I don't know about, sheriff," she said with an appraising gaze. "What I mean is, the noise bothers Mother. She hasn't been able to keep anything down."

Vomiting? That might explain the overripe smell.

Gina stepped forward, her hip brushing against him as she took the lead through the archway into the kitchen. The contact sent a physical jolt through him, like a static charge deep under his skin, causing him to shudder. Even through their clothes, he'd felt the heat coming off her body. And yet, hot as she seemed, he'd swear on the witness stand he could almost see his own breath as vapor before him. "What are you waiting for, sheriff?" Gina asked, looking back at him, hands on her hips, head cocked. "Mother's right here, sitting at the kitchen table. Come look."

Rest here on my web, said the spider to the weary fly.

From where he stood, the sheriff could only see Gina and the corner of the long kitchen table. Two more steps and he'd be able to see it all, including anyone else who might be waiting for him in the kitchen. Once again he thought about the Remington, mounted in the Jetta, loaded with seven flechette rounds.

With a slight nod, he took the final steps into the kitchen, not bothering to hide the motion as his hand dropped to his side and popped the holster snap.

The boy couldn't have been more than twelve years old. Not the typical Crystal Path patron. *Maybe he thinks this is a comic book shop,* Wendy thought. When he walked straight toward the cash register island, she changed her mind. *Needs to use the bathroom.*

"Is there a Wendy Ward here?"

She'd been about to tell him, *There's a gas station bathroom at the corner of the next block,* when she did a double-take and said, "What?"

"Wendy Ward," the boy said, holding what looked like a greeting card with her name written in block letters on the white envelope. "She told me to give this to Wendy Ward. This the right place?"

As Wendy came around from behind the counter, the kid slapped one of the oversized palmistry hands mounted on springs and suction-cupped to the countertop. The hand swayed back and forth like one of those inflatable clowns you punch only to have it spring back up again, ready for more abuse. "Who told you?"

The kid shrugged. "Don't know her name."

Wendy took the envelope from him. "What's yours?"

"Nick," he said. "Nick Shankin."

Wendy opened the card, a sick feeling lodged in the pit of her stomach. Not a greeting card, an invitation to a house warming party at 5 P.M., August 6th. The word *warming* had been underlined with a red permanent marker. Wendy opened the card, sure it would be the address of her rental cottage on Kettle Court, surprised when it wasn't. She suffered a disorienting moment of confusion, recognizing the address without having it register . . .

100 College Way, Danfield, Massachusetts

Then she gasped, her hand flying to her mouth to press against her quivering lips. She shook her head. "Oh, no! No, no . . ."

Kayla and Tristan had been in the back of the store, straightening shelves, vacuuming the rug with the push sweeper and all the other odd jobs that filled a slow day. They must have sensed something was wrong because they hurried to the front of the store moments after Wendy had ripped open the invitation. Tristan looked left and right as if expecting Gina to be lurking behind the magazine rack or to pop out of one of the candle baskets like a demented jack-in-the-box. Kayla's gaze settled on the boy as the source of Wendy's distress. "Who's the brat?"

"Hey," Nick said. "Don't kill the messenger."

Wendy thrust the invitation in Kayla's hands without a word and grabbed the boy by the shoulders. "Who gave this to you?"

"I told you I don't know her name."

Kayla read the invitation. "Wendy, is this—?"

"Yes, it is," Wendy said. Then, to the boy, "Describe her?"

"Tall, skinny, straight dark hair," he said with a shrug. "College student, I guess."

"That doesn't sound like Gina," Kayla said.

"It's not Gina," Wendy said, recalling the Crone's words. "But I know who it is." *We have been changed by past events, Wendy, but you least of all* . . . She looked at the boy again. "Is she outside? How long ago did she give this to you?"

Again he shrugged. "Two minutes." As Wendy ran for the door, he called after her, "She's gone. Jumped in a blue pickup truck."

Wendy ran outside into the August heat, crossing to the middle of Theurgy Avenue for the best vantage point. Several drivers laid on their horns, telling her in no uncertain terms to get the hell out of the road. She ignored them, taking a step forward, then back, craning her neck for any sign of Jen or the blue pickup. Two minutes . . . She shook her head. They were long gone. Pounding her thigh in frustration, she bolted across Theurgy and returned to the shop.

Kayla's raised eyebrows were question enough. Wendy shook her head. "Do me a favor? Take over here. I gotta bolt."

"Go," Kayla urged. "Don't worry about the store."

"Call nine-one-one," Wendy said as she grabbed the

invitation from Kayla and hurried backward to the rear of the store, toward the employee entrance. "Call the fire department. And call the sheriff. Tell him to meet me at the president's mansion."

"Sure, but—who was *she*?" Kayla called. "Who left the note?"

"Jen Hoyt."

Kayla frowned. "Jen?"

Tristan scratched his blond hair, puzzled. "The tramp?"

The boy yelled after Wendy. "Hey! How about a tip?"

"Here's a tip," Kayla said. "Don't take money from strangers." She gave him a little shove toward the front door. "Now get out of here before I call your mother."

"Wait a minute," Kayla called to Wendy. "If that was Jen, where's Alex?"

But Wendy had no answer. She turned, ran through the back room and out the employee entrance. She started the Civic, backed out of her parking space and sped past the row of Dumpsters and onto the street without braking, narrowly missing a rusted white Camaro as it turned into the lot.

She fumbled in the glove compartment as she drove, scattering maps, a packet of tissues, and a tire gauge before finding the cell phone her father had given her as a present. Moments after she powered it on, the LCD display blinked out. Dead battery. She cursed, tossed the phone on the passenger seat and went fishing in the glove box again, this time plucking out the cigarette lighter adaptor. Some awkward finger gymnastics as she pulled out the lighter, plugged in the adaptor and connected the other end to the base of the phone, all while trying to stay between the dotted lines on Theurgy Avenue.

She'd had enough foresight to program her parents' number into memory, and speed dialed it now. The pop and crackle of electrical interference almost drowned out the faint ringing at the other end of the line. It felt as if she were calling the other side of the world. "Come on! Pick up, pick up, pick up . . ."

A line of storm clouds rolled across the overcast sky, intermittent heat lightning illuminating the ugly, roiling mass from within. She was driving right into the storm.

Alex had only the vaguest recollection of walking to Bosch Hall the previous night, a fleeting memory of climbing into the back of a pickup truck, but no idea at all how he ended up bound and gagged on the floor of a finished basement. Not quite true. He'd rolled onto the floor all by himself, after waking on an old blue-and-white checked sofa. Whoever trussed him up had been thorough. Clothesline was knotted around his ankles and, from the feel of it behind his back, also around his wrists. A wad of cloth filled his mouth, trapped in by liberal strips of duct tape.

One reason he'd hurled himself onto the floor was to retrieve his cane, which had been dropped or tossed near an old treadmill. The other reason had been to get as far away as possible from the mutating corpse sprawled on the chair next to the sofa.

The corpse had once been a stout woman with reddish-orange hair wearing a black servant's dress—a domestic uniform—complete with sensible white, rubber-soled shoes. Alex would expect a corpse to rot, to decay, and stink, after time . . . but this corpse was mutating, and seemed to have erupted out of the binding clothes, trans-muting into some other . . . thing, which had what looked like a rubbery texture slathered with gobs of viscous fluid like thin mucus. This new substance, spawned from the corpse's flesh, stretched out in all directions, slimy tendrils climbing everywhere, fleshy creeper vines. One crossed the small table separating chair and sofa, another crept up the back of the sofa, a third had fused itself to the paneled wall, while a fourth was draped over water pipes recessed between joists in the ceiling, and still others spread across the floor. The corpse's head, covered with a green, patchy mold, had collapsed in on itself, with its two uneven and shriveled eyes staring vacantly at him. Even worse, the mutated and wandering flesh had exposed the corpse's internal organs, and they were all pulsing, rippling and had begun to dissolve and flow in all directions. Had Alex stayed on the sofa a few more minutes, he was convinced his own body would have been snared and used as human fertilizer for the expanding flesh creepers.

Keeping as much distance between himself and the blossoming corpse as possible, he'd inchwormed his way across the rug, then rolled over so he could grab the handle of the custom cane. Took him a moment to find the recessed button by feel alone, but he did and the carved dragon-head handle snapped up, allowing him to pull the eighteen-inch blade free of the steel housing. Flipping the blade upside down in his hands, he began to cut at the clothesline binding his wrists. A serrated blade would have been ideal. The short sword was designed more for thrusting than cutting or slashing, so his progress was agonizingly slow.

While he worked, he became aware of a soft, intermittent splat sound behind him, and worried the mutating corpse's roving flesh had caught up to him. Instead, when he craned his neck back to locate the source of the sound, he discovered another problem. The wood in one of the ceiling joists was melting.

At first he assumed water was leaking through from upstairs, dripping off the wood. But the rug told a different story. Brown goo—not water—was splattering the short-piled rug, goo with the consistency of hot tar. He focused on the joist in question for a while until he determined it was losing substance, becoming deformed. The dripping point was sagging, turning into a wooden stalactite before his eyes.

Not for the first time, Alex wondered if he'd been drugged.

The sheriff sat behind the wheel of the Jetta and tried to remember what he'd seen in the Gallo house. His curiosity seemed to have been satisfied—at least he had the feeling it was okay to leave now—but the details informing that conclusion eluded him.

He remembered taking the last few steps into the kitchen, expecting some sort of ambush, ready to unholster the .357 Magnum at a moment's notice, but then he'd relaxed . . .

Gina stood next to her mother, also dressed in black, but sitting at the table, head in her hands, a wide-brimmed, black hat casting her face in shadow. Even so, the woman seemed pale and sickly, despondent, but alive. Certainly, the sheriff felt sympathy for her. She'd lost a son and a husband, and then the memories of the husband had become tainted by the discovery that he'd been abusing her daughter. The sheriff couldn't remember what had driven him to intrude on this woman's misery. Nor was he capable of remembering why he'd thought Gina's abuse accusations might be false.

"Mrs. Gallo?"

Caitlin Gallo nodded, fluttered a hand at him. What little he saw of her face in the dim light showed pale skin stretched taut, a hollow-eyed look revealing the skull beneath the skin, an unpleasant hint of mortality. *She's been through enough*, he thought. *Too much. I should go* . . .

"Anything I can do?"

She shook her head, almost a feeble gesture, barely definitive, until she whispered in a hollow voice, "Please, go."

And so he had left.

Just like that.

Nothing more natural.

The sheriff stared at his hands on the steering wheel, held loose at ten and two o'clock, proper driving position, but his car was still parked and he had no idea how long he'd been sitting in it . . . no memory of even leaving the house. But he had been inside, that part he hadn't imagined, because Gina Thorne still had his hat. And, he thought, rubbing an itch on the back of his right hand, *she . . . touched me.*

One thing was certain, his aching thigh hadn't been wrong. The overcast sky was much darker than it had been when he'd entered the Gallo residence. A storm was coming and, judging by the wide front of dark clouds rolling across the sky, it wouldn't be pleasant. *Damned weather forecasters never get anything right!*

"... eriff, you there!" the police radio squawked.

The sheriff rubbed his eyes, massaged a strange numbness from his face. How long had they been calling him? A minute? Longer? He couldn't be sure. Shaking off the lethargy, he picked up the mike. "Nottingham."

Seemed Wendy Ward had finally placed the emergency call he'd been expecting all day, or rather one of her friends had placed the call for her, saying there was an emergency at the college president's mansion and he should meet her there immediately.

The sheriff started the Jetta and pulled out of the parking lane. A newspaper flew end over end down the street, an empty soda can, and a potato chip bag in hot pursuit. The trees leaned into the gusting wind, shedding weak branches. Farther down the street, an unlatched gate began to bang an irregular percussion in the howling wind.

Kayla had just finished making the last of the emergency calls when she heard the door chimes sound. Her heart skipped a beat. For a frightening moment, she was sure Gina Thorne would be standing inside the store.

Instead, Kayla saw two teenaged guys who looked like a couple of Harrison High's rejects, definitely out of The Crystal Path patron demographic. Tall guy in the lead was muscular, with short dirty-blond hair and a crooked nose. He wore a white T-shirt with a red biohazard symbol on the front, jeans worn through at the knees and scuffed, tan work boots. The other bozo had a shaved head, white goatee, silver hoop earrings, and wore a black muscle T-shirt to show off the snake coils tattooed up and down both arms, a snake head with crimson eyes and extended fangs on the back of each hand. He wore green cargo pants, the kind with thirty-seven pockets, tucked into black military boots laced up to the knees.

Kayla was about to tell them the body shop was two blocks down, when she noticed Tristan was already circling from behind the cash register island to usher them out. They had both decided regular business hours be damned. They'd close the store a few minutes early, hustle their butts out of there, and figure out how to help Wendy.

"Sorry, guys," Kayla called. "We're closing."

Shaved Head said, "Let me help, then." He turned back toward the door and flipped the open/closed sign over so *closed* was facing out. "All better."

Tristan stood before them. "If you know what you want, I can help you find it," he said, trying to be pleasant but sounding nervous. "Otherwise, I'm sorry, there's no time to browse. We have something of an emergency brewing."

Broken Nose grabbed Tristan by his gray knit shirt, bunching the fabric in his fists. "Get out of my way, pansy-ass!" he said and shoved Tristan back so hard he tripped over an elaborate display of candles and holders. Broken Nose stepped around Tristan, as he scrambled to his feet, and walked toward the cash register.

Kayla picked up the phone and was about to dial nine-one-one for the second time in ten minutes when she saw that Shaved Head had wrapped a muscular, serpent-coiled arm around Tristan's neck and was holding a hunting knife to his ribs. "Press one button and I'll chop his fucking heart out!"

Carol Ward placed the telephone back on the cradle. "Dead," she told her husband, Larry, who was peeling potatoes at the kitchen table. He'd been the one to suggest inviting Wendy over for dinner since she would be closing up the shop early on a Sunday. "Guess we eat alone tonight."

"Too bad," he said.

She knew the feeling. The empty-nest feeling, but on a much grander scale. At a cost of over five hundred and fifty thousand dollars, unanimously approved by the college's board of trustees, the president's mansion featured eight bedrooms and six baths and now just the two of them to live in all that empty space. Of course, the extra space was there for entertaining, but on a day-to-day basis, Carol Ward felt as if she were living in a vast, echoing cavern. *How could one daughter fill so much space,* she thought. *In this house . . . and in my heart.*

For a moment, Carol blamed herself. *Maybe if I hadn't been so critical all the time . . . What? She would stay with us forever? Just having a hard time facing the simple fact that my little girl is all grown-up.*

A flash of lightning bathed the kitchen, followed almost immediately by a window-rattling roll of thunder. The overhead lights blinked off for a long moment before flickering back on.

"Super," Larry Ward said with a shake of his head. "First the phone. Now the electricity."

"Wonder if Wendy left us any candles," Carol said. "We could dine by candlelight."

Larry walked over to the window, hands in his pockets as he watched the bruised, turbulent sky. "Look at that, Carol. Wasn't even supposed to rain today and just take a good look at that miserable sky . . ."

Carol stood beside her husband, leaned her head against his shoulder and wrapped her arm around his waist. From a distance, she heard the faint, mournful wail of approaching sirens. When Larry put his arm around her shoulder, a weird premonition made her shudder.

"What?" he asked.

"She's out there alone now," Carol said. "I hope she's okay."

"Wendy will be fine," Larry said, his tone confident. "We raised a good daughter."

Yes, we did, Carol thought. *But I'll always worry about her.*

• • •

"Fuck!" Wendy shouted for the third time and tossed her cell phone across the passenger seat. She'd dialed a half dozen times but nobody was picking up the phone at the mansion. *Maybe they're not home,* she thought, momentarily relieved. Then, *So why isn't the answering machine picking up?*

Several minutes later, she drove up College Avenue well above the residential speed limit, and she could see the white mansion up on the hill, just to the right, on College Way.

The sky was purple and black, with angry storm clouds roiling overhead, massing like an invading army. Fat raindrops began to pelt her windshield. But the lights were on in the house, and Wendy saw no sign of fires burning through any of the windows. Except for the violent storm brewing over the campus, everything looked normal.

Coming down College Way, she saw the sheriff's car and, farther back, a fire engine, red lights strobing in the storm dark sky, siren wailing.

Wendy sighed. *Thank God we're not too late.*

And then the lightning struck.

CHAPTER TWELVE

"Put it down, bitch," Broken Nose said, ripping the receiver out of her hand and grabbing the phone by the base. He yanked so hard, the line snapped free of the wall jack. He tossed the phone across the store, connecting with the top shelf in the tier of crystal balls. Like a row of dominoes, the spheres began to fall, one knocking over the next in a chain reaction, bouncing and shattering on the floor with dull *thunks* and muffled crashes.

Kayla held her hands up, palms out. "Look, guys," she said, trying to stay calm. *Freak out and you might freak them out.* "It's been a slow day. Not much in the register, but you're welcome to it. We'll stay out of your way."

"Thanks for the offer," Broken Nose said. "But we're not here to rob this dump, are we, Cecil?"

Kayla bit her lip. *Cecil? You gotta be kidding me.*

"Nope," Cecil said.

"Then what—what are you here for . . . ?"

Broken Nose shook his head and laughed. "You ain't gonna believe this shit. We're here to offer you a job."

"Uh, no thanks," Kayla said. "I like this one just fine."

"No, no. You see, there's no future here," Broken Nose said. "Right, Cecil?"

"Right," Cecil said and shoved the knife deep into Tristan's abdomen, up under his ribs. Tristan gasped, his eyes impossibly wide. Then Cecil pulled the knife out and shoved Tristan into the magazine rack. Blood smeared all over the rows of magazines as Tristan crumpled to the floor, pulling down half the shelf's contents on top of him. "Definitely no future here."

Kayla reached under the counter for the aluminum bat. She planned an overhead swing, no warning, right down the center of Broken Nose's head. She got as far as the swing, but the bat stopped in midair, caught in Broken Nose's palm. She hadn't even seen his arm move. *This is fucked!* she thought, just as he yanked the bat out of her hand.

"Plus," Broken Nose said, tossing the aluminum bat to Cecil, who snagged it out of the air, one-handed. "I hear a couple vandals trashed this place. Right, Cecil?"

Cecil went on a rampage with the bat, his first targets the tall, Galilean thermometers on the counter. His swing right down the middle shattered the elegant glass constructions, spraying fluid, shards of glass and pieces of the temperature-tagged floats across the front half of the store. Kayla had a moment's warning to turn her back before she was pelted with glass and fluid. After that opening salvo, Cecil smashed baskets of herbs and candles, gouged books and magazines with his knife, smashed bottles and hurled crystal sculptures against the wall, toppling any display racks in his path. Kayla looked on in helpless horror as the entire inventory of The Crystal Path was damaged or destroyed. The front window displays blocked most of the view into the store and the adjoining stores in their mini strip mall, if they opened at all on a Sunday, all closed at three o'clock. No chance anyone would hear the destruction and come to her aid.

Broken Nose stayed close to Kayla but nodded his approval at Cecil's work, a smug grin on his face, interrupted by the occasional chuckle of delight. When Cecil decided to piss all over a mound of gutted books, Broken Nose gave him a hearty round of applause.

Kayla palmed a box cutter and edged away from the register, drifting out of the periphery of Broken Nose's vision while he was distracted, ready to run at the first opportunity. When she thought she was in the clear, she sprinted for the door. Cecil yelled. Broken Nose ran after her, his boots thudding hard and fast behind her. She grabbed the metal door handle and started to push it when a hand clamped in her spiky black hair and yanked her head back. White spots burst in her eyes as she was dragged back and bounced off the magazine rack, then slammed into the wall, stumbling over Tristan's body in the process. She thumbed the razor blade out of the box cutter and slashed out at Broken Nose's face, if only to stop him from ripping her hair out by the roots.

"Fuck! My ear!" he yelled, and shoved her in the back with his boot. She stumbled and fell, the box cutter spinning out of her hand.

"I'm getting the feeling she doesn't want the job," Broken Nose yelled back to Cecil, who had zipped up his fly and was striding to the front of the store with an angry look on his face.

Kayla lunged for the box cutter too late, as Cecil kicked it across the floor. Ten feet or ten miles, not much difference at that point. In a rush, she climbed to her feet, noticed Broken Nose might just as simply be called Half Ear. She'd lopped off the top of his right ear, which was stuck to the floor like a juicy wad of bubblegum. Nevertheless, the wound wasn't bleeding all that much and seemed to be causing Broken Nose no discomfort. "Take your job and shove it," Kayla said. *Ooh, that's good. Piss them off some more. I must be a glutton for punishment,* she thought. *Shit, maybe in some sick way, I do enjoy pain.*

"Guess the pierced bitch don't understand," Cecil said. "If she don't take the job, she's just—meat." With the last word, Cecil punched her in the gut, doubling her over. She gagged, a long line of spittle dangling from her mouth. "You want to be meat, bitch?"

Unable to utter a word at the moment, Kayla shook her head. Vigorously.

"Good," Broken Nose said. "That means you're coming with us."

"Wh—why are you doing this?" Kayla croaked.

"Cause Gina says so," Cecil said.

Oh, *fuck*, Kayla thought miserably. It *had to be her*.

She was too weak to fight as they dragged her out the back door and tossed her into the grease-stained trunk of a rusty white Camaro. After Cecil slammed the lid shut, trapping her in pitch dark, she heard him say, "Now you're riding in style, bitch!"

Alex's shoulders and hands had cramped up more than once while he attempted to cut through the clothesline that bound his wrists. When he heard the creak of footsteps on the stairs, he had enough time to shove the cane sword and its housing under the treadmill, but not enough time to wiggle back to the old sofa. Instead, he worked himself into a sitting position, with his back against the front of the treadmill.

She came around the central staircase in a red silk blouse and a white linen skirt. Her lips, painted red to match the blouse, looked like an open wound in her narrow, pale face, framed by her sheaf of black hair. In one hand she held a serrated steak knife. Just the type of knife he needed to make short work of the rope around his wrists and ankles.

She crouched down beside him, laid the knife on the floor, then peeled the duct tape back from his mouth. "That's better," she said.

"Jen, what's going on? Get me out of here?"

She seemed almost incredulous. "You want me to help?" He nodded, confused. "Well, that's just stupid," she said. "Since I'm the one who put you down here."

"What are you talking about?"

"Guess you don't remember much, huh? Kind of a side effect of us taking mental control." Jen sat on the floor, hugging her knees. "Maybe you should tell me why you're way over here. I had Brett and Keith dump you on the sofa."

"Couldn't stay near that—that thing," he said, nodding toward the fleshy creepers sprouting from the corpse in the chair.

"Oh, Sylvia," Jen said, looking back over her shoulder. "She kind of spoiled, didn't she. Not very good meat, even if she were still warm. See, Gina is getting all these new . . . abilities and she's not sure how to control them all yet. Not like she has some kind of owner's manual. And all her Wither memories are in itsy bits and pieces. Like they went through a paper shredder. So, Gina, she kind of experiments, you know, trial and error to see what works, what feels good . . . what tastes good." While she was talking, Jen scooped up the steak knife and pressed the point against her fingertip.

"Wither? What's this have to do with Wither?"

Jen laughed. "Everything."

"Wither's dead," Alex said. "Wendy killed her."

Jen tapped his nose with the tip of the knife. "No, no, no, Alex. Wendy got lucky. She won a battle. But Wither will win the war. Wow, that was really alliterative, wasn't it." She chuckled. "Seems Wendy neglected to tell you Wither is back with a brand new body."

"You?"

Jen laughed, poked Alex in the chest with the steak

knife. "No, Alex. Wither is in Gina Thorne now. We're in Gina's house, in her basement. She specifically invited you to the party. You should feel honored. I was honored when she invited me to join her coven." She lifted her chin, then frowned. "Well, I really had no choice, but it's for the best, don't you think? I'm so much happier now." She slipped the knife blade between the top two buttons of his Hawaiian shirt. "Happier and . . . hungrier." She pulled the blade down, cutting the buttons off the shirt, exposing his chest. Looping the point of the knife around his chest, pressing almost hard enough to draw blood, she said, "You see, I dream all the time about the blood . . . and about fresh meat."

"What's this—this party? Why does Gina want me here?"

"Party's for Wendy, but it's really Gina's coming out party. Let's just say, Wither is real pissed that Wendy tried to kill her last year. Can you blame her? So, first she'll torment Wendy by torturing and killing everyone close to her, and then, when Wendy is thoroughly miserable . . . well, you know what they say, payback's a bitch."

Jen's lost it, Alex thought. *How long has she been insane and I didn't know? This must all be some sort of warped fantasy . . . but then how do I explain the mutating corpse and melting wood. If Wither is back and Wendy knew, why didn't she tell me, warn me?* "Where's Wendy now?"

"Oh, probably rushing to save her parents," Jen said with a dismissive wave of the knife. "But they'll be crispy critters long before Wendy can lift a finger. Gina can call storms, you know. Been practicing for a while."

"No, I didn't know . . ."

"She's left me all alone to guard you," Jen said, placing the tip of the knife in her mouth.

Alex had a wild thought to lunge at her, head butt her, maybe force the knife back into her throat, but he couldn't get past the gruesome image. Even if he could manage to lunge with his ankles bound and his hands tied behind his back, he'd probably land flat on his face.

"She wants you there at the end," Jen said. "So Wendy can watch you die." She waved the knife point over his chest again. "You know, I could slice you open with this . . ." Her eyes took on a glazed look. ". . . and see all the steaming, red meat."

"But you won't—right?" Alex couldn't back away any farther. "Gina—Wither—would get really mad, wouldn't she? If you ruined the surprise?"

"Gina might forgive me . . . if I told her how *hungry* she had made me. Filling my head with all those dreams." She shook her head. "No, I won't cut you with this," she said, tossing the knife behind her. "Because I have something better, more personal." She held her hand up, fingernails in front of her face as if inspecting a fresh manicure, then waggled her fingers. "I have these." She leaned toward him, pressed the edge of a nail against his bare chest. "I can cut so easy with these." To demonstrate, she raked her nails down his chest, slicing open his flesh. Alex winced at the sudden, burning pain. Blood welled up in the four parallel wounds. "That's because I'm different now. She changed me. Wonderful, isn't it?"

Alex saw the tip of her tongue protrude.

She pressed her fingertips to his chest, daubing blood, then placed them in her mouth, sucking her fingers clean. "So creamy . . ." she said, sighing with pleasure. "I could just eat you up."

"Remember," Alex said. "Gina will be mad—!"

Jen rolled her eyes, impatient with him. "Oh, relax," she said. "A few bites won't kill you."

Let's not test that theory.

"Besides, why do you think I took off your gag?" Alex shook his head, not wanting to give her any ideas. Turned out, hers was bad enough. "I took it off so I can hear you scream, silly," she said. "That's half the fun."

Alex clenched his jaw but thought screaming, under the circumstances, might be his best option.

She bared her teeth and lowered her mouth to his chest.

Later, much later, Wendy would admit to herself that the first bolt of lightning, smashing right through the kitchen windows with an explosion of glass and a deafening clap of thunder, had probably been the one to kill them. Her only comfort, that it had been over quick, they hadn't really suffered, not from blistering heat or smoke inhalation. From the position of the charred remains of their bodies, they had been standing together at the end, near the window. Wendy sometimes imagined they had been holding hands, affectionate as newlyweds. But all that speculation had come later . . .

When the jagged spike of lightning ripped into the side of the president's mansion, Wendy screamed and lost control of the car, jumping the curb and smashing into the wrought iron fence that surrounded the wide expanse of lawn. At the last moment, her foot found the brake pedal and slammed down hard. She was thrown forward by the jarring impact, snagged by the seat belt harness as the airbag deployed, white oblivion exploding in her face.

In a daze, she staggered from the car, stumbling in the rain, surprised in a detached sort of way that she hadn't totaled the Civic's front end. The wrought iron fence hadn't fared as well. One whole section was leaning at a forty-five degree angle. Rather than follow the line of the fence all the way to the front gate, Wendy climbed over the listing section, slipping on the wet bars, but managing to topple inside to the manicured lawn.

Along the perimeter of the lawn was a rough border of dogwood and maple trees, while closer to the sprawl-ing white house, marking each corner, were small stands of pine and spruce in various sizes. Connecting each stand of evergreens, in a dotted line, were regular clumps of rhododendrons. Otherwise, there were no sight line obstructions. To provide plenty of space for large outdoor gatherings, along with the occasional erection of tents and canopies as proof against rain, the vast expanse of fertile green lawn was otherwise devoid of landscaping. Even the vast array of sprinkler heads retracted into the ground when not in use.

Wendy raced across the unobstructed lawn now, her eyes drawn to the curling tendrils of black smoke rising from the back of the mansion on the hill. A little after five o'clock and the sky seemed black as midnight. An electrical charge in the air raised all the hair on the back of her arms, along the nape of her neck. That was all the warning she had . . .

Halfway across the wide lawn, she was knocked off her feet, the white hot afterimage of a lightning bolt, frighteningly close, still dazzling her retina. The blistering crack of thunder still ringing in her ears, she stared at the charred remains of the heavy front doors, dangling from ruined hinges.

She rose to her feet, just as another fork of lightning struck a second-story window, staggering her as she shielded her eyes much too late to do any good. Her vision danced with overlapping afterimages. Undaunted by the steady rain, flames began to rise from the second-story window.

Red light continued to sweep across the lawn, but the wail of the sirens was muted in her ears.

Another bolt of lightning struck the house, blasting chunks of stone from one wall. Then another bolt split one of the corner spruce trees in half. Wendy stumbled forward, the tears streaming down her face lost in the torrential rain that soaked her to the bone. As she neared the charred, burning front door, a hand grabbed her arm from behind.

She whirled, expecting a fight, only to find Sheriff Nottingham facing her down, shaking his head. "You can't go in there! It's too dangerous!"

"I have to," she said, twisting out of his grip. "My parents . . ."

"Wendy!" he shouted after her. "No!"

As she approached the doors, without even touching the quartz on her bead bracelet, she conjured a protective sphere and was vaguely aware of the sheriff, rebounding off its invisible surface, falling on his rear. At that same moment, another bolt of lightning ripped through the roof of the mansion, shaking the ground with its explosive concussion.

Wendy walked between the hanging doors, but her sphere was much larger than the gap and she was surprised to see both doors forced aside and ripped free, as if by invisible, giant hands. The first lightning strike had taken out the electricity, but the interior of the mansion was bathed in the flickering amber glow of fires, catching everywhere. Flaming debris collapsed from the ceiling, shattering on the floor, while red hot embers pirouetted downward, fluttering sideways, igniting wallpaper, paneling, carpeting, anything combustible. Yet within her protective bubble, Wendy was shielded from the heat and the accumulating smoke. Intuition, or the simple, deductive assumption that her parents would have been preparing dinner, guided Wendy to the kitchen.

More lightning rocked the house, shattering windows. With the influx of fresh air, the flames roared to new heights and the destruction accelerated.

Wendy hurried past the crumbling horseshoe staircase to the kitchen, which looked out on the back lawn, and found the room all but devastated by the combined assault of lightning, fire, and smoke. The walls were all aflame, and the ceiling was collapsing in smoldering chunks. Sparks danced from shattered appliances and the long oak kitchen table had been split down the middle.

They were both on the floor, charred beyond recognition and not quite whole, although her mind refused to assimilate all the details . . . just that their heads were toward each other in the grisly tableau.

Wendy screamed.

She rushed through the kitchen toward them, her sphere rolling with her, smashing into obstructions and blasting them aside. Kneeling beside their smoking remains, protected from the heat and the smoke and even from what must be the roasting pork smell of cooked human flesh, Wendy sobbed uncontrollably.

All the healing magic in the world wouldn't help.

Her parents had been blasted out of existence.

Above her sobs, she heard the insistent blast of a car horn.

She stood, almost unaware as a split beam crashed down from the ceiling and slid down the arc of her protective sphere, and stared out the gaping hole where the bay window used to be.

Standing on the roof of a blue pickup truck at the far end of the back lawn, waving her hands overhead, was Gina Thorne. Once she knew she had Wendy's attention, she extended both arms, flashing her middle fingers. Then, with a joyous howl, she slid down to the hood, dropped to the ground and climbed into the passenger side of the truck.

Wendy thought the driver of the pickup might ram

into the side of the house, hoping to pin her in the flaming ruins. Instead, he drove in a wide circle, digging up the muddy lawn, before Gina leaned out the window and shouted, "This is only the beginning!" With that, the driver gunned the engine, spraying rooster tails of mud and grass toward the house before gaining enough traction to lurch back onto the asphalt driveway and speed out the back gate.

Turning back to the dark, incomplete corpses of her parents, Wendy knelt down again and whispered to them, her throat tight, "I love you, Mom and Dad. Always. And she *will* pay for this."

As if to urge Wendy on to Wither's next act of revenge, several lightning bolts rocked the mansion in quick succession. The constant battering and the hungry flames were conspiring to rob the house of what little structural integrity remained.

Walls began to topple around her as she strode through the burning, smoking debris. Moments after she passed beneath it, the slanted horseshoe of the double staircase screeched and groaned under what had become unbearable weight, finally tearing free and crashing all around her. And the greedy flames roared higher in this preview of her own private hell.

Once outside again, Wendy saw the firemen, in heavy coats, with dangling oxygen masks, afraid to approach the lightning ravaged house. She couldn't blame them. Nothing could have ever prepared them for this.

The sheriff, undaunted or too stubborn to be cowed by the unnatural lightning, was waiting for her in the middle of the lawn. She shook her head, but her tears and the expression on her face told him all he needed to know. Just as he stepped forward to take her in his arms, she absorbed the energy from her sphere into herself, giving herself almost enough strength to stand on her own. "I had no idea she could . . ." he said. "I mean, the hailstorm last year was one thing. But this was . . . directed."

"Apparently, you can teach an old bitch new tricks," Wendy said, her fury rising above her grief and despair. "She's punishing me. She was waiting in back, standing on a pickup truck, just so she could watch the show."

The sheriff stiffened and stepped away, a hand dropping to his holster. "She's back there now?"

"Gone," Wendy said. "But she said this was only the beginning." Wendy stared him in the eye. "Time to visit her home."

"No, Wendy," the sheriff said, placing his hands on her shoulders. "You've been through enough already. Let me handle this. It's my job. I should have taken care of this while I had the chance."

As he strode across the lawn to the gate, beyond which his Jetta was parked at a haphazard angle, Wendy thought, *You took the words right out of my mouth, Sheriff.*

At last, the worst of the storm clouds began to move on, taking with them the barrage of lightning strikes. Even the heavy rain relented. En masse, the firefighters advanced across the lawn, snaking hoses behind them.

Wendy glanced back one last time at the mansion she had called home until a few short weeks ago. All the evergreens had been split or leveled, and the surface of the house was scorched almost uniformly black, flames lapping out through every window. The firefighters might extinguish the fires, but the battle was lost, there would be nothing left to salvage. One day the board of trustees might vote to rebuild on the lot, but Wendy had an empty feeling she wouldn't be around to see it.

The sheriff's car sped away, dashboard bubble light flashing red and blue, siren wailing in a Doppler fade as his taillights winked out in the distance. Wendy walked across the lawn, toward the canted section of fence, quickening her pace the closer she came to her car, praying the Civic was still drivable.

The left front bumper had crumpled, but not enough to impinge on the tire, and the radiator was leaking fluid, but the engine turned over for her. She gripped the steering wheel to quell the trembling of her hands, put the car in reverse and backed away from the toppled fence.

This is only the beginning!

She has Alex, Wendy realized. *He's next.*

She turned onto College Avenue, and floored the accelerator. While his intentions were good, the sheriff was no match for Gina Thorne. Maybe it was too late for anyone to stop Wither reborn. If so, Wendy had only herself to blame. But she refused to let anyone else die because of her. This was Wendy's battle. *And Wither, that bitch, is in for one hell of a fight.*

Alex was spared the torment of Jen's teeth tearing into his flesh.

Just as he felt her hot breath against the burning

wounds of his chest, she was interrupted by the sound of a slamming door upstairs.

"Oops," Jen said with a wry grin. "Looks like the boys are back. And me with my hand almost caught in the cookie jar."

Two muscular young men, one with snake coils tattooed on his shoulders and arms, the other with half his right ear missing, hustled a young woman down the stairs. With a nervous lump in his throat, Alex at first thought they'd kidnapped Wendy, but it was Kayla Zanella they held between them. *Why is she here?* Alex wondered. Then, *Because she's a friend of Wendy's, that's why.*

Kayla's white, sequined Betty Boop tank top was splattered with blood and the left knee in her black jeans had been torn out, exposing a gash in her kneecap. Otherwise, she seemed uninjured.

"Ah, it's the Keith and Cecil show," Jen whispered to Alex conspiratorially. "You know, they like to hurt girls." She clucked her tongue. "Pity poor Wendy."

Alex's rage got the better of him. "Shut up, you sick bitch!"

Jen backhanded him, the force of the blow rocking his head and splitting his lip wide open. *Gina Thorne changed her in other ways,* Alex thought miserably.

Jen climbed to her feet, forgetting about the serrated knife she'd cast aside in favor of her razor-edged fingernails as she approached Keith and Cecil, hands on her hips. "So she's the one?"

"You must be Jen," Kayla said. "Surprised Wendy hasn't already kicked your sorry ass."

Jen laughed. "Don't be bitter, dear. You've been recruited by the competition."

"What are you talking about?"

"Oh, you'll find out," Jen said, chuckling. "Can't you just feel the electricity in the air?"

Kayla looked down at Alex. "You okay?"

He ran his tongue over his bleeding lip and nodded. "Considering . . ." He mouthed a question, Wendy? With a slight shrug and a shake of her head, Kayla told him she had no idea.

"What do we do with this one, Keith?" Cecil, the tattooed tough, asked, his gaze fixed on the front of Kayla's Betty Boop shirt.

Keith gave Cecil's head a rough shove. "Get your mind out of her pants, you dope," he said. "She's about to move above you in the food chain."

"So, nothing?"

"Did I say that?" Keith took a roll of gray duct tape down from where it hung on a nail. "Here. We'll gift wrap her. Then wait upstairs for Gina."

Though she struggled, Kayla was little match for the two thugs. They bound her wrists in front of her, wrapping them in about two yards of duct tape. After they taped her ankles together, Keith picked up her feet and Cecil grabbed her under her arms, copping a thorough feel in the process. They tossed her onto the sofa and Keith warned both her and Alex, who was still propped up against the treadmill, that if either of them made a sound before Gina returned, Cecil would be happy to relieve them of their tongues. Jen's parting shot was,

"I bet the tongues are tasty. They'd almost have to be."

As soon as Jen, Keith, and Cecil left them alone, Kayla shifted herself as far away from the mutating corpse as possible and said, "Any ideas?"

Alex nodded. "There's a knife on the floor, beside the sofa."

"Excellent," Kayla said and flung herself to the floor.

ABOARD UNITED 612, IN FLIGHT
APPROACHING LOGAN INTERNATIONAL AIRPORT,
BOSTON

Hannah had insisted on the window seat and, as the Boeing 757 made its final approach to Logan International, she pressed her face against the window, alternately fogging the window with her breath and wiping it clear with the edge of her palm. "Look, Mama," she said, pointing.

Karen sat between Hannah and an elderly Asian businessman who had slept with his hands folded in his lap through the worst of the turbulence. Since they were two rows ahead of the left wing, Karen had an unobstructed view of the rolling mass of clouds, a dark bruise in the wounded sky, north of Boston. Recalling the freak hailstorm of last Halloween, Karen had a bad feeling this storm was poised over Windale. "Are we . . . too late?" she whispered, one small part of her wishing it were so, that somehow her daughter would be spared this nightmare.

In a tentative voice, almost too soft for Karen's ears, Hannah said, "I don't know."

WINDALE, MASSACHUSETTS

They almost had enough time. Small consolation. Kayla had just cut through the clothesline binding Alex's wrists when a series of footfalls thundered down the steps. Kayla whispered, "Shit! What now?"

"Quick—cut through the rope at my ankles."

Kayla shook her head. "Not enough ti—!"

"Just do it!"

Kayla scooted toward his feet, slid the serrated blade under the rope at Alex's ankles, while he kept his hands behind his back, as if still tied.

Four of them stepped down into the basement, a strawberry blond wearing a black slipdress in the lead, followed by a sandy-haired guy who looked like he spent long hours in a weight room. Bringing up the rear were Jen and snake-tattooed Cecil. No sign of the other guy, Keith. Gina was talking, her attention directed to Jen. "You should have seen the look on her face when she found their charred bodies in the kitchen. Priceless!"

Jen clapped her hands together, delighted, but her smile vanished when she saw the knife in Kayla's hands. Faster than Alex would have thought possible, Jen sprang forward and wrenched the knife away. "Someone's been naughty!" Jen turned to Gina, "Can I cut out her tongue? Please!"

"Let's not be hasty," Gina said. "Girl's got spunk. I like spunk in a girl. But that's not all." Gina turned to Cecil. "Care to do the honors, Mr. Kerr. If I'm not mistaken, our little Wicca will be here soon and we have an initiation to complete."

Cecil came forward, crouched down to grab Kayla by the shoulders. In the process, he made sure to rub his thumbs against her chest again. "One last feel for old time's sake," he said with a smirk. "After she *turns* you, I hope you won't hold this against me."

"She won't," Alex said, "but I will!"

Even as he spoke, Alex brought the cane sword out from behind his back, and plunged it deep into Cecil's ear, skewering what passed for a brain. Cecil's jaw fell and his eyes bulged in his shaved head a moment before he toppled sideways, twitching on the carpet.

Kayla screamed, falling back from the corpse.

Alex's mistake had been impatience. He'd planned to wait until he had a clear shot at taking out Gina, the ringleader of the demented group, the one who wanted to kill Wendy. But he made his decision the moment he thought they were about to torture Kayla, anything to buy them some time. Now his feet were still bound and his only weapon out of reach.

"Brett!" Gina yelled.

The weight lifter rushed forward.

Alex made a valiant attempt to lunge for the sword hilt, but never even came close. One moment he was reaching for the dragon-head handle, the next he was slammed against the wall, and while lying there dazed, a boot drilled him in the gut. He curled into a fetal position, retching.

"Enough!" Gina commanded. "I want him alive ... at least long enough for little Wendy Wicca to see him die. Now, bring the girl to me."

Alex looked up, helpless, as Brett hoisted Kayla off the floor, wrapped his arms around her from behind, pinning her own arms at her sides as he planted her before Gina. "Relax," Gina said to Kayla, who was squirming in Brett's arms. "This is to die for."

"Die and be reborn," Jen said fervently. "Become one of us."

"I'll pass."

"See," Gina said to the others. "Spunk. But, sadly, Kayla, you have no choice in the matter." With the fingernail of her left index finger, Gina sliced open the tips of all four of her right fingers and offered the dripping black blood to Kayla. "Down the hatch."

Kayla clenched her teeth shut.

Alex saw the muscles in Brett's shoulders and arms bunch with effort, then thought he heard one of Kayla's ribs crack under the pressure. Kayla gasped in pain—

—Gina shoved the bleeding fingers into her mouth.

Bite them off! Alex thought.

Then the most frightening thing of all happened.

As Alex watched from the basement floor, Kayla moaned in pleasure. Brett released her and stepped back. Kayla brought up her taped hands, seized Gina's wrist and held the fingers in her mouth, desperate to hold onto them, onto the sensation she was experiencing. Her knees buckled, and Gina accommodated her by dropping to one knee, continuing to let Kayla drink as much as she wanted. "That's a good girl," Gina cooed. "Or should I say, bad girl. Very bad girl."

"A whole new world of devilish delight awaits her," Jen said in a singsong voice, waving the steak knife like a conductor's baton.

"Wait!" Gina said, glancing at Jen. "Do you feel them?"

Jen looked up at the ceiling, her eyes unfocused, and nodded. "Strangers. Gate crashers every one of them! They weren't invited."

"Take care of them," Gina instructed her. "Provide a diversion for Keith to get into position, while Brett and I make the final arrangements." When she plucked her fingers from Kayla's mouth, Kayla swooned, too weak even to kneel. She rolled onto her back, staring at the ceiling with an ecstatic look on her face.

Alex closed his eyes and prayed it was all one big nightmare.

The sheriff had his deputies, Jeff Schaeffer and Hank Rossi, flank him as they approached the Gallo residence in the driving rain. When they saw the blue Ford F-150 in front, they'd parked their squad cars down the block, donned Kevlar vests and rain ponchos. Each of them carried a Remington shotgun loaded, as per the sheriff's instructions, with flechette rounds for maximum penetration.

The hell with being inconspicuous.

When several neighbors poked their heads outside, he cautioned them to silence and motioned them back inside for their own protection. He planned to kick the door in, search warrant be damned. Wendy had seen Gina Thorne behind the college president's mansion, reveling in her destruction, and that was all the confirmation he needed. Never mind he couldn't walk into a court of law and prove Ms. Thorne had destroyed a house and killed two people by hurling lightning bolts like Zeus down off the mountain. He'd witnessed the destruction, knew it was true; his only consolation now was knowing she wouldn't destroy her own home with lightning. At least he hoped not.

When he thought back on the next few minutes, the sheriff took full responsibility for not searching the bed of the pickup before approaching the front door. When the left side door opened, as they were about to kick it in, well they were all caught off guard.

"Hold your fire," the sheriff said reflexively, but only because it wasn't Gina Thorne standing in the doorway. Instead, they faced the girl from Wendy's party, the same girl who'd witnessed Jack Carter's abduction from the covered bridge, Jen Hoyt. She'd been the first to see the monster witch, Wither, and live to tell about it. "Step outside, please, Ms. Hoyt."

"Certainly," Jen said, stepping down to the landing. "But what's all this fuss about?"

"Police business," the sheriff said. "Stand aside."

"Oh! No, no, you can't go in there," she said, smiling

indulgently. "You see, we have this initiation thing going on and it really can't be interrupted." She glanced at Hank Rossi, pointed and said, "You've got something right there, under your chin."

Hank's left hand released the stock of his shotgun, patted his heavy five o'clock shadow, "Here?"

"You missed it," she said, reaching up with her index finger, then slashed left to right under Hank's chin.

"No!" the sheriff screamed, too late.

The deputy made a gurgling sound, clutching his throat as his yellow poncho turned crimson and he fell to his knees. "Oops," Jen said. "Guess it was an artery."

After that, everything became a blur of stroboscopic images, a reel of film where every third frame has been removed, every action a fateful step in an inexorable march toward disaster.

Jen plucked the shotgun from Hank's right hand and tossed it into the air.

Why—? the sheriff thought, half turning even as he leveled his own shotgun at the girl, and yelled at Jeff to stand back.

—a tall shape, bounding inhumanly fast up the walkway, catching Hank's shotgun in midair, raising it high and driving the butt down into Jeff's startled face—

Jeff collapsing—

—the sheriff firing a flechette round.

BLAM!

Half of Jen Hoyt's face whisked away in a flash of red, exposing bone.

As Jen screamed, the sheriff was already swinging

the barrel toward Jeff's assailant—the face registering as Keith Hoagland, Harrison High troublemaker, white Camaro, reckless driving, vandalism, underage drinking—before the stock of Hank's stolen Remington struck the sheriff a glancing blow, gouging his cheek and pulping his left ear. Dropping to one knee, the sheriff fired another round, catching Hoagland in the gut at close range. Should have been a mortal wound. But Hoagland kept coming, smiling even as blood trickled from his mouth. Tossing aside Hank's stolen shotgun, Hoagland grabbed the sheriff's and pulled it close to his chest. Happy to oblige the young man's masochistic tendencies, the sheriff began pumping round after round into him. BLAM! BLAM! BLAM! BLAM! BLAM!

All seven rounds spent, the shotgun was nothing more than an expensive club. Hoagland's chest was a glistening, bloody mess of shattered ribs, but he still wouldn't go down. Instead, he yanked the shotgun from the sheriff's nerveless hands, twirled it around and was about to stave in the sheriff's face. Until he pulled out his trusty .357 Magnum, pressed the barrel against Hoagland's throat, said, "Hey, you've got something under your chin, too," and fired. The round blew away the back of his skull. "Oops, guess it was your brains."

Hoagland was still for a moment—head back, eyes bloodshot and bulging from the sudden burst of intracranial pressure—then he dropped to his knees before toppling over with a satisfying, wet thud, the empty shotgun slipping from his lifeless hands.

The sheriff's moment of triumph was short-lived.

Problem was, even with half her face missing, one eye blown to hell and too damn much of her leering skull exposed, Jen Hoyt was still alive. And angry. Very angry.

Without hesitation, the sheriff fired his revolver at her, shattering her collarbone with his second round, blasting away the balance of her face with the third. Aimed high for a head shot, but his fourth round went wide of the mark. Before he could fire the fifth round, her hand chopped his wrist, shattering bone and dislodging the revolver from his numb hand. Grunting in agony, he staggered backward and fell on his ass. Her left hand caught his right heel and tugged him toward her with brutal ease.

In grim fascination, he stared at her ruined face. An amazing transformation had begun. A glistening film of black blood seeped from ruptured flesh and crimson gore to cover flensed and shattered bone, making repairs right before his eyes, with the mesmerizing speed of time-lapse photography. Her inhuman healing ability, more than anything, demonstrated the utter futility of the battle. *I've lost,* he thought, in despair. *My crack law enforcement team never got past the front door.*

The . . . creature that had been Jensen Hoyt raised her free hand, long finger extended, no doubt about to ventilate his throat as she had Hank Rossi's. For all the good it wouldn't do, the sheriff drew back his left leg and was about to slam his boot heel into her patchwork face, when he noticed the white, four-legged shape dart past the Ford pickup and bound across the front lawn in long, graceful strides.

As Jen slashed at his throat with her right index finger, the white wolf leapt and caught her wrist in powerful, grinding jaws. Screaming in frustration, Jen staggered backward, dangling the wolf from her arm.

Behind them, Jeff Schaeffer rolled over, groaning, blood streaking one side of his smashed face, gumming his left eye shut. Squinting to take in the scene before him, he fumbled his gun out of its holster and took unsteady aim at Jen's head.

"Not the wolf!" the sheriff yelled.

Jeff seemed to have trouble comprehending the sheriff's command and looked about to pull the trigger anyway. At that moment, Jen raked the wolf's flank with the claws of her left hand. It squealed, releasing her wrist and falling to the ground in an awkward heap before rolling over and darting out of range. Jeff pulled the trigger, missing high.

Jen whirled around, stalked toward him as he fired one round after another into her torso. The sheriff hurled himself low, behind her knees, toppling her. As she climbed to hands and knees, he snatched his gun off the lawn with his left hand, shoved the barrel against the base of her skull and emptied the last rounds into her, one after another.

Incredibly she staggered to her feet and plodded toward the front door of the Gallo house. Before she disappeared into the darkness of the house, she turned toward him, her head hanging forward at an impossible angle, one baleful eye glaring at him with hate and rage. The worst part was knowing she could probably heal even that much damage given a couple hours.

While my team needs to be airlifted to the nearest hospital.

Hank Rossi was dead. Jeff, who had passed out after emptying his revolver, would require several rounds of reconstructive facial surgery. The sheriff's right wrist was shattered and, with each heartbeat, the agony edged closer to snuffing out his consciousness, not to mention the separate torture of his blood-soaked right ankle. Jen's razor-sharp fingernails had gouged the flesh down to the bone. He could barely put any weight on it. And Abby . . .

My, God—Abby!

The sheriff looked left and right, then saw her pale shape breathing raggedly where she lay on the lawn, the heavy rain washing away four streams of blood that continued to well from her side. She had reverted to human form again and looked so helpless as the life seeped out of her fragile, naked body.

Unable to walk on his bleeding ankle and equally unable to put any weight on his shattered wrist, the sheriff dropped to the ground and pulled himself along by clutching grass and dirt in his good hand, and kicking off with his left foot. He twisted out of his poncho and tossed it over Abby, then huddled over her, hoping his warmth would prevent her from going into shock. But he had begun to shiver himself, and the world around him was receding, slipping away from his immediate consciousness . . .

Until a strong hand grabbed his shoulder.

She crouched beside the sheriff, grabbed his shoulder and rolled him off of Abby. "Let me help her," Wendy said.

He nodded, moving away just enough to give her access to the trembling girl. Wendy gripped the rose quartz bead in her left hand, then slipped her right under the poncho and pressed her palm against the bleeding wounds. Last time she had let too much energy flow from her into Abby, draining herself in the process. This time she released just enough to repair the internal damage and close the wounds. The golden glow barely radiated beyond the girl's skin, a subtle corona. *Abby will still be weak*, Wendy thought. *Maybe weak enough to stay out of trouble for the rest of the night.*

"What about—me?" the sheriff asked, grimacing in pain.

"Not yet," Wendy said, nodding toward the Gallo residence. "If I heal you now, you'll go in there, and she'll kill you. She and I need to settle this alone, before anyone else gets hurt."

"The pain—" the sheriff gasped, clutching her arm. "Please . . ."

Wendy nodded, crouched down next to him and placed her right palm against the side of his face and his left ear. The golden light began to suffuse him, but the sheriff noticed something in her face that alarmed him and he pulled her hand away. "Why?" she asked, a little breathless.

"You became pale."

Wendy held up her right hand. "This doesn't come without cost."

"Then stop," he said. "You have to be strong when you face her." Wendy nodded. "I've been a fool. Didn't want to admit this was something I couldn't handle. Even after I watched you walk through a burning, collapsing house without a scratch." He shook his head, as if still amazed by the mental image. "But I know now . . . for whatever reason, this all depends on you, Wendy. Get in there!"

"What about you? Abby? Your deputy?"

"You've taken away most of my pain. Ankle feels better, think I can walk okay, at least function well enough to get them clear of the house. The rest can wait."

"Do it, then," Wendy said, rising. She stared up at the house, at the eerie green light flickering in the windows of the second and third floor. "Because one way or another, this house is coming down."

CHAPTER THIRTEEN

Alex expected Wendy to arrive at Gina's house at any moment, primarily because Gina expected her. With his ankles still tied together, wrists now taped behind his back and a fresh strip of duct tape over his mouth, he was in no position to help her when she arrived. After securing Alex again, Brett had left the basement with Jen's knife and Alex's cane sword in his possession. *All tied up and not a weapon to be found,* Alex lamented.

With a shudder, Alex remembered the wicked grin Brett had directed at Cecil's corpse as he gripped the dragon-head hilt of the cane sword and extracted the blade from the tattooed man's brain. Brett's parting words, as he wiped gore from the sword onto the dead man's shirt, had a tone of cruel satisfaction. "Hey, Kerr, thanks for sharing."

Kayla was murmuring, even writhing a bit on the floor, as if in the midst of an erotic dream. Not only had Kayla been drugged with Gina's black blood, Alex had a sick feeling it was, at that moment, transforming her into a member of the away team. *The odds just keep getting better.*

Alex had regained a sitting position, his back pressed to the wall of the basement as he considered his dwindling options. Without the wad of cloth in his mouth, he was able to work his jaw side to side and push out with his tongue to work loose the tape on his mouth. If *nothing else, maybe I can scream a warning to Wendy.* His gaze settled on the serpent head tattooed on Cecil's nearest hand, with its fearsome red eyes and extended, poison dripping fangs. *Cecil!* Alex thought in a flash of inspiration, and scooted across the rug toward the dead man. Brett had made sure to remove the knife and cane sword, but he'd neglected to search Cecil for weapons. And Alex was willing to bet a semester's tuition that the serpent-tattooed Cecils of the world didn't leave home unarmed.

Twisting around, Alex reached out with his hands and began to pat down the many pockets in Cecil's cargo pants. In less than a minute, he found what he was looking for, pulled against the Velcro flap and removed a long hunting knife, the back edge of which had a serrated section. Alex flipped the knife over in his hands and started to work on the thick wad of tape securing his wrists.

"What are you doing?"

Alex froze, looked over his shoulder and saw Kayla on hands and knees, staring at him, a trickle of black blood dribbling down her chin. His own mouth was suddenly dry.

She shook her head, fighting the blood-induced lethargy. "What happened . . . ?"

Alex tongued aside a flap of tape from the side of his mouth. "Y—you don't remember?"

"She . . . shoved her fingers in my mouth, didn't she?" Alex nodded. "Blood—black blood. What the hell was it?"

"Something actually from hell, I'm thinking," Alex said. "A drug, a poison, a virus. Just a little something to make you join her exclusive club of psychotic witches."

"It was . . ." Her eyes almost glazed over with the remembered pleasurable sensation. "It was incredible." Alex just cleared his throat, waiting. "Too incredible to be good for me, right?" Alex shook his head, sensing her growing fear of losing herself to evil. "Alex, what do I do?"

"I don't know, Kayla," Alex said. "Maybe there's an . . . antidote."

"Fuck that," Kayla said. "Have to get this shit out of my system now!" She raised her hands, still bound with duct tape, and shoved her fingers back into her throat, triggering her gag reflex. She retched, but only spittle came out. Again, she shoved her fingers back into her throat, over and over, until finally it rushed out of her, black blood gushing out of her mouth and spraying the rug. She fell back, away from the dark, bubbling mess, panting while her limbs quivered with exhaustion, or maybe it was withdrawal.

"Feel better?"

Kayla shook her head, face pale as she stared at the soiled rug. "This will sound gross, I know, but I have this overwhelming . . . urge to lap it up."

"Take your mind off of it," Alex said. "Get over here and cut me loose."

Wendy stood before the double doors, on the doorstep of the Gallo house. She tried the doorknob and found it locked. Preferring a stealthy entrance, she clutched the agate geode on her wrist and focused on turning the deadbolt with her mind. She ignored the rain streaming down her face, blocked out the rolling bass rumble of thunder and concentrated only on the lock.

"*Wendy,*" called the voice of the Crone.

Wendy smiled, glanced back at the Crone's astral image, much more delineated than the last time Wendy saw her. "You're back."

The Crone glanced up into the stormy sky. "*I came closer to you. Proximity to push through the resistance.*"

Wendy smiled. "Your mother decided to ignore my warnings."

"*So you know.*"

"You've been defying the normal flow of time since you were born, Hannah. I just never realized how much. 'Hannah is a palindrome.' Backward and forward, it's still the same."

"*We've all been changed, Wendy,*" the Crone said, repeating her earlier statement. "*Abby, myself . . . and not in ways we would have chosen. But we make the best of it.*"

"Why couldn't you warn me?" Wendy said, her throat tight. "About my parents?"

"Because of temporal persistence, my memory of these events has always been . . . murky, at best. I exist here now only because of the Hannah of your time. She sees back through a . . . fold in time, with my eyes in my form, but it is her mind that informs you, not mine, not directly. And your Hannah has incomplete knowledge."

"And divination leaves a lot to be desired," Wendy said. "Gotcha. So let's agree to sort out the folded time scenario later." She nodded toward the door. "Any ideas what I'm up against?"

"Gina Thorne, the destructive creature you knew as Wither, has the ability to warp nature, to twist it to her will, raping it as she pleases. She will use that twisted nature to her advantage. Once you cross this doorway, don't trust what you know to be true, what you know to be physically possible, because she is making the rules."

"Just how powerful is she now?"

"She is a wild card, in every sense of the word. Through her blood-possession of Gina Thorne's body, Wither was reborn in a unique way." Last year, Wendy had been Wither's intended prey. Then the monster witch had made a failed attempt to swap minds, placing her ancient mind in Wendy's body to begin a new three-hundred-year life cycle, while attempting to cast Wendy's mind in her old, dying husk. The Crone continued, "And though Wither's mind and memories were ravaged by your attempt to destroy her, she may no longer be limited to the old three-hundred-year cycle."

"Meaning she might not have to be three hundred years old to become mega-monster-witch again?"

"Just . . . *expect the unexpected.*"

"Super," Wendy said, turning her attention to the lock. She cleared her mind of distractions, and willed the deadbolt back. CLICK! "Got it," she said. But try as she might, she couldn't master the subtlety of forming a mental key. Maybe if she had a copy of the real key in her hand to replicate with her mind . . . then again, if she had the real key, she'd just shove it into the lock. "Oh, well," she said. "Forget stealthy."

Stepping off the doorstep, she picked up one of the discarded shotguns, aimed, and blasted a chunk out of the doorjamb. Wendy pushed the door inward with the butt of the shotgun and stepped into the vestibule, peering into the darkness of the reception hall beyond. The unnatural chill inside the house raised gooseflesh on her arms. Pulsing green light flashed down the twisted staircase and the walls seemed to be warped, bowed outward and wet with slime. As she walked into the reception hall, her breath preceded her in little clouds of vapor. Her gaze drifted up to the strange green glow.

From her left, a skeletal figure in black lurched out of the darkness, butcher knife held high. Drool running down her chin, the woman shrieked, "Leave my daughter alone!"

Wendy blocked the woman's wrist with the stock of the shotgun, shoved her back a step, then slammed the butt of the shotgun into her face. With a sickening crunch, as if it had been cast from papier-mâché, the woman's head caved in. And with it, her entire body seemed to crumple in on itself, dry skin, desiccated tissue, and brittle bones.

"*Your protective sphere, Wendy,*" the Crone reminded her, drifting behind her like a ghostly wake.

"Right," Wendy murmured.

As she passed the staircase, she looked up and saw the stairs spiraling upward, seemingly much higher than the outside height of the house. *Don't trust what you know to be true,* Wendy remembered. *Good advice.*

As if alive, the walls pulsed around her, glistening with a white, viscous fluid that flowed upward as often as it drifted down. In places, the wood paneling was melting, running down to the floor and forming pools of liquid wood. A nauseating stench filled the house, a mixture of overripe fruit and decaying flesh. As she passed a closet, the doorknob stretched, reaching for her. With a little sidestep, she avoided the sharp point and crossed through the near corner of the family room. Some of the windows were bubbling, like the surface of a hot spring.

Sitting lifeless against the far corner of the family room, like a broken doll, was the body of Jensen Hoyt. *Not quite lifeless,* Wendy observed. Glistening black blood swirled around her shattered face and head in a feverish race to rebuild muscle and tissue. Meanwhile, her body had sagged into some sort of restorative coma. Wendy hoped to destroy the place long before sleeping beastie had a chance to awaken. *Kill two poisonous birds with one cleansing fire.*

Wendy peeked into the kitchen, glimpsed the gas

range and had an idea. *One way or another,* she thought. In a house thick with a sour miasma, she doubted one more unpleasant odor would draw undue attention. She fiddled with the dials on the range. From behind her, she heard the cautious tread of someone climbing the basement stairs. *More than one from the sound of it,* she thought and conjured her sphere. She glanced at the Crone, who nodded her approval before fading into the ether. *Three seconds flat and without a focus,* Wendy thought. *Imagine that.*

Wendy crouched out of sight, keeping her gaze on the basement doorway, conscious of the rushing hiss of gas, as the door swung open. She heaved a sigh of relief and stood when Alex came through the doorway, looking battered, a little bloody, but in decent shape, considering. Behind him, another figure—Kayla!

"Wendy," Alex said, startled, then dropped his voice. "You have to get out of here. Gina wants to kill you."

"The feeling's mutual," Wendy said. "Kayla, how—?"

"Gina's goons trashed the store and they . . ." Kayla paused, swallowed a lump in her throat. "They killed Tristan, Wendy! Then they kidnapped me." She shook her head, angry. "That sick bitch made me drink her blood, to force me into her coven. But I puked all of it up. At least, I hope that was all of it."

"I need both of you out of here," Wendy said. "Close the reception hall door on your way out and get behind something big. This whole place is gonna blow. I'm taking Wither out—this time with flames."

Alex glanced at the gas range, saw what she had in

mind. "Wendy, no! You'll be killed too. I won't leave you. We'll find some other way."

"Alex, remember the sphere?"

He was about to protest, then caught himself, nodded. "Make it big enough for both of us."

"I can't do that yet," she said. The truth was, she thought she might be able to now, but she couldn't tell him that. Size wouldn't matter because three seconds still wasn't fast enough. But the only way he'd leave her alone in the house was if he thought she'd be safe. "Take Kayla out of here and wait for me."

"I have a bad feeling about this," Alex said. "But I've seen what you can do." As he stepped forward, she absorbed the sphere energy and fell into his embrace. He squeezed her hard. "It's not enough."

"What?"

"If you want this whole place to blow, you're gonna need more gas. A lot more."

Wendy glanced at the four unlit, hissing gas burners, each turned to the highest setting. "I'm open to suggestions."

"I saw a toolbox under the basement stairs. All I need is an adjustable wrench. If Kayla helps me pull the range away from the wall, I can reach back and disconnect the main gas line in no time. That will flood the house with gas a lot faster than those burners."

"Do it," Wendy said. "Then both of you get out of here."

"Your sphere? It *is* strong enough, right?"

"Don't worry about me," Wendy said. "I know what I'm doing."

Alex stepped back, examining her face with unnerving thoroughness. Wendy forced a brave smile. *Have a good life, Alex*, she thought. "See ya soon."

Alex nodded, then returned to the basement for the toolbox.

Kayla grabbed Wendy in an embrace and whispered in her ear. "You plan on lighting this firecracker with your little witch flame?"

"That's right," Wendy said, maintaining her confident smile.

"You'll have to drop your sphere to ignite the gas."

Wendy whispered, "Do you want this bitch to survive?" When Kayla bit her lip, Wendy had all the answer she needed. Before letting go, Wendy whispered fiercely in Kayla's ear, "Keep him safe, Kayla, or I'll come back and haunt your ass."

Kayla backed away, wiped a tear and nodded. "Be good, Wendy."

The light showed her the way.

Wendy returned to the bottom of the spiraling staircase and looked up into the pulsing green glow. The Crone shimmered into astral existence beside her. "She's up there, isn't she?" Wendy asked.

The Crone nodded. "She'll try to keep you off balance."

As Wendy climbed the staircase, she felt the steps give under her weight, not so much straining as undulating. Higher and higher she climbed, and soon the banister railing ended, leaving only the posts, narrowed at the top to sharp points, like an endless procession of wooden stakes. If she should fall from the stairs, she could all too easily imagine being impaled on the way down. With that disturbing image in mind, she pressed herself against the wall and climbed ever higher, but soon even the security of the wall vanished, as it crumbled away under the slightest pressure, fragile as rice paper. She was so startled the first time the wall broke away, she lost her grip on the shotgun and watched helplessly as it plummeted into the dark depths below.

And still the spiral staircase climbed into the pulsing green light, unsupported by anything other than Wither's warped gravity. *I must be at least a hundred feet up already.*

Another possibility occurred to Wendy. That not all the changes to the interior of the house were real. Perhaps Wither was using glamour, an illusion to intimidate Wendy, to strike cold fear deep into her heart. The endless, unsupported spiral staircase had the hallmarks of an elaborate stage, a magical façade for Wither's revenge play. But Wendy didn't dare trust her senses until she could distinguish between reality and Wither's twisted imagination.

Above, the staircase vanished, lost in the hungry green haze, but no matter how high she climbed, there was another circle awaiting her. She heard a roar above her and the sound of heavy footfalls on the staircase, approaching fast, shaking the whole perverse construction. With no railing or wall for support, Wendy went down to hands and knees. "What is it?"

"*Brett Marlin,*" the Crone said. "*The one she trains to be her keeper.*"

Without the shotgun, Wendy had no weapons, either conventional or magical, other than her small flame, but she was determined not to spark the deadly explosion until she had Gina in her sights. No sense sacrificing herself if there was the slightest chance Gina had escaped. "You said I invented—will invent—some creative uses for protective spheres. Care to give me an example?"

Brett Marlin lumbered into view a half turn of the spiral staircase above her, flying down the steps two at a time, wielding what looked like Alex's custom made cane sword.

Startled, the Crone blurted, "*Other shapes!*"

Wendy only had a moment or two to assimilate that little tidbit of information, but as she watched the violent tremors Brett caused in the unsupported staircase before her, she had an idea. Brett clutched the sword over his head in both hands as he charged the final yards toward her.

She had already conjured her sphere, but a collision might throw her clear of the stairs and she might not survive the long fall. Instead of waiting to find out, she sensed the shape of the sphere around her and pushed a portion of it forward, like a pseudopod of mental force, and punched through the warped wooden stairs just ahead of her.

Brett's momentum carried him right to the gaping hole. At the last instant, he tried to hurdle the gap, but his stride was all wrong. He let go of the sword and flailed with his hands, but too late to stop himself from plummeting down through the hole, down into the darkness below. He screamed in fury all the way down.

Wendy ran up the stairs and jumped over the hole, but her right foot hit a weak section of wood and started to burst through a damaged riser. She flung herself forward, placing her center of gravity far enough forward so she wouldn't follow Brett down to her death.

Two more turns around the stairs and Gina Thorne, in her black slipdress and bare feet, was waiting for Wendy. Gina hovered in the air in violation of the pull of gravity, her strawberry blond hair a flowing corona around her head. "*Don't trust what you know to be true . . . she is making the rules.*"

Beneath Gina's skin pulsed a thick network of black veins, branching along her forearms and legs, up her chest, throat, face, and forehead, vanishing into her hairline. "Yes, I've finally learned to fly," Gina said. "Impressed?"

"Disgusted."

"Brave," Gina said. "I'll give you that. But in the end, courage alone isn't good enough. *You're* just not good enough. I've seen what you can do and, sorry, but not all that frightening. You don't scare me anymore, Wendy Ward. Not in the least."

"Then why go through all this trouble?" Wendy said, steeling her nerve to light her tiny flame, to touch off the tremendous explosion. Not much in the way of magical power, little more than a Zippo lighter, but it would be enough to torch the bitch.

"First I had to find out how strong you were," Gina said, arms extended, spinning slowly in the center of the spiral staircase she'd created and seemed to support with her own warped gravity. "Turns out, not very. I had a good laugh over your puny little flame. On to step two, make you suffer for past crimes against me. So I toast your parentals, corrupt your friends, flay your boy toy, all while you watch, helpless and hopeless. Pathetic."

"Getting ahead of yourself, Gina. Kayla and Alex are gone."

Gina cocked her head, then nodded slowly. "For now," she conceded. "But how far can they run? You'll die knowing I'll torture them after you're gone."

A *real conceited, confident bitch*, Wendy thought, then had an idea. *Maybe I can use that against her.* "I'm not worried, because I'm betting you're not all that powerful, Gina. Or should I pretend that you're really Wither?"

"I AM WITHER!"

"You're loud, but that doesn't prove much," Wendy said. "Wither had power, real power. You just put on a fancy lightshow. This is all probably a simple glamour, an illusion to trick the rubes. But I'm not falling for it."

"ILLUSION?" Gina roared. "I'll show you illusion!"

Wendy already had her protective sphere up. *Hold on*, she told herself, *this is just the warm-up act!*

The banister posts with their sharpened points ripped free of their mooring and shot through the air, every one of them aimed at Wendy's head or torso, flying from all directions with the speed of crossbow bolts. Every one struck and bounced off her invisible barrier. When the shattered spikes had all tumbled down into the dark depths below, Wendy's limbs were still trembling.

"Ha!" Gina shouted. "Defensive magic has its limits. I'll wear you down and when you're weak as a kitten, I'll crush you."

Within her protective sphere, cut off from the increasing volume of natural gas around her, Wendy raised her palm and conjured her tiny flame, acting as if she hoped to do some major damage with it. Ridiculous, of course. But Gina had a big ego and a showoff mentality. Wendy just hoped she hadn't overestimated the demon witch's abilities.

As Wendy expected, Gina laughed at Wendy's meager flame. "I'm shaking now, little Wicca! What next, a hotfoot?"

"Laugh all you want, pretender," Wendy said casually. "I don't see you conjuring any fire."

"You want fire?" Gina said, stretching both arms toward Wendy, fingers extended. "I'll give you a taste of hell."

"I was hoping you would," Wendy whispered a moment before the explosion. She had time only to close her eyes against the blinding flash of light. The roar of the explosion was muted by her protective sphere, but the concussion hurled her and the sphere end over end in a torrent of igniting debris.

Within the roaring insanity of the explosion, Wendy imagined she heard Gina—*Wither*—shrieking against her destruction in flames and, with her dying, agonized gasp of breath cursing Wendy, hurling a fiery brand on her soul that would bring death and destruction to her for the rest of her life.

Much later, Wendy regained consciousness on a front lawn, across the street from the Gallo house. She hadn't been hurt in the blast, the Crone explained, but the expenditure of energy to maintain the sphere's protection through an inferno had taken its toll.

Wendy rose and crossed the street on wobbly legs, determined to get a better view of the burning ruin that marked Wither's final resting place.

Fire is the only sure way to destroy her evil . . .

This time, Wendy knew, it really was over.

EPILOGUE

Sometimes I dream I'm protected—and trapped—within the sphere, spinning out of control, landing far from those I know and love. That which protects me also isolates me. My days are like that, too.

Six weeks since Gina Thorne, lately known as Wither, died in the explosion of the Gallo house and I still feel detached from everyone, lost in my own home town. Frankie loves the cottage, but for me it's lost its charm. My real home was destroyed, along with my parents. Of course, everyone is sympathetic. There's even talk of renaming the Danfield Library in honor of my father, The Lawrence A. Ward Memorial Library. And I've been promised a full scholarship to Danfield, assuming I choose to stay.

Alissa returned early from her European holiday soon after I called to tell her about the destruction in the shop. She assures me her insurance will cover all the damage, but I can't help feeling I've let her down.

Fall semester at Danfield is well underway and for everyone else, life moves on, same old same old, but things will never be the same for me. Once I realized I was retaining none of the lectures and my notebook pages remained curiously blank, I stopped attending classes.

Alex has been there for me, standing with me when they buried my mother and father in adjoining plots, and later, during Tristan's funeral, spending long evenings with me, trying to keep me entertained and far away from the abyss of grief and guilt . . . and yet, I have the feeling he's never quite forgiven me for keeping him in the dark about Wither's return. My intentions were good, if naïve. At first, I wanted to keep him out of Wither's reach. I knew she would come for me, but I foolishly thought I could keep those dearest to me safe by keeping them ignorant. Somehow I thought I could shoulder all the responsibility and take on all the danger alone. For that I've paid a terrible price.

Life goes on, for others at least. After Gina's destruction, I saw Hannah and Karen for several days. Curiously, Hannah could not meet the Crone. Apparently, the conjuration of her future astral body is something she does subconsciously. The intuition of the experience informs her, but not even as directly as the Crone speaks to me. For the most part, the astral experience is a mystery to Hannah, as is our future. Karen and Hannah returned to Art and Menlo Park after the funerals. Despite Karen's hopes, Hannah continues to age at an accelerated pace and, at eleven months old, is being tutored at the second grade level.

Magic has limits of its own. Weak as I was after the explosion, I healed those most in need of it, including the sheriff. He's kept Abby's secret, as have I, but he has a haunted look in his eyes, as if he won't believe the nightmare is really over. Can't say I blame him. It seems magical healing does little for emotional scars.

Abby continues to take her occasional midnight runs as her other self, the wolf, with the sheriff's consent, if not his blessing. For better or worse, the wolf is part of who Abby is . . . and she has now saved both our lives in her wolf form. During a recent Nottingham family picnic at which I was a casually honored guest, I asked Abby, when we were alone, if she's ever tried changing into any other animal forms and she said no, but with a wondering look in her eyes. Later I caught her staring at a spot above some pine trees, where an eagle wheeled lazy circles in the sky.

Kayla began to have what she termed "dark" dreams, participatory nightmares. Usually, in the days following these dreams, she would run a low grade fever. On August 30, during the first new moon after Gina's destruction, Kayla woke screaming in the middle of the night, certain she had blood all over her hands. The next day, at the Crone's suggestion, I attempted to "heal" Kayla, if that's the correct word. The golden aura suffused her, but I could sense no impairment. Moments later, she rushed to the bathroom and I heard her retching long and loud. Since then, she says the dark dreams have stopped. I believe her.

Unfortunately, my own nightmares continue. Troubled dreams of standing on that Daliesque spiral staircase, of the explosion and subsequent shock wave, of hearing Gina's tormented voice in those hellish last moments of her life, uttering Wither's dying curse on me. The most frightening aspect of these nightmares is that they seem more like pieces of forgotten memory than fanciful constructions of my subconscious mind. I've had lucid dreams before and I truly believe that, somewhere deep in my mind, the entirety of her dark curse awaits my discovery. Wither may be dead and gone, but I will always fear her evil . . .

Wendy Ward's Mirror Book
November 1, 2000, Moon: waxing crescent, day 4

Halloween 2000 is over.

Hadn't realized until this morning that I've been holding some sort of "psychic" breath all this time. I watched TV, gnawing on my fingernails, while Frankie made sure all our trick-or-treaters were well provisioned. Couldn't sleep until sunrise, but when sleep came, it was blessedly dreamless.

Exhale . . .

WINDALE, MASSACHUSETTS
DECEMBER 22, 2000

Wendy leaned against the wrought iron gate at 100 College Way, hands stuffed in her jacket pockets, watching as construction workers guided the cement mixers, pouring the foundation for the next college president's home. *From five miles up, she thought, they must look like a colony of ants, rebuilding an anthill damaged by the careless tread of a human. Whether careless or malicious, it never seems to matter. The ants always rebuild.*

According to the college newspaper, the new mansion's construction would be complete by the following May. By then, Wendy hoped to be long gone.

As light snow began to fall, she turned her back on the construction crew, and crossed over to College Avenue, letting herself be mesmerized by the simple wonder of lazy, drifting snowflakes.

Wearing a bomber jacket that complemented his Ray-Ban sunglasses, Alex fell in step with her, without the aid of a cane. Her healing had accomplished that much, at least. Secretly, she suspected her healing touch had also cured his oversensitivity to light, caused by the old hockey injury, and that he kept the sunglasses as part of his attire out of habit or acquired affectation. She reached out and felt a familiar thrill when his hand slipped into hers. "Rumor has it you dropped out," he said.

"Failed out," Wendy corrected. "Heard that kind of thing happens when you stop attending classes and skip those pesky exams."

"Take a semester off," Alex said. "Hell, take a whole year off. Nobody would blame you."

Wendy stopped walking, turned to face him, and pulled his sunglasses down the bridge of his nose so she could see his eyes. A stream of students flowed around them, not even pausing as they cast curious glances their way. "What about you? Do you blame me?"

"Of course not, the time would—"

"That's not what I meant," Wendy said. "I'm talking about Gina Thorne. The whole Wither business."

Alex sighed and looked away for a moment before responding. "Do I think you were wrong? Yes! You should have told me everything. Do I think your intentions were bad? No."

"The road to hell being paved with good intentions?"

"Intentions without appropriate actions, maybe. But your actions were understandable, honorable even. I just wish . . . I wish you had told me, that's all."

"I wasn't trying to be a martyr, believe me," Wendy said. "In the beginning, I couldn't believe it myself. Later, I felt responsible, that it was all somehow my burden to bear."

Alex walked over to a stone bench outside one of the administrative buildings and sat down, hands clasped together between his knees. Wendy joined him, giving him a frisky hip bump as she sat down. He looked over at her and smiled. "I'm all packed. Ready for winter break."

"Good," Wendy said, nodding. "Tell everyone back home I said howdy."

"Mom wants to know if you'd like to spend Christmas with us."

"That's sweet."

"But you're not coming?"

"I think I'll stick around here for a bit," Wendy said. "Karen, Art, and Hannah are coming out for the holidays."

Alex cleared his throat, looked straight ahead, and asked, "What then? Where will you go? What will you do?"

Her parents, she'd discovered, had invested wisely over the years and while they'd bequeathed a sizeable endowment to the college, the rest of their estate they'd left to her, their only child. More money than she really needed or knew what to do with at the moment, but she wanted to distance herself from the tragedy before making any donations or long-term financial decisions. Certainly, she planned to help Tristan's family, but beyond that ...

Alex was watching her, sunglasses in his hand, waiting for an answer.

"I think I'll travel for a while, maybe embark on a journey of self-discovery in the process." The Crone had lifted the veil from Wendy's magic, allowing her to glimpse the vast potential that awaited her. Yet there was so much to learn. "Whatever you do," Wendy said, giving him a peck on the cheek. "Don't you worry about me."

He arched an eyebrow. "Okay to miss you once in a while?"

Wendy flashed a wry grin, kissed him on the mouth this time, with slightly parted lips. "Not as much as I'll miss you."

"More," he whispered back.

She grabbed his hand and hauled him off the bench, then tucked her arm under his, leaned her head against his shoulder, and together they rejoined the flow of foot traffic. "You haven't seen the last of me, Alex Dunkirk," Wendy said. "That's a promise."

And a promise to herself: *Whatever the future has in store, I'll be prepared.*

ABOUT THE AUTHOR

In May 2000, John Passarella won the Horror Writer Association's prestigious Bram Stoker Award for Superior Achievement in a First Novel for *Wither*. Columbia Pictures purchased the feature film rights to *Wither* in a prepublication, preemptive bid. On Amazon.com, *Wither* was an Editor's Choice, as well as a horror bestseller in hardbound and paperback. Barnesandnoble.com named the paperback edition of *Wither* one of horror's "Best of 2000." *Wither* was also an International Horror Guild Award Finalist for Best First Novel.

John's second novel, *Buffy the Vampire Slayer: Ghoul Trouble*—a *Locus* bestseller—was followed by *Angel: Avatar*. *Wither's Rain* is his fourth novel.

John resides in Swedesboro, New Jersey, with his wife and three children.

Visit him on the Web at http://www.passarella.com or E-mail him at jack@passarella.com.